Odyssey of an Etruscan Noblewoman

Rosalind Burgundy

This is a work of fiction based on archeological data. Characters are products
of the author's imagination. Other names, places and events are intended to
give the fiction a setting in historical reality.

This book was printed in the United States of America.

Cover design: Rosalind Burgundy
Back cover: ornament on a funerary cippus preserved at the National
Etruscan Museum of Chiusi, Chiusi, Italy
Reproduced with kind permission of the Soprintendenza of the Ministero
per I Beni Archeologici e le Attivita Culturali della Toscana, Firenze

Map design: "Larthia's Cosmos," Rosalind Burgundy

To order additional copies of this book, contact:
Xlibris Corporation
1-888-795-4274
www.Xlibris.com
Orders@Xlibris.com
19582

Also by Rosalind Burgundy:

Song of the Flutist

Tuscan Intrigue

Dedicated to the Etruscan people
whose spirit is as alive today
as when they were
at the height of their power.

You may forget
but
let me tell you this:
someone in
some future time
will think of us.

Sappho
(Greek poetess,
sixth century B.C.E.)

Odyssey of an Etruscan Noblewoman

Before ancient Rome there was
Etruria, Land of the Etruscans . . .

Stars must have shone more brightly in that part of the world. From the eighth to fifth centuries, B.C.E. the Etruscans cast their charm upon the earth. In what is now central Italy, there lived a life-loving people who ate, drank and banqueted lavishly, held sway over the seas, had an abundance of crops and metal, and built afterlife tombs for eternity.

Of the twelve main cities, Tarchna and Cisra were the most powerful, controlled by nobility including the grand Vella-Laris family, four generations strong. The gods must have played tricks on that family for each was assigned distinctive abilities. Amidst them, Noblewoman Larthia had a unique gift. Magic was in her fingers! She could scribe the spoken word. Cleverness was in her being! She could quickly master languages. Her talents would lead her on a journey where there was no turning back . . .

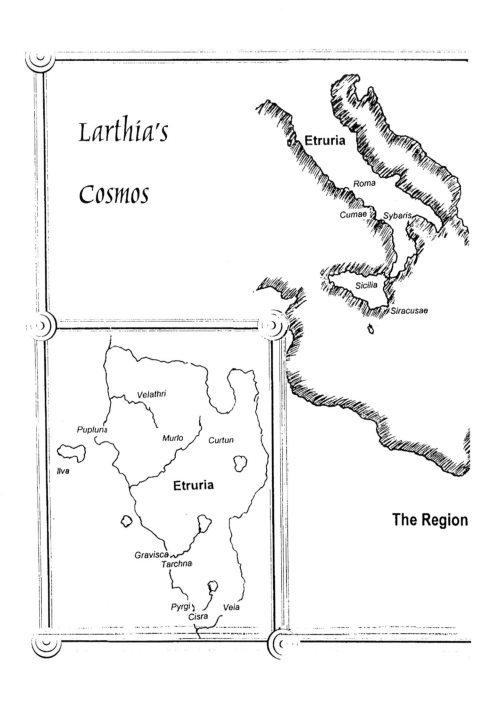

Larthia's

Cosmos

Etruria

Roma

Cumae Sybaris

Sicilia

Siracusae

Velathri

Pupluna

Murlo Curtun

Ilva

Etruria

Gravisca

Tarchna

Pyrgi Veia

Cisra

The Region

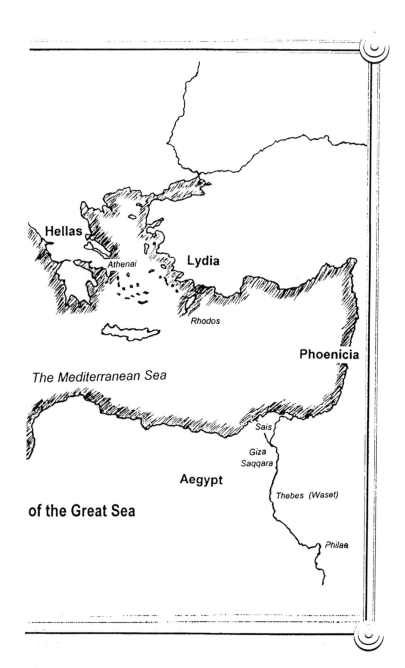

Hellas

Lydia

Athenai

Rhodos

Phoenicia

The Mediterranean Sea

Sais

Giza
Saqqara

Aegypt

Thebes (Waset)

of the Great Sea

Philae

1

Tomb of the Ancestors

"Who shall be the first to enter?"

No one stirred. None answered.

Supreme Etruscan prince-priests, magistrates from each of the Twelve Peoples, stood stiffly before the great dome-mound wearing ceremonial garb befitting the occasion. Lesser officials and court staffs crowded about them. Glad to be invited, I stayed happily in the outer circle with my fellow scribes from other city-states.

As well dressed as they, I blended in with confidence. My trim linen tunic, male length to the knee, met high-strapped sandals. Zilath's gift of gold clasp pinned fabric at my shoulder. The pouch with my prized scribing tools hung from a gold-threaded rope belt. My plain mid-length straight hair and nearly hairless jaw gave me a boyish appearance.

"It's a glorious day to be in Cisra's City of the Dead," the scribe next to me whispered.

Anxiously we waited for this event to begin. The enormous mound loomed above, an artificial mountain created by the Ancestors, topped with turf of brightest sod, on a base of large porous gray stone blocks. Sliced into the mound, a long path led to the place that held secrets.

Prince-priest of Veia rang out, "We gather to pay homage to our Revered One, Ancestor Princess-priestess Larthia, who brought strength to Etruria. I repeat, who shall be the first to enter? Who will step into The Shadows?"

Shrewdly the prince-priests eyed each other. Their delicate, gold-leaf crowns, representing their native cities, gleamed in Aplu's sunrays. Each canvassed the assembly, searching for a would-be candidate.

One stroked his beard. "After all, the tomb hasn't been opened since her death."

A second wrinkled a brow. "So moldy and dank."

A third smoothed the hem of his tunic. "Wet from rains."

All gave excuse but none said the true reason. They were afraid. What had started in jest among the boastful rulers had become a challenge: to open the grandest tomb. From vanity they would defy the gods and go against the laws of Tages.

Brave Prince-priest Zilath cleared his throat to gain recognition. Selection had been made. He was going to do it. How proud I was of him at that moment.

"My noble Scribe Larth is named after the famous Princess Larthia. I choose him," Zilath announced.

Trumpets blared.

Had I heard right? Zilath joked. He couldn't mean me.

"Intriguing." Maru, Cisra's prince-priest smiled.

"You're pleased that I would volunteer one of my court." Zilath returned the same kind of smile Maru had given him, one that showed intense dislike and intense rivalry. "We Tarchna are valiant."

I ducked low so I wouldn't be seen.

Zilath's piercing eyes searched the crowd and fixed on mine. "Step forward, Scribe Larth."

"Me?" I squeaked in a voice unlike my own. Sweat poured from my hairline to toes. *I'm not a magistrate, prince, augur or warrior. I don't rule, bless or fight.*

The way conveniently parted to let me pass. *Oh God Tinia! When Zilath commands, there is no choice. I must obey.* I moved solemnly toward my leader. *Has Zilath coerced the Fates to cast a curse over my head?*

"I am but a scribe, recording laws, transactions and accounts. Why would you want me to open a tomb?"

"Take the candle with you."

The magistrates encircled so close I could see each embroidered emblem of authority on their white linen tunics. Precious jeweled pendants sat on their chests like victorious trophies. Gold armlets draped over muscled biceps, marks of warrior status. Their high-laced sandals, appropriate for this heat season, reeked of foot odor. Hawk-like eyes devoured me. Wordlessly they screeched that I should be victim, the sacrifice to cross the threshold.

Hoping that they would see folly in sending a puny stripling into the tomb, I stalled by acknowledging and praising each magistrate with flowery speech, exaggerating his splendid contributions to bring about abundance and industry.

Please, Tinia, let some fearless hero step forward for this dreadful duty.

"Put us off no longer, Scribe Larth. Take the candle!" Zilath impatiently instructed.

This onerous task was unavoidable. "I'm honored, Zilath, that you have decreed that I be at this gathering, that you give me this accolade." Respectfully, I reached for the unlit candle and flint thrust in my face.

The necropolis mound threatened like a monster about to swallow its prey. Mustering dignity, I turned towards the path, seeing each uneven stone as a challenge to be conquered.

If a rock falls on my head, it is only an unimportant scribe to die.

The path within the *tumulo* narrowed, shaded by moss-covered stone walls. With my free hand, I touched the cold stone to support my inner trembling.

The downward path ended at the carved stone post that marked the closing of a tomb. One of Prince-priest Maru's slaves awaited, glaring. "Why are you here? Where's the warrior who enters the tomb?"

"I am chosen."

Startled, he asked, "Where are your weapons, youth?"

I held up the meager candle. "I have none."

"You're crazed to do this," the slave mumbled. Terrified by his own chore, he shakily managed to strike hammer and awl at the marker. The stone door that sealed the sepulcher unhinged and opened. Two other slaves, wild-eyed from this assignment, struggled with the cumbersome door and pressed it against the wall, leaving enough room for me to slip into the dark space. Jittering with fear, they retreated rapidly back towards the assembly.

Those slaves will die for knowing this entrance. What fate will be mine?

Alone, in deadened quiet, except for my own deep breathing, I struck the flint and set flame to the wick. Cautiously, I advanced with an outward braveness I didn't feel. One more step and I would be in the shadowed land of the Ancestor, my namesake, Priestess Larthia.

The cool darkness, refreshing after the humid heat of day, propelled me further to a carved rock hallway. Like the outside path, it was narrow with unornamented walls. I tapped my foot. Hard dirt. At a snail's pace I crept, unknowing its length or whether the floor would be even or not. Solid ground. Reflected on a speck of bright light, some obscure object shined. No smells of death. Damp, stale air permeated the walls. I saw that master builders of a century ago had already devised our system of wedging stones together without mortar. No masonry or rocks would tumble.

The candle flickered as the hallway forked into two passages. A sharp glimmer came from the chamber on my right. I held the flame high and peered in. That brightness had to be gold. A chariot sagged in the corner on wooden wheels splintered by time, yet its decorated lotus blossoms and palm leaves glittered. No, it was untarnished bronze.

In its midst—the metal funeral bier! Under shreds of manly cloth and worked bronze rings and plates, the bony fragments of a skeleton rested face up.

I'm wrong. It can't be Larthia. This is a warrior's chamber.

Breathing more calmly, I continued to the next chamber. Amphora-shaped, discolored silver vases guarded the doorway. Silver and bronze vases, dulled with age, hung above them from the vaulted ceiling. House wares were scattered across the floor: silver bowls and bronze plates, chalices, pitchers styled as ducks, perfume vials and oil burners.

A shadow on the wall of a woman arched acrobatically backward caught my attention. My candle provided meager illumination. She was not alive but a distorted image on a lid's handle of a cylindrical bronze bucket. The rusted lid was inscribed with myth of Goddess Turan casting her love upon mortals. Too irresistible to leave, I placed my candle on the ground and pried off the lid. Dried unguents, oils, lip and cheek paints in little pots stuck with spoons were at the bottom. Hairpins, combs, tarnished mirror and perfume vials were pinned to leather lining. This had to be Larthia's chamber for certainly these were her cosmetics.

Slowly I kept moving. My sandals brushed against something that rolled, its sound reverberating to the wall. I stooped down with the candle. An ordinary black-ware perfume bottle, durable enough not to shatter. Larthia had scribed a band of the Hellenic alphabet around its base. Underneath, a second band was written in Etruscan. She had converted Hellenic to our language.

The Ancestor was talented. Was she the one who created the Etruscan alphabet?

Carefully I tried not to stumble over other precious offerings, but there were too many. Rows and rows of statuary massed around the corner of the chamber, hand-sized metal votives. They were different from the usual safeguards of a deceased one. The women mourners clumped together in a ritual death celebration, dancing and wailing, arms outstretched with grief. These figurines expressed so much heavy sadness that I too felt sorrow.

And then I saw it. Had my gasp been any stronger, it would have blown out the flame. Those votives surrounded a shriveled form that lay on a bier of intricate, latticed bronze. In my candlelight, the form glistened as if Aplu's sun had brightened the chamber. Its leathered skin, sunk into decayed bones, was swathed in pure gold ornaments. Upon it were amber beads, once a necklace on threads. A frayed headdress rested on the skull. Long-looped earrings sank into voids where there were once ears. Gold link necklaces with pendants of silver and ivory were at the throat. Thick filigree bracelets pressed on forearm and wrist bones. Heavy gold rings were studded with oval gems on fleshless fingers. Brooches of imaginary animals rested on tattered fabric. I bent over the remains. Larthia!

Across the skeleton's chest, the gold-threaded garments were fastened with a large shining, half-moon disk. On its surface, lotus plants bordered embossed lions whose manes and tails curled artfully as they prowled about. Below it, two long horizontal fibulas etched with zigzag pattern were pinned to the cloth. Rows of tiny ducks studded with tiny gold balls formed the elliptical base. Jewel of all jewels! Gold of the gods! Larthia's sacred breastplate, her warrior's shield! The augur-priests had said, *"It was forged to protect the soul from powers of evil spirits by intervention of good."* Larthia was known to be the epitome of good—perfection.

From somewhere in the depth of my being, a violent urge sprang up, an urge to touch the sacred breastplate. How wrong it would be to violate it with my stroke.

How would anyone know? Not of my own volition, I covered it with my fingers, then my hand.

My fate is in the hands of the gods. Unknown heat seared up through each finger. *How blessed I am, the first in a hundred years to touch this wonder.*

Captured by Larthia's power, I tottered wearily, slogging back to the tomb's entrance. One last glance. Enough candle was left to see a woman's head sitting in a niche.

"Pick me up," a voice within it seemed to beg.

There was no voice, just my desire. Not a human head, but a container. I cupped it in my hands and rotated it. An inscription read:

"I am the vase of Larthia."

Her vase. Larthia's life image was depicted in finest clay. The black painted hair was incised with wavy lines, a handle extending from the back. Across her forehead, a strip of paint indicated checkered cloth. Birds perched along squared designs on the rim.

Her likeness. Smooth cheeks, forehead and chin, painted almond eyes and thinly arched eyebrows, a short straight nose showing the hint of nostrils. She must have been beautiful.

What a smile! Her upturned lips gave the impression of one who knew mighty secrets of the cosmos. I couldn't help but caress the lovely contours of her vase. This was a treasure I could love, one that I knew she had cherished. Larthia's tomb was marvelous, full of loving objects that brought her joy. *What will my tomb be like? Surely, it won't be as great a tomb as hers. I'll put in my scribing tools, the wedding goblet that the Syrian goldsmith made and an Aegyptian ostrich egg. My bed will be of carved stone, a lidded box like the famous sarcophagus of the married couple, my spouse and I reclining in loving embrace.*

The candle fizzled. I grabbed the stub, taking what little light I had to get out. *This place will consume me if I don't leave.*

Strong daylight burned my eyes at the tomb's doorway. Elation surged through my being. *Done! No wall collapsed. No god of the netherworld assaulted me. I've entered the cosmos of the dead and returned to the cosmos of the living. I live!*

Strangely, the daylight changed. Rapidly, Aplu's sun died and a thunderous roar came from above. A cloudburst, driven by a savage wind brought Tinia's most vicious rain.

What omen is this? Are the gods angry with me for entering Larthia's tomb?

Under the canopy of a large oak tree, the prince-priests sheltered to keep dry, eagerly anticipating my approach, waiting for my report.

Above the noise of the storm, I shouted, "Larthia rests with dignity. Her chamber astonishes with glory! Gold and silver dazzle! What superb workmanship of vases and trinkets!"

"Have care, Larth. You show frailty of character by your cravings for the sacred gold trinkets." Zilath yanked my arm and hissed, "What have you brought me?"

"I took nothing."

He frowned, but turned to the other prince-priests and beamed. "The Ancestors invite us to know their wealth! We enter tomorrow."

At the end of the evening's banquet for the prince-priests, Zilath drew me aside. "Tell of the treasures."

"So much gold that it hurts the eyes. Opulence beyond ours! Matchless. Everything for eternal life."

His eyes flashed. "Show me. Immediately."

"Now?"

"Without delay. A fine time when others banquet."

Yielding to his demand, I led Zilath on the moonlit path. Since Tarchna had been the city to enter the tomb, our guards were on watch. At Zilath's presence, we were let in. Candle in each hand, I steered the prince-priest through the hallway, first to the warrior's chamber.

The warrior had to be Larthia's husband and protector, less appreciated than she by his less opulent chamber. More clearly, I saw the grave goods. On the floor, a four-wheeled cart with a basin in the center, surrounded by dancing satyrs, served as an incense burner. Bell-shaped fumigation vases dangled from the ceiling. it held venerable remnants of war. Tiny metal votive figures, solemn and stiff warrior gods of defense, lay methodically placed on the floor by a bundle of rusted darts. A round embossed bronze shield was stacked against several others. Piled high were warped arrows, stringless bows and dented helmets. The venerable remnants of war.

In Larthia's chamber, Zilath silently examined the cache, going from one to another, holding, stroking and weighing each for worth. I too had another chance to look. A delicate gold flower petal cauldron lay empty on the floor. I sniffed inside. The aroma had evaporated. There was an extraordinary plate painted with ducks, storks and herons that would be perfect for banquet. Last, I picked up a womb-shaped vase of a winged goddess, with big belly and very short legs, dappled with rounded stars. It sparkled with humor.

"A joyful, lively collection, Zilath!"

He hadn't heard me at all.

The prince-priest crouched over Larthia's bier, a spark of intense pleasure on his face, a glint of rapture. "What a vision!" Disregarding Larthia's skeleton, he was enthralled with something he found more precious. His fingers explored the breastplate's polished surface, touching the granulated gold shot balls. He plucked at the edges, prying it loose, sighing and muttering, "Elegant. Magnificent."

Eyes glazed with passion, Zilath jerked at the plate. The ancient cloth disintegrated with a puff of dust. The golden plate remained on the corpse, but the brooch of ducks flew onto the floor. He retrieved it and held it to the candlelight. As swiftly as a hummingbird, Zilath stuffed the brooch into his pouch. "So small. It won't be missed."

In front of me, Zilath dishonored the Ancestor. In lust he had seized the sacred. His justification made me uneasy.

I could say nothing.

By the next dawn, I was renowned for bravery and appointed to guide the formal procession of prince-priests to Larthia's eternal netherworld home. Two of Cisra's guards slouched at the entrance, oddly not hearing us walk on the gravel or rousing at our presence.

"Never mind," Maru of Cisra kicked one. "They'll be punished later."

In all their noble finery, the prince-priests stepped in, humbly awestruck. Unafraid, I led them through the grand tomb. What curious effect occurred! Their humbleness dissipated. Hungrily they ogled at the pieces, calculating which ones would suit their own afterlife tombs. Yet none marked a trinket.

Absorbed in their inspection, they left me free to thoroughly admire the Ancestors' treasury. Wandering about, I grasped something was askew. A silver vase was turned over. The bronze votives were no longer upright. The warrior's ring was missing. So was the winged goddess vase. At the niche where Larthia's vase had sat, a ring of dust stained the ledge.

Dismayed, I went to Zilath. "Gone! Thievery, an insult to the gods, Zilath!"

Haggard, not his usual self, twitching his beard with nervous fingers, he ignored me. I knew he hadn't slept, for he was bleary-eyed, pensive and withdrawn.

The other magistrates exited and became unexpectedly vigorous, excited and agreeable to each other, unified by the sweetened atmosphere of death.

"Most venerated Princess-priestess Larthia, last of the female line of priests, was celebrated for her wisdom and knowledge of the <u>Book of Tages</u> and the <u>Code of Discipline</u>," Aule of Veia said gleefully.

"We must tell our people how advanced the civilization of the previous saecula was," Maru of Cisra pronounced with delight.

"Did you see the stone-encrusted necklaces, gold armlets and rings, the bronze chariot and weapons, crafted more as works of art than tools of war?" Zilath drooled to the other prince-priests. "Let's see the chamber once more."

Incessantly he spoke of Larthia's wealth. What unquenchable appetite he had for her treasures.

The tomb has aged him. Could the Ancestors will him to death for entering it?

"So much beauty," Zilath prattled as he goaded his fellow prince-priests towards the necropolis on the second procession to the tomb. Abruptly they stopped at the tomb's entrance. The same guards of the night before lay twisted into agonized knots. Froth bubbled from their contorted mouths.

"Poisoned," buzzed one prince-priest.

"The hemlock herb," agreed another. "Ghastly death. Trembling. Loss of movement. Loss of breath."

Horror replaced thoughts of splendor. Averting my eyes from the revolting sight, I focused on the loveliness of the garden where living cypress and ilex trees blended into the score of mound tombs. But the guards' oozing dribble penetrated my mind.

Do we suffer the anger of the gods for opening the Ancestor's chamber?

Commotion followed. The prince-priests crumbled and their previous dignified behavior faded. They scrambled away from Larthia's tomb as if they too would be poisoned by proximity. Through incantations and offerings as homage to Gods Tinia, Uni and Menvra, they attempted to find means to examine the Ancestors' tombs without retaliation. They found none.

Other Cisra slaves were summoned to shut the entrance, resealing it with stone and mortar, hammering the marker into place.

Hastily the prince-priests dispensed with all ceremony, ceased the Celebration of the Ancestors, and sensibly dashed to their cities to order citizens never to desecrate the Ancestors again.

2

Duplicity

"Word is out that you've been to Cisra and seen the
Tomb of the Ancestor," Arun grumbled irritably, sprawling face up on our matrimonial bed watching me undress.
"I was the first! The magistrates were afraid to go in!"
I shed my costume, and folded it into the keepsake carved
ivory chest, gifted by my seafarer uncle who ventured
throughout the Great Sea. With relief, I unbound the cloth
that suppressed my breasts and pulled off rags that
thickened my waist. "I couldn't get a message to you of
my whereabouts. You were on a hunt and not in need of
me."

"My family worried at your absence. I made excuse
and told them your mother beckoned. Too long this has
been going on. I'm weary of your secret jaunts to the
court."

"You're as loyal to Zilath as I am, though you tell untruths
to everyone on my behalf." I pulled the floor-length, wheat-

colored linen tunic over my head and belted it with a wide bronze chain. "Yes, Zilath selected me to go into the tomb. I couldn't deny him."

"You could have said 'no' and revealed your womanhood—your nobility."

"How unfairly you tease! Zilath expects my obedience." I wrenched off the clunky men's sandals and donned soft feminine leathers. "Besides, Zilath will favor us with rewards for our tomb."

More wide-awake, Arun sat up, eyes blazing, his angular tanned cheekbones highlighted by the candle. "That's better. Now you wear proper attire for an Etruscan noblewoman. You may be a scribe, but you're also my wife, Larthia."

"I haven't forsaken you for a scribe's clothes and habits."

He laughed scornfully. "My wife poses as a man to scribe for the prince-priest."

"No one knows."

"Not even Ranu or Velza?"

"Not even them, my best friends."

"You say you love and are devoted to me, as I you, but you slink away from home at odd times to do bidding of another."

"Don't be liverish." I began the arduous task of weaving strands of old shorn hair into braids on top of my head. "Our gods bestowed me with the gift of scribing. I honor this gift and discharge my duty as Zilath orders."

My fate is difficult, my role one of constant trials. I am forced by circumstances to live a life divided by duplicity. What a curse!

"You're dutiful to Zilath. Are you as faithful to me?" Arun snapped.

"Of course I'm faithful!" I exploded. "If you had demanded from the start, I would have given up being a scribe, albeit, unwillingly, but you didn't. If I stop now,

Zilath would be angry and not have me scribe again. Why are you fretting?"

Would he be pleased to have me stay home? Might he love me more? Deliberately, I dallied in arranging my hair. Problems of our union surfaced grimly and angrily as I recalled my plight.

Married in youth, season after season passed without offspring, not from lack of trying. Some ten years had gone by, childless years without children's voices. *Why had I not squeezed out children like other Etruscan women?* Old Birthing Woman of the Hills said I wasn't ripe, and my mother, Risa, urged patience. She told me of her own difficulty in child bearing. *Had I inherited a curse from my mother?*

Since childhood I scribbled, starting with crushed soft white stone on black clay slabs that Grandfather Vel invented, the bucchero he created as he experimented with clays and ground stone. I persuaded Grandfather and Ari to teach me simple images so that I could keep household accounts. Then I took stylus and waxed board to copy the Hellenic alphabet as well as words scratched on pots and vases that Uncle Venu and his Hellenic craftsman, Nikothenes, brought to Tarchna from Euboean colonizers in the southern city of Cumae. I loved the lines of each letter, mysterious symbols that joined into words, then sentences containing important meanings. I could read and say them out loud fluently.

"Young girls use hands for chores, not for writing. Shame on you! Scribing is the sacred task of the prince-priest's court, not to be mocked by a girl child," brother Culni taunted with superiority of being older.

"I don't care. It's a stupid law," I retaliated.

"Rebellious you are!" he spat back nastily.

We were never to think well of each other after that.

Brother Ari defended me against him as I continued to enjoy my passion. Brazenly I listened to how the Tarchna spoke, and scribed sounds I heard, realizing that Etruscan scribing was actually Hellenic, with a few minor corrections and revisions of the Etruscan tongue.

As a noble wife, I relied on my servants for chores of home and market, disdaining the spindle. To fill my childless, empty days, I immersed myself in scribing practice. Arun pitied me and so was not offended by my insatiable need. Nor did he prevent me.

Numerous seasons ago, the gods changed my fate on a day so extraordinary that I couldn't forget it. I was at market. Near the stone steps, a group of magistrates were in heated conversation. They disbanded. I noticed one left behind his slate with words and numbers clearly written in chalk-market accounts—important ones to my eyes. My arms were loaded with vegetables and herb bunches, so I couldn't see his entire face as I called out, "Magistrate, you've left your orders for grains here."

"'Magistrate' you name me? Don't you know who I am?" the man asked kindly. "A noblewoman like you must surely recognize me. What family is yours?"

I dropped my bundles. "A thousand pardons! How could I not know you, Prince-priest Zilath of Tarchna, the greatest magistrate of all!" As gracefully as I could, I bowed, although my tunic was dotted with herb leaves and twigs. "I'm humbled by your presence. My father was your road builder, my husband is your hunter."

"Your family serves me well. Wasn't your grandfather, Soil Sampler Vel Porenna, and your grandmother, the Healer Anneia?"

"Yes, Zilath."

"You read my slate. Who taught you?"

"Please don't ask me to inform."

"If you can read, you must scribe."

"Yes, Zilath," I said reluctantly, wondering if he would be angry for my insubordination.

"Fascinating," he laughed and held out another slate. "Can you read this?"

"It's the sheep count."

He drew a scroll out of his tunic's belt and handed it to me. "And this?"

I unrolled the scroll gently, printed letters on linen disclosing some text of the *Book of Tages*, Etruscan laws. I whispered, "These are sacred words, Zilath."

"Can you copy them?"

"Perfectly."

"Ah!" the prince-priest chortled. "Magic is in your fingers."

That's when I learned the word, 'magic.' My long, tapered fingers curved naturally as if I held stylus between thumb, pointer and middle fingers—not coarse, for I rubbed them daily with liquid of olive. Maybe my hands held magic for I talked with them as if they had a life of their own. Late into nights when I couldn't sleep, I would sit in our courtyard by candlelight, scribing songs and stories of the gods remembered from banquets. Thus I strengthened my right wrist for endurance. Words flowed through me onto whatever scraps of linen, stone and slate I could find.

Zilath picked up my writing hand and stroked it. "Too bad you're not a man or you'd scribe for me."

My hand tingled from Zilath's touch.

Thrilled by the encounter, I rushed home earlier than foreseen and threw back the curtain to our matrimonial room. Arun was lolling on our bed with an unknown woman by his side, both moving like two serpentine creatures sinuous in ecstasy, bathed in the sweat of coupling. Intense in lewd positions, they didn't see or hear me. I closed the curtain and retreated to the courtyard to obliterate the repulsive sight.

*As I bore him no children, he has found another who
might. Perchance it was a vision that I saw him fornicating
in our bed.* Perhaps it was a curse imposed by the gods,
or perhaps it was love Goddess Turan at work, but that
sight of my husband and the woman changed my course.
*Without children, I'm more a man than woman. If Zilath
needs a scribe, I will accommodate him.*

Furiously I chopped my hair to a youth's length, and
let it fall without braiding. Under the loosely belted
tunic, I bound my breasts and hips. In borrowed boot
length shoes to the knees that concealed my feminine
calves, I practiced swaggering like a man. With pumice
and cold embers from the fireplace, I roughened my face.
In the pretext of a youth I sneaked into court, hatless, a
cape covering the tunic I wore, made of men's cloth and
color.

No one paid heed to me as I waited in the public line
to speak with Zilath. This chore must have disgusted him,
for at my turn he drummed his fingers with irritation, and
said abrasively, "What do you want?"

He hadn't recognized me. Boldly, I asked, "Do you
not remember our meeting?"

"No.—Yes! Your flesh was different. You've put on
weight." An amused smile crossed his face.

Of course, he knew who I was. The great leader teased.
His authority didn't frighten me, nor did his humor.
Proudly I replied, "Prince-priest, I came to serve you, to
scribe for you."

"Why?" he demanded.

I had to convince him of my sincerity for his decision
could change my life. "Every being holds a reason for
existence. The gods must have willed that mine is to
scribe, for my head, heart and hand can lay down symbols
I mouth and think."

More alert, he looked at me with interest, as I went
on. With each word, I grew more confident. "Fast my hand

moves across stone or scroll, forming numbers and letters. You will be pleased that I can record your every word. Humbly I come before you to plead for my fate." Then I trembled.

"Your explanation marks well. Noblewoman—tsk— youth . . ." He seemed to be mulling over my speech. "You shall be known as Larth, my clever new scribe."

"Larth?"

"Your name must be used in the male gender," Zilath chuckled and pulled me closer. "Scribe Larth, you must come whenever I command. How you manage is not my worry. You will have tools and a seat, far away from others so they don't spot your sex."

So began my secret life. I, Larthia, became Scribe Larth. It made sense to be named one so similar to my own. I sat on the stool behind Zilath and copied his messages, using charcoal and chalk on bucchero or stone. My proficiency improved with practice. With fine bronze styluses dipped in sea anemone ink I scribed orders for grain on linen scrolls. As my techniques advanced, I was summoned to inscribe treaties with Phoenicia and Hellas with sharpened bronze knives on stone pallets.

At first I questioned my ability, but going to the court became familiar and routine. I was accepted as expert and moved closer to his side. How I delighted in my craft! Zilath saw this too and was amused.

My skills brought me importance. I became privy to codes from the *Book of Tages* and the *Etruscan Discipline* of the augur-priests. Promising discretion, I accepted this honor. Zilath had metal crafters make the best quality bronze styluses with needle sharp points to imbed prayers into gold plates. Handles of my styluses were of smoothest fir wood and decorated with the prince-priest's symbol of authority.

"You're a valuable asset to Zilath." Arun would peek over my shoulder as I took care in forming cursive letters.

"You have miracle of translating what came from the inner tongue and lips, through hand to slate."

"You aren't jealous of my joy? You don't hate me for this talent?"

"Hate you? Never. You're my wife, as loyal to me as the day we wed."

I am loyal to him, but he was not to me. Goddess Turan plays with us. Does our union stand with Turan's strength or not?

"Larthia, do you hear me?" Arun's voice broke through these background thoughts. "Your hair is a mess. Your mind is elsewhere."

With hand-held mirror, not only my contemplative frown was reflected. Hair strands I connected to my shorn hair were too loose, tangled, unruly braids to be redone. My usual solution would be to insert sprigs of recently picked field flowers.

"Be quick! We're late. Cover your head in the old style." He brought my mantle and laid it over my hair and bare shoulders. "The temple gods call us. Come, forgive my temper."

"We Tarchna have been foremost to see the princess-priestess's tomb!" Zilath gloated to all, his court newly popular, the fashionable destination of magistrates, nobles, landowners, and sea and land merchants. Even Italic cousins of Zilath's family came from Roma. Day after day all would arrive with the same curiosity as they pledged new commerce ties.

"And by the way, what was found in Larthia's tomb?" visitors asked, slyly questioning as they negotiated new transactions. "What have you taken out?"

"Nothing. Nothing to barter," Zilath replied slickly. "The sepulcher has been resealed, intact, to honor the Ancestors."

He omits the truth, the demise of the guards. Had Zilath drugged them the night we went into the tomb? Did he poison them?

"My noble scribe went to see the Ancestors! Ah, yes, here he is." The Prince-priest threw out his arms in a histrionic gesture, flashing ringed fingers. "Fragile looking, isn't he, but strong of mind and purpose. Without hesitation, he entered Larthia's tomb. The best scribe in Tarchna! Larth, meet Magistrate of Construction from Velathri."

I was famous! Not only did they come to learn of the tomb but to see me, a scribe who entered before royalty. Respectfully, I went forward to bow, and caught the shimmer of Zilath's ten rings shining in daylight. His middle finger held one that was new. *The warrior's ring!*

"Larth, here's the merchant from Ilva to trade iron. Copy our accounts with him."

Bothered by seeing that ring, I grabbed my pouch of tools and marked transactions on linen scroll as efficiently as I could, not looking directly at Zilath. He hovered over me, clamping his hand on my work, forcing me to turn around. On the prince-priest's tunic, a clasp drew the cloth on his shoulder. *Larthia's brooch of golden ducks!*

"My cousin Senacus from Roma, Larth. Speak with him in his language to show your aptitude." Zilath paced around the court, rearranging rich ornaments as he spoke, his way of letting the Roman know of Tarchna's power.

As I recited a common myth in Italic, Zilath stood in front of his table of ornaments. Rashly, he clutched one of his prizes and darted back to his throne. *Larthia's vase!*

Shocked at seeing it, I stuttered in recounting the myth. But Senacus seemed truly excited by my abilities to recite, even with my mistake.

"Well done," Senacus approved.

"Yes, well done," Zilath agreed with the Roman. "You know so much. You're quite the scribe, Larth, aren't you? You even know the *Etruscan Discipline* and *Book of Tages!*"

The tone of his voice made me mumble back, "Zilath, only at your instruction."

In turmoil, I left the court. *I can say nothing of these treasures. Zilath's intentional comments and his thievery distress me. He would deny any accusation. His smile says we're conspirators.*

The howl of a dog greeted me and then stopped after I passed. It howled again, alerting me that someone else walked in the night as Tarchna slept. Probably a night watchman or guard. Deliberately, I rounded a different corner to obscure my identity and home. The man rounded the corner too. I changed the course of streets, and he trailed at a distance, but still there. I leaned against a recessed doorway and as the man continued, I saw that he was neither watchman nor guard, nor of Tarchna, but someone on search.

Does he seek me? Why?

"Landowner Pumpu from Clevsin and Vintner-Merchant Marc from Curtun. Meet my noble Scribe Larth, the one who courageously entered Princess-priestess Larthia's tomb. My scribe will keep the best accounts with you. They want our Gravisca vines, Scribe Larth. Inland, they're becoming wine makers."

"Not yet," the vintner-merchant said amicably. "Our crops have failed for two seasons. We used the wrong vines, I think. If we can exchange sheep for your vines, we may succeed."

The man's deep rich voice reverberated through me even though he stood across the court's platform. *His words are straightforward and honest.* A bolt of Tinia's lightning seemed to penetrate my being as my eyes were drawn to the vintner-merchant. *He's the most attractive man I've ever seen. I could melt in his arms.* Fidgeting with stylus, I dropped it, almost blushing. *Whatever am I thinking? I'm married to Arun.*

The vintner's sparkling eyes, vigilant and intelligent, looked back at me quizzically, studying my ears or was it my cheekbones, then my eyes. He appeared confused by what he saw and turned away.

Does the vintner know of my deception? Perhaps I've been seen too much. Surely someone would know I'm a woman and reveal my true identity if they looked closely. How long I've been a scribe! Am I foolish enough to suppose it will last my life? Did I ever think I wouldn't be found out?

After the last guest left the court I packed my tools.

"Tinia's sky has darkened. I need rest after these long days."

"Long days, you say? You're popular with our visitors. Perhaps too popular."

"I'm tired, Zilath."

"Go, then." Zilath gave one of his magnanimous smiles. Impetuously he kissed me on the lips. "Good bye."

Surprised by this unpredicted endearment, I managed to stammer, "Even the gods bed down for the night. Good night to you, Zilath."

Out of the glare of Zilath's temple lights, I crossed the courtyard and went down steps to the market place, more cautious since the night that man had followed me. Uni's moon shone behind a mist rising from the edge of the uplands, throwing eerie shadows over the square. The shadows mocked my nervousness. Covered grain stalls and vendors' parcels stood deserted, lonely without crowds of day.

Arun will be angry that I'm so late. I quickened my walk, scraping my boots on the paved empty market place. Somewhere behind me, I heard the slightest sounds of footsteps. *Not again! Please Tinia, let it be a servant or slave finishing toil for his master. Don't let it be the same one who pursued me before.* Those footsteps followed, hurrying, getting closer until I could hear the person breathing strongly.

A sudden gust of cloth whipped across my face, blinding and gagging me with a strong unpleasant smell. Unable to scream, I struck out weakly with my fists. Strong hands firmly pinned my arms to my body and dragged me on the stones, scraping my knees raw. With little remaining strength, I resisted and struggled against his heavy weight, but he punched me in the stomach, knocking out my air. Energy drained from my being and I faltered, slumping awkwardly into an unnatural position. Depleted by this attacker, darkness overtook me and I remembered no more.

3

Arun, The Hunter

Larthia didn't come home last night. She's been late
before, sitting at banquets, feasting on Zilath's delicacies to celebrate Tarchna's bounty. Is she fornicating with
him? Much time they spend together especially since she
opened the Ancestor's tomb.

All Etruria talks of that tomb, crowding Zilath's court
with new commerce. The noble Scribe Larth is fawned
over, accoladed with privilege, recording new orders like
a magistrate. Larth, ha! Larthia's new fame makes her
careless of who she truly is.

Last night was the longest night of my life, lying in our
bed after the oil lamps had been dimmed, missing her body
next to mine, despite my fury. I couldn't sleep, for every
conceivable memory tortured me. Sentimental thoughts I
never knew I had, romantic, emotional and maudlin.
Awake, I thought of our years together, our courtship and
fierce lovemaking that hadn't produced children, leaving

her despondent. How unusual she found solace in scribing! How many seasons and years we've been together, joined in union since youth, now in our cresting. Larthia was special! Smitten, I, Hunter Arun, not a nobleman like Hunter Culni, married her before another youth could.

What thoughts I had in the dark! I paced back and forth in our small, cramped marriage room until I could no longer stand it. Who could I tell that my wife was this famous scribe? No one. I dressed in my leathers and went to the stable to groom my stallion, calming him with a handful of barley before taking the brush to rub him down. As I combed his flowing mane, I remembered how Larthia detested riding. The wind from the speed bothered her. She didn't like that I conquered wild beasts either. Equally, her marking slates and scrolls with gibberish writings didn't interest me. *What does that matter? We were paired by the gods.*

My household was awake and I went into the cooking room to have some puls. It wasn't ready. The servants were still pounding and grinding grain, preparing it for our daily meal. My mother and sisters spindled wool by the hearth.

"Larthia is to cart wool today. Where is she?"

"Asleep," I answered bluntly.

"She is needed now. Get her up! It's her duty!"

"I must hurry," I said evasively. "I'll eat later."

The hour was changing from dark to dawn when I started for the Laris-Vella household, not far from the court. My in-laws' dwelling, Tarchna's most lavish and wealthy home, was second only to the prince-priest's palace in size and opulence. Risa inherited it from her father, the famous Soil Sampler Vel Porenna, who made Tarchna rich in copper and tin, along with his deceased wife, Healer Anneia Laris, who introduced herbs to tend the sick. It was logical that Risa owned it even though her older sister Arith and younger brother Venu were raised there. Merchant Seafarer Uncle Venu, was always sailing off to Hellas and the East to bring imports to Tarchna. Aunt Arith had married a nobleman from Cisra and lived there. That family! Always successful, smart, fired with varied purpose! I supposed they'd be snobbish and condescending, but they were agreeable and vigorous, all except Arith. How proud I was to marry into this prestigious family!

It must be some restless trait that carried from ancestor to descendant, striving for some unknown reason that made each one of them achieve recognition. Larthia was no exception, scribing and learning strange languages.

Now that Risa's husband, Road Builder Parth, was dead, a tragic death at the hands of Umbrian rogues, Larthia's brothers, Culni and Ari, along with their families moved close to protect Risa. Not Larthia and I. A wife stays in her husband's home.

Culni Laris was ready to quest for stag when I arrived at the house. We always rode together, he, Master of the Hunt, on his stallion, and I on mine. Without him, I, as a young hunter just learning the trade, wouldn't have met and married his younger sister.

"Did Larthia stay the night here?"

"Ask Mother. She's mixing paints in the shed."

Brave Risa ignored how scandalous it was to defy a widow's life and paint tomb scenes with Master Crafter Asba. Risa's hands and smudged face showed her to be absorbed in her craft. She greeted me vaguely, not wanting to be distracted from her paints.

"Risa, is Larthia here?"

"Haven't seen her since last market day."

She wasn't upset about not knowing the whereabouts of her daughter. Larthia was like Risa, eccentric, with peculiar needs and habits. Even though Larthia slyly scribed for the prince-priest, she must have told Risa.

"Risa, do you think Larthia has been acting odd lately?"

"Not more than usual. Ask Ranu."

Ranu was wife of my best friend, Ari, a noble road builder as his father Parth had been.

Ranu was in the dining place, plumping cushions and arranging fresh flowers.

"You remind me of Larthia. You both like to do the same tasks."

"That's why we're friends."

"When I first met Larthia she was doing what you do, slapping cushions with happy abandon. When she saw me, she instantly stopped and stared steadily at my face, then walked straight towards me and touched my cheek. 'I like you,' she said. Noblewoman Risa heard Larthia and quickly apologized for her daughter's rudeness, yet she was laughing! 'My daughter's been around her brothers too long. She talks as if she knows their friends well.'"

"That sounds like her," Ranu said.

"I was delighted with her directness, her attractiveness. Not seductive or sensual but honest in her statement. Pure, charming, joyous!"

"Why are you telling me this now?"

"Where is she, Ranu?"

"You don't know?"

Her retort made me think she did. "I've been out on hunts for the court. Hasn't she been with you?"

My innards throbbed as concern for Larthia increased. She hadn't shown up all day. At twilight, I waited for magistrates, advisors and court to leave so I could see Prince-priest Zilath alone.

On his royal ivory chair Zilath sat chewing quail meat left from a recent feast, its juices running at the edges of his mouth.

"Prince-priest, where's Larthia? Where's my wife?"

"Larthia? There's no such person here." Zilath laughed, obviously tickled by what he had said, until tears poured down his cheeks.

His little joke made me realize that last night's imagination had overrun itself. I went along with his game.

"Well then, Scribe Larth."

Zilath indulged on a bone, crunching with wolf-like jaws. He choked and sputtered, "Ah, yes I had a Scribe Larth."

"So where is he?" Incensed by his nonsense, I sourly cut the matter short. " Not to be impertinent, yet I must ask, did you have your way with him—err, her?"

He spit the bones noisily into a bowl, regained his posture and roared, "I don't fornicate with scribes! Scribe Larth was the culprit who stole treasures from Ancestor Larthia's tomb."

"Stole treasures?"

"A few trinkets-necklaces, armlets, a golden brooch. A valuable vase."

"Impossible! Larthia has no need to steal. She's a noblewoman of high rank."

"Is she now? Noblewomen don't shear their hair and wear high boots. They don't scribe nor read. I use male scribes as decreed in the *Book of Tages*."

"But . . ."

"My Scribe Larth saw the Ancestor's tomb in Cisra. He became greedy." With a linen cloth, Zilath wiped his greasy hands from his meal.

"Greedy—no. There must be a mistake."

"That scribe didn't come to court today. He disappeared." His point made, Zilath flung the stained cloth on the floor and pushed it off the throne platform.

"Disappeared?"

"Gone. Where is anyone's guess." Zilath flicked his thumb and middle finger together, his sign of power just as God Tinia was known to do when creating lightning. "Don't contradict me."

I was dismissed. Embarrassed by my own suspicions and stunned by Zilath's cruel accusations, I shuffled away from his platform like a wounded animal. As Uni's moon rose high, I raced to the widow.

"You say she didn't come home last night?" The widow, sultry and ripe as a sweet melon, stroked my brow.

Widow Matulnei didn't know that Larthia was a scribe, only that many of Larthia's days and nights were filled. The widow and I were often together after a day of seasonal hunt.

"It gives us extra moments this eve." I relaxed under her ministrations. It was safe to go to her. Her two children were usually asleep and didn't disturb us no matter how loud the widow shrieked.

That Larthia had become a scribe was convenient. Most eves she labored at Zilath's court. When she was home, there was no newness in our bed. Why should I waste my lonely nights without her? I needed relief that the widow offered.

"A quick romp!" I told the warrior's wife next, the other woman who serviced me discreetly. She was usually available, for the warrior was at sea for long spells and she was lusty and lewd in her movements. I would mount her like a stallion. Once, in her itch, she sneaked into my home bed. Just once, for I would not have Larthia discover my amusements.

The widow smears honey as precaution, but I question the warrior's wife. What scandal would arise if I impregnate either or both of them! I must take more care.

Both women are unlike Larthia, well-bosomed, not boyish like Larthia, she who had once been my warmth, my life-long desire, now too clever and brilliant to bed. Yet, if I were to go against Larthia, her noble family would have me hunted down like I hunt deer and boar. They'd go one step further. They'd have me mutilated.

Does Larthia know of my dalliances? Is that why she didn't come home? Our bedchamber was still unused. At least I was comforted that Larthia hadn't bedded with Zilath. And, for all of her foolishness in dressing as a man, she wouldn't pilfer. She wouldn't steal from Zilath. So unpredictable lately, detached, almost haughty with power after going into that tomb, almost possessed when talking about its contents. What did he mean that she had disappeared?

From the courtyard came the clamor of children running, my assorted nieces and nephews. Giggling and joking, they washed up from daily chores, splashing in the gurgling water of the communal cauldron. Their parents soon arrived, admonishing them for spilled water while praising cleanliness. So many of us living under one roof in a compound of connected rooms.

"Arun! Larthia! Evening meal is upon us!" my mother called at our bedroom curtain. "Come eat!"

I joined the family in the courtyard—parents, two sisters, brothers and spouses and their children—sitting on cushions at table, waiting impatiently to begin.

"Well, where is Larthia today? At eve last night she also missed the family meal," my father griped.

"She's off to Old Woman of the Hills to get childbearing herbs," I lied, a natural lie considering our childless state.

"She goes so often. By now you should have many offspring of your own," my younger sister tittered.

Those kinds of biting remarks angered Larthia to get away and scribe for Zilath. I, too, was humiliated, for Larthia's barrenness was much discussed.

"Let's eat or the stew gets cold," mother ordered. "Tell her she's needed to weave new linen cloth."

Were they becoming suspicious? It was usually easy enough for Larthia to absent herself with so many relatives. Busy with their own labors, they didn't know of her daily employment. Did they think, with her infertility, she hadn't enough chores to do, an empty existence for a noblewoman?

"Ari is here, Uncle," a small child interrupted. "He wants to see you."

"Eat without me," I excused myself, heading for the door before he could be invited to join the meal. "He probably needs provisions for his road crew."

How will I explain to the Laris family that Larthia is not to be found?

"Where was my sister today?" Ari demanded, annoyed.

"At your family's home, I thought."

"Of course not. She's your wife. She should be here."

"Then she could have been at market."

"At market!" Ari scoffed. "Not so."

"She comes and goes at whim. I don't know where she is." The lameness of my own words unsettled me further, weary from lack of sleep and food, my face pinched into a scowl. "Surely, she'll be home by dark."

"Is she missing, Arun? Zilath's scribe is missing, too. Word is out he's a thief."

"Zilath's scribe a thief!" I could feel my voice go hoarse with tension. "No!"

"Zilath said he's disappeared."

"What?"

"He's gone. Larth's his name. Larthia's gone. Are they missing together?"

I almost retched at the craziness of Ari's ideas. He had put the scribe and Larthia together and come up with a preposterous conclusion. Others could think the same.

"Can you not keep your wife, Arun?"

I should have argued, but I was too discomfited. A part of what he said was the truth.

"Don't fool me." He threw his mantle around his shoulders and stalked out, gritting his teeth. "Find Larthia. You're the hunter."

4

Revenge Of The Gods

Trussed like a stag on a roasting spit, I rolled from side to side, slamming my forehead against wooden slats in one direction, bruising the back of my head in the other. I couldn't stop the rolling; my arms and legs were bound with hemp. A wet rag was stuffed in my mouth, bitter from a taste I didn't know. My eyes were blinded with a scarf.

I'm in a box, no, it's a cart. The smell of barley straw went up my nostrils and I floated on a cushion of needle-like old stalks. The cart bumped along uncontrollably on a deeply rutted road. My pouch of scribing tools on my belt pierced my skin. Each movement made more bruises. The constant rolling made me drowsy again and I lapsed into semi-consciousness.

"Skinny, he is. Not a warrior bone in him."

"That's why he's a scribe. Not much of a man."

The cart jolted and stilled. Low and rough, the first voice said, "We'll stay here. We're far enough from Tarchna. Let's pull off the road and sleep. Uncover the scribe. Give him air."

The black canvas tarp was furled up and light from an oil lamp streamed under my blindfold. I could feel their eyes upon me, peering into the box. *Who are these men? Who has done this to me?* I wanted to scream, but the rag jammed too tightly against my tongue. *Why have they taken me?*

"Get some flax from that field there. The scribe groans in discomfort. He needs a better bed. Chain his foot to the hook. We'll take off these binds. No one could hear him yammering anyway."

I moaned within. *Is this a jest, Arun? Do these men work for you? Are you jealous of Zilath's hold on me? That season past when I came home unexpectedly to find our bed warmed and perfumed by another, in despair I became loyal to Zilath. I promise to quit. Don't expose me, don't plot to get rid of me. I'll come back to you, Arun, to our families, to our home. Please come, Arun!*

One of them was talking to me. I couldn't tell one voice from the other, still drugged from some noxious potion. One captor removed the blindfold and took the wet rag out of my mouth. My vision of the man was blurred from the darkness to sudden light, but he spoke Tarchna dialect, although not natural. "Make water if you must behind the tree, scribe. Don't try to run. Hemp ties your foot to my arm."

It's to my fortune they are discreet or I would be discovered as a woman.

Once relieved, I collapsed into the fresh flax, unable to keep my eyes open, falling into an abysmal slumber. At dawn, my captors awakened me with puls cake and wine, allowing me privacy to repeat my relief behind a tree. Odd that they hadn't taken my pouch of scribing tools. If someone had followed us, they might see a sign where I was. I whipped out a stylus and quickly scratched L-A-R-T-H on the trunk.

Thrown back into the flax, my foot was chained to the hook. Before another rag could be pressed into my mouth, I pleaded, "Take me back to Tarchna."

New wet rag in hand, the man hesitated, balled it up, snickered, and then leaned against the side of the cart.

"You've made a terrible mistake. Zilath protects me for I'm his loyal scribe. Arun—my family—all will miss me."

"They won't miss you after awhile."

"They will. I'm needed." Through my haziness I asked frantically, "Do you work for the vintner?"

"The scribe babbles. 'Arun.' 'The vintner.' No one will miss you, especially since you've been disgraced for stealing the hoard from the Ancestor's tomb." Dropping the rag into the cart, he scooped out some flax and brushed off an odd shaped sack. Reaching in, he withdrew an object. "How virtuous, scribe. You took this chalice. And this armlet." He dangled them before me. "You stole them, didn't you?"

"No! These are objects from Ancestor Larthia's tomb that were beside her bier!"

The man snorted. "Surely you wanted this armlet of entwined serpents, too."

"I've never seen that one."

The second man came around to the other side of the cart and held up a perfume vessel, juggling it from hand to hand.

"Don't do that! It's precious, delicate!"

"What a smart scribe to recognize your own thievery."

"I didn't steal anything!" I strained my eyes to better see both accusers. They had crudely shaved beards hiding their features. They wore soiled tunics as if they had been working in the field. No, their tunics were intentionally soiled, but of good quality, worthy of wearing at court. *Court? I know who this man is! He was once at Zilath's court. I'm not sure of the other. Had these two been at court yesterday, or was it last season?*

"Who are you? What do you want with me?"

Without reply, he packed Larthia's tomb goods back into the sack and jammed the rag into my throat.

Pungent smells from the rag softened my being like sheep wool. Seeing my limpness, they stretched the tarp across the top rim, closing off my light, leaving me to my flax bed.

"Let's be going," one growled and lashed the horse with the rein.

The cart lunged forward, rolling as before on the broken road. Tied as my body was, I rolled closer to the side, constraining myself from added motion, but my chained foot was chaffed from strain. They hadn't blindfolded me again, for which I was thankful, and a slit of light blazed from a knothole in the wooden slat. Bits of landscape skimmed by. Tarchna's land was gone, for there was neither heath nor corn or their smells. As I lay deadened during the night we must have passed Tarchna's boundary ridges. Inland we traveled, away from the Great Sea for there was no watery breeze, just hinterland air. My belly lurched with each spin of the cart's wheels, wearing off the potion until I felt more clearheaded, bringing a dread that crept up my spine and made me rigid.

The cart labored up a hill, stopped at the top, then tumbled down the other side as if drunk from too much sweet Etruscan wine, almost throwing me into a washed out gully. Both men swore on the gods as they righted cart and horse away from a thicket of thorny bushes.

"At least the scribe's hands are fine."

Today they're concerned about care of me and treat me better. Peculiarly, they're even worried about my hands.

They lifted me out of the cart and carried my strapped up body to a shade tree, then sat me against it as they inspected the cart for damage. I had a chance to view the road cut from tufa rock. The wild gully threatened me with its ugliness. Gnarled shrubs sprouted upward from the rocky hill, the color of charred wood, interspersed with oaks and dense vines. If they wanted to kill me, this lonely and remote gully would be the place.

After the men pronouned the cart fit, they drove on. We came to mossy banks of a stream, butted under a steep, craggy cliff draped with foilage. Mouths of caves yawned at me from the other side, menacing, darkened spaces, skirted by a weeded path.

Where are they taking me?

"We climb from here. Let's get there before Aplu's sun dies," the more talkative man looked up at the cliff. He wrapped a hemp cord around my tunic and the other end around his hand, "Don't bother to call out. No one lives here."

Calm. I must stay calm.

Obviously they had planned this journey well before abducting me for they both knew what to do. The second man cleared some uprooted bushes, uncovering a cavern, big enough to hide the cart and horse inside, quieting the horse with grain.

We crossed the stream on foot. Small and big, irregularly shaped, grotesque caves loomed at me as I was pushed up the path. One cave after another lined the cliff above. My entire being quivered. *What creatures are in them?* Further on, some were boarded. Masonry incised with fake columns and door frames covered the more finished ones. Man-hewn. The higher we went, I saw what they were, niches carved into the rock. Sepulchers!

We halted at a closed tomb.

Why else would they bring me here except to kill me? I squeezed my eyes shut, standing as tall as I could to show

dignity at death, bracing myself, waiting for the knife to
be plunged through.

"This is as far as we go. "

I opened my eyes. I still lived.

Using wedge and hammer, the two men pried wooden
boards away from the wall and pushed me in. With flint
they each lit an oil lamp. Inside was a chamber with beds
molded into the rock wall. From the leather bag he carried
on his shoulder, the taller man withdrew a stake, and struck
it with the hammer, driving it into the stone floor. "You'll
stay here tonight and others will come for you tomorrow."

"Others will come for you," I repeated stupidly,
reeling from amazement that I wasn't dead. "What
others?"

"We'll leave ewe's cheese and mash with your Tarchna
wine, and a pot for your relief. Our work is done."

"Done?"

They laughed like demented wolves, and chained my
left arm and leg to the bed. "We satisfy our Prince-priest
by getting you. Your hands and wrists were not damaged,
scribe."

'*Your Tarchna wine,*' they said. With sudden
recognition, I knew who they could be. Not of Tarchna
but of Veia. *They were at the Celebration of the Ancestors
with their Prince-priest Aule. Most likely they are his
advisors, no, his henchmen. And they've brought me to their
City of the Dead.*

"Fear not. You'll get enough air from the door. This
oil lamp will light your supper. Here's your sack of
thievery." Wrapped in softest cloth like a gift, the bottle,
chalice and jewelry were laid at my side. Saluting me
with evil grins, they banged the door shut, dimming the
chamber. I could hear them crashing down the hillside.

As bruised as I was from being attacked at the court
and from the dreadful cart, they hadn't mistreated me
brutally, nor killed me. I slumped onto the stone bed,

sore and out of breath from the climb, and hugged the cape around me, glad to be protected from the dampness seeping into my bones. With my free hand I lifted the lamp and saw decorated walls, dulled with age. Painted bands bordered the top part of the wall. Underneath, the Ancestor figures were drawn. This was a magistrate's tomb. Depicted was a man holding the double axe of a prince-priest across his shoulder, preceding a slave. The slave led a crimson-colored boy on a spotted horse with a dark mane. On the horse's rear flank a tailess cat rode, one paw on the boy's shoulder. Other beasts were painted below, a standing sphinx with a snakehead for a tail and striped wings. A panther sat on his haunches with his paw on the sphinx's tail. Another beast, catlike, with his tongue hanging out, stalked a bird. *How distorted these figures, elongated and pinched in the wrong places. These paintings are different from those in Tarchna's tombs. Mother's paintings are joyous.*

Two sculpted lions crouched on either side of the entrance door. Usually, sculpture was at a distance from worshipers, on the sacred temple platform or on the roof. Here it was different. The Veia were distinct sculptors. *Did they put their modelings in tombs? No, that can't be. They must have been taken, stolen like the chalice I've been accused of stealing.* The words sunk in. *I've been accused of being a thief!*

Shards of broken pottery lay on the floor and with a chip I scribed a prayer in large letters: SAVE ME TINIA. SCRIBE LARTH. Plain bucchero jars for offerings to the gods were by my bed. From the charcoal stains on the ceiling, it was evident that ancestors had been cremated here in olden days, although the practice no longer existed. *This tomb was used and abandoned. This place is of the forgotten dead. That's why they brought me here. No one will come.*

My belly rumbled with hunger. I hadn't eaten much since I was seized. "They brought no banquet food for me," I said to the guardian lions and drank thirstily from the wine flask. A wave of nausea overcame me with its bitterness. "I'm getting used to tombs," I giggled to them as my eyelids drooped. Before I slept, I recalled what these tastes and smells I had been given were from— valerian root, an herb that grandmother, Healer Anneia , used to sedate wounded or dying patients.

"Wake up, Scribe!" Coarse hands shook me.

"You've come back. You didn't leave me here to die," I said groggily. "Welcome!"

Bleary eyed, I tried to focus on the men. These were strangers, bigger than my first captors, one stocky, the other tall, both sinewy and tougher. "You're not the same . . ."

A stinging slap crossed my face. "Those oafs know nothing. One drop is enough. Get water from the river and boil it," the stocky man ordered. "Squeeze a lemon from yonder tree. That will do it."

The taller man prepared the liquid and then sloppily poured it down my throat. I vomited it back into one of the empty tomb pots and stared. "Who are you?"

No response. He towered over me and jerked my arm, pulling me from the niche that served as my bed. "Where's the treasure?"

This ruffian knew of it too. He snatched the cloth sack away, packed it in his sling shaped bag, then pushed me forward out of the ancient tomb. The other, clad in a foreign style tunic, rested his hand on his knife belt as he waited at the tomb's entrance. He led while the taller one shoved me ahead so that I was caught between them, compelled to move at their pace.

If I make a wrong move, these men will knock me down and stab me. I hold no contest for them.

As I followed the stockier man, I tried to control my panic. One at a time, we scrambled down the side of the cliff that I'd climbed the day before, past the caves, to another part of the stream where it gushed forth as a river.

More sheer cliffs of yellow, gray and white tufa rock edged the river. Ahead, ilex, ivy and brushwood hung over a mass of rock, covering the river's passage into a hollowed archway. A violent noise came from within and bounced off the outer walls.

"What's this?" I yelled, shaking, terrified by the sound. "What netherworld god lives here?"

Neither heard me. Strong hands of the tall man steered me ahead into a tunnel, along a narrow dirt walkway that fringed roaring swift water, and funneled into a man-made canal, as long as the prince-priest's courtyard and as wide as a double cart road.

The cause of the roar brought me to my senses. The initial shock of being abducted was over, replaced by a new fear. *I'm forced to go into the unknown, powerless to escape.* Wearied, I collapsed on the path in the tunnel, unable to go on.

Swirling water crashed against the flume's bank. My momentary fall gave respite in this nightmare dark cosmos.

"We can't haul a dead man." The sarcastic voice of one of these thugs came from close by. "Especially not such a fragile scribe."

Like Veia's henchmen, these miscreants have a mission to take me somewhere, but where I don't know. They've used a knife only to slash away at branches that block the path, not point at me.

"Your language isn't Etruscan, although you try to be."

"Smart you are, scribe. Speak to me then, in Latin."

"In Latin? What's this place?" Defiantly I asked in Etruscan.

"You don't know? You, the knowledgeable Etruscan? It's the drainage ditch that runs south. We're at the southern entrance, away from Veia. Hurry, now that you're lively," the tall man urged and poked my back with his finger.

We left the tunnel and continued along the ditch, into timbered forest and toward the open sweep of countryside. Patches of wood and tufts of grass interspersed cone-shaped hills and pastureland that thrived from Aplu's hot sun. The day wore on, the season's heat intensified, even more humid and hotter.

The path intersected a well-trodden, dusty road as the land flattened, passing peasant huts and grazing flocks of sheep. We had to be out of Etruria into barbaric Latin's domain. The two ruffians changed formation, guarding me from escape, and walked beside me as if in supposed friendship, should anyone chance by. Mud from the wet tunnel mixed with road dust. Sweat caked on my skin and tunic, bringing no dignity to my appearance. I must have looked as much a ruffian as these thugs.

On the horizon of hills and valleys, a settlement emerged. No, it wasn't a settlement, but a sprawling town—not just a town, but a city. It could only be Roma, city of Etruscan roots, separated from Tarchna a saecula past. Our enemy, our rival! The Elders told of its treacherous leaders, conniving, manipulating kings who defected south, leaving us, denying the ways of the Ancestors.

"It's Roma," I said aloud, wilting at the thought.

"None other," came the cheerful reply.

How desperate I was to retrace my steps, back through the tunnel, hills and ravines, to go over that hard, stony land to Tarchna. Anger welled up in me as my ruthless abductors locked me between them. *In less than a quarter moon's time, my splendid life has been wrecked, destroyed first by two Veia thieves who drugged me with poison, then these two Roman ones who guard me like I've committed treason. They take me away from my cosmos, all that I love and care about.*

What could I do but trek forth with these two ruffians? We drew near Roma's perimeter walls, slowed by cowherds and stray goats, then throngs of Latins on the road.

Oh, God Tinia! Have you anger at me for opening Larthia's tomb? I did it, not of my own volition, but coerced by the prince-priests' conspiracy. I, an innocent, who couldn't fathom the consequences of violating a sacred space. Have you no feelings for me?

Joining a cluster of city folk, we surged through Roma's gates, winding our way past windowless brick buildings, some grand and ornate, others slovenly or deserted, into a labyrinth of dark narrow streets, crowded with bedraggled people. These two knew their destination well, tightening their grip on my arms, holding me as a trophy in triumph, thwarting any attempt for my escape.

Now I saw the true nature of my folly, of my dishonest life. I had been cast out. As a scribe, no one knew my background as I claimed no family. But what if I was found out? All Tarchna would know of my disgrace.

What have I done in my selfish pursuit? Have the sight of the Ancestor's tomb cursed me that I should be punished in this manner? Have I angered Gods Tinia, Uni and Menvra for dressing as a man and being a scribe? What more punishment may the gods have for me?

5

The Power Of Jupiter

"My prize!" Tarquinius Luscius Priscus, leader of the Roman people, boomed heartily in the Etruscan language. "You've arrived. So you're the famous daring scribe who opened the Ancestor's tomb!"

Wedged between the loathsome men who forced me to this palace, I stared, in shock, at the white-haired man sitting in a golden chair on a raised platform.

"You've brought gifts, slaves. Where are they?"

He was questioning my captors! *Slaves? These scoundrels are mere slaves?*

Reverently, both men bent on their knees and humbly offered the possessions of my Ancestor, Princess-priestess Larthia. The bucchero chalice. The perfume bottle. The armlet.

Priscus examined each item, laughing at the bottle's inscription, biting the jewelry to test for true gold, picking at the gems to see if they were paste copies. "You chose your thievery well, scribe."

"I didn't steal them! I'd never steal from the Ancestors!"

I could hardly bear this painful exchange. *What am I doing in a place I don't belong with people who don't know who I am but call me a thief?*

"Put these gifts in the treasury, Balbus." To the sentry guards, he waved an order. "Take those two away. Dispose of them. They've seen the scribe."

The incredible scene that ensued spewed out foulness, like an evil dream. Before my abductors could struggle, they were seized, deceived by their own king who owned them. Eyes aghast at their new fate, they glared at me with hatred, as if I were the cause of their downfall.

Weren't they the cause of mine, too? They ruined my life as I ruin theirs. What of the first two men who captured me? By whose hands will they meet death?

"You've come to the city of your Etruscan Ancestors." Switching to Latin, his tone changed and he sneered, "They've died out and we Romans survive."

"My Etruscan Ancestors dwell in the tombs on Tarchna uplands! Defectors of Tarchna's noble family immigrated here two saecula ago," I burst out, my schooled Latin not much practiced, but adequate enough to be understood.

"True, but I'm the first Etruscan to rule Roma. When I learned how clever you are, good scribe, how devoted to your work, I knew we needed you. I can see you understand my every word."

Priscus stood, smoothed the folds of his heavy tunic and stepped down to approach me. "You, Scribe Larth, will enjoy my hospitality here as my guest. Beautiful Roma is warm and sunny while mists on your uplands bring chill." He glanced at the massive court's platform supported by sizeable columns. "This is the core of Roma, the arx. Paths that lead to our temples and market stalls surround us. Beyond are shaded gardens on the hill." He flung out his arms to emphasize his own words. "We've just begun, but some day Roma will be a great city with more temples, many public buildings of commerce, and countless columns soaring skyward, even on the opposite banks of the Tiberis."

Construction was everywhere. Naked slaves were frantically digging out rocks to fill in the courtyard between buildings. Workers laid hewn stone, framed walls by hoisting columns upright, and hammered cornices in place. Others balanced on scaffolding of wooden branches lashed with hemp, dabbing mortar on sun-baked brick.

"Send me back to Tarchna."

Vehemently, he shook his head. "I'm an old man. Indulge me with Etruria's secrets. You will scribe your *Book of Tages*, and those laws of *Etruscan Discipline*. Your skill has kept you near Zilath and now I will profit from you."

"My being is dull. I'm weary from the treachery your henchmen put me through."

Disregarding my words, he leaned towards me and poked a crooked finger into my shoulder. "You're a small scrawny youth for a manly profession."

"I was castrated for leering at a noble's daughter," I lied, recoiling from his touch. There was no escape from here, only further complications to this life of deceit I had created. Anxiously, I searched for words to delay being discovered. "Please, I'll serve you well if you don't send spies to watch me in my personal preparation. My castration was brutal, my scars still raw."

"Pity," he said impassively.

What kind of ruler is this man? Vicious. Less than human. An animal.

Balbus re-entered unobtrusively. Since I was delivered to the king, he had watched me. Awkwardly, I quaked under his inspection.

The king told Balbus, "Have the scribe cleaned up and better dressed. His clothes stink from his journey and his hair must be washed of its filth. Give him a chamber to rest and fatten up. Return him in five days, before the celebrations."

Glad to be dismissed, I degraded myself, so as not to undergo the same fate as those men. "Many thanks, Prince-priest."

"Prince-priest I am not! Here I am king, most supreme leader of Roma. No magistrates rule with me or advise me," he boasted. "And, by the way, you cannot flee our guarded city. If you try, you'll be hunted and suffer dire consequences. I tell you this for your own safety."

Escorted from the king's court by the silent Balbus, I was led to a chamber within the royal house, simple in its necessities but luxurious and restful after my tortuous abduction. Left alone, I sagged onto the feather-cushioned bed, wanting sleep for my aching bones and bruised skin. *First a flax box and then a stone bed niche. This so-called king imprisons me in royal chambers, plying me with soft, inviting cushions, to betray Tarchna's secrets.*

Uneasily I slept, thrashing about in dreams filled with horror of being named traitor, torn limb from limb by Zilath's men. The foreboding dream awoke me. It was almost dusk. Only when I put my feet down and thumped on the solid floor was I convinced I wasn't dreaming. I was alone. No one guarded me as the king promised.

All neatly arranged on the bench next to the bed were a pail of warm water, a bowl of finely ground sand to scrub, and razor and cloth. A basic man's tunic, longer than our style, was laid out on the table, with a belt of loose leather ribbon. *Should anyone intrude, I must be costumed.* I couldn't wait to change those smelly clothes worn since

Tarchna. Quickly, I ripped my old tunic into strips, re-bound my breasts and hips until I appeared boyish and donned the new tunic. My Etruscan boots of oxen hide, although mud-clad upon arrival, had withstood my journey and had been cleaned and polished without explanation. I pulled them on and laced them at the knee. Carefully, I smudged charcoal from the hearth onto my cheeks and trimmed my hair with the razor to make me appear more mannish.

I had no sooner finished than Balbus came in.

Could he view me through a secret peephole?

Balancing a tray of roast duck with juniper berries, a mound of grain cakes and a flask of wine, he set it on the bed. Greedily, I tore meat from bones, crammed berries into my mouth with my hands, filling my empty belly to capacity.

"You Etruscans consume great quantities of food and dance recklessly, showing off weirdness in your fingers and toes."

"Dance recklessly? No! Weirdness in our fingers? No! Nimble rhythmic movement we do. We're filled with song and laughter." Restored by sleep and food for the first time since my capture, with yesterday's poisoned wine eliminated into a toilet pot, my courage recovered. "Weirdness when we dance? Our enchantment is that we delight in precious life on this earth, in the abundance we are given."

"I see you're no different from a lot of Etruscans, thinking you're better than us Romans," Balbus said angrily.

I must soften my words for he is one I need to help me. I can't anger him. "We're no better or worse."

When he didn't answer, I went to the open balcony and beheld the site they labeled the Forum. It was like Tarchna's market place although much larger and in the state of being built. Constant dust filled the air, the result of hammering and pounding, scraping of mortar and crashing of rock, mixed with smoke from hearth fires. On the hillside, buildings of stone with tiled roofs were replacing mud and straw huts.

Like a servant would, Balbus came after me, offering a goblet of wine and plate of figs. "Not tainted. They drugged you to bring you here but no more."

"You serve me finely," I complimented with as much tact as I could, hoping to sound lighter than I felt. *How loyal to me he acts yet he guards me. He surrounds me at every turn! I have been well plotted against. The gods must hate me to have done this.*

"My duty is to make you well for the king."

And spy for him too, I wanted to add.

"We aren't a backward village. Our king has many plans to make Roma a great city. This place was once a swamp. We drained it. It is a sacred spot, choice for Roma's central buildings. I will show it to you."

I studied the people in the Forum below. They appeared energetic in a different way from the Tarchna, less graceful, not refined. *Loutish they are, savage in their demeanor. When they laugh or argue, it's as if their belly explodes. Men and women don't mingle, nor do women walk alone on the streets. I must be careful what I do or say.*

Balbus and I walked along the Sacred Way, a cobbled street that extended from one hill to another, lined with altars, courtyards, an assembly hall and temple. Wailing came from an enclosed building, groans of despair, of impending death.

"Those men who brought me here—are they within?"

"Those slaves? No. They're dead. Died the next dawn." He pointed up to a shiny white stone building at the hilltop. "The condemned are jailed there. They'll be dragged up those steps to be judged. It's the fate of those who displease the king."

Sweat poured through my garments in reaction to his words. *I'm as responsible for those slaves' deaths as the king.* The day was hot and humid already. The tunic stuck to my bound breasts and I picked at the sticking cotton, my gesture more womanly than it should be.

What thought is behind the look Balbus gives me, staring at my body?

"Roma has breasts—seven hills shaped like women's breasts. Actually each hill was a village that became Roma." He poked me in the ribs. "Women's breasts are beautiful, are they not?"

What would a man say to such lewd talk?

"Beautiful melons," I agreed, keeping my movement masculine. To get respite from Aplu's sun, I strode to a shady path. "Can we refresh ourselves under the trees on that grass-covered hill?"

"Scribe, you Etruscans talk too poetically. Speak plain language, like us Romans."

As Etruscan Scribe Larth, I was permitted to tour Roma's Forum, accompanied by Balbus whose grim countenance matched his stern lessons on Roman society.

"The king rules over all who live here, he, the highest patriarch, just as every father in every family. We owe obedience and respect to him. His power is great enough to name life or death as he chooses. The king before Priscus sold his son three times as a slave, and then on a whim freed him. Priscus himself exposed his second girl child and threw her out in the street to die."

"We Etruscans owe obedience to both father and mother, not just the father," I replied, mildly although I boiled from the unjustness of Roman practice. "Our girl children are cared for and protected."

"Priscus expelled his wife when he suspected her of 'foreign superstitions' and sent her into the wilderness."

"'Foreign superstitions? What are they?"

"I know of you Etruscans! You spend your days mixing magic herbs and searching the skies for omens! Your haruspices sneak into Roma and tell everyone of your strange ways!"

He knows too much to be an ordinary servant and guard.

True to his word, Priscus waited five days for my convalescence before summoning me to his private quarters. The king lazily reclined on a cushioned bench staring up at the ceiling as if he just awoke from a long nap. Until he stirred, I had time to peruse the room. Waxed tablets framed in wood were stacked on a table. A pile of styluses sharpened at one end, flattened on the other, was readied for use.

Despite the heat of the day, by law not permitted to go out, the goddess' hearth fire in the room was lit. Statuary surrounded the hearth, chunky god-like male and female forms with solemn expressions, stoically clutching draped cumbersome robes.

Their votives and customs are similar yet there is less joy and lightness to their ways, not lively or merry. I coughed softly, politely, to let him know I arrived. "You have household gods, too."

"We call the spirits of departed ancestors watching over the perpetuation of Roma, 'Lares.'"

I nodded. He rose tall and eyed me, I suppose searching for any lies I might tell.

"Our Penates household gods help and protect the family."

"Those are our names, too."

"That's why I need you, Etruscan scribe, to tell me of your gods, and your revered cities. You must tell, for example, of that wizened creature, Tages," Priscus demanded pleasantly.

"You want the story of old, the founding of Etruria?" I asked incredulously. *This is a common story, not a secret to us.* "Why?"

"This city is rooted in your heritage. Yes, I must know the story."

I hesitated, seeing him for the first time. His wrinkled face, chiseled and hardened by conquest, then made tender with age, seemed almost kindly.

"I've gone to great lengths to get you here, and I treat you well in my palace."

By showing me his household ways, he's softened me to do his bidding.

"Well?" he said, becoming impatient.

"Our great Ancestor—" I began. *I wouldn't be a traitor telling this story, would I?*

"Our great Ancestor," I repeated. "Tarchon, a grower— who could have been the son or brother of Tyrennos of Lydia in Anatolia's realm—was digging in a patch of soil. His plow scraped into the earth's crust, creating a deep hole that stretched to the bowels of the cosmos. Suddenly a wisp of a spirit rose up, a child's face topped with hair of an Elder. He could have been a dwarf, a misshapen half man, half-animal or a god. He said, 'I'm a messenger from gods of the heavens, sent to show an earthly man how to set boundaries of the land. Since you, Tarchon, have been chosen for the love of land beneath your feet, start at the early morning's first light, gouge the plow's blade into the soil at the point where I have risen. Yoke this sacred white bull and cow together with plow,' Tages instructed as two oxen mysteriously appeared from nowhere. 'Drive out from this spot to the farthest distance that your strength endures where you cut a perimeter. Encompass as much land as you can until the sun dies at end of day. That shall be your land, consecrated 'Tarchna' in your honor."

"Tarchna, not Etruria?"

"Tarchon became prince-priest and beckoned other leaders to set the land with oxen in the same way."

"That's how I consider the story, too," the king said, satisfied. "Farming is the noblest and most useful of all occupations. We have done the same thing with Roma, but it was the brothers Romulus and Remus who gouged the land—our arx where our central court dwells—and set the perimeters around our public areas and the Via Sacra."

"When was that?"

"Less than two hundred years ago. Here are your tablets." He gestured to the table. "Copy that in Latin."

"In Latin? If I refuse?"

"You won't," he said airily. "Surely, you will do as I say."

I stood fixed, yet my being pounded as fast as the hammering of distant workers. "I cannot, King Priscus."

"Cannot! What say you?"

"I cannot go against my people and give out our holy myths and customs. Our ways are sacred."

"As your prince-priest owned you, now I do! You're my scribe, my property!"

His scribe! His property!

"You repay my hospitality with obstinacy!" the king yelled, jumping up and turning over his chair. Aware of how undignified he appeared, he straightened up and smoothed his tunic. Absent-mindedly he reached for a pear and bit into it, looking at it thoughtfully as if it connected to a new idea. A smile flitted on his face and he clapped his hands for service. A servant hastened in and Priscus said something to him, too low for me to hear. Raising his voice, the king said nastily, "Bring food to the scribe."

Sent to my chamber, I was rationed meager portions of thin gruel, the main staple of Roman common folk, the same given to lowest Etruscan slaves who misbehaved. For drink instead of wine, murky rancid water was delivered in a rusted cup. No longer did Balbus usher me about Roma nor did the king demand my presence. I waited in my room alone, staring bleakly out at the Forum, thinking of the wonderful life I had led in Tarchna.

Arun cares for me. In my daydreams, his likeness appeared, his lithe body taut with raw muscle, moving gracefully as he mounted his Arabian steed. *He must worry about me, look for me, doesn't he? I even cherish his petty clan who gossiped about our lack of children, reproaching me that I was barren.*

Scenes of my family, the happiness shared when I was a child flew through my mind. *Mother, Ari and Culni must wonder where I am. Aren't they all looking for me?*

My night dreams changed from ones of fearful encounters with enemies to visions of delectable banqueting. I could almost taste savory venison and wild boar, roasted whole on the spit, dripping with tasty fat, and herbs intoxicating the air. Images doused my eyes, trays laden with juicy grapes garnished with ewe's cheese, chubby roasted ducks, stewed geese and chickens in gravies topped with ripened olives, hare and figs, pheasants with eggs, glazed fishes in sauces, boiled carrots, beans, peas, barley cakes dribbled with honey, all washed down with sweet Etruscan wine. Oh what feasts! How I waited for those special occasions, anticipation and excitement growing as banquet nights drew near. Guests would sweep into the dining courtyard, women speckled with golden rings and necklaces, dressed in their most elegant tunics, displaying stylish leather shoes. Bare-chested men with skimpy skirt-tunics would fling their cloaks down, laugh gaily as they reclined on soft cushions, listening to a flutist play, or watch naked dancers whirl into frenzied postures. We would gorge ourselves until dawn. How many nights I celebrated at my own cresting feast or those of family and friends, wearing my noblewoman tunics. Or, in the last season of Tarchna's society, how I had gone costumed as a scribe for Zilath's banquets after my success of entering the tomb of Ancestor Princess-priestess Larthia.

One dream after another, rich in detail, obsessed me as I remained confined to my room, not knowing what would be my fate, salivating for the unattainable.

Balbus came for me. Without a word he yanked me off my bed and prodded me forward. I shrugged off his grimy hand with as much propriety as I could, and walked ahead of him to the throne room, my head held high.

"Perhaps you need more food to sustain you." King Priscus cackled with a high-pitched laugh when he saw me. "Bring the scribe to our banquet room so that he may join the court to celebrate Jupiter's worship."

I nearly swooned. Bowls and plates of splendid meats, fowl, fish, and a bounty of greens, olives and fruit and nuts, differently prepared than Tarchna's bounty. It didn't matter what it looked like or tasted. So hungry, I craved all.

"Sit here," Balbus ordered. "Neither eat nor drink."

Drooling men and women milled around the table, rudely jostling their way to platters piled with foodstuffs, grabbing and stuffing morsels into their gluttonous mouths as fast as they could. They dipped cups into great bowls of wine and bolted down drink, dribbling and staining their clothes.

This is Roman nobility! How different from Zilath's. So serious they are, eaters not delighting in the provisions as we Etruscans do! All wear the same draped tunics dragging on the floor. Dull clothes. Not elegant. I was repulsed by how they consumed the food, grunting like wild boars to devour whatever they could get. *Perhaps*

*they are often given gruel as I am. Yet I did the same when
I first arrived, hungry as I was, now hungrier still.*

At the front of the banquet room, the king's voice
called out, "In honor of Jupiter's wine harvest, serve the
Etruscan scribe!"

A hush fell on the company, silence settling with his
command. The nobles froze in place and stared at me
with what must have been curiosity. Unquestionably I was
an oddity in this court, a foreigner, pale, gaunt, bony, not
as coarse and corpulent as they.

From the hallway, scratching sounds echoed off of bare
wooden floors followed by a chase of thumping feet that
ended with a bang of a mallet.

"Your meal is ready, Scribe Larth," the king
announced.

No one moved. A burly cook brandishing a large silver
platter shuffled in. With flourish, he plunked it down
under my nose. A dormouse laid upon it, head and eyeball
gaping at me, blood oozing from its bashed skull and
bushy tail stiff in sudden demise.

I controlled my urge to gag, to vomit forth my
abhorrence of the king's ploy. *I mustn't be squeamish. It
wouldn't be manly.* Faking the haughtiness that Zilath
used with undesirable food, I said coldly, "It's a lean one,
not plump and certainly not properly cooked."

"Ah, yes. True. Come feast tomorrow, scribe," Priscus
offered.

For four days I was invited to banquet and tortured
by seeing masses of banquet food displayed for the court,
then given inedible creatures, a moldy owl, a rotting sea
gull, putrified entrails of a hare all of which I refused
jocularly, trivializing his attempts to disgust me.

In my chamber, the daily pail of water to cleanse with
became my sole food, leaving me listless and dizzy.
Delirious dreams of Zilath's banquets faded me with
hunger. Dehydrated, I vomited water.

"Would you prefer this succulent chicken?" the king dangled the grilled meat before me at the next banquet.

Its aroma wafted up my nose. *This hunger is unbearable. My life is not secure and pampered as it was as a noblewoman, my existence full of opulent luxuries. God Tinia has doomed me to suffer.*

"Yes, please," I begged weakly.

"Recall Tages's story." He pushed stylus and tablet at me.

If allowed, tears of misery would have fallen down my cheeks. But they weren't. I would have more strength if I didn't cry. *I've no choice. I'm starting to die already. My survival depends on what Priscus desires.* I picked up the stylus and began. "Our Ancestor . . ."

"We will destroy our ancestral links with Etruria if we aren't told of the *Discipline Codes*. Tell of them, your laws given for all of Etruria. There are three books, are there not?"

"They are sacred, King Priscus."

"You know them, Scribe Larth. Have you not helped Prince-priest Zilath master them by your writings?"

I bowed my head in self-loathing for my weakness at giving away the most hallowed Etruscan secrets, scribing words translated from Etruscan to Roman Latin.

Look not badly on me, God Tinia, but I will starve to death if I don't obey. I must reveal our secrets to these barbarians.

I began to inscribe: "The first is of the haruspex, the augur-priest. There are many haruspices who tell of divination from entrails of freshly sacrificed animals."

"And?"

" . . . of the fulguriator, the augur-priest who tells of omens—of flights of birds as they go across the cosmos.

Likewise there are many fulguriatores who study the skies." *Priscus knows of them already. He cannot scribe.*

"The second book?"

"Of divination by God Tinia's lightning."

"The third?"

"It's of Etruria's social and political life. Our ritual practices."

"Hmm," he purred. "Scribe every bit."

"I forgot. There's one more," I volunteered so as not to be further deprived of sustenance. "But it's lesser known and hardly spoken of. It tells of animal gods."

"Commendable," the king burbled. "Soon I will have the power of the entire cosmos. Zilath gave me a scribe and your ancestor's treasures in compensation for gold. And I have purchased the Oracle of Cumae's pronouncements, dictated by the Hellenic Prophetess Sibyl. Know you of them?"

I shook my head, fatigued from my labor, his words then spinning into clarity. *What has he said—something about giving Zilath gold in trade for me? Impossible! Zilath would never do that. I'm his most trusted aide, knowing more laws of the cosmos than the priests and magistrates, scribing the most complicated details. Why else would he have me go into the Tomb of the Ancestors? I am loyal to Zilath, so loyal that even as he took the brooch and warrior's ring, I said nothing. Aplu's sun rises and the stars set with him for he is all knowing master of my cosmos.*

My throat closed and I choked. *Yet, is it possible? I am accused of stealing treasures, delivered to Roma, a curiosity to this court. Priscus paid for me with gold.* The image of Zilath's face came to me, his laugh turned to a cruel sneer. In that instant I knew what I denied to myself was truth. Zilath betrayed me, sending me on this unwanted journey because I knew not only of his thievery but that I knew too much, more than my place.

"Do you hear me, scribe?" Priscus was saying. "The *Sibylline Books* of Hellas are of ceremonies and prayers to Hellenic gods whom their priests consult. You will translate them for me . . ."

"Name your gods of the heavens, Scribe Larth," Priscus commanded, "so that we may compare."

"Tinia, god of the cosmos." *I am in Priscus' charge, no longer a whole being.*

"Jupiter, the sky god."

"Uni, wife of Tinia."

"Juno."

"Goddess of Wisdom Menvra."

"Minerva. Yes, they're the same. Our gods tower over us on the temple in the Via Sacra. Majestic, are they not? We cherish them."

There was always an array of clean tablets and writing tools at the marble table where I recorded the Discipline. Completed manuscripts were bound and stacked to the side. *At least, Priscus accommodates and recognizes my abilities.*

The king continued, "Our gods prophesize that Roma will ruin Etruria. The power of Jupiter will be stronger than Tinia. Surely, your augurs must advise you of this."

I shuddered. Tarchna had laughed at that very same rumor, for the prophecy would be in a saecula when the present population would be ancestors.

"I must know all about Tinia to make Jupiter more powerful than he, and you will tell me."

I am disloyal to the gods as well as my people. "Tinia is best and greatest," I said faintly. "He rules the skies by the flick of his fingers and lightning comes. He roars and thunderbolts strike."

"Ho! By his fingers! We must make Jupiter do that!"

"Uni helps him. She is goddess of the night sky and moon, and tells him how to make Aplu's sun appear or go with storms."

"Go on . . ."

Priscus stopped requesting my attendance even though I wrote every law, legend and story I could remember, from dawn to end of day. As I became adept at Roman Latin, I realized how much it pleased me I was learned in this language besides Etruscan, Phoenician and Hellenic.

Engrossed in my work, I could ignore that something was amiss but I wasn't told any particulars. Bonfires lit the night sky, and people raced along streets outside the palace as if hunted. Old women wailed, wild dogs howled, loud slurred voices carried argument. Afraid, I stayed in my room.

Balbus knocked on my door and announced after much lapsed time. "The king wants you, scribe."

"He finally summons me after passage of a moon."

"Follow me," Balbus smirked as he led me to the court, only it was not at the arx but in another part of the palace. On the same golden throne where Priscus had once sat was a young man. Balbus bowed and said, "Behold and bow to our esteemed King Servius Tullius."

"So you were my father's scribe, taken from Tarchna, land of the Ancestors."

"Where is Tarquinius Priscus?" I asked daringly, not bowing, bewildered by this new ruler's presence.

"He's dead. After all, he was an old man."

The night fires. People shouting, running through the streets. Warriors marching through the Forum. "He was old but not sickly."

"I can see he trusted you. I don't. You're not manly, eunuch that you are." He got up and walked around me, observing me closely. "A lot of dust on your face for one who otherwise keeps so clean. No beard stubble. You are hairless."

Servius Tullius brusquely wiped my cheek. "As I thought."

I stood as a statue, unable to breathe. From the sheath in his belt, he pulled a sharp knife and slit the front of my tunic, showing my bound bodice. "What is this?"

"Bandages. My wounds heal slowly from my ordeal with my captors."

"I think not. You fooled the old man but not me." He sliced away my bindings, freeing my breasts. He caressed my taut nipples and pinched them until tears came to my eyes.

"Small breasts you have, but firm with full, finely shaped nipples. Not a man's chest. Lovely spy for Zilath of Tarchna," he hissed at my ear "Are you whore of Zilath? Or were you whore of Priscus?"

He motioned the guard. "Well done, Balbus. Now get rid of her!"

"Shall I take her back to Tarchna?"

"Never! She's part of trade. It would provoke war with Tarchna! Rid us of her and her deceptive ways. She's a whore. Send her to the land of whores. Where else but Hellas?" Meanly he shoved me down against the stone floor. "Take her to the barge. Get woman's clothes for the journey. And, by Jupiter, give those fine Etruscan boots to my son."

6

Zilath, The Law Maker

"Seek the flutist of my cresting banquet, Arun," Risa
begged, smearing her paint encrusted hands on my arm.
So distressed, even her face and tunic were smudged with
bright hued stains. With Master Painter Asba, Risa's days
were occupied, composing scenes on underground tomb
walls for the dead to rejoice in their eternal homes. Her
paintings were good, no, beautifully lively in capturing
the moment. An odd occupation for a noblewoman, but
who was I to judge, one who had a scribe for a wife?

We waited for Larthia to appear, Risa and I. By day, I
was on the hunt. Nightly my mother-in-law and I sat in
her courtyard mulling over what to do. By now, all Tarchna
knew that Noblewoman Larthia disappeared a half moon
ago.

"The flutist will play the tune he did for me, the one I
taught Larthia. She'll remember it and come out of
hiding."

"If she is hiding," I replied.

Early next morn I rode outside Tarchna's third gate to where those of base occupations banded together against Tarchna's outer walls. Performers, acrobats and dancers lived in wood reed huts. The most renowned flutist dwelled among them, his hut more substantial, structured with sawed wood. Aloof, elegant and mysterious in his command of calling animals from their lairs, he met me at his door without inviting me in.

The flutist was certainly a different breed. To seal his discretion I gifted him with hare and ewe's milk cheese. "Tell no one of this request."

With this exchange, the flutist climbed Etruria's verdant hills, trilling the love song he had composed for Risa's banquet many seasons past.

"I calmed the wild beasts along the way to alert them not to emerge. This isn't their season to be hunted. The woods were silent," he reported. "Larthia wasn't concealed there."

"My haruspex prophesizes about love's ways. He wouldn't be helpful to find Larthia. Perhaps another kind of augur-priest. A fulguriator," Risa sighed flatly.

Without rage, she considered one idea after another. Her eyes were fearful, pained by sorrow, yet crinkled with joyful lines around the folds. Risa had suffered the ghastly death of her husband, noble Road Builder Parth, ambushed and cut down with his men by Italic bandits in the road near Etruria's boundary. She suffered again with Larthia's new mischief.

"A fulguriator? They predict the gods' storms and winds!" I said.

"Yes, but they know what direction causes are from," she reasoned. "One could divine Larthia's whereabouts."

I couldn't refuse her suggestion. I visited the fulguriator who lived on Tarchna's precipice. A hot wind gusted at our encounter. The augur looked blankly at me and pointed randomly in the air towards Cisra. "Cisra! Of course it's possible that Larthia went back to the priestess' tomb! She must be exploring it again." The ray of hope in Risa's eyes when I told her that, spirited me on. With a thrust of duty, I'd search for Larthia, bring her home, put her in her place at my side and make her give up the scribe's nonsense.

In haste, I galloped my prized stallion along the coastal route to Cisra, so sure that Larthia would be there. I wasn't prepared for what happened next.

The gates at the City of the Dead were sealed, and sentinels patrolled at the walls as if it was a fortress instead of a cemetery.

"I'm Zilath's Hunter Arun from Tarchna."

"Tarchna, you say?" a sentinel asked. "It was Tarchna's scribe who made this a popular place. We're besieged with worshipers who pester for glimpses of our treasures, not knowing the Ancestor's tomb was resealed. That's why Maru of Cisra orders our patrol."

"Has the scribe returned here?"

"How could he? We've heard that your Zilath crows over him and that he'll open other tombs."

"Where would that be?"

"Why are you interested, Hunter? Go before we rope and drag you to Prince-priest Maru."

It was useless to give further purpose. Now that the Celebration of the Ancestors caused such turmoil, Cisra suspected all new strangers, including me. Rudely, the sentinels ordered me to walk my horse in front of them. With spears at my back, they escorted me out of Cisra.

Embarrassed that this journey to Cisra brought no news, I shunned immediate return home. North to

Pupluna I headed my stallion, avoiding the coastal lowlands and swamps, stopping at villages and Etruscan towns. Then I galloped east to woodlands and mountains, thick with beech wood trees and conifers, steep with rocky ledges. An early cooling season snowstorm thwarted my attempt over the mountain pass. My horse would have become lame on its hazardous crags.

Skirting the base of the metal bearing hills and clay slopes, I hurried south, east of Tarchna through settlements and the smallest places searching for my wife, asking the same questions of all I met. "Have you seen Noblewoman Larthia Partenu of the Laris clan of Tarchna on this road?" When people said no, I probed further. "Have you seen Zilath of Tarchna's Scribe Larth?"

I met with vacant stares. Suspicious dolts. They doubted my cause. There was no one to explain or tell the truth to, and my queries sometimes brought not only hostility but ugly taunts as if I was a spy. Sometimes, village folk with nothing more to do than chatter, pulled my ears to theirs.

"The Veia road is deserted this season when fields must be cared for," said an old peasant whose cottage was on the road, "except for two men driving a cart of flax which they . . ."

"covered with a black cloth," his wife tattled. "Odd that those men covered the flax when Tinia's clouds weren't in sight."

"Those men didn't look like growers," the man reflected.

So what? I wanted to shout, my wits exasperated. *I don't want to hear everyone's gossip. I just want to find Larthia.*

Hard crusts of old barley cake and gristly meat of an old stag, the only kill since my search began, kept my belly raw. Spent from another hard day's ride, I sprawled on my mat, dejected from no further place to search. Perversely I imagined my favorite meats, young boar, moist and tender to the bone. *Larthia is wild, untamed like the game I hunt.*

Tarchna's fields and orchards were being harvested as I led my stallion through the city's main gate. I hailed workers I knew, but they averted their eyes and went back to tasks, loading carts with baskets of ripened grapes, hauling bundles of flax to market. Others strolled about, coming or going from Zilath's court or market, pretending they didn't see me.

Respectfully, I visited Risa first. "No one has seen a sole Tarchna traveler or a stranger they remembered, for most citizens remain in their communities. They find it unusual that people would be alone in woods or on roads. No one is interested in a woman who runs away from home. No one cares about a scribe."

"I don't believe she's gone for good," Risa insisted stubbornly. "Her loyalty to you and Tarchna is strong. She'll come home."

In my family's courtyard where we ate our noon repast, the clan gathered to greet and question me about my journey.

"We also have no news of Larthia's return in your absence," my father declared.

A silence fell upon us until my sister blurted out derisively, "You lied to us, Arun. You and that wicked wife of yours. Our city buzzes with the story! When Zilath disapproved of how the columns of the new temple would be built, Magistrate of Construction Pevthi spitefully said he knew who Larth really was. He told everyone in sight that a leader who had a female scribe could not be expected to make good decisions, that Noblewoman Larthia was Zilath's Scribe Larth!"

"And then Zilath announced that his scribe had stolen from the Ancestor's tomb and slunk away so that no one could prove the scribe's gender," my brother interjected.

"The magistrate is no more. He lost his footing from where he worked on the temple's roof and fell to his death."

"What sensation that caused!"

"Our family was shamed. We denied that Larthia and the scribe were one and the same. We told all that she visited the Temple at Voltumna to plead for a child's birth and that you were on the hunt. No one believed us so we held a feast to show our nobility is hardy."

"You've done what you could." I slumped into a cushion, wiping the road grit from my brow. "She's disappeared."

"You must get back into Zilath's good graces or our family will be destroyed," my father sternly demanded. "There's rumor that Zilath's court is in an uproar. Some advisors would oust him if his closest magistrates don't support him. Go at once."

Long brewing resentment at Larthia flared up in my chest, enough for me to pound my fist on the table and dismay my family. "What right has she to ruin me! By Tinia! Larthia has harmed us all."

"So here is Hunter Arun Partenu, back from a chase. Did you bring fresh venison for banquet?"

Flabbergasted by Zilath's insulting question, I gaped at him. He looked different; hair and beard lightened, brows wrinkled and eyelids veined and squinted. A flabby thin paunch had become evident. Carbuncles sprout on his face. "You know where I went, Zilath. I searched the length and breadth of Etruria. I cannot find Larthia."

"Larthia?" Zilath toyed with the name, saying it slowly then quickly. "Larthia? You mentioned your wife when I last saw you and I remind you—I never saw her."

Zilath lied through his teeth. Disgust rose within me. *Where's the brave victorious warrior-priest I've known since youth, who took the throne at his father's demise, showing truth, prowess, competence, mastery of his citizens. Zilath has aged. His mind is not what it was, twisted in his twilight.* Without asking for leave I backed away, but Zilath strode to me and snapped, "Listen, you! Stop this futile pursuit. You, my brave Hunter of stags could not flush the hare. Look no more. She brought trouble to my court and vanished. So has my Scribe Larth. The thief sneaked away with other Roman spies. I've told everyone that if he returns, he must bring my treasures. But he won't return. Roma now threatens war with us if they can't keep my scribe. They want our knowledge and think Larth knows all. I have schemed back and revealed that Larth is female. What will they do? They will feel duped and kill her, if the deed is not already done."

I fell to my knees revolted by the impact of Zilath's words.

"Your loss troubles you? It shouldn't, for it's a good omen for you. Tarchna cannot go to war over a faithless woman. I demand your service. Your fidelity, Noble Hunter, remains with me. Marry another. Have children with my blessing."

I raised my eyes and saw the iron will of Zilath in his weaseled countenance, the finality of his cunning plot.

"Better she is dead from her follies," Zilath contemptuously mused, "for if they let her go and she returns to Tarchna, she will die."

7

Ships Of Horror

"I'm a Tarchna noblewoman, chained to a post like a slave!" I yelled at Balbus, terrified by the dark water under the hull. "Free me! Don't let me sink to the bottom!"

Among racks of stretched sheep carcasses and corn grain, I stood tethered with an iron ring around my bare ankle, cloaked in Roman-style woman's cape and tunic. Living in Tarchna, I had no cause to go to the river, for my servants cleansed me in an iron tub. Never had I been on water, not a boat nor ship, only having seen them from a distance when I accompanied Zilath down to Gravisca Port. This working 'barge' of that malicious tyrant, the new Roman king, was nothing but a slimy, rail-less, flat vessel, six horse lengths by two, an uncovered platform that drifted on water.

The barge sped from its moorage on the swift current of the River Tiberis. I waited for it to suck me into a murky netherworld. But the barge floated, rocking gently, not plunging down from weight. The deck stayed firmly under my feet. The river curved and widened before heading downstream. Miraculously, the current slowed. *Surely some river god holds up the barge!*

Treated as if I didn't exist, the barge pilot and his men concerned themselves with tasks to maneuver this sail-less boat. Everyone had become my enemy, the guard, pilot, and the men who steered the barge with long metal rods.

"Free you!" Balbus taunted sarcastically.

He fooled me. Loathing filled my being, swift and sharp, a mood never felt before, displacing whatever kindness I had known.

"Spare me your words. A woman!" he sputtered contemptuously.

Obstinately I willed away tears of melancholy. *I need strength, not weakness. If only I had someone to talk to. No husband, family or friends, all going about their lives in Tarchna, forgetting me. Here I am on a barge, on a river in unknown territory with a merciless guard.* I couldn't stop blood from trickling down my leg.

Balbus saw the mess, dipped a bucket into the river and sloshed its water at my feet. "Women's mysteries. That's how I guessed. I was well-rewarded for finding your true nature."

Momentarily forgetting my fear of the river, though I detested him, I realized I shouldn't have demanded my freedom but pleasantly enticed it. Once won over, I would flee his stifling guardianship. *I must escape from him!*

Remembering how Zilath's women at court flirted to win favors, I cooed, "We were friends when I was a scribe. I trusted you. You brought sweet figs and made me well. You were my protector, my friend. Now you're angry. If you take me to my homeland, my family will reward you with gold and jewels."

He jeered, "I've more reward than that, a better one, to know what your hapless fate will be."

His palpable hatred made no sense. I couldn't help but question, "Why do you dislike me so?"

"You made my brother die."

"Brother?"

"One of the slaves who brought you to the king. The taller one. We came to the palace together, poor boys from a hill village. The king picked and chose. My brother became slave laborer and I a court servant."

Hate your king, not me. Those were his orders. The Fates gave you a different purpose. You were the lucky one. Yet I couldn't provoke him further with spitefulness.

The waterway narrowed and the current quickened again, rushing the barge out of Roman territory. The boat's sturdiness encouraged me to calm to its motion, to lower my panic enough for me to scan the bleak countryside past the river's banks, a grim region featureless of fields or vines.

To distract him from other revenge, I asked, "Where does this river go?"

He continued smirking, self-satisfied that he bested me. "To the outlet of this channel, the Mediterranean."

"The Great Sea of the cosmos?"

"The 'Great Sea'? So that's what you Etruscans call it. Ostia Port lies ahead of that, where they give us salt."

"They?"

"Veia—your Etruscan neighbors."

The river broadened to where mud and thatch dwellings lined rock and clay banks. Some similar barges appeared heading towards Roma, filled with salt bins, baled straw, stacked amphorae or crates. Small boats crossed from one side of the river to the other picking up new loads, tying up at wooden docks that looked like they would collapse under any weight. Seafarers uttered commands at each other between boats, while overseers ordered laborers to stack heavy goods.

Over this water, their cries sounded like lamentations. *No! Those lamentations come from my being.*

In stages, the Ostia settlement came into view, a few buildings, then substantial baked brick warehouses and a small temple, familiar with Etruscan columns and portico. The merchants in front of it weren't praying, but bartering for goods, some arguing, others smiling. There was no mistaking that those men were either Roman or of Veia, by the plain Roman-styled or fancier Etruscan tunics they wore. *Veia and Roma are allies. Etruscan or not, I'll find no protection here.*

The barge pilot signaled one of his men. The boatman threw a hemp rope to a dock near the temple, nimbly leapt between the gap of water and the bank and deftly reeled in and secured the barge. Laborers from the dock arrived in commotion, vying to earn food to cart off the king's trade.

Without waiting for the barge to unload, Balbus bounded off the side and scampered away. I looked in the direction he had gone—towards the sea. Great colorful flags on ships identified homelands: Roma, Phoenicia, Hellas, Etruria. Anchored in the harbor, with furled canvas on their masts, the ships bobbed on the waves, at rest between voyages, probably waiting for the next load. Just their sight made me queasy. I became more frightened by Balbus' unforeseen action. *He's deserted me!*

The laborers ogled at me as if I were a common harlot. How I lapsed into such degradation! To their insulting gibes I lifted my chin high and kept my face blank, until they became uncomfortable seeing my pitiable state. Resuming work, they unpacked the grain and sheep racks, shoving the guard's sack out of the way, in my direction.

When completed, the barge pilot gave them leave, glanced distastefully at me, and went with them.

The sack! Balbus had forgotten the leather bag he always carried, filled with an assortment of provisions including my ration of barley cakes.

Daylight faded and sea winds swirled. Dusk descended and the port men of Ostia from other barges dispersed, most probably heading for evening meals and lodgings. Left alone, I strained against the tether, bending from my waist to touch the deck. The sack was more than one arm's length further, but the tether cut too painfully into my ankle to reach it. Frustrated by my useless effort I pulled myself upright and leaned on the post again, desperate for any comfort.

The song of slapping waves mingled with the increasing sea wind. Gusts blustered up the river, whipping at the hull. A brewing storm. The barge rocked and the sack slid closer, just enough to extend my hand to retrieve it, unlace the string and withdraw a moldy barley cake. *Praise the wind gods!* Gluttonously, I stuffed it into my mouth, licking crumbs off the palms of my hands, the taste of no matter. I dug in and took out a wine flask, tore off the stopper, and swigged down the liquid, quenching my thirst, as giddy as uncouth Romans at banquet.

Rummaging further into the sack, I fingered a piece of round metal stick and remembered its use. *This opens the iron ring.* Sliding down, I poked the ring with the flat end of the stick until it fit the nail. Excited, anticipating escape, I jammed it and forced the nail out the other side, leaving the ring loose. Footsteps along the dock made me quickly regain my stance, the ring still on my ankle.

By the light of his swinging oil lamp, Balbus staggered towards me, joined by a large brawny man. Judging by his walk, this companion was less inebriated, but he was a disturbing, savage-looking man with hair, woolly like a sheep, sunburned forearms, and stained tunic. His mean countenance gave me greater fright. He stared straight at me, up and down, nodding, then opened his mouth. Garbled sounds came out.

He has no tongue. New anxiety entered my being. *A luckless omen! He brings no good to me.*

"You must be tired from standing all day." Balbus exhaled wine-soaked fumes at me, obviously in his cups. He stooped to unhinge my shackle, and cursed when he saw it loose. "First a scribe, then an iron-man! May the gods condemn you for doing man's work!"

My chance! As forcibly as I could, I jerked my knee to his chin, and threw the iron at his forehead. Balbus catapulted backward, striking his shoulder on the barge's edge, splashed into the river, and gurgled, "You hussy! You unchaste, faithless harlot!"

Unshackled, I shot over the deck and flung myself from the gap between barge and land as I had seen the boatman do. With the darkness of eve for protection, I ran up the grassy bank and sought cover, my breath rapid. At that same moment, Tinia unleashed his rain in annoying, inopportune torrents.

"She's not my charge anymore! She's your property!" Balbus surfaced at the dock and whooped.

Balbus' mission was unmistakable. He would be faithful to the new king and expose me. I would be part of the next load to sail.

The mute reacted and fumbled up the bank, then, fast as an athlete, started chase. Never having run so quickly in my life, I sprinted like a frightened deer, crossing a field of spelt, looking for an Etruscan land marker, a grower's hedge. To my relief I found one, unfortunately a thicket of thistle. Separating the branches I huddled within, scratched by prickly spikes, the rain pelting down heavier.

Some noise rustled in the hedge not far off, a grunting angry snort. A foraging wild boar had caught my menstrual smell. The mute heard the animal too, and charged across the field at the speed of a hunter's horse. Before I could untangle myself and run further, the hairy, long-snooted animal led him to me. The mute lunged at the bush I hid in, crushing the thorns into my flesh. He grabbed my arm, almost disconnecting my shoulder joint, and pulled me with him for what seemed like a saecula.

"Great Tinia, save me!" I screeched, slithering into the rain's flood. "O Sacred God, hear my prayer!"

The mute clasped my wrist in an unyielding grip to re-cross the field that I had just run through. I tugged against him, swinging at him ineffectively with my free arm. In this grappling fashion we skirted the settlement under pouring rain. No one saw us. No one intervened. Everyone must have sheltered in the stormy night, finished with labor. Huffing from our struggle, we reached the far side of the harbor. At the bottom of a hillock he kicked me to make me climb upward.

At the top, the squall abated and ceased as if it had never been. The moon ascended from milky clouds casting shadows on the ground. Not shadows but men. They lay like logs, lifeless to all but sleep, near the shore of the Great Sea.

The mute grunted like the wild boar, an inarticulate command and lumbered away. *Thank Tinia for that!* Every part of my body throbbed, worn out and limp. It didn't matter whether the ground was wet or hard. I swayed and pitched into a heap next to a sleeping body. He didn't waken. Neither did the others whose bodies smelled of sea as they slept soundly.

Too exhausted to move far from them, I curled into a tight ball, should anyone attack. Pain shot through the length of my body, spasms darting in and around skin and muscle. My being sank lower, disheartened, mortified. *Why has no one come looking for me, in Veia, in Roma, in Ostia? Why has no one followed my abductors?*

*   *   *

They speak Hellenic! The men I was thrown in with
were seafarers, sleeping on land at night, sailing the
waters at day. I listened to the rhythm of their low dialect
until I pieced the words together. *I've been traded to a
mute for an Athenian vase!* Unaware that I understood
them, the seafarers joked over why I was there. Their
bawdy remarks chilled my bones. They mocked how the
mute's dreadful face contrasted to my comeliness. For
the first time, I wished I were an ugly hag.

The mute must be as important as he is strong.

Intermittently he left to trade and that was when I
heard about him from the crew who thought him as cruel
as the nastiness etched into his cheeks and jaws. His
tongue had been cut out for lying, but they didn't know
why. One thing was certain. He'd never tell another
falsehood. Yet they admired him. His mutilation made
him honest among merchants and he had prospered,
owning one of the ships in the harbor.

It was before the mute's ship was to sail that the
cruelest marks of the Fates focused on me. On that
grassy hillock, the horrible mute came at me with
menacing eyes, and threw me down. He forced me on
my back, and straddled me like a rider does his mount.
I fought him off as I could, punching at his chest until
he pinned my arms against the ground, and grasped my
wrists together. While the crew witnessed, he roughly
pawed at my skin and squeezed my breasts with his huge
callused hands. With malice, he ripped the cloth of my
tunic until he found the opening and slid his hand to
my belly.

"Love Goddess Turan! Husband! Come, Arun, save
me! Our marriage falters with this violation!" I screamed,

fevered with outrage, humiliated by the mute's crudeness. "Away with your filth, you warped imbecile!"

He struck my face to stop my sounds.

"Wisdom Goddess Menvra! Give thought to this mute. Make him leave me alone," I resisted, squirming futilely under his weight only to have him press harder.

Drooling like a starved beast, the mute rammed his finger into the hole of my sacred mound. Releasing his engorged member, he beat it against my mound.

"Gods Tinia! Uni! Help me!" I pleaded, my resistance fading under his clumpish pounding.

Liquid smeared on my skin, seeping under my tunic, onto the menstrual rag. He turned to his men and raised his fist in triumph. The men cheered and so did I, silently. The mute had finished, but not inside me. Not even the crass mute would take a woman during menses. Fury entered his eyes but he swung off me.

What god can I thank for this rescue?

"I'm a high born, a scribe, not a harlot! Balbus' barter was false!"

At that last gibe, he struck my face again, then my shoulders, back and breasts. I shielded my body with weakened arms, cowering into a heap. He battered me until I neither felt nor saw more.

Muffled voices came from somewhere. *Etruscan voices? Roman?* I opened my eyes to blackness. *I am dead and meet the netherworld.* I touched airless walls around me. Cloth! Bagged in a sack like the salt. A cold silence entered my being, emerging black and repulsive, a void remaining there. *I do live! Why do the gods give me trials to stay alive? Do they harden me, strengthen my resolve to live for some unnamed reason?*

Under me the floor rocked, then surged. I couldn't move for I was wedged between something, on top of something. As my breathing slowed, I smelled grain, sacks of grain, my new companions. Confined in this cloth bag, afraid that the mute would attack me more, I stayed inert. Those voices that I was heard were the mute's crew gossiping as they went about chores, about how I had been carried senseless to the vessel, and left on deck piled among the sacks to be watched over by them. Lewdly they guffawed on how the mute tamed me.

Charred wood, then grilled fish smells blew at me as the seafarers ate their meal close by, ignoring my bundled form. The food made them agreeable to generously congratulate themselves on their bounty.

"We benefit from our dealings with Veia and Roma."

"What about Simonades' dealings? He may not talk but he's promised we'd have a turn with her."

Almost good-naturedly they laughed at what they assumed would happen, and then disbanded to continue ship tasks. As if they were talking of some common pleasantry, they discussed what they could do to a female.

Then I realized whom they lusted for. *Me. They prepare to violate me.*

The vessel slowed and moored within a lagoon. Only Hellenic voices spoke from what could be land. This must be Cumae—foreign territory! Placed on a cushion bed of salt sacks that one goodly seafarer put under me, my bruised limbs were crumpled in the bag. By hearsay at Zilath's court, and through King Priscus, I knew more about this Hellenic border city then I cared. Their Hellenic gods had empowered them to colonize, and settlers built an acropolis. It was only by treaty that the Cumae kept peaceably to their southern territory because Etruscan and Roman warriors would otherwise repel them. All Hellenics traded throughout the Great Sea from there. *And it's the mute's homeland.*

"Simonades! Take her out of the bag! Are you an idiot as well as voiceless?"

Humbly, the mute sensibly unwrapped and presented me. The person who spoke was a bulky woman, an older version of the mute, but with baggy cheeks and a bulging forehead. She picked at my bloodstained tunic and tangled hair, sniffing my foul breath. "At least you didn't drug her."

Even in my stupor, I recoiled at the woman's rough jabs. Aplu's sun worked its magic and his light began to revive me. My hazy vision cleared and I saw that a few other people clustered around me, all resembling the mute and his mother.

"You're right, son. She's nobility. Etruscan, you think? A fine trade you did with that Roman guard. You have a good eye for seeing her worth. Whatever was she doing in Roma? Whoring for the king, no doubt. Except for her filth, she's a pretty thing. We'll clean her up and fix her looks."

At her sordid compliment and disgusting ideas, the mute puffed out his chest and opened his tongue-less cavern of a mouth to agree. The relatives clapped.

If only I could kill him. He dishonored my sacred womanhood and tormented me with vile conduct.

Worried by their despicable words, I hardly breathed. Stunned by their slyness, my knees buckled. The mute's sisters dragged my weak body to the mother's house, a group of rooms piled from floor to ceiling with amphorae, crates and packages, more a storehouse than a home. Into one of its stark rooms, the two women lugged a cauldron of cold water and ladled it over my body. So what if they tittered over my nudity? I reveled in the clean, fresh water, dissolving the mute's dried liquid, my old blood and muck from abuse. The women draped a tunic over me, cut unlike that of Tarchna or Roma, less bulky in its folds than Roman style.

The mother waddled into the room with the mute. "Proper clothes she'll need. A pretty chunk of silver we'll make. Simonades, return her to your vessel."

Obediently contrite, the mute whisked me out to the ship, leaving me on the deck. Salivating like wild dogs, the seafarers gathered close.

"My turn!" one called.

"No, mine!" another pushed forward.

"No one gets her!" Breaking through their ring, the sharp voice of the ship pilot interrupted, "She's trade— valuable trade."

"If the female comes, we won't go!" one growled.

The mute edged next to the ship pilot, communicating some gesture.

"She means trouble!" one yelled, starting to push me.

"You'll be well rewarded," the ship pilot assured.

"Only a bit, then Simonades will want us to barter with Magna Hellas."

"After, you can re-trade with Mother Hellas!"

"Wealthy goods are our business, not females."

"At Athenai's temple you can pray for more wealth, " the ship pilot argued.

Furtively, the mute gave other signs to his spokesman.

"Wait," the ship pilot ordered. He looked at me apprehensively, then at his seafarers. "Before heading south, we consult the prophetess. Bring the female."

8

Perilous Waters

Guarding me in their midst, the mute, the ship pilot and seafarers marched, as dignified as they could manage, wearing their best tunics, each banded with a ribbon of Cumae. At the base of a gigantic boulder where an ancient temple stood, we faced a hollowed darkness underneath it.

"Go forth," the ship pilot prodded.

Uneasily I walked over rutted ground. Inside the entrance, oil lamps fastened to walls of enormous height unevenly lit the darkened way. We tracked deep into a tunnel, then deeper. How long I didn't know for time was becalmed until we reached a vaulted chamber. More oil lamps were on a massive stone slab, brightening the path.

"Seafarers, why are you here?"

"Simonades wants this female for our voyage. The crew is scared she means bad luck," the ship pilot lamented. "She threatens our ship."

"Come, Larthia of the North, come!" A high-pitched she-voice played a thousand utterances one wall then another, repeating those words, lucid and resonant, then low and cloudy.

How does she know my name? Is this she-voice in my imagination?

"A sign! The female has been called! Go to the table! The prophetess beckons you." The ship pilot solidly thumped my back and I dropped, face down, on the cold table.

Reverberating from loud to soft, the prophetess began to sing a welcoming tune, singsong in its sweetness, weaving my name within it, echoing.

A hideous fear seized me. Not of my own volition, I rose and glided towards the voice. No one was at or near the table. "Who calls my true name? Who are you?" I whispered.

The she-voice boomed, "Who am I? I am the Sibylline Prophetess. I know all. No corner of the world escapes my sphere. Your fame, Larthia, precedes you. Your folly trails you."

I trembled. "Are you of the netherworld?"

She laughed, a silvery tinkling sound. "Not I! I give only pronouncements of destination. The ship is old and waterlogged. It can sink in stormy seas. You sail with the sea gods through dangerous waters."

"The prophetess is a sorceress! Don't heed her words!" I pleaded with the mute and the ship pilot.

"Your presence will make this voyage safe if these seafarers abide by the right course. This night, shelter in Pithacusae Island's caves. Tomorrow sail past the Phlegrean Fields—the fields of fire—then to the Messina Straits. Never leave sight of land. Sail close to shore," the prophetess cautioned.

The mute gargled appreciatively at the Sibyl's instructions.

"Hurry! We leave Cumae immediately," the surprised pilot nodded. "The female will bring us luck!"

"The prophetess favors her own kind!" I yelled.

The mute grabbed my arm. The pilot clutched the other, both hurrying me back through the tunnel, taking much less time than going in.

"Don't take me with you!" I thrashed in their locked arms. "It's against the *Book of Tages*."

"What's Tages?"

"Laws of my people. Tarchna women don't go to sea."

They chortled like goats.

"I can't oppose the laws of my country."

"We live by different laws."

They didn't care about my anguished pleas, laughing at my anxiety, celebrating their victory. Fed cheese, olives and the sourest wine I had ever drunk, I was led back to the mother for inspection.

"You speak Hellenic, don't you?" she asked.

Seeing a wicked gleam in her eye, I said nothing.

"My son won't tie you up, unless you give cause," the mute's mother warned harshly. "Have you not heard of the tyrant's famous bronze bull? Perillus of Athenai constructed it for Tyrant Phalaris of Sicilia. Should you try to escape, you shall go into its metal shell and be roasted. They say that victims scream through its holes and it sounds like a bellowing bull." She laughed hysterically, slapping her thigh merrily.

Sickened by her awful description, my spirit dwindled. I became too cowardly to take the knife to her or the mute, rip them apart and destroy their lives as they planned to do to mine.

God Tinia! That rat-infested ship will go down without me saying goodbye to my kin. If I have to die, why isn't it

*in my own bed with my family around, not fed to God
Nefluns' fish in some harrowing, mighty waters? How I
would welcome death instead of this horrible fate, a destiny
of exile.*

In the next days, we entered a wide half moon bay on
flat shores, surrounded by lush shrubs and trees. A cone-
shaped mountain loomed, frighteningly high and gray,
fronting a cloudless sky. Black smoke belched from its
top like too much smoke from a damp wood hearth fire,
becoming more furious with each puff. Unexpectedly as
we crossed the bay, rain started, a rain of fine sand, not
of water, obscuring the clear heavens. Acrid smells filled
the air, stifling and heavy, almost suffocating my breath.

"The mountain erupts! Make haste and quit this sea
before we're engulfed." The ship pilot lashed the rowers
with leather whips to gain speed. "It's the fault of the
female!"

"That can't be!" I protested. "I didn't know that awful
mountain existed until today!"

With prayers to Poseidon, the Hellenic god of seas,
and curses at me, the seafarers shoved the vessel from
that shore land towards a series of cliffs covered with
flourishing gardens of hanging vines and abundant
foliage. Waves slammed at the boat, furiously tossing it
high and low at its will. I heaved over the side, not able to
keep even water and bread cakes down. Drained of bodily
fluids, I collapsed on the water slick deck.

It must have been Hellenic gods who ushered us south
from that wrathful mountain, thrusting us to fresh climate.
Suddenly we sailed calmly along this coast on gentle
waves, with a delectable breeze at our backs, warm and
soothing. Aplu's sun sparkled on sea so clear that bottom
was visible.

Amidst my wretchedness, the shore gave me momentary pleasure, a respite from my body's pain. The scent of lemons wafted from high jagged cliffs, connected to beautiful mountains covered in an array of blossoming deep-hued flowers. A multitude of trees covered the terrain, different from those I had ever seen, some with fan-like leaves branching out, others thick with good tone, and shine. Waterfalls cascaded down sheer rocks and crevices descending into the sea. I wanted to stop this sailing and seek refuge in this wilderness of wonder. *This beauty, so vivid, so intense, gives me cause to exist. I don't want to poison myself to death. I don't want to drink the hemlock. The power of that beauty keeps me going. If it is so, I want to live!*

We passed ships of all cities, hailing rival merchant traders, staying free of potential enemy ones that could be pirates, marauders who boarded the enemy's ship to steal booty or take passengers for slaves. The ship sailed during the day, finding safe harbor at night at Hellenic immigrant settlements. Overhearing the crew's talk, I learned why Hellenics colonized the Italic peninsula. The soil was better than in their motherland.

Once, a distant warrior-vessel plied the coast, running fast with sail and current.

"Ho! A raiding Etruscan ship!" A crewman shouted from the mast. "The flag's from Tarchna!"

"Put your back into it, oarsmen! Heave on!" the ship pilot commanded. "To port!"

The mute's ship sought refuge in a cove, hiding between mountains that met the sea, waiting with weapons to stave off the raider.

They're coming for me, my Etruscan rescuers. How excited I became. *They'll overtake this ship and take me with them.* They must have seen us.

But I was deluded. On the horizon the Etruscan ship sailed on, chasing a Phoenician vessel.

"The prophetess is wrong about the straits! Where we should have gone east, a wild wind blew us south west, towards the Sicilian coast."

Is this where they roast live enemies in the metal bull?

"The fault of the female," the crew ranted again, discontented with this change of direction.

"A woman doesn't belong on this ship." A seafarer stepped forward and spat at me.

Another swaggered, leering at me. "Women are different from men. Made from sows. Slovenly like you! Vixens in bed. Spiteful. Bad-tempered. Make trouble like you've done."

The men inched around me, lusting for my death.

"Not true! I'm not a muse or sorceror but a noblewoman, unjustly denounced. I didn't cause the mountain to spew forth. Nor can I change the winds. Leave me be! The ship is safe. I brought no harm," I said defiantly, backing up to a mast.

Or at least I thought I had. But it was the mute who stood rooted there. Enraged by my audacity, he roared his disgust. With his huge arms and fists he shoved the men aside and pushed me to the part of deck where amphorae were tied down. After me he threw a lice-infected cushion for my bed, not much of a relief from the grain sacks.

The mute concerned himself at other stations, apparently assigning the crew to rotate watch over me on the deck, each seafarer wary that I would cast a malevolent curse on them, or the ship, or both.

The ship pilot spoke for the mute. "We anchor in Siracusae with gratitude to Poseidon. Surely good trade welcomes us. This mighty city is as big as four. For now, our merchant Simonades makes the female stay on board."

The seafarers bolted for shore, leaving one watchman and me. Too weak and thirsty, I couldn't escape without being caught. And where would I go? Low cliffs bordered a wide harbor of this Corinthian colony with two elaborate temples built opposite grand white houses. Bare hills were beyond.

"I've been here on another voyage. Siracusae is wealthy. That is the Temple of Artemis and the other is dedicated to Athena. Can you see the gold and ivory doors? That golden shield on its roof was the beacon to our ship to get us here." The watchman shrugged his shoulders. "Perhaps you'll be left . . ."

"This is where the metal bull is, isn't it?"

"Surely."

"Have you seen it?"

"Never! Nor do I want to!"

Does he know what Simonades plans for me? How clever of the Romans to sell me to him, he who can't speak but enslaves me.

Heat of day burned at the deck. With little water in my flask, I sipped sparingly. Commotion of clopping feet and idle chattering came up the gangplank. And then, looming like giants, the ship pilot and mute shaded me, lending my only cover since dawn when they left for port.

"I haven't tried to escape, Simonades," I croaked, parched and scarred by Aplu's sun.

"What have we here?"

Others crowded around. Five unknown men from the city! *They've come to fetch me for the bull.*

One simpered, "Your men gossip about the woman on this ship. Let's see her!"

They're here to seal my doom. They'll cook me for stew.
Blankly, I stood up, empty of life already.

Rudely the ship pilot paraded me in front of them and
bantered, "She's strong of body, isn't she?"

"She'd be good for my dog to chew her scrawny bones."

He showed off my legs and made lewd motions of
copulating.

"Is she good?"

"Foreign born are good whores."

"She stinks!"

"Been on our vessel too long."

"Of low birth."

"No. Her teeth aren't crooked. Take her for a slave."

"Would make a great sacrifice for the tyrant. He
searches for the likes of her."

They relished my panic. I waited to be trounced upon,
roped and carried off. *The mute punishes me. He thinks I
brought the storms and volcano. This is his revenge. How
exulted he'll be in watching me roast!*

One man nudged another, idiotically grinning at me.
"Enough of her! Let's get on with it."

They went to the far side of the deck, finished with
jest. Not officials of Tyrant Phalaris, but trade merchants!
Hagglers! With the ship pilot and the skilled, silent
Simonades they argued over rare Cumaen vases, made
by some of their most gifted potters. In exchange the
Siracusae waved ivory tusks and precious stones
begotten from the Phoenicians as temptation. In their
bickering, I was forgotten, not worth their concern. *Is this
the way of humanity, one more uncaring than the next?*

The sea winds died, and the newly stocked merchant
ship made for the north. "Sybaris, we go to!" the ship
pilot declared jovially to his men.

"Sybaris! Sybaris!" they imitated enthusiastically.

When the ship docked on a polished stone quay, I could see why it was a choice port. Kept to the ship's deck, I breathed in its aromas. Near the dock, food sellers displayed fish with creamy sauce, fruit syrups, artfully piled cabbages, and freshly netted squiggling eels that the townsfolk praised and purchased.

From that distance I saw plentiful gardens surrounding terraces and paved streets. Vines draped over charming tile-roofed dwellings. Slow moving chariots carried men wearing robes of purple and their women wore sheer linen tunics, hair braided with gold ribbons. What a stylish life!

The barbarous mute hadn't cared for me as his mother advised, not letting me cleanse myself, not dressing me properly, making a joke of me. Conscious of my own shabbiness, I wrapped myself tighter in my ragged clothes to become less conspicuous.

Never had the ship pilot spoken directly to me. Now he did, accusingly and bitterly. "I've heard you Etruscans are just like these Achaeans, who descended from Mycenae. Decadent. So you were the Roman king's whore that Simonades claims?"

"Never! I'm a married woman."

"You look at these Sybarites, lusting at their fineries."

"Only because they're so beautiful."

"No! These Sybarites are all decadent whores, swaddled in whatever luxury they can afford. I trade them ivory and gold for the best wine to be found in all of Magna Hellas. Their secret, I hear from rumor, is that they flow wine through pipelines from vineyard to port."

"I am Etruscan, Tarchna high born! I see beauty here as with my people."

"Lie all you may, but if you hazard my ship, you'll be the first to go down in this briny sea!"

*   *   *

"This passage will take a quarter-moon, with luck of the gods." So it was said. Open waters between the Italic Peninsula and Hellas approached and the crew became dejected and grumbled more. The boat creaked in its resistance to choppy waters. My guts wrenched with each new wave. Oarsmen below deck cursed their work and sang vulgar songs in unison. Intent on keeping sail lines tight from Poseidon's wrath, none of the seafarers bothered with me. I had become the dark cloaked, ugly hag of my wishes, pressed close to the mast, eyes closed, in and out of dreams.

Land out of sight, nothing but sea surrounded us. I was going further from my homeland on a Hellenic vessel bound from Cumae to its motherland. The sea sprayed up and left a salty crust on my skin. I felt shriveled up, wrinkled and stained. The need to see Arun and my home kept stirring within me.

Visions of my joyful home softened my discomfort. I saw it differently now, a lovely compound of rooms decorated with garlands and cushioned couches where the family lounged after gorging themselves on venison and ripened fruits, downed with sweet Etruscan wine. The crowded family home, happy with singing nieces and nephews, sounds of slaves rhythmically pounding grain into daily mash, servants bustling around its rooms, sweeping out the dust, polishing copper pots. How cheerful were the in-laws, not pestering Arun and me to have children of our own.

I awoke. The vision was shattered when Simonades brought a bowl of porridge. *My life hadn't been like this dream. It wasn't zestful. I had too many daily tasks and the in-laws nagged me to tend their children since Arun and I had none. Bored by routine, scribing for Zilath opened my heart.*

Violent winds shook the waves before sheets of Tinia's rain pummeled. I held onto the ship's railing while the boat crashed down on voids between gigantic waves and crests.

"You've brought the storms!" the crew whined repeatedly. "You're evil, consorting with underworld gods!"

"How could I have done that—what power could I have, I, a female," I replied bitterly.

They would not be convinced. The mute shunned me, leaving me destitute of the most common necessities. Incredible I had lost value because they thought I was the harbinger of storms! With each new flash of lightning or thunderbolt, my value lessened further and my cosmos split apart.

What gods I pray to in my dilemma—Goddess of the Hearth Vesta, or Gods Lares and Penates who protect all. Please do not banish me from my home. Land God of Wine and Field, Flufluns, please save me from the mute. They give no answer. Instead I was driven from land to these deep waters. What god have I left for appeal, but Sea God Nefluns? Nefluns, have you made me the hazard on this voyage? Are you angry enough to exile me from my brethren and roughen the waters to sail me on? Save me from drowning in this sea.

Still there was no sign that the gods heard. Petrified that the ship pilot would make good his threat and feed me to the depths, fear coiled around me like a sea serpent. Swiftly I grasped the unthinkable. The gods made the rules and ordained my fate. Once they showered me with love, then cruelly twisted my life. I might not be saved. If I should die, what effect would it have on Arun, or my mother who had grieved so much, or Ari and Ranu, even Culni? How could I still believe in Etruscan gods? None had answered. None had delivered me. Worship of the great sky God Tinia, of the wise Goddess Menvra, of love Goddess Turan faded away and vanished, leaving a void, as thunder, lightning and gigantic waves spilled over the deck.

9

House Of Delights

For what new torture am I destined? Death would be better. Numbed and confused by this unwanted perilous voyage and soaked to the bone, I shrank down on the deck and turned my back on the gods, no longer seeking their help. Despondent I was with the violent sea's undulating surf, the dark clouds, thunder, and lightning. The crew's safety was more important than food and I wasn't given any.

And then, good fate! Next dawn, the squalls changed direction, the storm abated, the unpredictable sea calmed and sparkled brilliantly. The mute Simonades, ship pilot and crew dropped to their knees and gave thanks to the gods who saved their lives. I couldn't give praise.

The ship entered the rock-lined coast bordering dried wheat and barley fields, and we were within the Gulf of Corinth. At the harbor, pulleys hoisted the vessel's hull, dripping with barnacles. Reckoned seaworthy, the crew swayed, pushed and lowered it onto the pebbled road through Corinth. A load of pottery, the famous Corinthian geometric pottery, was exchanged for Cumae's grain, olives and wine, and ironically, some Etruscan iron and copper.

As the seafarers conveyed the ship overland, bedraggled in salt covered clothes, I tramped alongside Simonades, my wrist attached to his with rope. How the mute humiliated me! He had left me to suffer in sun and rain. My uncombed, matted hair was incrusted with brine. My shoulders and arms blistered, then peeled. The stained tunic was the same since Cumae. Only a mantle shielded my head, face and shoulders, given by the ship pilot during the great storm.

It took an entire day to cross that neck of land they called an *isthmus*. Next dawn, with triumphant shouts, they dumped the ship into the Aegean Sea and we continued sailing, staying close to the rock-lined shore until we reached the promontory, the main sea port, Piraeus. Uncle Venu's sea stories were true for here I was repeating the journey that merchant ships made annually.

Once again my wrists were roped to the mast. Impatiently the mute hurried down the ladder secured to the dock where the cargo was unloaded. By the time the last parcels were stacked on land, he returned with a bag he tossed at my feet. Slashing off my ropes with a knife, the mute gestured dispassionately that I open it. New garments, the color of setting sun.

At least the mute realizes that clothing changes with the seasons. How many moons I've been away. It's the cooling season, when Aplu calls for harvest. Being at sea, I've lost sense of the seasons.

"Put them on," he gestured with his threatening look. Submissively I draped the new tunic over my head and down my body, wiggling out of the rags I wore on this endless voyage. The tunic adhered to my flesh, showing breasts and nipples. The new skimpy mantle barely covered my shoulders. I opened my mouth to protest this costume, but he shoved me ahead of him off the ship.

A two-seated cart, not a chariot but a serviceable vehicle used for basic transport, was on the road. Boosting me up and seating me at his side, he whipped the mule harshly into a docile trot. Unlike a beautiful Etruscan stallion, the mule was a misshapen animal for labor that plodded along wearily on the bumpy stone road. We ambled through Piraeus, out to a better paved road between bleak fields. Going inland, the first glimpse of high mountains with the silhouette of a temple against the sky appeared on the horizon. Athenai, the Hellenic polis, a fortress, unwalled and ungated.

What do people see when they look at us, an odd pair, a bestial looking man and an unkempt woman with troubled eyes and blemished cheeks? I wondered in shame as we went through the rowdy city, past chalky-colored, squared dwellings perched haphazardly on narrow, crooked streets that slanted upward. As the mule made its climb, there was less noise and fewer children and animals. Flowers and shrubbery adorned doors and gates. The mute stopped at the largest house in the neighborhood. A columned portico framed its entrance, and its walls extended back until it met the mountain.

A woman came to the door and stood there, not bidding us entry. "So, Simonades, this is your beauty. Bring her here."

She was unlike anyone I'd ever seen. Her fitted tunic, the colors of brightest sky, was trimmed with bands of embroidered flowers. Adorned with long polished silver earrings, layers of stone necklaces and bracelets coiled around her upper arms, she jingled as she moved.

How garishly dressed for daylight she is! She must be that kind of woman who gives her body for food and shelter.

The woman inspected my body and ran her hands over my breasts and down my belly, smoothly checking hips and feeling the strength of my legs. "She's not worth what you ask. I don't want her."

This woman touches me as if I'm a priestess.

The mute shrugged and scratched another line on a piece of stone. He pointed at my cheeks.

"You're right. Her bones show nobility but she's scraggly. You've starved her!"

Indignantly, falsely outraged, he waved his palm a little downward.

"No. Impossible. Not worth the expense."

"What have we here?" A man stepped casually out of the house, and perused me with interest as he would a prized warrior's horse, although he didn't touch me. Elegantly clad, he wore a starched white tunic trimmed in purple, a sign of high rank. After consideration he whispered into the woman's ear.

The woman's patron.

"Very well. I'll take her," the woman told the mute. She handed him two small bars of silver. "Get you gone."

The mute looked at the meager amount in his fist, and a low grumble came from his throat. Grudgingly, he accepted the bars. Mounting the cart, he drove down the steep road, not glancing once in my direction. With repugnance for him, I stood rooted to the same spot on the portico where the entire transfer of me as property had just taken place.

My being churned with distress, no, with hysteria. *What has befallen me now? Ill-fated, I am.*

"May larvae crawl up your ass!" she cursed the departing mute.

As if the sun had broken a cloud, the woman's startling comment made me giddy. I coughed to suppress my laughter, the first time I felt humor since the night of my abduction.

Smiling warmly, the woman continued inspecting my teeth, nails and joints, pressing my parched skin carefully so not to bruise, softly, almost caressing me. All the while she realized my panic and spoke gently. "I'm not a common whore, not a harlot. I'm a 'hetaera' carefully trained in the ways of making love."

I must run from this harlot, away from this place.

"After the voyage she's been on, she'll need a bath. And meat and wine, honey and goat milk, cakes with nuts and raisins to bring back her flesh," she calculated, speaking to the man as much as to herself.

"A decent bed, Ariela, will also help."

"Of course."

"Her eyes are beautiful."

"Your advice is always good, the only reason I took her in."

To my discomfiture, they discussed what to do with me as if I were unseen.

"Has he broken your spirit as he's broken your body?" Ariela murmured as she and another woman put me on a cushion. Numb, waiting to be violated, I lay stiff like a wooden board while they stripped me. But no one attacked. They covered me with a goat hide blanket and I sank into the softest bed I had ever laid on. With a wave of comfort, I closed my eyes to sleep.

"Dehydrated," Ariela diagnosed, standing above me. "Poseidon has taken her water for his own. Bring a carafe of purest water from the gods' spring. Sponge bits to her lips until she can sip from a goblet."

The women obeyed like servants, rotating their care over me. Each in turn sat on a stool near my cushion, accepting this duty as if this were her only place to be. Ariela came at intervals, monitoring my treatment. She spoke with each woman individually, admiring or correcting her unique personality, habits or manners, posture or way of speech. The woman would acknowledge Ariela's criticism that was given like a teacher to her pupil, not cruelly.

In my delirium, I sobbed, "Arun, have pity! What need you, Zilath? Mother, help me! Guard, don't betray me!"

Ariela whispered in my ear, "To whom do you speak?"

Dreamily, I answered, "I am Tarchna. We hold secrets of the cosmos."

Ariela shook her head. "My newest purchase speaks not in Hellenic but in a strange tongue. It doesn't sound Phoenician, or Aegyptian nor any language I've heard."

My bodily water restored, they remedied me with broth or boiled mint water. Dizziness and nausea ceased; the ache in my bones diminished, and my bruises felt less sensitive. Lying on my back, I opened my eyes to a high ceiling propped up by marble colonnades. Painted men and women, no, gods and goddesses copulated in various positions, lusting in glory. I knew some of the myths, for Etruscans loved them also. The room faced an open central courtyard within the house. Thrushes and larks twittered throughout the courtyard as they came in from the fresh cool morning air—air that smelled of the changing seasons.

One of my attendants spoke caringly in hushed Hellenic. "Your illness is over."

Younger than me, her foreign features, generous sensual lips and almond eyes, were exquisite. *A hetaera, certainly.* Weakness abated, I sat up at the bed's side, flexed my toes and spread my arms in relief. *I'm whole again!*

"I understand your speech, sweet lady. I am versed in Hellenic," I confessed. "Grateful I am to you."

The hetaera's response was immediate and joyous. She called a servant who promptly brought a bowl for my cleansing. Not permitted to attend myself, both did the ablutions like practiced rituals. My hair was combed, my mouth, nostrils and ears washed.

The others must have been waiting, for when I was prepared, the most beautiful women I had ever seen sauntered in and surrounded my bed. Diaphanous cloth draped their graceful forms. Jeweled, coifed hair framed faces painted with artistry.

More hetearae!

They lifted and carried me above them to a marble pool, then lowered me into water perfumed with rose oil. Their hands massaged my skin with herbs until I breathed evenly. Daintily they toweled and led me to my couch.

One by one the hetaerae curiously touched my face and stroked my limbs, laughing at my quick recovery, rejoicing, "The gods wanted you to live."

"A changed woman she is."

"What's her name?"

"Larth or Larthia it could be," Ariela said as she joined them. "I couldn't understand the mute's communication."

As if nobility, they introduced themselves, naming their origins. I studied the women, mostly Hellenic, one Phoenician, learning that the one with the exquisite features was Aegyptian.

"Their names are easy to recall for they were renamed when they came here. 'Sama' from Samos, 'Naxa' from Naxos, 'Chia' from Chios. The twins from Athenai are both 'Helena.'"

When it was my turn to answer, I blurted out in perfect Hellenic, "All of you go with men, don't you?"

Mirthful laughter greeted my query.

"The best in our polis of Athenai." Ariela proudly lengthened herself to her full lissome height.

"Were you all bought, like I?"

"Some came willingly, glad to be away from beastly families and foe," Ariela retorted. "I choose my hetaerae as prudently as young girls from noble families are chosen to be Athena's priestesses. Are you not grateful to be rid of that callous mute?"

The gods forsook me no matter what prayers I gave them. They might have saved me from the mute but delivered me to these women! "Forgive my impudence," I said humbly. "You saved my life."

"And you?" Ariela ignored my compliment. "Why are you not on your native soil? You are Etruscan, I guess?"

"Yes. I am Tarchna, a noblewoman married to a hunter of the prince-priest."

"Married, you say?"

"We were separated by a storm at sea," I lied thinly, "but the mute saved my life. Then he tricked me, forcing me to go with him."

"Your story is much like Homer's *Odyssey*, journeying over the seas with ordeals to overcome."

"No. *The Odyssey* is heroic legend, not real," I answered.

Ariela dismissed my explanation, knowing it to be false, and replied sweetly, "My women are courtesans, the finest in all Hellas."

They laughed and pinched each other in glee to be so praised. Ariela ordered them, "Tell of yourselves to our newest companion. Name your virtues."

When they did, I could only think: *they are all slaves turned concubines. And I join them.*

The Phoenician recited a memorized prayer. "We are blessed by the gods to be here."

"Blessed," repeated the Euboean reverently, "Our fortunes increase with Ariela's tenderness."

" . . . and yours will too," clucked one of the Helena twins.

The hetaerae, in unison, rose from their haunches and circled my bed, serving foodstuffs arranged on huge platters, feeding me morsels like I was an infant. Naxa plunked the lyre as Chia poured wine. In chorus with voices reminiscent of gods frolicking in the cosmos, they entertained me, laughing and dancing, sweeping arms through the air, pointing toes forward.

Ariela's eyes locked on mine as she set to tune:

> Like a sweet red apple
> ripens
> on a top branch
> unseen by pluckers
> unnoticed
> untouched . . .

The voice of another hetaera broke in:

> Like mountain rose petals
> trod by shepherds
> until only
> crimson remains
> on the dew.

They give lament for a maidenhead. I am meant to participate in their ways.
The hetaerae smiled at me, waiting for reaction.
It would mean nothing to tell them I'm a scribe, but better my lie covers truth. I live a life of lies, abashed for being a Tarchna scribe. What has my vocation done but bring trouble, abduction, more lies, tossed from one city and country to another?
"Do you like our song?" Phoenicia asked. "Poetess Sappho has taught us many."
"Poetess Sappho?"
"She is a goddess, a seer, a poetess, a prophetess. We sing her words and we are soothed, inspired to be the best courtesans. Give us a lyric, Euboea."
Euboea brought out her lyre, and strummed as she warbled another verse. The others danced around me as I sat back on my bed, my sacred mound quickening from intoxication of the melodies.

"We go now." With that amiably given command, Ariela led her well-trained hetaerae. They filed out singly. "You are not to enter those doors until you are ready, and I will tell you when."

Faint voices in the distant night, wisps of music and deep laughter came on light evening winds. Those sounds repelled yet fascinated me. I envied the hetaerae's acceptance of who and what they were.

A servant, supposedly my attendant, curled half-asleep against the colonnade. *She guards to keep me here. That is how Ariela lulls me into subjection, to make me ripe for men to pluck.*

"Ripe for men to pluck," I repeated out loud, gazing at the ceiling, a familiar study to me after being confined to this pleasing room. "Daily, this blissful setting is more appealing."

"Click your fingers like this. Raise your hands as if offering grapes to the gods and click as the lyre is strummed," Ariela instructed and danced across the marble floor.

Euboea played. I closed my eyes to hear the melody and snapped my fingers. "Etruscan women dance, of course."

"Then you are like us."

"No. We're different. Our men and women are not separated. We always banquet and dance together. Nor do we have a house of delights where men go to women. And our women are not secluded like the Hellenic behind closed doors."

"Click your fingers, Etrusca!"

I persisted. "We would never click with our hands when dancing, Ariela. It's a sign of disdain, to get rid of a servant or slave."

"We dance with our hands and feet, Etrusca. You saw Sama and Chia dance. Euboea plays so well. We entertain our guests and enrapture them to bed."

The hetaerae lounged on plump feather cushions in the courtyard. They watched my instruction and pointed out what gestures should be included or omitted.

"You learn quickly," Sama said hospitably and took up the lyre and continued when her turn came.

"We sing not of Homer's *Iliad* here. That's epic tragedy," Ariela insisted, "but Sappho is peaceful and feminine. She suits us."

The hetaera began to sing to me like a mother to her daughter:

> Hear me out,
> my dearest girl,
> By Aprhodite,
> I swear
> that I, like you,
> chastely left
> the house of my father
> without fear.
> When Hera beckoned me
> And cast away my maidenhead,
> I sung sweetly.
> My own night
> was not of thorns
> but made life glad.
> And you,
> my dear girl
> have nothing to fear.

"I'm not a virgin," I said. "I married Arun when I was twelve."

"He is past and you are here now. With my training, you will be the sensation of Athenai. You must sing and dance, touch and caress as if the gods set you on fire."

It's to my advantage that I'm not a virgin for I would grieve more.

The curtain to my room was tugged back and Ariela swept in, resplendent in a sheer ivory toned tunic, belted with gold sash. "Tonight, you are requested."

"Requested?"

"The Judge Councilor wants to see how you fare. He is the one who selected you the day you came."

"He's a councilor?"

"The very best. He follows the *Laws of Solon*, our great philosopher who set Athenai's politics and encourages democracy."

"*Laws of Solon?* Democracy? What does that mean?"

Ariela laughed and handed me a shimmering gauze tunic, the color of violets. "You have much to learn of our polis. In my house, we know of government, discreetly of course, before the citizens do."

"How powerful you are, Ariela." As I said that, I knew it to be fact. *She who holds me slave and hostage is my enemy as well as my benefactor.*

"You are ready, are you not?"

I nodded. Yes I was ready. No longer a wife or a noblewoman, I would go on and find some kind of happiness and contentment. We Etruscans reach out for joy, not sorrow for there is enough grief in the cosmos. Tired of my sorrow, I had reached the edge and capitulated. This was my fate—to be a harlot.

As if Ariela could read my thoughts, she said, "Come while the night calls."

By holding on to the doorway jamb of the great hall, I steadied my nervousness and awe. The room where the hetaerae met guests was two stories high, held up by columns and lit by wall torches. Painted figures beautified

the walls: God Dionysus held grapevines in one hand, a
drinking bowl in the other; Sappho strummed her lyre; a
piper played his tune; Zeus and Athena posed in their
famous legendary stances. Wood carved couches with
plump cushions invited guests to sit. Bowls of fruit, flasks
of wine and candelabra were displayed on tables. What I
had expected were some tawdry harlots' rooms. Instead,
an elegant, tasteful living space, luxuriously appointed.

All of the hetaerae were dressed in finest transparent
cloth, nipples tipped with gold paint, and shoulders bared
to suggest pleasures their bodies could bring. Men and
women stood or sat as they talked, nibbling on sesame cakes
and draining wine from bowls cupped in their hands, a
noisy group, enjoying the night breeze that filtered from
another courtyard at the opposite side of the room.

Ariela mingled with guests, smiling graciously,
offering libations, inquiring after their comfort. She
beckoned, "Come, Etrusca, this is Judge Councilor of the
Areopagus."

Agog, he brushed my arm provocatively with his fingers.
"This cannot be the same woman! You were a mangy waif when
we last met."

"Had you not argued for her, you can imagine what
would have befallen her with the Cumaen mute," Ariela
chimed in, then sashayed away to other guests, stirring
the air with her essence of flowing clothes and tinkling
jewelry.

*She sets an example for me to be vivacious, exciting,
stunning.*

The judge ran his fingers to my shoulder then up to
my neck and cheek. "You are desirable now, Etrusca."

I shivered from his touch and dripped my wine bowl
onto the marbled floor.

"What, Councilor? Have you undone a maiden before
the evening songs?" a different voice growled.

The judge glowered. "You're here in Athenai, again. What trade you now?"

"The usual. Rhodian pottery for household weavings. Introduce me to your companion."

"Find another, Merchant of Rhodos."

I looked at these men, trying to figure out why they had such animosity. Both had muscular bearded jaw lines, intense dark eyes but the judge's were crafty while the merchant's were unreadable.

"Stay away. I saw her first."

"Come now. Can she not speak?"

What hatred is between them? They aren't arguing over me, but over some past rivalry.

"Excuse me but that patron holds fresh grapes." Hastily I crossed the room and smiled at the seated bewildered youth munching grapes apprehensively. I picked a grape from the cluster, making sure the two men noticed my flirtation.

"You look as I feel—scared and alone. Is this your first time?" I smiled sympathetically at the youth. "Pretend I'm your sister and we chat at evening."

The boy seemed relieved. "My father made me come for instruction."

"Women also are scared at first. The unknown frightens."

Surprise crossed the boy's face. "You don't act like a hetaera should. You don't frighten me."

"You remind me of my brothers, but they thought more of food than courtesans at your age. Are you hungry?"

"Yes."

"Let's eat together," I suggested and then whispered, "Those men think you are my lover and are jealous."

The boy blushed. "Perhaps I will be."

*   *   *

Last night you charmed Judge Councilor and Merchant Alexis. Even the boy's eyes opened wide when he saw you," Ariela approved as we met for the noon meal of olives and bread, a meager contrast to the evening feasts.

I flushed. "We Etruscans enjoy banquet. Food and drink give us time to talk. It's what we do well."

"There was much talk of the workings of the polis."

"I learned the meaning of the Council of the Ageopagus, that past archons then become what we Etruscans would call 'magistrates.' I heard that one year the Judge Councilor had been Archon of Athenai."

"You understand some politics already," Ariela marveled, "and that will make you a good courtesan. In this season government officials debate in assembly during the day and spend evenings here to refresh."

Abrasive winds blew over Athenai. The polis readied for cold storms, covering courtyard rooms, storing grains, drying vegetables and meats, domestic chores that were no part of a heteara's life. My instructors involved me in mastering arts of song and dance, the artistry of lovemaking. Ariela herself guided me on how to touch, caress and chose men with whom I would pair.

The evenings' routine parties became less shameful as long as I could forget who I was. Arun hadn't rescued me, nor had my family, nor had any other Tarchna come to my aid. When my bitter fate welled up in my being, I would pick at pomegranate seeds, the gods' acid-sweet fruit, and remind myself of my bounty, that at the least, I was alive and sheltered.

My sister hetaerae had taken me in, nourished me with care and affection. I could do no less for them. Playfully I braided their hair in Etruscan fashion. With leaves from the garden, I made wreathes to crown their heads. My sisters were thinner than I and I gave them extra morsels of figs, dates and cheese for I ate and drank well enough. Curiously, my body bloomed with new womanliness.

At every eve's end, couples paired off and moved to couches in their quarters. So it was that Ariela pushed me in the direction of my room.

"How fortunate you are wanted by the judge. He will bring much business with him."

"I'll please him, Ariela, and use the love techniques you've taught."

Inert as a statue, the judge's nude body lay on my bed, looking up at the same ceiling paintings I saw nightly. I stroked him with my nails, ran my hands over his arms, chest and down his thighs, but he was flaccid. No matter what I tried, he remained unmoved.

"There are many thoughts on your mind." I nibbled his ear. "Tell me of them."

"Today there was an assembly in the Agora."

"How interesting these assemblies must be!" I feigned excitement, having heard that the Hellenic held long tedious arguments in developing philosophy, so unlike Zilath's preordained, enlightened laws given at Tarchna's market place.

"Yes. The citizens banded together, finally free of slavery from wealthy nobles and spoke of their needs and desires. What they wanted was lower taxes."

"Can they not pay?"

"They always pay. They demanded the wealthy to pay their share. As strong and rich as we are, the Council of the Areopagus doesn't like that. Yet to see if the rule of the people works, I voted with the citizens and we won."

"Were you upset?"

"No! Democracy works. They cheered me as they had Solon." As he told of the day's action, it reinforced his convictions and bolstered his powerfulness as a statesman. In his excited mood, his limp organ enlarged and he rolled over onto me.

"You talk of Solon with praise." If I urged the sophisticated judge to expound on his genuine passion, Athenian democracy, before I did my duty with him, he would be content with me.

"He was our chief Archon, Solon the Lawmaker who brought democracy to Athenai. We became citizens from all classes of wealth, not just nobles or property holders." The judge ran his fingers over my nipples. "Solon went around Hellas and saw how corn had worn out soil. He saw discontented farmers sold into slavery to pay debts when scant crops couldn't support them and released them from enslavement, breaking them from debt."

"How did he do that?" I reacted to the pressure on my breasts by diverting his attention with my question.

"The land was well suited to olive groves and vineyards, so he encouraged farmers to change plantings. With his knowledge of foreign trade, he began to export olive oil and wine. In his poetry, he spoke of how greedy nobles were unjust to farmers. He created the law of popular assembly in Athenai, and rallied as its champion."

"Is that why they called him 'Archon'?"

The judge nodded, and raised himself up on his elbow. "Hellas prospers now. You coax my manhood with talk of Solon."

"You admire him much. Did you know him?"

"I was his lover when I was a boy."

As long as I keep talking, I can tolerate this embarrassment of being a hetaera. When the judge and I bedded, I listened to the theory of individuals and laws of the polis.

"So farmers are citizens," I deducted.

"Yes. Farmers are landowners. We have four classes of citizens according to wealth, not just property."

"What class are the hetaerae?"

"You? You aren't counted. Women aren't citizens."

"Not citizens! Why not?"

"Women are nameless. Just 'wife of Andros' or 'wife of Theos.'"

"Nameless!" I gulped in dismay. "How different from Etruscan ways. Your democracy is less than ours for Etruscan women are named. They're citizens." *He would be shocked that I am a noblewoman.*

"Women are for home and bed."

What disrespect! ! For home and bed only! I wanted to shout, but contained myself not to spout too much Etruscan doctrine. *Our class system isn't in upheaval like this polis. We know our place but it is honorable. Etruscan women would laugh, if not cry, over the dilemma of poor Hellenic women. What place women have here, not citizens but servants, treated as poorly as slaves. I was a tranquil noble and now I am worse than a slave!*

"You said that freeing an individual is the first level of democracy. Yet is not a woman an individual?"

His face bloated with sudden hate. "Trying to be shrewd, are you? You anger me with your sniveling drivel."

He left, not to return.

None of the hetaerae left the house. Either servants did their bidding or patrons came and went. It was forbidden that we should be exposed to the polis or to even weak sunlight, kept in our world of luxury, opulence and lovemaking. The others accepted confinement within stone walls that enclosed the house compound and its gardens, but I couldn't. Restlessly I paced its inner perimeters, seeing only the roof of the acropolis temple, higher up on the mountainside. I asked one of the Helenas, "What's on the other side of this wall?"

"I don't know. I've never been there."

"You are of Athenai and have no thought?"

"It is not my place to go, nor is it yours."

"Everyone talks of this wonderful polis." *But we are locked in here like prisoners. I want to see it.* It would be dangerous to share that thought with my sisters. In pretense of picking lemons from the tree in the garden, I leaned the ladder against its trunk and climbed up. The full slope of the hill was visible, the Agora at the bottom where servants scooped water from its well, the polis marketplace teeming with people. A man stood on a platform, and others surrounded him, listening intently, sometimes clapping or shouting, but the words were too distant to hear.

So that's the assembly. Citizens are all men, making laws that I must abide.

Uphill I saw a white columned temple, the sacred temple of Athenai's highest priestesses, worshiped by all. People strolled about in the sacred grove, women arm in arm. *They walk freely, like I used to do with my mother, with my nieces, with my sister-in-law, Ranu.*

While Judge Councilor was my first, there were others, a warrior lately home from the sea, an Athenian landowner, a former noble. One of Solon's law advisors was followed by another Athenian landowner, then a famed Corinthian potter. Not the youth I had met at my first party. Naxa captivated him. Nor the merchant of Rhodos, Alexis, who stayed in the polis for the cold season, talking with me when he came for Ariela. I asked all of them of their views on democracy.

"What good is your democracy if it's for the chosen, and only for men?"

"Act not belligerent when you speak of ideals," Alexis cautioned when I broached the subject with him.

The cold season became gloomy. In solitude, I sat on a cushion in the great hall, scratching Sappho's words into a piece of stone, pondering, *Was it her poetry that first softened me to my sister hetaerae, renewing kindness to my spirit? Or was it the kindness my sisters exhibited? Among them I feel more gentle and serene.*
The merchant of Rhodos interrupted my musings. Alexis saw the stone before I could stuff it under me. Nosily he inquired, "Are you sculpting?"
"No."
"Let me see," he teased, his hand diving under the cushion. "What's this? Hellenic words!"
"Don't tell anyone," I pleaded. "Please."
"What words are they?"
"Poetry of Sappho. It soothes me with its beauty."
"Who are you? You're not a hetaera by calling. That first night, I knew you were quick-witted. You saw through that quarrel with the judge."
"It doesn't matter anymore."
"You speak Etruscan. Did you scribe this?"
"Yes."
He looked at me, dumbfounded. "A woman who scribes. I can only scribe numbers for my trade, not words."
"Women can do many things."
"Have care what you do—and say. I give you warning."

During the Feast of the Cold Season, Ariela gave a lavish banquet, inviting favorite clients to join the hetaerae and be entertained by musicians and acrobats. I sat on a couch, bored with the naked performers, wondering if my next lover would be fat or thin.

"For you, Etrusca." The merchant of Rhodos sidled next to me and slid a parcel under my seat. "Don't crush it."

"I can listen to your troubles, but we hetaerae can never take gifts from those we don't bed," I reminded him, "You're Ariela's lover."

"I bring you not jewels but something more valuable to you."

"Not jewels!"

"Because your talents amaze me, I will keep your secret." With that he rose brusquely and joined Ariela's guests as if continuing the conversation.

I hid the parcel among my clothes and waited until all the women and servants were busy with tasks. Memories flooded in. The parcel sat on my lap, layers of papyrus, with a sharpened quill and jar of octopus ink. I started to memorize Sappho's poems for myself, not for a lover or my lost life. As if the cosmos had sent its gods to replenish my spirit, I rehearsed songs of the poetess Sappho.

When the house was quiet, I copied her poetry, bringing an enjoyment lost to me since my abduction. What pleasure Sappho's words brought, full of women's opinions, similar yet different to men—an understanding of how the cosmos should work. The Hellenic loved her and sang her praises. She inspired me by lending sanity to my troubled being. *I never thought such pleasure could come from a single gift. But his gift makes me sad, too. The sorrow that I thought would leave, never does, the hurt of separation never dies. Yet I have survived. To leave here and return home is my greatest wish.*

What was Alexis's true motive in bringing the papyrus? Perhaps he wants me to be of use to him? If so, I had a plan.

*   *   *

The merchant observed me on his every visit to Ariela's house. I had to find out his true interest in me by showing disinterest in him and went out of my way to let him see me fawning over the clients as if I loved them.

"Your false brightness shows," Alexis whispered to me during an evening party. "Why do you stay?"

"Stay? You confuse me, suggesting my freedom. I was sold and bought. Ariela is my owner, my benefactor. I am her slave without position to leave. A hetaera's life is fair, certainly better than I supposed. I enjoy the song, the dance."

"There's danger in your actions. You act the hetaera but you ill-pleased the judge. You bring trouble with your talk of women citizens. If he finds you're a scribe, too, your life is worthless."

"Will you reveal my identity?"

"To the judge? No. Are women not people? His politics and mine disagree."

Happiness at his confession made me smile, an authentic smile, not my usual polite vacuous one. "I've misunderstood your intentions."

"My intentions?"

"I thought you were perhaps interested in me sexually. I see it is my intelligence and talent for scribing you care about."

I had planted the idea in his mind.

The next part of my plan was to listen to the hetaerae's prattle, gleaning what I could about the merchant's business and his birthplace. Finally I became desperate. I spied on Ariela and him, sitting under their chamber's window as they made love. Not the most honorable activity, but I learned what I needed.

Thus I told small lies. "Ariela says you sail from Athenai through the Aegean when the storms rest. Where do you go?"

"To my home, Rhodos."

"A grand island, I understand. The polis there has much commerce and farmlands. The school where scholars scribe for the Dodecanese is so powerful that your trader's league controls the region and commerce from Anatolia to Phoenicia."

Alexis looked at me in astonishment. "How did you know that?"

Modestly I drawled, "I know. Have you a scholar to scribe for you?"

"Whoever is about."

"You're a merchant! There's more to accounts than just numbers. How do you know they're reliable? You might be robbed!"

His lips thinned as he thought over my suggestion.

"You need your own personal scribe! A scribe like me, honest and discreet, who could watch over your accounts, write contracts with your league, scribe homage to your gods, figure your losses, and help you profit. "

Never having done so before, I wept fake tears, and then slyly interjected, "Would you take me with you?"

"What?"

"You see I'm not who I pretend. Bring me no more pain, Merchant. Help me leave. I will scribe for you if you send me home when transport to Etruria comes to your island."

"By thunder!" Alexis wheezed. "Stop your sobbing! I will think on it. You're the most persuasive hetaera of all!"

10

Ariela, The Hetaera

Alexis bit my neck playfully. The merchant of Rhodos was my most devoted lover and friend.

"I have a new hetaera, Alexis."

"Not so new. You've been wanting to tell me about her for ages." He rubbed his nose against my ear.

"'Etrusca'—that's what I named her—was sun blistered, and thin as a stick when I first saw her, yet I saw potential. Judge Councilor was here that day—the great judge he is—thought so, too. He would know, a magisterial justice who sees every member who goes against society."

"Ah ha. Go on, Ariela."

"I paid less for her than I would have, but that disgusting mute infuriated me to haggle. He was a heartless one, treating her like an animal." I slipped away from Alexis' embrace and picked an olive branch from the bowl, offering it to him, then took one for myself and sucked on its tartness, working my tongue around the pit to practice dexterity. "The tongue is a source of pleasure. I will have to instruct Etrusca of it."

"Don't you think she knows?"

"Perhaps. She is somewhat like my younger sister, Helena. In some ways Helena was innocent before she became a hetaera, but she was knowledgeable of the universe. Evidently, Etrusca is knowledgeable. She was no virgin. Too old. She intrigued me with her foreignness."

"Me, too," Alexis agreed, sucking on his olive like he would my breast.

"You've met her!"

"When you were with the councilor."

We laughed compatibly.

"So tell me more," Alexis implored.

"She's the first Etruscan woman I've seen. When she toppled in my doorway, she didn't smile but still contained some secret charisma. Scared, of course. For two days she slept. Feverishly she dreamed in her native language. Yet with the past locked under all that sorrow, there was a liveliness that emanated from her body. I think my hetaerae felt her pain for they were drawn to her and took care of her. In a few days, she ate again and bloomed like a spring flower."

Alexis nodded thoughtfully. "At the docks in Piraeus I met Etruscans—men, not women. They're evasive, self-possessed, with big fat smiles like they know all the world's secrets. The ones who come here claim to be merchants but they're highborn pirates sailing sleek ships. It is said Etruria has rich land, abundant gardens and huge amounts of stock."

"Many Hellenics went to Sicilia and defected to Etruria," I replied and joked, "Disloyal Hellenics! Traitors!"

"Etrusca's loyal to you."

"Sometimes I trust her, sometimes I don't. She acts too loyal."

"She has hubris."

Annoyed that he seemed overly interested in Etrusca, I nestled up to him and flirted. "My dear, are you jealous of the judge?"

"Only that he comes to you regularly," Alexis took another branch of olives.

"The life of a hetaera is never easy, fawning over those we dislike to make our way, crying over those we loved which is a mistake." I suggested to Etrusca when her turn came during my daily inspection of the women. I re-brushed her hair, coiled and piled the thick waves into a becoming style, and pinned it down.

"You and I are alike, Etrusca," I said. "We're survivors. My own life's struggles have put me where I am."

"Survivors? Is that what we are?"

Determined to let her know that my life was as unhappy as I surmised hers to be, I launched into my personal saga. "I'm the daughter of a once wealthy aristocrat. He opposed Athenai's new system of government for he and other rich patrons would have to give up crops and goatherds. To save his family from danger, he sent his wife and grown boys to colonize the new settlement of Megara in Sicilia. That's near Etruria, isn't it?"

"Far south," Etrusca shuddered tersely.

I continued my story. "They perished on the voyage. My father was grief-stricken. He had no one else, so he consorted with a woman servant, my mother, who bore me. She died in labor. My father raised me on his own, lavishing attention with gorgeous tunics, gold armlets and earrings, beaded necklaces and exotic foods to compensate for lack of family in this huge house. His noble Hellenic ancestry became my own, my mother's peasant lineage obscured."

"You must have been lonely." Etrusca sat like a stone goddess as I worked on her body, examining her teeth for cleanliness, blending powder on her unblemished face. I rouged her high cheekbones, and dabbed scented oils behind her ears. Her watery eyes told her sympathy. Her reaction spurred me on.

"I acted as hostess to his social obligations, listened to his politics, knew all of the polis leaders, and understood how this new society was blossoming with democratic concepts."

"Democracy," she murmured. "There's so much talk of it here."

"You are interested in our philosophy?"

"It's different from ours. We don't argue or think of changing it constantly."

"Change is inevitable," I said, wanting to lash out at Etruscan complacency. "My father changed. In his elder years, his mind narrowed further as interest in accumulating wealth and rank diminished, until his fields were in ruin. Feeling sorry for his life-long losses, he debased himself with too much wine, ate too much grain, and fattened. The more he drank and ate, the more he wanted to destroy his wealth, inviting any who would come to imbibe with him, thus attracting the low class to his home. He forced me to sit by his bed and watch him amuse himself with dancers, harlots and young boys. Tainted by his whoredom, the house was in shambles from lack of care."

"Yes, you're right of course. Fate changes our lives."

She agreed humbly like she accepted her inevitable situation, becoming an outstanding hetaera. I hoped she would say more, confide in me. She didn't.

I went on. "At Father's death, I inherited the house, but nothing else for he had become a whore master, and I, by inference became one too. Not able to survive without family or means, I paid with my body to restore this home, sleeping with carpenter, stone worker, weaver, painter, warrior and politician. My reputation grew with my skilled techniques of carnal love, until my house was most cherished by the polis' patrons. That's how my position was elevated to the highest title of "Hetaera, Courtesan to the Patrons."

I painted Etrusca's nipples with gold leaf, holding each small breast in hand, concentrating on my work. Her nipples hardened with the brush stroke, a sensual reaction to hearing my history. "Other desperate women of comeliness sought my protection and shelter within the walls of this house, which is majestic, don't you think?"

"Yes it is. How convenient to Athenai's acropolis, next to dwellings of rich citizens. You are indeed fortunate to have a satisfied life," Etrusca said, almost glowing from my ministrations.

She was happy to be in my house! Like a trapped beast, she was brought to me to domesticate. Resisting no more, she joined my feasts, mixing in with my delectable group of courtesans, never discussing her background. The Hellenics brood, quarrel and debate over their lot in life. But not her! What kind of people did she come from?

"When you touch a man's flesh, run the tips of your fingers across it. Your fingers must show a sweet breeze, a ripple of refreshing air." My hands skimmed over Etrusca's face in demonstration. "Start at the crease between his brows and forehead, down to his cheek bones, circling the lines of his face."

She sat at my feet, looking upward as I stroked her face, her neck, down to the bared shoulders where her tunic hung loose, draped seductively, although I didn't think she noticed.

"Your skin has rejuvenated. I wish mine could," I told her. Daylight hours showed my aging skin and I had to remember to stay away from sunlight. At night it was easier to cover my flaws. I applied unguents and cosmetics to keep my beauty, for I would be a hetaera until death.

Etrusca quietly took instruction, closing her eyes in surprised contentment. She sighed. "Yes, this is a perfect way to soothe a man."

"Good. There is a variety of poses to sit or lay in when one caresses her lover," I went on. "Think of how the gods frolic on the potters' bowls, their movements supple, turning this way and that in rhythm of lovemaking. You must work your limbs. Arch your back in practice."

To the Judge Councilor, I told of Etrusca. "I could not help but like her. She became hardy quickly and learned her circumstance. Remember her first night when you saw her? She mocked your game and smartly stopped a fight. And the boy? She treated him as if he was family and passed him to Naxa who was delighted."

"She's clever, Ariela," the judge nodded, "and she beds well, but she speaks against the polis."

"How could that be?"

"She says there must be slaves so nobles will have their place."

"Could that be the way of the Etruscans? They are strange, locked into mysterious traditions of the ancients, I've heard."

"She prods me with questions of our politics, of Solon, of democracy."

"She is curious. And when you tell her, what then?"

"I am overcome with emotion and explode into her."

"The judge likes you," I complimented Etrusca. "He comes frequently and you quench his fires. Others ask for you. Your popularity grows."

"I do what you say."

"You bring more success to my house this season than I've ever had before." With those words out of my mouth, I felt a premonition that I had spoken too soon.

"Phoenicia, Sama, Naxa, Chia, Euboea, the twins Helena, Aegypta—all prizes." The judge and I lounged on the cushions one evening after my hetaerae danced for the patrons.

"And Etrusca?"

"Etrusca can be . . ." He searched for the right word. "Volatile."

"What do you mean?"

"She twists words to her liking, talking of women as citizens!"

"Impossible."

"It is so. She will bring you ruin," he predicted.

"She's a delight."

"You are loyal to the polis. The polis protects your establishment. Get rid of her or I will."

Etrusca had vanished, her clothes and bedding still intact. Was she taken by the judge as he threatened, or did she sneak out? I didn't know. My servants scoured the neighborhood and down the acropolis road without tracing her. *Ungrateful harpie! All that I've done for her! When I find her she'll be beaten.*

Until I could get her back, I would have to lie. Thus I gathered my women in the great room, not what I usually did. They came as bidden. Tension tied them together, these beautiful cultivated women whose lives I carefully managed.

"Etrusca's not here," Naxa sprang up. "Shall I fetch her?"

"You can't." I laid my hand firmly on Naxa's shoulder, directing her to face the group. "I must speak to you about Etrusca. She's gone. I sold her."

Euboea gasped. "You sold her!"

"Etrusca was with that hoplite from Sparta. Maybe he wanted her on his military campaign," Sama guessed.

"No, it must have been that handsome poet from Samos," Chia suggested. "He liked her more than me."

"I bet it was Merchant Alexis," one of the twins Helena deduced. "He's rich with gold trade from the East, and his house in Rhodos is staffed with servants and laborers he bought from his voyages."

"Will she be his hetaera?" Phoenicia asked.

"Of course not, silly one. He's Ariela's special lover," the other Helena chimed in.

My hetaerae were becoming loose-tongued, speaking out of turn. Before they could harm my house and destroy my labors, I had to regain control. They had to be kept disciplined. "A hetaera of my status cannot be careless. I must please the patrons so that I can ask for favors when needed. We, as hetaerae, must work together. Etrusca was sold because—"

"Why her?" Aegypta cried out. "Why not me?"

"She never truly adapted." I snapped, turned on my toes and exited, my announcement finalized. Silently I cursed, *May Etrusca mate with an oceanid and produce a monster!*

11

Island Of Moonlight

"Come! I bring you freedom!" A shadowed form stooped next to my bed and whispered in my ear.

"Freedom," I repeated stupidly, groggy with sleep after another night of nightmarish, disconnected dreams that plagued me since my arrival in Athenai. "What is freedom? I am like Prometheus. Bound. Not to a rock but to this house."

"It's me, Alexis." He tugged at my blanket.

Somewhat cleared of sleep, my body tensed as every small sound grew louder. My dreams may have created these appalling noises—insects crawling in the garden, scratching as they climbed over leaves and dirt—owls shrieking from the heights of the acropolis. The regular breathing of my sister hetaerae increased into a chorus of harmonic song as they slept, rustling on their cushions.

"Etrusca! Larthia! Hear me! Please, hurry. We sail at dawn."

I awakened fully, accustoming my eyes to the dark. My body resumed its breath, my dream state over. "You're mad, Alexis. Ariela would be livid, not only at me but at you. I can't go."

"You will. Now. Cover yourself with these. Take nothing."

I tumbled out of bed, adjusting to the usual shadows of my room. Alexis had come to help me escape. His urgency was infectious. He thrust a heavy wool tunic at me, durable after the delicate ones of a hetaera. I tugged it down over my flimsy gown. Ready to be off, he quickly wrapped a thick homespun cloak around my shoulders. My sisters' snoring continued.

I'll miss them.

"Wait. I must take my scrolls."

He gave a short laugh. "You're a true scribe."

The merchant and I bolted out a side door, through a gate that led downward through the Agora's paths, leaving Athenai. Without a word to each other, we walked until dawn streaked across the eastern horizon on a road that smelled of the sea.

I bunched the cloak close to my throat. "If someone from the polis sees me, I could be seized."

"No one will. We're close."

He led me down the slope to a sleepy harbor. As we neared the dock, I heard the all-too-familiar lapping of water against ships. Ropes strained and ground against wood. How else could I leave except by sea?

"Worry precedes me at every step. I'll be found out and missed."

"Proceed through the unknown with awareness to glorify it," Alexis grinned, much delighted by our night's clandestine adventure.

"What bit of wisdom is that?"

"Known to seafarers," he quipped.

As the sun broke through the end of night, the outlines of anchored ships spread over the sea. There were none from Etruria. A slim hope I briefly had that I could find some sympathetic Etruscan to take me home.

"We board my ship for Rhodos."

His was a bulky merchant vessel, similar to the mute's. It bumped the pier in cadence with the waves, co-existing like old friends. On deck the crew scurried about in final preparations, securing bundles of cargo with ropes. Alexis signaled the crew and they hoisted the sail and prodded the ship, floating it from the mooring with long poles.

"Am I your prisoner, Alexis?"

"No."

"Your hetaera?"

"No. I breathe not a word of that. The men would riot to have a piece if you were."

"What will you tell them about me, Alexis?"

"Understand that to us, a used woman is for pleasure. A married woman's duty is to procreate and oversee the house. You are neither."

"Many thanks for your slur!" I exclaimed grimly, appalled that his attitude was like the judge's, not tolerant as he had pretended at Ariela's house of delights. I burst forth, "From Roma to Athenai, the mere mention of women turn men disdainful and rapacious with lust. The fate of women in this country is to be used and scorned, shut away behind walls to cook, clean and produce offspring! My people, both men and women are considered of equal importance. We banquet together, walk together, sing and dance together, one not better than the other as here."

"Fireball you are! Unwisely you spout! Do you not remember you promised to scribe for me? You will be addressed as 'Distinguished Guest, Respected Scribe.'"

"You protect me by giving me title?" I questioned, feeling both doubtful and grateful. "My word is honorable. I will surprise you and show you my worth."

"Is this Etruscan fortitude?" Alexis asked.

Cast asunder by the gods of my youth, all powerful
Tinia and love Goddess Turan, carried forth by Hellenic
gods, supreme Zeus and sea god Poseidon, into unknown
waters, embarking for a further land, I sailed on Alexis'
vessel. How lonely I was, engulfed in renewed grief for
my past home, knowing I was going east, not west, south,
not north.

For days we shunted among islands of rock, sometimes
populated with goats in search of grass, or poor fishermen
drying out the day's catch in front of lean-to shacks.

"These Carpathian Straits are hazardous waters."
Alexis squeezed my hand in reassurance. "Most of this
coast is barren with those vertical cliffs."

"My Uncle Venu was a seafarer. As a boy, he ran away
to sea and stowed on a ship. He was here, I know, for his
descriptions match these desolate islands."

"What did he say about this coast?"

"He described it exactly as we see. Treeless settlements
of fishermen who make their living from the waters. The
hot sun beating on huge boulders. Useless white sand
beaches. Brilliant, clear water down to its depths. Venu's
ship stayed at these islands because villagers were friendly.
They offered shelter and hospitality. He felt an affinity for
this part of the cosmos and believed our Ancestors came
from east of here, Lydia in Anatolia."

"I've met a number of your people because Etruscan
ships ply these waters. Your seafarers are skillful, even
polite, but close-mouthed to us, secretive about your
heritage. Why is that?"

"We don't shout our ancestry! Our stories are for
ourselves."

"Tell me anyway. The day is sultry and calm, and, we sail until dusk." Lazily, Alexis slouched against a sack of pungent onions whose smell didn't seem to bother him. "Give recess from my watch. I've heard the Etruscans are known as a splendid society. Your stories beg to be told for the entire Mediterranean is in awe of mighty Etruria and wants to know how it has become powerful. Indulge me with a tale. I'll keep your secrets."

Like the Roman king, Alexis wanted answers to the cosmos, answers to the meaning of existence, holy stories and philosophies. What a dilemma I felt. If I didn't tell of my people, he might return me to the hetaerae or feed me to Poseidon's fishes. *Would it harm to tell him?*

"There are old legends of the Ancestors. I'll tell you one to you as a gift."

"A gift?"

"It's the least I can do since you rescued me from living out my life as a hetaera."

He cheek twitched like he had been stung, an extreme reaction that disturbed me.

"The story of King Attis was my favorite, how Etruria came to be."

"I thought you said your people came from Anatolia."

"Yes. Lydia in Anatolia. Long before Athenai was a city, Lydia was a great city, wealthy with gold. Its palace and temples were grand, stone buildings with columns and polished stone floors, elaborately ornamented with statues. And then a drought came upon the land, drought that plagued the people, not for seven or twelve years, but eighteen. With the drought came wretched famine, cursed by Tinia's anger."

"Tinia?" Alexis asked. "Man or god?"

"Our greatest god, god of the sky, thunder and lightning. Like your Zeus. Once, Lydia's garden bloomed with fruits and fields of ripened wheat. Greedily the people picked everything without tending or appreciating their bounty, forgetting to renew the soil by setting aside Tinia's rainwater. Tinia was furious. His powers could give nourishment, but he could also punish. He cursed them with drought and famine.

"Because of the drought, the soil crumbled into sand and it crept into the palace, covering the lord of the city, King Attis, his tunic, cloak, feet and even his beard. His people, the Lydians, in their distraught state, were covered with grit in every crevice. They waited for the sand to smother the entire city and suffocate them. The sand became dust and dust was everywhere."

Alexis looked across the sea to rocky shores. "Drought, yes. There's much of it in these parts. Perhaps Zeus has done the same with our land."

"The eighteenth harvest was smallest and grimmest. Ever since, it's been called 'the starvation of Lydia.' Meals were curbed to every other day. King Attis' people loved games, especially dice, and everyone played constantly to ward off hunger. At least the polished stone floors were good for something—dice rolling! The old king, thin as a wheat stalk, played with his son, Prince Tyrrhenos. Hunger made their game violent. With vengeance the king rattled the dice, and said, 'this last game decides our fate. Half of our people must leave our parched city, wasted by these endless droughts. If you lose, it is you who must lead.'"

"And then?"

"Tyrrenhos lost. Attis told him, 'Seek out a new life, a land of plenty that will fill our people's empty bellies and make them sing and dance joyfully again.' Tyrrhenos was clever. He had already consulted the high priest for his prophecy and learned that this would occur. Unbeknownst to the king, Tyrrhenos had built ships along the coast. He chose the strongest men, the smartest overseers, the cleverest crafters, the finest artisans, the most serious engineers of water courses, the most enduring child bearers, males and females who could carve cities out of wilderness and guide his people out of Lydia."

"How many ships?"

"Sixteen."

"A fleet. You didn't mention warriors."

"They were too hungry to fight! Ships, jammed with gold and traded ivory, but scarce of food. They sailed along many coastlines, never losing sight of land, searching for harbors to build new cities, pausing for shelter, looking for wild food stuffs and good soil. The first terrain that cheered them yielded temporary harvest, only to be replaced by drought as severe as Lydia's. Death of the less hearty demoralized them in their plight."

"Where was that?"

"Somewhere along the Hellenic coast. They had to journey on or the Hellenics would fight them."

"Of course."

"The high priest had prophesized that they would find what they sought. How unkind the gods were! A fierce, turbulent storm whirled the fleet from the coast, pushing them westward into bottomless waters, disorienting them, ruining their task and disillusioning them. Tyrrhenos pleaded, 'Gods of the cosmos, of sky and sea—desert us not. We pledge our utmost loyalty to you and do your bidding.'"

The very words I had just uttered silenced me. *Those were my words, too, when the mute took me on his horrible ship, uprooting from my cosmos. The Fates ignored my pleas.*

"Why don't you go on?"

My eyes filled with tears. My throat ached from so much speech.

"Finish," Alexis mopped my tears with his scarf. "Please."

Miserably, I kept up my narration. "The oceanid Fates must have heard his urgent prayers and righted twelve of the wood clad ships. A blessing that only four were lost in the awful storm. Aplu's sun broke the clouds in their path, and a new coast, a vision of beauty, came into view. Tyrrhenos felt his burden lifting. 'Explore this land' he directed his people. 'Spread out over plains, into valleys, mountains, ravines, extend up and down this coast, push inward to high mountains.' What they found were savage hunters and pastoral tribes who lived in squalor, who marked territory only with funerary mounds of bones and old broken pots. The Lydians, smart in the knowledge of battle, but toughened by struggle, pushed these Ligures and Umbrians to the northlands and east of the mountains."

"So the Lydians became the Tyrrhenoi—Etruscans."

"Yes." Before Alexis could rise, I moved forward to the prow of the ship. For a long while, I watched the sea billow and glide us forward.

"You didn't tell the whole story. There must be more," Alexis said a few days later. "Your tale was like stories the Hellenics tell, a bit of Homer, and of the gods. King Attis was like Priam of Troy. Tyrrhenos was like Odysseus. How could that be?"

"It's in our sacred books."

"Not many females read! But you do. And you scribed it, haven't you?"

"I copied the books for Prince-priest Zilath."

"You're a high scribe!" Alexis chuckled. "What other services did you provide?"

His question annoyed me for he almost leered. Reluctantly I mumbled back, "Zilath used my talents where he saw fit."

"How did your people get so great from that sorry past?"

"Tyrrhenos found good land," I answered, relieved that this question was more artful. "Fertile land that produced grains to sustain them. They hunted wild animals for sacrifice and food. Then copper and tin for industry were found in the mountains., the same mountains where they got beech and oak trees to mill into ship hulls used for trade with Hellas, Carthage and Phoenicia. Of course Tyrrhenos became king, having been a prince since birth, and they were called *Tyrrhenians* after him. He went to the Ancestors a happy man, having brought his charges out of famine into this garden of wealth and prosperity, providing good fortune to his descendants."

"Surely your sacred books lie. The gods are not so benevolent to give forth land so abundant anywhere," Alexis said truculently.

"My stories must agitate you."

"They charm."

I replied with generalities, giving stories that the entire cosmos knew. I couldn't be a traitor again! I wouldn't reveal more of the glory of Tarchna, of all Etruria. I remembered them, only to myself. *Tyrrhenos came upon a verdant glade, a place he acclaimed to be of sacred goodness where the gods wielded their powers. Humbly, he fell to the ground giving praise to Volumna for safe passage to this newly found land. The sacred glade became part of his legacy. There were no more kings, but prince-priests and they went to the glade to thank the gods for well-being. And then the little old wizened creature Tages appeared to a prince and taught him the secrets of the cosmos in his book, the Discipline. That has been the real strength of us.*

After that, during the day, I stayed in the shelter of the deck's cabin, not wanting to be persuaded to tell more stories.

*   *   *

How odd it was to be dragged about on sea journeys, I, a land-bound noblewoman. It was not that I sought to learn the workings of the vessel and the secret rhythms of seafarers, but it had become part of my fate. One dawning as I awoke to the gentle rocking of the hull, I named to myself each action of ship, the routines of every crew member, the sea currents, the air's climate. How similar these activities were to the mute's ship although the sea differed. Ships kept similar rules. Thus, with purpose, I scribed observations about mariners with a seagull's quill on papyrus that Alexis gave me from one of his barters, with excuse to practice Hellenic writing.

Sometimes, the merchant vessel would dock at certain islands for barter, cargo, to gossip or drink and rest. While Alexis kept his men away from me, he was only one man among many. My biggest fear was to be violated by lustful men who hadn't had a woman in many moons. What saved me from the seafarers was that Alexis was too skilled a seafarer to be caught at night without ground. They slept on land at night, in settlements or on a beach, or even on rocks or hillocks, for there was no space on the vessel. Their seafaring lives uneasily reminded me of being ravaged by the mute and his coldhearted men. To keep away from possible attack, I slept on deck under the stars where I felt safe.

Every eve, Alexis and his ship pilot studied positions of the stars to navigate the journey, and I listened. Once, when stars blazed across the sky, Alexis gazed up and said, "Our sky holds the most stars in the universe—you call it 'the cosmos' but it is 'world'—so we've named them after the gods. Our gods shine in the stars and constellations."

"The Etruscan augurs study the flight of birds in the sky," I replied, "and divine the movement of the cosmos."

"Your thinking is tainted. How could you divine life from birds when it is the night sky that defines our world."

Tired of insults and mockery of me and my people, I said, "Our truths are not like yours. You are raw, serious. We are refined and forgiving."

"Nonetheless, you are wrong."

Beware! Alexis troubles me for he is sure his convictions are right.

The night came that a round stone tomb loomed out of the dark sea, a tomb perched majestically from a mound of jagged rocks at the end of a spit of land, ringing a small bay.

"It's a monument to one of the seven wisest men of Hellas, Kleovoulos. It honors Lindus with its presence. We've arrived."

Across from Kleovoulos' tomb on the opposite cliff was an astounding sight. "What is that? It's magnificent!" In wonder, I was captivated by its sheer height.

"A temple to the goddess of the moon by our Minoan ancestors."

By moonlight, we entered the sheltered waters of the crescent-shaped harbor and the ship anchored. Squared flat buildings lodged around the base of the high sacred cliff. Along the shore, black rocks scattered along the sandy beach.

"My eyes play tricks! What kind of rocks move?"

Hooting with laughter, Alexis passed my words to the crew. "They aren't rocks but our women"

A bad omen not to know their ways. Swathed in dark cloth, sitting on their haunches, the island women sang.

I laughed along, to ward off a growing discomfort. *What new worry comes?*

"So many customs I don't know in the cosmos! What do they sing, Alexis?"

"A song of welcome, of relief and gladness that the sea has spared the seafarers, of pride in the seafarers' endurance."

A woman stepped forward and waved. Imitating Alexis, I waved back. The woman picked up her long hemmed skirt and tromped away into the trees that lined the beach.

"She's your wife, isn't she?"

"Yes, and displeased at the sight of you, I'm sure."

"Why, I cannot guess. After all, you are my benefactor."

"Women don't sail the seas in Hellas. She will think you're a witch or . . ."

"Or what?"

"Larthia, how is she to know you're foreign born, that you're an Etruscan scribe? I'll explain as soon as her temper cools."

The other women came forward bidding welcome to the seafarers who dived from the deck and splashed to shore. I remained at the railing, watching the reunion. *What will it be like to return to Tarchna and be greeted by Arun and my family? Will they be as loving as these people?*

"Stay on board tonight," Alexis directed, a frown creasing his face. "Tomorrow you will come to my house and your work will begin."

On sight of his homeland, Alexis had become unpredictable, not the same man who was Ariela's soft, gentle lover, nor the rugged seafarer of our sailing.

Sharp, staccato, deep men's voices mixed with melodious singing reverberated across the water, the seafarers and wives or islanders celebrating the safe return after two seasons gone. There was a vulgarity about their reunion, riotous and base. I hadn't been around many ordinary people. I didn't know what they did or talked about. To be fair, they weren't nobles. In Tarchna, we stayed with our own kind. When warriors returned, we banqueted and feasted at Zilath's court, but seafarers, except Uncle Venu, stayed separate.

Unable to sleep, I leaned against the mast. Stars showered across the night sky, quieting me with magical luminescence. I had never seen so many of them at once. Some had been there eve after eve, glistening, unmoving in splendor, tonight more bright.

Light came from a not-quite full moon on its rise. *This moon so white against the darkened star sky is most beautiful of all. How many moons I've seen! On land. On sea. I'm comforted by its reliability. It assures me of my existence, amidst the trials I've had. Now the moon and stars are my only joy.*

Except for the night watchman, a seafarer who sat on the prow eating cheese and drinking wine, the ship was abandoned. The seafarer hadn't looked at me, knowing that my presence on the ship hadn't tainted it, that I wouldn't cause trouble. Someone had always been watching me since my abduction, a servant, guard or hetaera or seafarer.

Hot, salted breezes drifted into Lindus' harbor and rocked the ship. *The breeze of the heat season,* I thought dreamily and curled up in the wad of cloth that was my bed. *These hot winds and waves bore me here. It was the last heat when so many changes began. Opening the tomb of Ancestor Larthia. My fame at Zilath's court. And then the darkness, those miscreants who destroyed my life and dragged me to Roma. Was I with Priscus for the whole cooling season? No, I was exposed to the mute before it turned cold. How long with Ariela? The cold season and the warming? Once again, heat. A whole cycle.* I quivered at those reflections. *These days are but a dream. I'll awake beside Arun, his arms rocking me, not the sea.*

But it was Alexis, not Arun, who shook me awake. "So you slept, after all. My people are curious about you."

"And your wife?"

He shrugged his shoulders. "She is but a wife and will contain herself soon."

Everyone in the entire town lined the beach, the seafarers I had known on board standing in front of wives and children, the islanders who heard of the foreign woman who crossed Poseidon's waves. Alexis' wife stood apart, arms crossed, her face masked by her head covering.

"The Distinguished Guest is from a land far to the west where the sun sets. Etruria it is called," Merchant Alexis, now in command of his village, announced. "She is a scribe."

"Why did you bring her here?" a man called out.

"She's not one of us. Send her elsewhere," another barked.

"She speaks our tongue and writes it. She will do accounts for my cargo."

"Show us your scribing, Etruscan," someone goaded.

They assembled closer to me. With straight spine, I held my ground against them. Most seafarers were of babarian stock, but these islanders were a breed apart, neither slave nor servant, ragged and unclean.

Alexis controlled my steadiness, pushing back the offending crowd. He picked up a smooth pebble stone from the beach and took his knife from his belt. "Write the name of the wine and oil, its destination and what it will be traded for here."

He shows force to his people, but can he protect me from them? Nervously, I sat down, cross-legged and began.

"You see?" Alexis held up the stone for all to admire.

The villagers passed the stone around, looking at it incomprehensively, solemnly nodding anyway.

They can't read!

"Welcome her as one of us."

Now I understood why Alexis had become different in his homeland. He had stopped treating me as equal. He hadn't rescued me from being a hetaera just to set me free and do his scribing and accounting until an Etruscan ship came. The man was a landowner and I was to be his servant. Where was that ship that would sail me home after no more than another season? I didn't see any on my voyage to freedom. *Until one arrives, how long would I be stranded on this island?*

No longer would I call him Alexis, just "the merchant". Ordered to stay at his house, I followed him through narrow alleys that twisted and went up the slope to the village. The merchant's wife trailed us as a submissive Hellenic wife would, her face covered by veil. I turned to smile and talk with her in friendship but no hospitality came from her, only a thick hot rage.

Every morning I went down to the harbor and boarded the merchant vessel to count cargo. The fishnet menders watched covertly from the beach. At the sun's height, I would go to the village center where the merchant made me copy Solon's laws onto a plaque to placate the islanders. As Aplu's sun faded, scholars from the other side of Rhodos would arrive, specifically to meet me. My reputation spread quickly for I was known as the Scribe who knew Etruscan and Italic as well as Hellenic.

At night I slept in a cubicle of the merchant's house; my restlessness accompanied dreams of netherworld gods.

"She runs with sorceress Hecate, goddess of Hades." The islanders stalked towards me, snatching for my scribe tools, tearing off my clothes and ripped my right arm from its socket. I screamed in agony. They laughed in pleasure. Alexis' wife hissed, "Alexis has been cast with the evil eye," and the village women chanted, "Ban the Etruscan from staying in Lindus."

I awoke with a start, the dream active in my thoughts, still seeing the vicious eyes of my tormentors.

Hate is a powerful disease. Or did the moon awaken me? A full white moon loomed above the town outlining the Acropolis Temple of the Moon Goddess. I slept again, and dreamed, not of the moon goddess but of another. *In the moonlight, Aphrodite, the Hellenic goddess of love, stood at the acropolis. I climbed the mountain to reach her, to appeal to her grace. "Save me, goddess!" I pleaded. "Send me home with your love." Aphrodite spun around in her transparent cloth garment and paused. Her tunic and body turned into clear liquid and crystallized, with a countenance full of malevolence.*

The moon came in through slits in the wall and glared across my face, not touching anything else in the room. How its intensity petrified me after the ghoulish dreams! It didn't shimmer with beauty that I saw from the ship. Now, this same moon radiated its strength, seeking to devour me. *Why does the moon choose me?*

A silver flash sliced through the night towards me. To avoid it I rolled onto the floor before a knife split my cushion.

The attacker realized the mistake, withdrew the weapon and cursed, "You will die, Etruscan."

"I'm no harm to you!" I sobbed, but my attacker had gone. *I'm not wanted here. I'm not wanted anywhere. Is this what the moon goddess decrees?*

*   *   *

In the morning I thanked Aplu's sun for rising. *Here it's God Apollo who rises, not God Aplu. It is the moon goddess, not Goddess Uni. The cosmos churns my life as it wants. 'Proceed through the unknown with awareness to glorify it,' the merchant told me. That must be if I am to survive. Courage must replace my fear.*

The merchant's ship reloaded with new season wheat and Rhodos pottery. "I trade new cargo with the hexapolis and will be bound for Aegypt," the merchant said offhandedly as if it was a daily event.

"Aegypt?"

"The sea isn't rough now. Our six cities profit from the Aegyptians whose land grows desert sand."

"And me?" The terror of my nightmare attacker returned. "I came with you seeking respite from a hideous life whose attitudes were not mine."

"You're right to be afraid."

My apprehensions surface anew. "It was false to bring me here."

"And now we depart. Soon you'll be at sea."

"At sea? I'm not a seafarer who welcomes a watery tomb. Aegypt! What place is that, further off? It is home I must go. Ruthlessly, you toss me to a new fate, condemning me to more chaos."

"You can't stay. My wife plots to have you killed."

"She has already tried," I answered.

12

Great Antiquity

It was hot, hotter than any day I had ever felt. No sea breeze, or drops of rain relieved the sun's harsh glare. The oppressive heat slackened any exuberance in my being. But I welcomed this journey after Athenai and Rhodos. Hellas was an austere country, ignoble and dangerous for all its talk of fine politics and democracy.

Drenched by my own body's liquid, my tunic clung uncomfortably against arms, legs and breasts. Brine from splashing waves coated the sun scorched wooden deck. Water from the amphorae was hot as broth, but moist, alleviating my dizziness. In my daze, I recited the merchant's wise words over and over, as if they were a prayer to guide me onward: *Proceed through the unknown with awareness.*

"Keep that black cloth on your head and cover as much of your face as you can, or you'll blister," the merchant said ill-humoredly.

How cold his voice sounds in contrast to the heat.

After leaving Rhodos and the Ionian Hellenic Islands in the Aegean Sea, the vessel sailed directly south into Aplu's sun and the open Mediterranean Sea.

For three days we saw a vast tranquil seascape. Without breeze to sail, the oarsmen rowed. Mercilessly, the heat bore down. My one satisfaction was that neither rain nor storms blocked our journey.

That burning heat caused me shame. I could not endure the sun's fire. Yet I had gained strength in another way and told the merchant, "I've gotten used to the sea finally. I don't fear it anymore."

"How innocently you speak! To travel is a hard necessity and one who journeys by sea must fear it. Seafarers are doomed if they don't always respect Poseidon's waters." After his sarcastic jab, he jounced back to running the ship.

I saw land first! Weak from climate and dripping sweat, the mist ahead seemed more a vision than land emerging from the sea on the waves' horizon. I wasn't the only one to sight land. The crew saw it too and cheered. Not the lash but promise of ground under their feet made the oarsmen row faster, a difficult task in the heat.

The vessel left the Great Sea, and we soon entered quiet waters of a lagoon. Thick marshlands sprouted papyrus reeds, buzzing with insects. Wild fowl peeked out of tall rushes. Clusters of lotus leaves floated by on the shiny surface. The lagoon swelled to become a river.

"It's a tributary of the Nile delta." The merchant squinted at the iridescent glaze upon it.

"Legends of the Nile are inscribed on prized vases that Etruscan nobles covet," I mumbled, remembering Zilath's Aegyptian alabaster tomb treasures. I had recorded description of their details and quality, and how they had been bartered. Then, it meant nothing to me. Now, it came alive.

Muddy banks passed by as we pushed through the current towards a deeper channel. Date palms, acacia and carob trees grew among fields of tall budding stalks. Set back, grand civilized homes interspersed vineyards.

At the water's edge, a rounded smooth rock seemed to levitate. A moving rock! *Not again my eyes play tricks on me.* Where I had last foolishly thought rocks moved was in the merchant's harbor when they were actually women hunched over like servants on a beach. The water rippled and the rock moved again. It lifted, revealing a hump, not a rock, and a huge sagging face bulging with nasty eyes. *More tricks! My eyes deceive me again.*

"A sea monster, Merchant!"

The broad-bodied animal wallowed towards the bank, grazing on tufts of shrubbery.

"That's a hippopotamus."

"Ugly thing. Will it come after us?"

"On the contrary. It attacks fields at night, ruining crops. It's a river horse, a plant eater, thick-skinned and hairless."

"We Etruscans would make shoes of its hide."

"Shoes? You Etruscans think of fancy things, not of serious ones."

"Shoes are serious comforts, necessary to withstand walking on bare ground, climbing or hauling."

"Aegyptians kill that animal for its hide and use it to make shields and helmets for war, whips for punishment."

Another monster shot its triangular head out of the water, jaws snapping, eyes glaring. A snake bubbled up from the mud and hissed at it. The monster retaliated and thrashed out at the snake with its horny skinned body.

"Even at a distance those beasts frighten."

"It's a crocodile, the 'lizard of the Nile.'" The merchant wiped his sweating brow with the back of his hand. "Aegypt's waters are not like the Aegean Sea. This country exists because of the Nile. Now it's shallow. Soon it floods and people will happily plant and harvest enough crops until the next flooding. The Nile is both a blessing and a curse. Too high a flood means ruined crops, too low a flood means famine."

"You know much about Aegypt."

"To trade with them, I must. Ancient Aegypt was once great, but no more. For all its riches, it's old and crumbles. The people are weary and solemn. We Hellenics have grown stronger than they. Our colonies are settled throughout the Mediterranean. Already we have mercenaries stationed in the delta, and have even built our own Ionian temple. One day we'll conquer Aegypt and make what's left of its wealth, ours."

He wants something more than he has. He yearns for this land to be his own.

On the widened river, small wooden slatted boats with singular sails bobbed with the mild shallow waves, while long-robed, turbaned fishermen dipped nets and retrieved them filled with squirming fish. Intermittently, long narrow boats glided by, gilt with golden and bright blue carved railings, manned by oarsmen working against the tide. On their decks, fan bearers stirred the breeze with plumed feathers for the regally clad men and women who stood calmly surveying the landscape. Envy warped me. *If I hadn't contrived to scribe for Zilath, I would wear fancy garments as befit a noblewoman.*

Among ripening stalks, sun-baked mud huts and palm trees lined the banks. In the fields, workers tended crops, picking and sorting harvest to be loaded onto donkeys. Some black-draped peasant women, balancing earthenware jars the size of a child on their heads, walked gracefully on a path along the river. Others toted overflowing baskets of reeds or corn. Men shouldered yokes steadying water jugs. All purposefully moving their loads toward market, for along both banks the bustle of vendors and crowds of thousands came into view. They seemed undisturbed by the heat. Small naked children shoveled silt from the water, dumped it into buckets, and lugged away. Young boys jumped up and down waving at us on the boat.

"Never had I imagined this Nile, this country of diverse activity. They're so intent on what they do that they ignore your ship on the river."

"They're just common folk."

"But what about the administrators? No one bothers you. They welcome you Hellenics," I said. "The Aegyptians let you pass safely."

"We bring much needed wheat. The sand produces nothing but death."

"I see abundance, not wastelands of sand."

"The wastelands are past this valley, over those hills."

"Do we go there?"

"Not you. You'll go on an Etruscan ship to your homeland."

"If that was truly so! No Etruscan vessel sails to this river. Phoenician sea vendors do and trade us Aegyptian ostrich feathers, painted eggs and alabaster vases to put in our tombs."

"Tombs! You Etruscans are as strange as the Aegyptians. We Hellenics cremate our dead. The pyre is a swift ending, not the slow rotting of a corpse."

I winced at his words. From the moment we had entered Rhodos he toughened and our friendship soured. Away from his people he became despicable in this heat. "Please, Merchant, don't bicker over my words."

"I shouldn't have taken you from Athenai. There you called me by name. Now you say 'merchant.'"

"I was desperate to leave."

"Ha! Desperate enough to connive with me. You, an enslaved hetaera, even spoke of freedom for women. What nonsense!"

"Etruscan women are proud and our men treat us fairly. I scribed for you to earn my keep, and then your wife tried to kill me."

"You brought trouble to my house and my people. My wife thought you my hetaera. You would have been, but you were hard to tame," he spit out, smirking at me like the men at Ariela's had.

As if the searing sun scorched my brain, I cried out, "Hard to tame? Am I a wild animal? So it was you who brought me misery in Lindus. I am not yours to control."

"I control everything you do. Where would you be without me—in the hetaerae garden fawning over some simpering politician or being rammed by his shaft? I've coddled you too long." A mean, hard expression crossed his face. "Why should I try to find you passage to Etruria? I'll get you out of my sight and gain a profit. They need hetaerae in Sais. I'll sell you to a house." The merchant knotted a rope over a bulwark to prepare for docking then boomed instructions at his men.

He had once been handsome, but now seemed as hideous as the repulsive crocodile. *Another house! Why could I not have seen his contempt for me? How stupid I was to ever trust him! He toys with my life, bantering with me at whim. As a whore master would, he speaks with vile tongue. He was my protector.*

The crew came forward, dutifully dragging ropes to tow the vessel to berth against a decrepit stone quay, as old as Aegypt must be. On the landing, a crowd gathered, curious to see our ship. Simultaneously, small river craft drew alongside, jamming fisher boats and vendors' rowboats, locking against one another in a riot of competition to sell wares. The merchant tried to steer the ship forward and drop the rope lines, but plainly couldn't. Vexed, he ordered the crew to reel the ropes up to the railings, cursing them for their clumsy handling, cursing the nuisances who obstructed his passage to dock.

His unexpected nastiness jarred me out of complacency. My mood became as bitter as his. "You rogue! I'm nothing but barter to you." He couldn't hear me through the chaos. *I must try to get away from him.*

The commotion on land and water amused not only me and the crew, but people on the quay. What entertainment! Seeing how useless their efforts would be, one seafarer threw a sack of grain to a vendor who hoisted up a bucket of beer to the crew to wait out the dilemma. A small, dilapidated boat filled with rusting pots and pans rubbed against the hull, the tradesman banging pans together to gain attention. Other little boats swirled around it and our vessel, connected together like stepping-stones.

Suddenly, a bolt of the gods' lightning was hurled at me! What twist of fate! *Little open boats swirling around us like stepping-stones.* Ropes for tying up to the quay lay askew. Stealthily I chose one and secured it around a bulwark as the merchant had. *Have the gods granted me another chance?*

"Worry no more, Merchant." It was well he hadn't heard my ire for he might have slapped me. Frantically I scrambled about for my bundle of clothes, found a black scarf and covered my head, then wrapped it around my neck and brought it over my chin and lips in the same fashion as Aegyptian women. Swiftly I raised my tunic to my knees, boosted onto the railing and tested the rope's strength. Swiveling towards shore, I gripped it tightly with both hands and rappelled down the hull's side, until I felt the decaying edge of the cookery tradesman's boat. Amazing how that splintered boat ever stayed afloat! If I stayed too long, it would probably sink. Bouncing as lightly as I could, I jumped over a bench and nets. The tradesman raised his pots to shield himself from me, maybe thinking I was an evil spirit from the netherworld. From the far side of the boat, I crawled to the next craft, a small skiff piled with sacks of grain. From the grain, I hurtled to the rocks fortifying the quay.

I've done it! Not a complicated dance. *Surely the gods joke with my fate. Or is it a cruel prank?* My knees shook and I leaned against the rocks for support. *I escaped from Balbus to be captured by the mute and then from Ariela and her hetaerae only to end up with the merchant!*

Mayhem at the ship's docking continued. While the crew poked oars at the surrounding boats to gain space to the pier, vendors shouted trade offers from the quay to the harassed merchant. Hundreds of spectators gathered, openly laughing at the frustrated crew's predicament. A horn blasted from the quay. Another, then another. Aegyptian officials, somber, gloomy faced men, trooped to the docking.

Of course, they couldn't be searching for me yet. The officials had arrived to welcome the Hellenic vessel. Along the quay, half the population was engrossed in scooping up corn and onions, while the other half examined rich assortments of fabrics, clay statues, bedding and pottery. Enough activity for me to leave the rock quay and plunge into the crowd. I blended in with some women and slowed my gait to match theirs, all the while walking away from the river towards mud huts and peasants' gardens into more stifling heat.

Think clearly, Larthia. I commanded myself. *Not back streets. He'll track me down there, cornering me at the edge of the desert.*

I circled back to the river to the end of the stone quay where a handful of boats were moored parallel, some of which I had seen earlier gliding on the Nile. *'Barges of the elite'* the merchant had mocked insolently.

These weren't working barges carrying cattle and grains like Roman ones. They were gleaming, formal boats of fine timber, with cabins and floorboards, all decorated with vivid intricate designs. Each was the length of an Etruscan temple. Banks of long oars slanted against the sides, secured in holders.

How quiet and clean after the dusty, dung-smeared market quay. No one was about. The nobles could have gone for a stroll or to feast. Some dark-skinned oarsmen, spotlessly clothed in long white dresses, with white turbans, stood on this polished stone dock, talking among themselves, oblivious to me.

One barge drew me closer for it appeared vacant. On the prow, a carved image of a woman with a disk and horns on her head glittered in the hot sun. The stern was carved with cornstalks, the cabin's walls painted with scenes I couldn't understand, and cloth streamers tied along the railings.

I leapt on, slinking along a shaded wall to crouch against the cabin and catch my breath. *Leaping! Jumping! Running! I think like an acrobat, not a noblewoman nor scribe! My escape gives me giddy thoughts. First, a short rest in this humid, scalding climate. Then I'll plan how to leave Aegypt, how to get back to Tarchna.*

The dark oarsmen were quicker than I thought, or I must have slept, drowsy from heat. They surrounded me and spoke soft gibberish to my ears. Impudently I stared at their almost black skins. *They could club me to death with oars and no one would know.*

A female voice hushed the oarsmen. They backed away politely to let her through. A dark-eyed woman with lengthy, black straight hair looked quizzically at me. She wore a collar of beaded blue stones around her neck. Her starched-white linen tunic was spotlessly clean down to her sandals, belted with a gold-knotted tie decorated with lumps of garnet beads.

"I saw you sneak aboard our barge. Your life is in danger, isn't it?" she asked in Hellenic. "Are you a spy for Amasis?"

Before I could answer, two strong arms seized and lifted me off my feet, swinging me between them.

"Take her to the goddess."

A deep groan set into my being. *How careless I've been. Again a captive.*

13

Call Forth The Flood

The goddess sat loftily on a high backed seat, balancing a headdress of a pair of bull-horns holding a golden disk. It must have been of great weight for veins in her neck bulged, but she displayed a peaceful, poised demeanor. In her left hand she held a staff whose top was a carved wooden lotus. The elliptical back of her chair emulated her position, her same image repeated in wood. "Put her down," she ordered the oarsmen.

Thrown down on the deck, I lay prostrate.

"They won't hurt you. The Nubians are surprising, aren't they? They're the backbone of Aegypt."

Awkwardly I turned over and got to my haunches, already hurt, bones stiff from being dropped. Not only this goddess, but several women with similar garb hovered over me.

The woman who found me whispered to the goddess who then conveyed, "Paheri says that a Hellenic seafarer searches for you. He raves that you were stolen from his ship by one of the officials."

"I escaped."

"I can see that."

"I went through the village."

"Sais isn't a village. It's an honored town where Pharaoh Amasis rules, where sculpture is inspired in the likes of our ancient ones, where painting is created. Our procession was there to assure Pharaoh that Aegypt prospers this year. Sais is past us now."

"Past?" I sprung up and looked over Paheri's shoulder, for she and I were about the same size. The barge no longer moored but floated mid-river.

"You dared to board my barge, Hellenic."

"It was a mistake. I just meant to calm myself," I explained. "I'm not Hellenic, but Etruscan."

"What then, a barbarian from the west?"

"We call the Italics and Phoenicians 'barbaric,' but we're a proud and civilized country. Our laws are just."

"Outspoken you are. If you are thrown into the river, the crocodiles won't show pity."

Thrown to the crocodiles! I must watch what I say. Bowing my head, I hoped, would show humility. "I mean no rudeness, Goddess. Your customs of speech are different here."

The goddess looked quizzically at me. "Amasis must have a new scheme. He gets his spies to speak in foreign tongues. Is that why you speak Hellenic so well?"

"Who is Amasis?"

She sighed. "You exasperate. Unfold your tale as we go. Amuse me. My priestesses can speak Hellenic but rarely do, so your talk is practice for us."

"If your story is true, we will protect you as sisters. If it is untrue and you lie to Goddess Isis, you will die, and I, Paheri, will kill you."

Kill me? A strong punishment for lies. "I'm a noblewoman of Etruria, and a scribe to Prince-priest Zilath."

The other women came near to listen. All were beautiful with long, black, straight hair and bangs cut across their foreheads, cosmetics high-lighting their striking features. Like the woman who brought me in front of the goddess, they dressed immaculately in white floor-length ceremonial tunics, collars fanning out at the neck.

From that ghastly abduction to my reckless arrival at their barge, I told my saga, and concluded with my most charming smile, "Is my story too incredible? I'm ashamed of my clothes and tangled hair, and beg food and shelter until I find my way back to Tarchna."

"Do you know who I am, who we are?" The goddess threw spices and flowers over the water, scattering them evenly like it was a well-practiced task, not speaking directly to me.

"No, but surely you are royal and respected."

"She is our beloved mother-goddess Isis, corn-mother, reviver of the seasonal winds, the wind of dawn from which Ra's Sun is born. We are her devotees, Priestesses of Isis, revered throughout Aegypt," the woman who found me sang out.

"We can't go downstream again nor can we leave you on the way, for a woman like you would not fare well among the people," the goddess cautioned ominously.

"A woman like me! What does that mean?"

"You could be bondaged by the pharaoh," a priestess piped up.

"Or die of thirst and hunger . . ." another interrupted.

"Or killed by desert creatures." The goddess gestured towards the western lands and emphasized her next words. "We hurry up the Nile to Thebes and our Temple at Philae before the flooding. The waters of mother river are late this year and we have sailed the mighty Nile to call forth its deluge with our prayers."

"We feed and comfort you in your travail." Priestess Paheri spread a basketful of food on the barge deck: roasted goose joints, spongy cheese, gourds, wheat breads, figs and wine.

Hunger and thirst do odd things to the spirit. I salivated at the sight of those delicacies, so starved for anything other than fish caught by the seafarers aboard the merchant's vessel. With the wet cloth given me, I wiped desert sand that lodged in my eyelids and crept up my nostrils. "Praises to your gods. This festive repast will nourish stomach and spirit."

Not the goddess but the priestesses sat down cross-legged and waited for me to gorge, and then politely nibbled some morsels.

"We have already indulged this day," a more heavy-set priestess sniffed.

"Hotep eats like a hippopotamus," another giggled.

"She's jealous that you might take another portion," Paheri interpreted.

"I have big bones." Hotep defended herself.

Congenially they chatted until the goddess broke in and commanded, "Shave her."

Before I could jump overboard, I was pinned down on a stool. A bucket of warm water was sloshed over my hair, the dust and grit streaking down my dirt-encrusted tunic.

"You must appear as one of us. First, you need a wig." Paheri shortened strands of my long hair to stubbles, then oiled and shaved my scalp expertly.

Weakened by the assault on my being, I sat numbed under the boiling sun.

"Don't cry, Noblewoman Larthia. You are newborn. Now your wig will fit snuggly." A shadow of hanging spider-thin ropes came above me as the goddess crowned me with a human hair wig, fashioned like those of the priestesses. Carefully she placed it like a crown, smoothing it to my head. It was as snug as she said it would be.

Without animosity towards the goddess, a few of the more lively priestesses left and returned with what must have been their personal possessions. Generously, they held up an assortment of long tunics, belts, armbands, wigs and scarves. Eagerly, they examined my shoulders and arms like they were looking for warts or moles. Distressed at being shaved, then threatened by their hands on my body, I gently fended them off, not wanting to be ill-mannered but not wanting them to find Sappho's poems under my tunic.

"Where is your skin stained?" the goddess asked harshly, standing as far away as possible, at the barge cabin door.

She distrusted me. I felt tainted, like there was something weird that I should know about but didn't.

"Stained?" Confused by her choice of words I answered, "I'm covered only with dirt!"

"Not dirt, but signs. Marks. Inscriptions. Designs. We search for your signs. Those who wear signs are dancers, singers or harlots. Where are yours?"

"I have none."

As she fanned away the heat with bird feathers, she grumbled, "Not of lowly birth, anyway."

Clutching at my wet, filthy tunic, I stood among them, mortified to be the object of interest.

"The human body is beautiful and must be shown. Perhaps Etruscans don't dress each other. Paheri will attend her," the goddess said.

"Take these. Soiled clothes aren't acceptable." Paheri offered a stiff-white linen tunic with an overlay apron, similar to the other women but with a roped belt. She also studied my exposed skin as if indelible marks would magically appear.

"Our servants bring us clothes but we Etruscan noblewomen dress ourselves." I patted the scrolls under my tunic, damp but hopefully not damaged. Temporary distraction was all I lacked to hide them. A common gull flew alongside the barge. The idea came swiftly and I pointed at one. "What bird is that, Paheri?"

As she looked skyward, I quickly slipped the fresh tunic over my head before she could stop me, wiggling out of the Hellenic one underneath. Freeing myself of it, I rumpled it into a ball, stuffed the scrolls within the folds and shoved it to the side. When Paheri turned back to explain the bird, I played the untaught, exclaiming over the wonders of wild animals in Aegypt.

How well I had chosen my ploy! Enthusiastically, Paheri searched sky and land for others, naming birds and beasts that were along the river. The one called Ankhfret sat on the deck next to me, busily stringing stone beads onto animal gut. She held out the finished necklace she had fashioned, delighted to adorn me as I dressed.

"Sleep here." The goddess indicated a reed floor mat under a canopied deck next to Paheri.

Once again I was amidst a society of women, not hetaerae, but priestesses of a religious cult of which I knew nothing, in an ancient land whose life was tied to a river, a temperamental stream that was feared. Dressed cleanly and well fed, a feeling of temporary safety appeased. I no longer looked Etruscan, Hellenic or Roman. The merchant couldn't find me, but neither could anyone else.

Fumbling about for a way to express thanks, I suddenly remembered the childhood prayer my mother taught me. "May the gods grant you peace," and then added, "How grateful I am for your kindness, Goddess."

*   *   *

Have I done nothing more than exchange one bed for another, one ship for a barge, albeit a lavish one? This sojourn will be brief until the heat abates and I find passage from Aegypt. Lulled by the water's undulating current that night, satiated after the ample meal, I lay awake. With sweet-smelling clothes and a cloth over my bald head, I was comfortable. At least the cult didn't sleep with the stifling wigs.

Earliest dawn awakened me more fully. Isis' barge bumped against the western riverbank, rocking the boat. No one steadied it for the oarsmen slept on the land's reeds, exhausted from their furious rowing. Obviously used to the side-to-side motion, the priestesses slumbered on, unaware of our docking.

Night rode above the dawning that illuminated three peaked mountains, grand imposing forms that soared from the desert floor. These mountains sculpted into summits, towering over fields and palms. *What image is this, that my eyes see an unnatural sight, pointed mountains? The sun's rays must be playing tricks on me in this sweltering land.*

Unsettled by the view, I rose from the mat as noiselessly as I could to ensure that Sappho's scrolls were in my laundry. With even a quick reading, her poetry of wisdom and fortitude consoled me.

"They are wondrous, aren't they?" Delicately, Paheri padded up in bare feet to join me, looking towards the same mountains. "The tomb dwellings of our ancient ancestor pharaohs. The greatest pyramid is of Cheops, the second of Chephren, the third of Menkaure."

"My breath skips in amazement."

"You're not the first. The sight always makes my blood rush."

*   *   *

Six carts pulled by donkeys waited at the river edge for Goddess Isis and priestesses to board. Paired together, the priestesses clambered into the first five carts, reminding me of Etruscan nobles on parade.

"Take the last cart with me. You must come with us so you won't alert the nearby villagers by your presence. Swear never to reveal our rituals or you will be buried alive in sand that spirals downward."

"I am honorable, Goddess," I stammered my oath to her stern demand, as images of oozing sand sucked me to a horrid death. "I do as you bid."

The goddess' intimidating last words were enough to keep me obedient. I stood behind her in a heap of corn stalks, discomforted by their prickliness. Majestically upright in posture, the cult priestesses rode silently, amulets and charms around their necks glistening in the sun. Muzzled to keep from braying in labor, the silent donkeys trudged along the sand road on the course that was once a canal, plodding in steady beat, then stopped short.

"Wait, Priestesses. Observe only. Make not a sound until I say so," the goddess instructed.

What frightful beast is this?

In front of us, an incredibly huge, carved-stone, human head on top of a feline's body, crouched on elongated paws. Its perfectly symmetrical painted face with wide-open eyes stared straight ahead. A regal nose turned upward to face the rising sun and under it the broad mouth and firm jaws relaxed in total harmony. Attached to the face, behind human shaped ears, a striped headdress stuck out like sails. Each feature was bigger than a human body and, moreover, the huge limestone sculpture was larger than six royal barges combined.

"We pay homage to the Great Sphinx of sun god Ra, guardian of Pharaoh Chephren's pyramid."

Summoned by the goddess, the priestesses meekly knelt at its paws, like children to a parent who would give advice. But I cringed at sight of the monster and couldn't approach, for it threw its power in all paths, blanketing all within reach. On a slight desert breeze its pale voice came at me:

Foreign Lady—what is in your soul that carries you here? Do you exist only to wander the world? Do not deny an answer for I can seek out your thoughts.

It was talking, questioning me! It knew my thoughts, my predicament. Reeling from its authority, I cowered next to the cart, isolating myself from the priestesses, dolefully reiterating its words, unworthy of a clear response. *Have I become only a wanderer, passing through one horrid situation to another, doomed to journey for the rest of my life? Why haven't I died or been killed?*

The priestesses stood up quietly, deep in prayer and turned towards the greatest pyramid, not indicating, nor perhaps aware that the sphinx spoke.

Am I the only one to hear the monster?

They began crossing the rocky expanse on foot and I trailed, while the goddess drove her cart at the rear. So this is what the desert was! From afar it was flat. But walking was difficult, for the treeless, lifeless soil was uneven with rippling hills of sand. In my new unbendable leather sandals Paheri had bestowed to complete my attire, I crunched onward. The sun mounted higher and heat radiated from the ground. The image of the sphinx and its mocking voice blended into the rhythm of my steps.

We didn't go to Chephren's pyramid but to Cheops. Closer up, the massive structure changed appearance, no longer the smooth lines of a triangle, but huge dressed stones, man hewn, its square base resting on the desert floor in oneness with the sand. How overwhelming it was!

"The ancient pharaohs were mortal gods, so holy that it was decreed they should reach the heavenly stars in death. We are mortals, but pray for immortality when we come here. We ask our gods to bring fertility to our land with the river's flooding. Gladly we sing this morn as God Ra watches over us," the goddess intoned loudly, but the desert absorbed her voice so that it became an intimate invocation.

Gathering clumps of dried corn stalks from the cart, the priestesses left me to watch from afar. At the great pyramid's base, they stacked the stalks and Goddess Isis climbed upon it. Hotep lugged a basket of fresh corn to Goddess Isis and offered ears, one at a time. The goddess shucked the corn, produced a knife and sliced off the kernels, sprinkling them around herself. The women linked hands together, chanting unintelligible words, and danced in a circle. When the dance ended, they scooped up the kernels and threw them upward. Neither solemn nor glad, this was a ritual they performed deftly and neatly. Finished, they collected the stalks, piled them back in the cart, and we returned over the old pharaoh's causeway to the barge on the Nile.

"We live by custom. What I do shall be done by you," Paheri, my designated instructress, informed as the barge docked at a pier where there was a solitary stone hut but no settlement. "Our procession stops for rest and water, and you shall receive two jars, one of drinking water and the other to wash. You must use them sparingly."

I was indebted to her, yet knew if I displeased the cult, she would be first to crush me down in that abominable sand hole.

From the barge, I sighted more monuments that rose skyward, these not as spectacular as the three majestic pyramids, but somehow beguiling.

"How unfortunate you saw the greatest pyramids of Giza first," Paheri frowned sympathetically. "You are deprived of a great loss, not to see Sakkara, the royal cemetery before them. There was no other possibility. We came from Lower Aegypt. Our afterlife homes arc on the Nile's western shore, less fertilc than the east. The ancient ones built these before Giza. 'Stepped pyramids', they are. Pharaoh Zoser didn't know the secret of the sacred triangle's strength, so he only built stairways to the heavens. There are other noble burials—*mastabas* and *tombs*—some better than others, some started but never completed, some destroyed by the sand's infidelity. Yet, more marvelous than the outer buildings is what is within. The ancient ones must have been very wise for they wrote in pictures painted in vivid hues. Hieroglyphs."

I knew something about those picture words written by ancestor scribes. When I scribed for Zilath, I had seen some on an alabaster statue that he acquired for his tomb. He jested that I could write any language, including hieroglyphics, if I set myself to do so. "How do you know they are there?"

"When the greedy ones—tomb robbers—unsealed the graves, we, the honored Cult of Isis, were permitted to see the chamber walls."

That night I dreamed that those mysterious hieroglyphic symbols flowed through my fingertips.

Waiting for the first rays of daylight, Goddess Isis and priestesses repeated the corn and prayer ceremony in the courtyard of Zoser's funerary complex. They sang of the mystery of the Nile's source and pleaded for its mercy to bring fertility to their crops, lest there be famine. Listening to their chants and daily talk, I began to learn Aegyptian.

We traipsed away from the Sakkara cemetery, back to the river, passing mastabas and smaller pyramids than the greatest ones. Inside them would be the hieroglyphics that Paheri mentioned. *They're so near! How it would delight my being to see them. What has the sphinx done to me? What has the desert done to me? I've begun to crave the sight of hieroglyphics.*

On our return to the barge, the chief oarsman awaited the goddess. "There is leakage in the boards of our vessel, Mother Goddess. We must get resin for repair."

"How much time is needed?"

"Two suns and moons."

"Then it be so. We will reside at Memphis across the river and worship at Sakkara each dawn."

No one protested the delay, a normal occurrence of wood rotting in hot desert air. The priestesses chittered happily like newborn birds, bouncing about the barge with vigor that hadn't been before, sorting and storing belongings in bins, arranging foodstuffs and wrapping bundles to carry.

Paheri gushed, "Respite from our duties! Memphis is lively. There we retreat to the palm groves and revere the colossal Ramesses statue. Its polished alabaster gleams in the sun at Ptah's temple. The goddess permits us to stroll through the city, to be admired and attended by worshipers of our cult. They are prosperous and lavish us with offerings for our own Temple at Philae."

I, too, became excited. Had some god answered my wish that had fast become an insurmountable need, to see the hieroglyphs that might guide me through this extraordinary land? *If we return to the royal tombs, there must be a way for me to view them.*

The goddess spoke loudly to her priestesses in Aegyptian and kept her eyes on me. "I want proof of her story. Take what she conceals under her clothes."

Preoccupied by wondering of how to get into a tomb, I gripped my waist belt under the tunic that held my treasures. My movement was too spontaneous.

Isis' eyebrows rose. "As I thought. Say something in Aegyptian, since you understand me."

"You're good to me, O great mistress of corn fields, protecting me in your journey." I could only hope the flattering words would hold effect on the goddess and priestesses.

"She's a fast learner. Intelligent," the goddess announced to her cult. "She's no spy for the Hellenics or Aegyptians."

"What made you think me a spy? How relieved I am you believe me!" I smiled.

Isis smiled back. "We priestesses speak old Aegyptian of Pharaohs Hatshepsut, Thutmosis and Seti. Everyday Aegyptian is of more recent dynasties since Assyrians invaded us five generations ago. You have begun to know my dialect. Where else could you have learned it but with us? What talisman of magic do you hide under your cloth? Give it to me!"

Reluctant to part with my scrolls, yet unable to disobey, I undid the belt and handed them to her. "It's not magic, just words."

The goddess unraveled the papyrus and studied it. "These are Hellenic words."

"In truth they are poetry of the cosmos. The poetess Sappho is admired for beauty in her reality."

"I'd like to examine them." She took and sealed them in an ivory box, locked it with a key and tucked it into her tunic.

That was as good as if Goddess Isis claimed them for her own. The scrolls would add to her knowledge, to her power. She had garnered my source of inspirational words of wisdom and poetry.

*   *   *

How uncanny it is that the goddess gave me permission to see Sakkara! Perhaps it was more than uncanny. She tested me with that consent.

"We have a ceremony to perform, more secret than others. You may wander, but take care not to fall into unknown spaces," she said. "Choose your path. One takes you to the pyramid of Unas, the other leads to the mastaba of Ti and the cemetery of Apis bulls. Be here when Ra's sun is highest."

Wordlessly, the goddess and priestesses left, all concentrating on balancing headdresses of disks and bull-horns. As they headed to their ritual, I shed my sandals. Calluses had formed on the balls of my feet from them already, but that didn't stop me from hobbling on the cool sand of morning towards the crumbling pyramid that the goddess named Unas. Peaceful, welcoming silence came with distance from the Nile. A fox howled from somewhere in the vast funerary complex, but no other humans were there. The Unas pyramid was further than I realized, and the sand heated with the sun's height.

What madness causes me to desire to see tombs after all that befell me since I opened Larthia's tomb?

A lone falcon's cry broke the desert's calm when it circled the mastaba pyramid. I hurried towards its call as it landed at the doorless entrance. *What omen is this?* Although of obdurate sand, the pyramid's stepped sides had deteriorated, rounding the structure to become a mound, a shape resembling tombs at Cisra's City of the Dead. Made of sandy earth, not rich loam or covered with grasses, there was a likeable, familiar, sacred feeling, similar to Princess-priestess Larthia's tomb.

One look and I'll go. The sun cast light into the chamber, enough to see a column of birds, lines and figures. My foot stumbled over something hard. Just a common object not to be afraid of, a wax lamp and flint left by some tomb guard. I stooped down and lit it. The wick of light shone on the entire wall covered with more of the same figures. "Bewildering! Baffling! Thrilling!" I must have gasped, for a reply came behind me.

"They are magic spells, hymns and rituals, offerings to my brother god of the underworld Osiris," a well-known voice said. "They bring safe passage to the pharaoh as he goes to the afterlife."

"Goddess Isis!" *How did she get here so quickly, unseen?*

"You seek out your obsession?"

"Obsession, no! Only interest." *I lied. I am obsessed.* "What is said can be written. The symbols intrigue me, be it these pictures or the lines of my language." I touched the carvings, looking upon the brightest blue pigment I had ever seen, contrasted against white walls. "How meticulously they're rendered. They are read vertically, aren't they?"

"Yes, so that the viewer's eye will look up at the ceiling of golden stars."

For what purpose did she chase me down, she who is most famous of goddesses?

"Come. I guide you to other places of glory."

Across sands and rubble of ancient tombs and monuments, we walked together, the highest priestess of the Cult of Isis, and an Etruscan woman dressed as an Aegyptian.

The goddess stopped at the outer court of a burial chamber. "The Mastaba of Ti."

In another courtyard one wall depicted a procession of women bringing food to the tomb, another of Ti's wife, the third of Ti himself.

"He begs visitors not to desecrate his tomb." Her eyes betrayed her slur.

"You misunderstand! I'm not a vandal or tomb robber!" I protested grimly. "I have knowledge of sacred behavior. Desecrate a tomb! Not so!"

From the courtyard's sides, hallways branched to chambers. The goddess led me through this imitation of the home Ti's family had in life, preserved as their afterlife dwelling.

"We are much alike, Etruscans and Aegyptians. Our tomb chambers are built like our homes to comfort us when we become Ancestors. Only we have not sand but fertile earth and trees enclosing our cemeteries."

Isis didn't respond to my comparison but steered me to a sunken stairwell. "Its beauty is below."

Now her intent shows. She will bury me in this grave. We descended. To my surprise, she entered a chamber without furnishings or statues. Wall paintings showed Ti as a hunter, sailing his barge through marshes of the Nile filled with fish, seeking his victim, a hippopotamus.

One scene after another told stories of Ti as master: watching cattle driven through a stream, rams trampling on crops, fishermen catching fish, artisans working on leather, wood, metal and stone. Other scenes told of life's pleasures: musicians playing, tables displaying food, lissome nude women offering gifts while dwarfs, monkeys and greyhounds walked among them.

"These reliefs are more than beautiful! They're the gods' gifts to the ages." In awe, I examined one after another, relishing the colors, the delicate line work, the complicated interwoven designs and patterns. "I'll cherish the memory of having seen them."

"You are insightful as well as intelligent," the goddess complimented and swept on. "We pass the cemetery of the bulls. Have care to whisper so that you aren't sucked into their underground labyrinth. It is said they prey upon liars."

Dramatically, like with her other lessons, she implied that I wasn't trustworthy. *That's why she hasn't let me out of sight. She tests me constantly.*

Serviceable again in its repaired state, the flat bottomed-barge was lowered into the river, floating contentedly in the water. The priestesses seemed wild, not contented from that night in Memphis. Under the glare of their maternal leader, they subdued themselves regretfully and boarded the vessel in single-file dignity. Knowing my place, I tagged on last, nonetheless elated from seeing the wonders of Sakkara.

"We commence again." Goddess Isis signaled the oarsmen to depart, not wholly sympathetic to her charges' laments.

We resumed our voyage, the barge dipping into the water and heading for mainstream. A few priestesses plunked down near the prow, some at the stern to balance the barge and watch the changing landscape as we floated in the late morning.

"This is the valley of the Nile," Paheri pointed at dusty sand, "a long and narrow strip of land, dried up until the flood. Unsafe to us now if the flow starts and our boat is swamped."

"I can't swim," I admitted.

"Neither can we. Only the gods can save us."

The head oarsman surveyed the river, a proud look on his face as if he was responsible for the goddess and priestesses. With his responsibility as overseer, sixteen oarsmen paddled effortlessly with such discipline that they didn't sweat. This wasn't the first voyage that he was entrusted with the task of going downstream and up, nor did I think it would be the last. We had left Sais and the delta, passed Memphis, Giza and Sakkara, fighting the shallow currents and sandbars to the parched desert lands invading the Nile, sailing towards Middle Aegypt.

"I fear this journey for the foreign woman hidden aboard is not a priestess," I overheard him say to his oarsmen. "I'm not sure what city she comes from, but beware! Do not look or talk with her! "

"She looked too boldly at me," one of his men agreed.

Had I looked at any of them? No, not more than a glance!

Without being told, I sensed that the journey would be of interminable duration. *What does it matter? My need to escape weakens. I can no longer dispute my fate. If I am to survive, I will do what I must on my own, and defy notions of others.*

The Nile ran sultry, as if pouting for thirst, its shallow bottom silted with desert sand. Aegyptian words for bearings confused me. The puny current flowed in what I supposed was north, but we headed south. When the river curved, its colors changed, sometimes turquoise, mud green, or rust-toned along village shores. Those poor villages were bleak, squalid with mud huts, but with friendly, lean, sun-pigmented folks. As the barge docked at night, the people would offer whatever food and drink they had and make us welcome.

"The Black Land on both sides of the Nile is the rich dark soil thrown up by the river to keep it fecund and give us harvest. The Red Land is barren soil where towns and cities are, as well as graveyards of our ancestors— lands of the dead and living. There is less confusion if you know what part to tread," Goddess Isis taught.

"How clear it becomes! Aegypt needs the river to surge over its banks because the flooding brings life. When it recedes, crops grow in fresh soil."

"Of course." A taut smile crossed her lips as she repeated, "the flooding brings life."

*   *   *

The goddess gave passionate speeches on Aegypt's antiquity, that it existed because the desert kept enemies out, convincing me to become her student.

"Aegypt overwhelms me with its history, its step pyramids and mastabas," I admired.

"Past glory." Goddess Isis looked at the crumbling stones of the pyramid of Meidum, rising in eminence. Surreptitiously she watched my every movement. "We imitate our ancestral buildings and sculptures now but have no new ideas of our own in this dynasty."

"You must have new ideas. That is what birth brings!"

"We are a dying culture," she said with finality.

The merchant had said similar words. This wasn't the thought of a random few but of many. This country had decayed, and pitied itself, yet still teemed with life.

Every day the oarsmen rhythmically forced their paddles against the slight waves, advancing upstream as quickly as the current let them. Both shores were always in sight, closing in with sloppy waves as the river narrowed or spread out to meet villages. Relentless sun! Relentless heat! Neither storm clouds nor raindrops broke our journey. When limestone cliffs and date palms changed the landscape between settlements, I revived some interest of this unwanted voyage, learning that rock-cut tombs, square holes cut into its cliffs were homes to ancestors more than one thousand years before.

"Away from the Nile more tombs are hewn into the mountains, with entrance ways like our palaces. But we only stop at one, to the east, the ancient city of Khmun, a city built by the gods, where God Thoth is worshiped." The goddess looked at me for reaction. "You don't know of Thoth?"

"No, forgive me," I replied humbly. "I'm ignorant of your gods."

"You shall know them in due course."

*   *   *

A messenger from Thoth's cult waited for us at Khmun's dock. "Make haste! Thoth, god of Ibis beckons you to the Temple of Karnak. You have detained our procession and the ceremonies cannot continue without you. The inundation has begun in Nubia and will reach your Temple at Philae before you."

"Karnak! Karnak! We go to Karnak!" The priestesses hummed the words to each other.

Since this announcement, each priestess took extra care in dressing, primping like meeting a new lover, applying thick pastes to cheeks, kohl lines to eyelids, paint to lips. Only in my fantasy did I envision them meeting lovers, for they were virgins brought to the cult in youth to remain pure forever.

"Karnak is most special, the home of our triad, sun god Amun Ra, his wife Mut the world mother, whose sacred animal is the vulture, and moon god Khonsu," the goddess recited her vocabulary of gods. "They honor our procession there."

The oarsmen stroked faster as if in combat, battling the rising river's waters that almost reached the top of the embankment, stopping periodically to take on drinking water or for a quick night's rest.

Languishing from heat, I lost count of how many days before the Cult of Isis disembarked at an ordinary stone quay. Escorts wearing the temple's insignia converged to greet worshipers, tenderly guarding us like fragile gifts. Donkeys led the stately carts, clicking wooden carved harnesses and jeweled reins, ornamented with symbols of Upper and Lower Aegypt, the lotus flower and papyrus reeds. How strange they had no horses or chariots. No procession in Etruria would be without them.

We caravanned through an avenue of ram-headed sphinx statues. Each held a miniature statue of an ancient pharaoh between its legs. A crowd of townsfolk resplendent in noble clothes stood between them, clapping joyfully, singing:

> Welcome, O great Goddess
> Divine mother, mother of the gods
> The mistress of charms and enchantments.
> The living one.
> You are at the house of the father, Amun,
> Creator of daylight, nurturer of life.

To which Goddess Isis and priestesses answered:

> We are but travelers
> Brought by Hapi of the south, Hapi of the north,
> Great god of the Nile.
> To worship at the house of the father
> And call forth the flood.

Vitalized by the welcome, I, too, smiled at the crowd. My benefactor was revered more than I believed and so I was accepted, an imposter priestess. The nobles roared in delight but remained on the avenue, coming behind us until we approached a wall so high and enormous that I felt small and insignificant.

"The Temple of Karnak shows great strength with this first pylon," Paheri told me with pride as we alighted from our cart. "This wall starts inward as it rises, and is the width of our barge's length. Its front is wider than our own temple."

On tiptoe, I glimpsed the carved reliefs that sculpted the pylon depicting the god Amun Ra, but we were whisked through its high wooden doors, leaving behind our greeting hosts. Standing within its frame was a huge leathery gray creature with a snout of a snake, twice the size of a hippopotamus, horns protruding from the snout's side, and flapping ample ears drooping almost half the size of its body.

Attendants rushed to goddess Isis in welcome and carried her to the animal's back where an ornate box sat. Isis knew the beast well for she petted it as she would a cat, stroking its sides as she ascended.

Terrified at sight of this creature, I shied away from its locus. Paheri grabbed my arm and held me fast, linking our arms together. "The elephant is endearing, isn't it? Now I train you to be part of cult Isis' procession. Together we'll go to the Holy of Holies."

We entered a great hall of pillars that reached mountainous heights, dwarfing our parade below. One after another, too many to count, each pillar was etched with reliefs. I gazed upward but couldn't see the pillar tops or the sky. *Nothing in this land is of human size! Even these columns are darkened in shadows by massiveness. Their purpose must be to frighten or impress, and I feel both.*

Isis, the priestesses and I walked solemnly forward to the next section, the inner temple avenue. Shafts of sunlight beamed down through courtyards set with palm trees, a series of pylons, honey-colored glazed sandstone temples, and endless statues and obelisks. My being trembled from these stupendous structures in their eerie monumentality. We were not the only ones proceeding along the path. Group after group led by masked men or women portraying gods and goddesses, less important than Isis, paraded through the complex after us.

The procession halted, hushed by the sight of a small temple. Paheri breathed, "It's the Holy of Holies, the sanctuary of Karnak's high priest, the incarnate of Amun Ra, he who blesses us and thanks us for bringing the Nile's strong flow."

Amun Ra lorded over the other mortal gods and
goddesses of the procession, unmasked, a bearded man
wearing a crown of two long plumes that rose straight up,
one red, one blue. His tunic was of sand-toned linen, an
animal tail hanging down his back. Necklaces adorned
his naked chest. Bracelets jingled as he spread his arms
in greeting the worshipers with a magical spell. "Cast out
evil serpents and crocodiles. Away with monsters of night.
Bring on day's light, the sun of the heavens."

As he prayed, so did his audience. They swayed and
chanted after him, enlightened to be in his presence. How
strong their faith was! I pretended to be impressed with
their gods and worshiped alongside. *I have no choice. I
would be dead without Isis' cult.*

Throughout the day, the gods incarnate invoked the
spirit of sun god, Amun Ra, to bring the inundation from
Nubia. Goddess Isis sang clearest, "The hearts of the gods
rejoice when mother river floods."

Then each god ascended to the platform and
expounded on his or her virtue, vying for popularity as if
in contest to see which one was most influential. All the
while, we of the assembly, sat or stood as ordered, drinking
and passing scoops of Nile water to ward off faintness
from the heat.

"He who once drinks from the Nile will return to drink
again," Pahari intoned, making sure I kept moist.

Drinking this water bonds me to this life.

The procession disassembled in the great courtyard,
each cult assigned to its quarters, free to wander through
the massive temple complex or rest before their next
sojourn. The goddess was speaking with a mortal god,
dressed in white linen, animal headed. Isis held my wrist,

her strength manly. "We meet the Ibis, God Thoth, with reason. You who judge the underworld with my brother god Osiris, you who know of numbers and letters, secure me the knowledge that this woman is true."

Thoth snapped his fingers and his servant brought papyrus and reed. "It matters not what language, Hellenic, Phoenician or Italic. I know them as well as Aegyptian. Scribe these words," he challenged from behind slits in the animal headed mask. "I count the stars. I measure the earth. I am the scribe of the gods."

"Those are your sacred words." *Will I be doomed if I scribe them?* Tensely, I hugged my sides, missing my comforting talismans of Sappho's copied scrolls.

"Therefore, can you not?"

Rage, as hot as the sun's scorching, overwhelmed me. I snatched up the papyrus. "Have you ink and tablet to scribe on?"

Thoth snapped his fingers again and his servant reappeared with a stool for me to sit, and an array of writing instruments, clay tablet, water and cloth to wipe off mistakes.

I can take no more of these tests. I wrote the required words furiously yet carefully, first in Etruscan, then Italic, Hellenic and lastly Phoenician, forming each letter as if it was an old friend. As I wrote, my resentment subsided. The pleasure of holding reed and papyrus became a reward. *Even if they punish me for impudence, I prove myself to them finally.* "I don't know Aegyptian."

Thoth read my scribing.

"Is she true?" Isis bristled from over my shoulder.

He drawled under his mask. "She has added that Thoth is god of wisdom."

14

Isis, Goddess Of Abundance

"One of my priestesses set fire to Larthia's tunic! The others resent her."

"Ah, the Etruscan! I expected some disaster. Her smartness brings trouble," God Thoth commiserated. "She is from an unusual country."

"Give me your wisdom. A spell, a prayer."

"You flatter me, Isis."

It was good to be at Karnak and see Thoth again. Mostly we met to invoke the gods' pleasures or worship at seasonal festivals together. How I loved these encounters! We would gossip or tell each other what we could not divulge to anyone else. But this event was different, dire. The Nile trickled from Nubia, not rushed in its annual flood.

Slowed by the heat of day, we walked together now that the procession was over. Even under the boiling sun, as incarnates Isis and Thoth, long wigs covered our shaved heads, wigs topped with headdresses, impressive enough for others to look at us in admiration and reverence. Masked in the manner of our legends, mine was painted with gold leaf, as corn mother goddess, his, molded with leather skin, a long curved beak for nose, the ibis. Our natural faces were unknown, which pleased me, for my thoughts could remain private.

"What a striking pair we make!" A low, seductive tone crept into his voice.

The wings of my swallow costume fluttered as Thoth grazed my side. I didn't mind. His body was not disguised as a beast but of the man he was, tall and slender, naked at the chest and shoulders, muscular like a young man. His skirt fanned out from waist to knees showing bare legs. A sensual god.

"How lovely your breasts and belly show through your gauze sheath," he whispered.

"Provocative you are." I raised my winged sleeves to give him a light, friendly punch. "Give respect! Should anyone hear you speak thus, word would get to Amun Ra and he'll be unpleased. Remember who I am, 'Goddess Isis, Swallow,' transformed to rescue god Osiris back to life by fanning him with these wings."

"I take back my compliment. Your power over life and motherhood arouses me." He sniffed at my sleeves. "Your fragrance is of Aegypt, of flowers and spices that you've attracted. Have I provoked you sorely?"

"A bit, you long-legged wading bird."

"So now you belittle me! I can be as pompous as you." He reeled off his attributes—moon god, counter of stars, measurer of time by the moon, measurer of wetness and rain. For ancient priests, he measured the worth of souls and knew of right and wrong, teaching secrets of life and death, inventing writing so that he could give Aegyptians the *Book of the Dead.* His myths were of an all-knowing god who could change faces at

whim to even appear as a sacred monkey. He was source
of wisdom and learning, master of inventing and scribing
the alphabet, knowledgeable of history and laws, numbers
and medicine.

"I'm more mystical than you," I rejoined, tired of his
speech.

"Surely. Let's not argue. No one will miss us if we walk
only to the sacred pool."

"My women await me for this eve's rituals."

"We won't stray long. After all, we lodge close to the
Holy of Holies. The lesser cults have already scattered
to their assigned quarters."

"There are advantages to be at the most revered
sanctuary at Karnak."

"Now tell of this 'Larthia.'"

With his slight persuasion, I gave account, relishing
the curious details that changed this journey from boring
to refreshing. "Paheri, my favorite priestess, had her
brought to me as we started up river from Sais. I knew
she wasn't Aegyptian before she spoke."

"How odd your oarsmen didn't kill her upon sight!"

We left the temple compound for the more open
ground of Karnak where no ears could hear us. "Her
boldness made them meek. Like a chameleon that changes
color, she adapted to the situation, which must be very
different from where she had come. She blended into my
cult from the start. Larthia walked with the gait of an elite.
That must have been the secret of why she survived in
those places she called Roma, Athenai, and that Hellenic
island of Rhodos. She would take on what her gods
ordained and use it to her purpose. Survivor she is."

"Survivor," Thoth agreed.

"Not only that. Her experiences had polished her,
sophisticated her and I knew that a certain type of truth,
self-dignity, drove her onward."

Thoth nodded. Our walk brought us to where a grove of trees surrounded the sacred pool. Narcissistically, he admired his reflection in the water's edge. "Dignity. Self-dignity. We know of dignity, don't we?"

My reflection joined his, two masked creatures hidden from public scrutiny under paint and leather. "We've been raised in dignity. We're masters!"

As old friends and past, lawbreaking lovers, we laughed. I confessed, "Of course I had to test her—test her will and stories—for I was compelled by a force greater than I to shelter her, one so far away from her homeland."

Silently, I tried to imagine being anywhere but in our sand-coated world.

"Could you ever leave Aegypt?" he asked.

"No." Without a word to each other, we understood the reason. If one dies in a foreign land, one wouldn't be swathed in linen wrappings at death, mummified for eternity. The soul, the *ka* would forfeit survival. "I never felt sorry for her for she wouldn't accept pity. She felt not sorrow for herself, not openly lamenting her fate. Yet a flicker of pain would cross her countenance and I knew she remembered her past and what was denied her."

"You've gotten sentimental, Isis."

"Larthia learned everything so quickly—rituals, customs, especially language—it took my breath away. She spoke no Aegyptian. How could she? But we communicated in Hellenic. When I caught her listening to our chants and daily chatter, I knew she also learned our speech patterns. I was right, for by the time my barge journeyed to Waset, she was almost conversant in Aegyptian."

"I don't believe it!"

"Nor could I! After hearing a word once, she could use it. First, she mastered words for food, garments, then birds."

"Birds?"

"The priests of her country divine by the flight of birds."

I supposed Thoth ruminated over that one until he asked, "What did you tell her of us?"

"I told her of Aegyptian gods and goddesses' cults, and that Thoth and Isis are male and female components within the complex pantheistic system, steeped in history and myth of more than two thousand years."

"I don't mean that. I mean 'us.'"

His meaning is as clear to me as had been long ago. Both descended from pharaoh's viziers, he, the son of a scribe, and I, daughter of the Washer of the Pharaoh's Hands, had met at the Pharaoh's main dwelling in Sais. I was a young maiden and he was a low-ranking scribe of my father's generation. We had known each other, unmasked. There was an attraction between us then, an excitement that had to be contained. Forbidden. Priestly authenticity depended on purity of purpose, and we rose against the attraction, negating it.

"Nothing," I answered.

"Oh,' he exclaimed flatly.

Was there a twinge of sorrow in his tone?

The usual temple attendants and worshipers weren't in sight. All had disappeared to prepare for the evening's fires and sacrifice. From his side pouch, Thoth withdrew the half-filled flask of ceremonial wine that had been used at the sanctuary, produced a goblet, poured the wine and offered it to me. "It's a complicated problem with the Etruscan."

Gratefully, I sipped the tepid liquid. Rancid wine, soured from too much heat. "She gets too much attention. I must restrict her."

"Do you want to keep her in bondage?"

"Perhaps. The other priestesses are jealous."

It was his turn to drink of the same cup. He drank thirstily, at length. "Let them resent her! Lavish attention on her!"

"I ask for advice, not agreement."

"See reason, sweet Isis. Since the Eastern foreigners invaded us three generations ago, people have lost faith in our gods, in our myths, in our history. Even Pharaoh Amasis is caught between old and new. But this fair-skinned stranger comes! From where? From nowhere! She's a gift to us. Tell your priestesses that she has been sent by *he who cannot be viewed by mortals, he who is invisible,* king of gods, Amun Ra. It will make our cults popular again! It will invigorate your cult!"

"Sent by Amun Ra," I echoed. Thoth's cunning dawned on me. My mind raced. Neither he nor I would be blamed if Larthia proved to be an enemy. God Amun Ra would be the one burdened. If Larthia could be glorified, I would be praised. "Gladness to you! You arouse dormant thoughts in me. If I devise new ceremonies for my priestesses, they'll be inspired and can thank Amun Ra. In curiosity, people will flock to see Larthia's fair skin, and in tribute to the hidden one, they'll pay homage to Isis."

"You could instruct her at your Temple at Philae."

"I should isolate her there until the next flooding to turn her into one of us, to build her reputation . . ."

"I'll come teach her how to scribe in Aegyptian."

"Her presence will give the Cult of Isis more power and prestige among cults. We could be held dearer to our Pharaoh. Then he'd bestow more wealth on us that we sorely need to build the complex at Philae, smaller than Karnak, of course, but definitely grander, more elegant," I mused, then remembered his previous words. "You would teach her to scribe! Why would you do that?"

"You're too vain, my enchantress. Are we not of same stature, my cult the worthiness of yours? Remember we complement each other."

From various palaces and dwellings within Karnak's temple complex, smoke filled the air. Smells of sacrificial offerings, geese, duck and pheasant, the only animals left before the annual inundation, swirled up like a signal for us to hurry.

"We're not rivals," he rushed on. "Rejoice! I, too, need the backing of Pharaoh Amasis."

15

Retreat To Philae

Mother River gushed her waters forth and the river rose, spreading her liquid wealth over the valley of the Nile, lapping at the Avenue of the Sphinxes, entrance to the Temple of Karnak. The Nile's sudden deluge stranded us at Karnak's complex along with other mortal gods and goddesses. They had miscalculated, waiting too long for the flood's appearance, believing that potent spells would bring it as Amun Ra dictated. The god had been wrong. It came two days earlier than expected, leaving the embarrassed cults frustrated, too late to return upstream.

"Grave robbers grow rich across the river while we sit here," Goddess Isis fussed unhappily, stopped from departure to her beloved shrine of Philae.

"Why does Isis say that?" I asked Paheri.

"Whispers abound of a valley beyond the hills across the Nile where pharaohs of old are buried. Thieving villagers are said to plunder sacred tombs, and then wear holy gold amulets at their throats. Even we of Isis' cult cannot go there. We must stay here in the Black Land," Paheri said.

I, for one, didn't care about any dilemma. I had no sympathy for I was at their mercy. Since God Thoth confirmed that I could scribe, the cult had enfolded me as one of its own, yet I was guarded night and day so that I couldn't escape.

When I saw my appearance in the river, the change alarmed me. The straight, black-dyed Aegyptian wig, with its long bangs at the forehead, was my crown. I was embellished with bull-horn headdress, armlets and nameplate cartouche. I had turned into a copy of a priestess.

"Trust none of the women except Paheri," Isis advised after that miserable second procession at Karnak.

At that procession I had been standing close to a sacrificial fire, crowded among the others, when a hand shoved me forward. Sudden heat engulfed my ankles. Flames licked my tunic as I fell into the blaze! Sena, who had been walking with me immediately shouted, then quickly yanked off the animal skin costume of someone to her left. Forced to the ground, I was rolled in the skin, my legs whipped to beat out the flame.

Afterwards, the twelve priestesses were divided about how to treat me. Some shunned me because they were jealous that the goddess had become my mentor. Along with Paheri, a few befriended me. Sena, Hotep and Ankhfret were probably ordered to do so. They were so different from I, that I practiced patience and tolerance by counting the stars at night, and remembering my own errors.

As we remained in Karnak's shelter, when released from duties or worship, some ventured forth to the nearby town of Waset, on the same side of the river. I, too, was permitted to go. Paheri and I jostled along with my three priestess allies, crammed into a donkey-drawn cart, driven by one oarsman, loyal enough to extend his duties to dry land. The cart paralleled the river on a road lined with dark rich soil and crops that stretched out to the Red Land where barren desert began.

"Why does this town we enter have so many names— 'Waset,' 'Newt,' more often, 'The City of the Hidden One,' after Amun Ra. The assortment of names baffles me," I said, hoping to develop a more convivial friendship with the priestesses.

"That's because it's a fallen city. The Assyrians ransacked it at the beginning of our dynasty," Paheri said.

Sena tapped my arm to gain attention. "Waset has its diversion. It holds charm in those gilded statues and gold topped obelisks."

"Those pieces were hidden from the Assyrians when they razed the city. I suppose they will be hidden again when the Hellenics invade it. Already they have renamed the city, 'Thebes,'" Ankhfret commented knowingly, looking straight ahead.

"When will they attack?"

"Larthia, it's foretold by the priests that it won't be for many years. Not in our time," Hotep assured me with a laugh that mocked my stupid question.

"Our Etruscan augur-priests say the same of our people, that the Romans will overpower us in four saecula. Perhaps great nations cannot be sustained forever."

"We are great! Aegypt has a glorious history," Paheri continued her tutorial. "It thrives not well now, but our duty is to keep the spirit of our people alive."

The priestesses were so practiced in their history, mysterious to me because their ceremonies were unlike ones I knew. There was much to think about with these Aegyptians, an older people than mine, whose ancestors had built monuments at the dawn of the cosmos. Antiquity clung in the air, in the sand and dust, in the worn-out skin of peasants, in the speech of the priestesses, god-priests and nobles.

We wandered through narrow streets of tightly packed, mud-brick houses. Taut as a harp's string, I looked around, expecting some Hellenic to jump out at me.

"You still watch for that man you escaped from," Paheri keenly observed. "Only Hellenic warriors are here, not seafarers. Worry not. We protect you."

Protect? No one protects me. That horrible fire would not have happened if I were truly protected. Whose hand pressed me forward, if not a priestess'? Had it been Sena who pushed, then showed bravery by saving me?

For my own good, I had to win favor with all of them, lest I be set on fire again. Death by fire was not the method my people advocated.

"Hapi, great god of the Nile, Hapi of the South, Hapi of the North, life-giving waters out of which sprang our divine gods," Isis prayed frequently, "bring about prosperity." Finally the river listened to her, slowing its flow.

"Isis is more complex than you think," Paheri proudly told me. "It was her helping prayers that caused the Nile to flood. Now she must control it and let the land fertilize with corn seed. As bearer of new seasons, she beckons harvest. Furthermore, she is responsible for annual birth and childbirth."

While we waited for the waters to recede, God Thoth, as scribe, began my instruction of written and spoken Aegyptian, sitting in the shade of a grand pillar in the hypostyle hall at Karnak. He was a good teacher, patient with my mistakes, but wary of me.

"Why is your face masked even as we work together? Are you mortal?"

"Constant work is my life," he answered brusquely and hurried me to Isis to announce, "She has procured enough words to perform her chores. She shall be deemed 'Scribe of the Goddess.'"

Upon hearing his declaration, Isis chirped in front of the others, "You delight me with your productivity."

Isis flatters me, yet I fear it is for her own enhancement.

A cool breeze blew away the atrocious heat and lowered the flood of the temperamental river. Arrangements for the cult to return home to their Temple of Philae began again. Another barge would accompany us, stocked with vegetables, grain, date fruit of the palm tree, house-ware goods, chisels, hammers and crafting tools. Offerings from worshipers—flax and linen cloth, gold threads, weaving spindles and whorls, bedding—or even a new throne for Isis, gifted from Karnak's high priest, Amun Ra, piled higher in the daily search for necessities.

Driven to the barge by Thoth's slave, I recorded supplies and amounts that were brought on board, much as I had for the merchant Alexis, but its purpose was to record staples to keep the cult active. I ached more as each item was loaded, for I could see my fate—I would have to go with them.

When done, in ceremonial procession, we priestesses reversed the process of our entry to the temple, leaving Karnak's great walls and rode to the river on carts.

"Farewell," Thoth bid me formally. "I'll visit Philae after I journey to Khmun."

"Khmun?"

"The city of my trust."

"God Thoth, what is this 'Philae' Isis goes to?" I asked, but he disappeared into the crowd of admirers who were loudly applauding our journey.

My excited sisters ascended the barge ramp. The lead oarsman bowed humbly as each priestess daintily pulled herself over the barge railing. I trailed like a sheep would its master. The oarsman slackened ropes, releasing the barge to dip into choppy waves before signaling the other barges to do the same.

"North with the currents, south with the winds," the priestesses chanted, renewed with purpose as we began forging upstream.

Under the blistering sun that illuminated a desolate, vacant landscape, with nothing but rocks and sand at the Nile's shores, we continued our journey. I looked back towards Karnak, and from whence I had come, northern, distant Etruria. Tears brimmed in my eyes. Pangs of welled up hysteria shot through me. A burning gloominess entered my being. *I must go home yet the direction is opposite, away from my cosmos.*

On the fifth day, the barges approached a high embankment of boulders supporting walled-in stone block buildings, no more than two streets wide in any direction. Philae wasn't a city, just a remote place in the hot desert, in the middle of murky rushing waters of the seasonal inundation.

Laughing and singing a song of passage on the river, the priestesses cheered with happiness. "The beauty of Philae is not to be denied."

"It's an island!" I gasped, terrorized by the isolation. *They are merry while I'm hollow with sadness.*

Enthusiastically, Isis whisked me onshore and led me to the fore court of the temple where columns rose in brilliant dignity around a square with a pond of floating lotus leaves. Flowering plants and date palms interspersed statues of Isis in mythic poses, winged or kneeling, holding the symbolic lotus blossom.

"Isn't it splendid? We'll build the outer court and a pylon lining the opposite wall. Each pillar's top will be sculpted with lotus petal, date palms and decorations. Our craftsmen are creative. You will sleep under stars and moon with the others here."

"Isis sleeps in the Holy of Holies, and stays within her sanctuary for prayer. She greets us at meals, for she is busy with her work," Paheri taught. "Along with her duties, she oversees those who tend the island. They live on the Nile's banks—servants, Nubian slaves and the oarsmen. All row over to plant, prune and harvest crops, bringing a daily supply of drink and wash water."

If only I could find one of them to trust and help me escape from this island.

More powerful on her own ground, Isis lorded over us with nagging rules should we forget our purpose. After her other obligations were finished and the priestesses were once more settled, Isis commanded, "Come forth to my chambers and receive instruction, Priestess Larthia, for you have become worthy."

Her darkened chamber was small and windowless, except for slits of light that penetrated where roof and wall met. Isis sat on her dais, fingering a scarab amulet. "Here is one of Isis' stories, my favorite myth. Osiris, my husband-brother, was murdered, torn limb by limb by Uncle Seth, an evil warrior. I grieved deeply for Osiris, lamenting, crying over his painful death, deafening the child I nursed, so that he died of fright. Overcome by my own disconsolation, I fanned the dead Osiris' body with my wings. What's the ending, Larthia?"

"I don't know it."

"Osiris lived again and became lord of the underworld."

"How did he do that?"

"He's a magician." Placing the scarab amulet on a stone table, she picked up a delicate vial of amber liquid. "To complete each instruction, you must drink this honey wine."

The wine coated my throat, stinging my tongue with bitter, then sweet flavor, making my head light, my tongue talkative. "A wonderful story," I mused, "yet strange, for you show two sides, devotion and struggle."

"It's loved by the people."

Her voice became melodious, reminding me of the Sibylline Prophetess of Cumae, as she told me more myths of the gods, of Aegyptian ancestors, and of herself. Superb stories, full of magic and wisdom.

"Our immortal life requires depiction of our story on these walls. You will scribe them and crafters will sculpt images and carve what you have written on pillar bases and around doors."

"I don't know hieroglyphs. I am just mastering demotic Aegyptian."

"It will be your life work."

Her words struck the core of my being: *life work.*

Rays of dawn started the cult's ritualistic day. Attendants served us meals of cumin seed bread shaped sometimes in the form of an ox, a lotus, or a crocodile, and corn beer spiced with leafy bitters. During and after each meal, Isis solemnly lifted the wooden image of Osiris as a human mummy. "Osiris reminds us that earthly life is of short duration and pleasure, and that we are blessed with our existence." We ate heartily to this mummy's warning, coming through Isis' voice.

This peculiar food affects me in ways that disturb. My head lurches from its potency. I want to sleep. I want to dance in the mid day. I did neither, compelled to worship the mother Isis, memorizing myths and stories, rehearsing new ceremonies to Amun Ra. How drowsy I grew as I listened constantly to this lore that wove mystically into my thoughts until they were part of me. My Etruscan heritage fell away, and I quickly, oddly, took on the manner and speech of my benefactor.

"It was *He* who has brought forth renewed abundance through his gift of you, the fair Etruscan," Isis announced to me in front of the priestesses. The others laughed, acting as if they knew something that I didn't.

I am a gift? What does that mean? I had no chance to mull over that question, for my mood changed rapidly and wildly. As fast as I had thoughts I forgot them, not in control of my being.

With imported cedar wood that the Phoenicians in Sais had traded Isis, the priestesses carved triangular, oval and curve shaped lyres, harps and other stringed devices I hadn't seen. Holding an instrument under arm, each priestess would dance and pluck the cat gut, making up note patterns and testing sounds, singing excited praise to the gods, particularly Isis. Occasionally I was allowed to strum some notes, learning rhythm and chants, but then, with not a moment of respite, Paheri would hurry me away to a temple pillar for my work.

One day I spoke out, "There's no joyousness in your song, just discordant thrill."

Paheri slapped my cheek hard. "We are serious."

Truly they were. The priestesses' disciplined routines had as small variation as the cloudless sky and stifling heat of the sun. So confined to our boundary, when tasks were finished there was little to do except make up games with a hand-sized, cloth ball wound from shreds of linen. In boredom, I joined in, throwing and catching like a

child. A wayward ball rolled past me, but I chased it into
the Nile, just out of my grasp. I watched the river absorb
the cloth until it sank. *My life sinks, too. If I try to flee, the*
waters or desert will be my tomb.

"Priestess Sena is dead," Isis announced tearlessly,
eyes and voice emotionless, not revealing what she may
have felt. "She drank of the wrong jar, of the water jar for
cleansing, then walked in contaminated water and mud.
Her body's fluids became impure, unholy to Ra."

The priestesses moaned in grief, real or not, I didn't
know, for Isis walked among us, pouring honey wine into
our cups to satisfy our craving for it. Before I went under
its influence, the thought struck, *how troubled I am with*
that explanation. Each priestess has two jars, one of Nile
water for cleansing, one of well water for drinking. How
could there be a mistake, for the Nile is contaminated with
excrement and offal? What violent death Sena met,
convulsing with pain! Is there another reason she died?

As Isis poured honey wine for me, she hissed,
"Seventy days to prepare for the afterlife."

Without warning I was surrounded. Paheri and Hotep
clamped my arms and rushed me to a back chamber of
Isis' complex of rooms. On a stone slab table, Sena lay
head up. In death, her face grimaced in pain.

Isis strode in and studied the body, lightly clawing it
with her long fingertips as she spoke to me. "You are
called upon to scribe *The Book of the Dead* for her *ka.*"

Numbly, I stared at Isis as she paced.

"Death is a transition of the body," Isis warbled. "The
ka is the spirit of the dead one, able to move and dwell in
tomb or statue, or receive offerings of meat, wine, and
unguents. The *ba* lives an eternal existence in a state of
glory in the heavens. In all, the whole person was a

complex unit, the life body, a spiritual body, a heart, a double, a soul, a shadow, a spirit, a form and a name."

"Seventy days!" I looked around this chamber, a room of thick sand walls, cool to the Aegyptian desert heat, a closed room with a corpse on a table, buckets on the floor, some filled, some empty. Torches propped at the walls lit Sena's form.

"You will learn names for each body part and master the picture forms. A laborious work to write hieroglyphics, yet you will come to love the ritualized words, for they are potent, poetic prayers to Osiris, god of the dead."

Hotep grinned almost malevolently. "You must watch what we do. We purify Sena. If, perchance, we make a mistake, molds and spores fill the air if the tomb is opened. Whoever enters would get bedsores. It's known as 'the mummy's curse.'"

"The rituals are for the well-being of the spirit, preserving the body from decay," Paheri added, saying this to comfort me.

For those seventy days, I didn't see daylight. I left the chamber only to eat, defecate and sleep, imprisoned as I was by my task.

The rituals were disgusting. My being sickened when Paheri and Hotep made incisions into Sena's torso, withdrew soft organs speckled with dead bugs and worms, and dropped them into a bucket. Her heart and lungs coated with sand were pulled out and put in alabaster canopic jars. With piercing instruments, gray masses were drawn through the nostrils, causing a putrid st ench that wouldn't go away. Horrid sweet embalming oils masked those obnoxious odors, but they weren't enough to filter away smells that rose from the corpse. Sena, the corpse. Not human. A shell whose spirit had gone elsewhere.

The embalming continued with strips of linen cloth dipped in natron, then wrapped tightly around the body before it could decompose. All of this I had to watch, for my task of scribing was done at this death site.

Seventy days! In my own sorrowful state, I kept jumbling the terms *ka*, the double of the deceased, and *ba*, the soul of the departed, for they were close in pronunciation. Those concepts absorbed me as my skin took on the color of death, whitening from the closed chamber.

Seventy days! How many leaves of papyrus I wrote to complete this book! How many images I drew! My styluses were crows' quills, my ink made of carbon from fires, replenished repeatedly for my scribing. There were standard symbols, beautiful in design and I scribed then with satisfaction. The symbols for sound were perching birds of Mother Nile or of prey. The symbol of curved shapes was the Eye of Horus, walking or sitting man.

To amuse myself, sometimes when I was alone with the corpse, I read aloud what I had written:

"Unlock the jaws. Open the mouth so that the Eye of Horus can enter." *The Book of the Dead* was a fascinating account, and I concentrated on it to ward off my nausea. On behalf of Sena, one prayer after the other was offered to Osiris:

> . . . Rejoiceth the boat,
> advanceth the god great in peace,
> Behold, grant to come forth
> this soul of Osiris.
> Sena, Priestess of Isis,
> triumphant before the gods, before your persons,
> from the horizon eastern of heaven
> to follow to the place
> where she was yesterday in peace.
> May she see her body,
> may she rest upon her mummy.

At the seventieth day, the door was thrown open. Dawn never was so beautiful! Fresh hot desert air! All of the remaining priestesses quietly filed in, not greeting me in their sober task. Those selected to carry Sena's corpse to its resting place obediently picked up the pallet on which it lay, raising it to their shoulders like servants carrying platters. We followed Isis to her royal barge—the only time we left Philae since we came from Karnak two floodings before.

Guarding the boat as if defending it from an enemy, the oarsmen rowed across the Nile to the western shore where the dead were always buried. Rhythmically, the oarsmen rowed as Isis sang a funeral dirge and we recited her words with bittersweet sadness.

From there we trekked to the hills, first past the verdant fields of crops that villagers grew for us, then past sand dunes to low rock mounds, devoid of trees and shrubs. Vultures, lords of desert rot, circled us as we strutted to the tomb's entrance. It was carved from the hill cliff—an open doorway that anyone could go into.

We descended steps into the bowels of the desert earth. Paheri and Hotep placed the stiff, lifeless mummy into a human shaped cedar casket, wood that came from a northern country.

"Her casket is plain for she was not of high royal blood," Isis explained in her eulogy. "It's the best we can do. Our tributes received this year are meager."

When death comes too soon to the young, it is always suspicious. But never a word was mentioned against Sena, never an objection to the cause of her death. I gleaned the reason. Sena had resented me for being favored by Isis. She disobeyed the goddess' orders that I should be well treated. *Disobedience was always punished with death.*

*   *   *

Lengthy days of ceaseless toil dragged at my being, the enforced learning of rites, music and scribing of myths, while sand and dust swept across our island in the Nile. With my past obliterated as an Etruscan noblewoman, happiness and joy no longer ran within me, just the grinding relentless chores of the cult.

"You must worship our gods since you're one of us," Isis had insisted.

"As you wish, my Goddess." Those words I repeated daily, outwardly. Inwardly I worshiped none. Faith in the gods had been destroyed when they tossed me to evil fates. Who had given me strength in my loneliness? What gods could I honor? In every place of this journey from Tarchna there had been gods. Even though God Tinia was Jupiter to the Roma, Zeus to the Hellenas, Nu to the Aegyptians, all with different labels and legends, they were all the same, worshiped by their native people. None instilled a response in me. Gods of my former life were dead to me.

From the priestesses to servants, planters, and oarsmen, I had found no one to trust. All were faithful to Isis. I gave up any scheme of escape that I ever had, too listless to make further attempts. With Isis' aphrodisiac, the honey wine given as reward for our toils, I took some pleasure in my oppressive fate. The potion weakened my will and made me come to love the goddess, her fortitude, her kindness and the prestige of being her scribe.

Without that potion, I wouldn't have survived. With that potion, I would forget my unhappiness, indeed, I felt enveloped with beauty. It made me recognize new truths gradually. Wisdom. Isis gave me the wisdom to survive. Endurance. I learned the secrets of survival in the cruel Aegyptian burning heat of Ra. Patience. Survival depended on these three ingredients. How strict the codes were! Grim and humorless, but thoughtful. Much wisdom I learned in being an Aegyptian scribe of the Cult of Isis, and still more wisdom from Sumer, the Mesopotamian civilization who lived prior to ancient Aegypt. How enchanted I became as I copied passages from old texts, the wisdom literature, writings that told of scribal values, and prudent and moral instructions passed down from their ancestors.

By the mere use of a stick, reed or whittled stone, scribes held high status and I was valued among them.

What a divided life I led. Even greater pleasure came to pass, not only as scribe, but as Priestess in the Cult of Isis. On feast days, I was revered under the protection of our mother goddess. Made to look beautiful, kohl lined my eyes, creams smoothed my cheekbones and my lips were reddened with cinnabar. Daily ablutions of the body became routine, washing with rose water and lotus oils. Like the others, I shaved my head frequently for my scalp prickled and I wanted no lice to fester. I brushed the tresses of each wig I owned. For all the poorness that Isis said the cult had, we were lavishly collared in gemstones and cleanest white elegant gowns that were strapped around the neck and touched the feet. Gold disk earrings with the image of Isis were bestowed upon me. Silver and gold armlets and bracelets jangled on my arms. Amulets of scarabs and ankhs dangled from delicate chains around my ankles. I became attractive outwardly, and it thrilled me inwardly, rejuvenating my organs and body fluids with unusual vitality.

*   *   *

Days became seasons and the annual inundation came again, this time according to the constellation of Orion, when the three stars glowed brightest. There was no cause for us to journey to Lower Aegypt and we didn't, for the flood waters in proper seasons gushed around the island bringing fertile soil for corn to grow.

Once, after eve's darkness came, my vitality withdrew, and even honey wine couldn't lull me into servitude. I could gain no quiet. In the corner of my being, a part of my past would erupt, enough to sadden me into a peculiar despair. I lay on my papyrus mat, under a patched animal hide blanket to ward off the frigid desert night, alongside other priestesses in our walled ceiling-less shelter. Encompassing a stark cold moon, the stars spread their luminescent glow across the ebony sky. Instead of comfort, I felt their menace, that I was unimportant in the spectrum of the cosmos, insignificant, lonely and unwanted.

As that intolerable night bore on, I could only imagine that the same moon gleamed on things in the river—slimy things that slithered under the surface and burst out of the water. Wet, scaly crocodiles with protruding, stealthy eyes hunting for prey! Gurgling at me! Threatening to tear me apart! I awoke, cold and shivering.

Then those stars vanished, leaving total thick darkness. A black wind flared from the river. Soon roving hyenas struck up chords of incessant howling joined by roaring starving lions. I held my tortured ears against their wailing. Those desperate creatures could devour me and pick my bones clean! In panic, my body's heat soaked my clothes. My internal water poured forth like the Nile's flood.

Exhausted by those images, I dozed fitfully. There was Arun ambling towards me! Mother and Father trailed behind, my brothers skipping after them with their wives and children! All almost reached me out in the desert night! Suddenly they stopped and hastily retreated from what they saw—an army of crocodiles slinking onto shore, snapping their long salivating jaws. "Rescue me, my beloved family!" I begged, but it was too late. Scores of yelping flesh-eating jackals pounced down from the desert hills and drove back my kin, until they vanished into the mist.

With these visions, my despair became enormous. I longed for death to take me.

16

The Breath Of Crocodiles

God Thoth had come only once to teach me the
scribings of demotic Aegyptian and more hieroglyphics
of the ancients. Other visitors came. The pharaoh's viziers journeyed to the island to collect tribute. Worshipers from Karnak and Weset paid homage before and after
the annual inundation. Seasons blurred with the unchang-
ing, scorching sun and burning sand that held no life.
Stark, cold nights contrasted to those hot days. There were
no storms, cool or frost, just two seasons, the flooding
and the dry.

Embarrassed that I could no longer mark with
precision how many seasons I'd been away from my family
and Tarchna, I secretly scratched three lines in the top
cornerstone of the temple, one for each inundation I
witnessed, counting each line to be equivalent to four
Etruscan seasons. Isis and her cult laughed at my concept

of time, for their lives would be of one eternal time, of this world and the next.

Squinting away at Amun Ra's sun, I carved intricate symbols into the grand stone pillars. My legacy. How would future generations know that an Etruscan, not an Aegyptian, was the artisan? Was this a joke of the cosmos? In the shade of a doorway, in respite, sometimes self-pity distracted me to hope for death.

Death menaced but didn't take me. I tottered on high scaffolding between two pillars, intentionally slipping, landing in thorny bushes, gouged and bleeding for my efforts but alive. With knotted cloth around my neck, I choked my breath, but Paheri, blundering in from her chores, giggled as she thought I was fashioning a new style, undid the cloth and played it around my waist as a game. How foolish I felt, yet I lived, destined to be teased by the afterlife.

Afterlife would be preferable to this one, but I was repulsed by thoughts of a fiery death, mangled by crocodiles, or drowned in a stormy sea. With Sena's ghastly demise, I wanted no murky Nile tonics to fill my being with worms and bugs, or to be dissected, separating my spirit from body.

The truth was I craved the afterlife of my Ancestors, of the celebrated Princess-priestess Larthia, whose tomb I had unsealed in the mists of my past. If only I could be laid on a bier with breastplate of jewels and gold, to reach afterlife surrounded by cherished possessions of my marriage, scribing tools, tablets of poetry and words I had written.

Over and over again, after night dragged by and dawn seeped through the eastern sky, I awakened stiff from the hard mat that I lay on in the fore court, sobbing from horrific dreams of slithering forms emerging from the turbulent Nile.

Most restless on nights when Isis plied me with excess drink or when my blood flowed, I went to the river for respite. One night, however, the river taunted me with its erratic currents. *Are those ripples crocodiles? How long would it take them to smell blood? How long would it take them to devour me, to end my misery?*

It happened that one dawn as I drew water from the well, a voice drifted across the windy expanse from the courtyard, a voice strained but familiar.

"Have you not seen her face age with grief since Karnak?"

"The sand ages us all," Isis's voice crackled. "Why should it be different for the Etruscan?"

"She is a different breed."

"She's one of us," Isis retorted.

Resonant chanting in the fore court suspended that terse conversation.

"My presence has been announced."

Here was diversion! Thoth's unplanned arrival hastened my step, enlivening me to halt my daily worship and tasks. The others, too, buzzed with his landing on Philae as visiting mortal gods and goddesses always did. Obliged to meet Thoth, I hurried to the courtyard and joined.

We dropped down at his feet and proclaimed, "Welcome, most revered Moon God Thoth, he who measures the universe with numbers, who first wrote words."

Even with his ibis mask, he dressed as scribe, and won my envy. A crocodile-skin pouch of sharpening stones was on his belt, dangling with ivory styluses and alabaster-handled carving tools. Around his neck, a wide, circular, crenulated collar fitted, and a loose robe covered his bare chest. His knee-length skirt slung low on his body.

And then this magnificent god did the unthinkable! With a jerk of his hand, he removed his ibis mask in greeting, and exposed his clean-shaven head and face.

Thoth was older than I first thought, as old as my dead father Parth would have been, an old man balding with age.

Charitably, he scrutinized us but spoke to Isis. "They adore you, Goddess. You are popular here."

"Of course." Isis shifted her weight next to him, and swatted a droning fly with her fan.

"Popular, but in need of more than bread and beer."

"We have our corn, our quail and pelican meats. Worshipers from Karnak gifted us with provisions until next harvest."

"A temporary measure. Your clothing becomes threadbare, your barges in need of constant repair. You don't have enough to provide for all. The Etruscan is an extra burden."

"Larthia does well," Isis said firmly. "She knows of us. There's more scribing for her to do. I cannot let her go."

At Isis' command, we priestesses rose and danced a song of welcome to Thoth. Their argument continued, loud enough for us to hear..

"I beg you, Isis. Give her to me for this season."

"She is needed here. She must serve the gods."

"How can you serve the gods without food? I can relieve you of her, and she can serve the gods otherwise. Possibly by serving the royal one."

"Pharaoh Amasis!"

My life is at stake with their scheming.

"Unfortunately the hands of my assistant scribe became painful with disease." Thoth sighed deeply. "I must scribe for the royal house at Sais. Larthia could journey with me and help scribe for Pharaoh Amasis."

"Ridiculous!"

A new tone crept into Thoth's speech, one of childlike innocence. "What if you had followers elsewhere?"

"Elsewhere?"

"Yes. If you want to expand your cult, perhaps the Etruscan can help."

How sly Thoth is! What does this mortal god who plans my fate want with me now?

"How can that be?" Isis angrily slammed her fan down on the table.

Mid-dance, we stopped to listen.

Thoth ignored her outburst and searched for me among the priestesses. His eyes bore into mine. "The gods have chosen to challenge you, haven't they? To send you forth on a journey. You have been assigned a sacred task to carry words of the Etruscans to the rest of our universe."

He waited for me to respond, rolled his eyes towards the river, then hinted, "Crocodiles."

He knows my fears. He's come to ward off the crocodiles! Crocodiles. I moaned almost inaudibly. *Crocodiles!* Inspired by his insight, words peeled off my tongue, unknown that they were inside me. "While Etruria has good soil, we have no corn goddess, no mother earth to bless it . . ."

"Messenger," he murmured so lowly that I would be the only one to hear.

Messenger? I felt his power reach deeper into me. "I could spread the word of Isis to my homeland and all will worship you, Goddess. Your myths will inspire the need. Your storehouses will be filled with offerings, your wealth tripled."

Thoth smiled his approval.

Does he help me? He schemes one-way and then another. Have I not been helped before, help that has driven me here?

"Ah, yes, she could board a Phoenician vessel from Sais and sail to Carthage where an Aegyptian priestess would be revered, one as beautiful as she. And then . . ."

My breath deflated. Carthage had a reputation for changing enemies at whim, sometimes with Etruscans, sometimes with Hellenics or Phoenicians.

"She could go and win Etruria and the Romans will be next, those barbarians who look for enlightenment."

"No," Isis protested again, but less firmly. "She is needed here."

"Send her home."

Strengthened by Thoth's encouragement I rose up and bravely moved towards him as noble as the Etruscan woman I once was.

Thoth drew my hands to him. A serene smile played on his lips as he spoke. "In a dream I saw crocodiles swarming around you, snapping jaws in hunger for your flesh. You floated calmly in their midst, an expression of resignation on your face, looking heavenward, unresisting death."

"What then, great Moon God, did you see?"

Entranced by his intuition, I let him lead me.

"Your sadness so irritated the crocodiles that they swam to the mud, scavenging for snakes."

My eyes squeezed shut; I wretchedly relived the repulsive scene. "I too, have seen crocodiles in dreams. Their vile breath hissed at me. Their tails lashed my body."

He donned his ibis mask again and clutched my hand in his. "Get her adornments and garments. Have the crafters chip a carving of Goddess Isis from the temple wall. Larthia will need proof of your cult to show her people. Bring them to the barge. We depart at daybreak, and Larthia will be protected as my guest."

Could anyone see my throbbing being? Did anyone hear the music resounding in my head? Yet how quietly we strolled to his barge, a half-animal half-human figure, and I dressed as a priestess of Isis!

"You can't do this to me, Thoth! She's mine," Isis screamed. "Bring her back!"

Thoth gave Isis a threatening frown. "Comfort her in her hysteria," he ordered the priestesses who stood in the slopes of the river too amazed to even babble about what they had just heard and seen. "Give her some drops of her own mystery potions."

Lit by a crescent moon, Thoth's stately barge was docked in sight of Isis' temple. From the deck, we could see priestesses dancing near an open pit of fire, singing frenzied incantations to fend off the unholiness of my departure. Gyrating shadows of arms and legs reflected against the walls.

I had to talk of anything but the unpleasantness of Isis and Thoth's disagreement. "The moon and stars are bright in Aegypt."

"The stars rain their light on this desert for they have no moisture to give." Thoth chose a piece of meat that would have fed four priestesses.

A sumptuous repast of ostrich eggs, joints of antelope and lentils with anise seed had been provided by Thoth's silent attendants. Eight priests sat with us, wearing standard black wigs cut shoulder-length, and loin cloths of finest linen with gold thread. They didn't question that I ate at their board. Every aspect of Thoth's cult showed more wealth than Isis'. His gilded barge was longer, curved higher at prow and stern with three cabins on deck, ornamented with a tall, colorful embroidered sail, checkered squares and zigzag line designs bordered by knotted fringes.

He no longer appeared formidable, more a friendly father than a god. Perhaps it was because I hadn't eaten as amply since banqueting in Tarchna.

"You tricked the Goddess," I said softly.

"Yes."

"You want me to scribe for you, not spread the word of Isis's cult."

"A half truth. I don't know the future." He withdrew a stone from a basket next to him and reverently put it on the eating table.

Not a stone but clay tablet broken from its sealed clay envelope, by Thoth, the receiver. I read the demotic script: *She is grown up and manageable now. Send for her.*

"It came from Pharaoh Amasis."

"The pharaoh of all Aegypt! How does he know of me?"

Thoth shrugged. "There are eyes and ears everywhere. Gossip is on the wind."

"So be it. I couldn't tolerate another day. The crocodiles would have had my being this eve."

The barge, as all riverboats, would remain until the first signs of dawn. No one sailed the Nile at night with dangers of hidden rocks, debris and creatures lurking under water. As Thoth made ready to depart at the sun's light, Paheri rushed to the dock and tossed a bundle onto the barge. I grabbed it and undid the cord. Some of my garments were wrapped around my scribing tools.

Paheri called out, "Isis is bitter. She refuses to part with Sappho's scrolls."

"Never mind. I memorized them to tell my husband."

"Farewell," Paheri waved limply. "May your days prosper. I'll miss you."

"And I, you, my dear friend."

Going downstream, Thoth's barge ran swiftly with the current, and he said with satisfaction, "With the flooding, it will take half the days to reach the royal house at Sais. There will be few obstacles."

"The river seems to know its mission, to give speedy journey to the wise God Thoth, god of letters and science of the universe," I complimented.

"It's not the river that knows its mission. It's the work of the gods who control it. If the gods are perverse or capricious, they change the flow to slow or fast. They permit the water's color to change or make the land verdant or not," he replied cheerily.

"I was at Sais once, at the time of—difficulty." I breathed freely, already feeling more at ease to potentially confide in him. The memory came back strongly, of dodging the merchant Alexis, of escape and capture into Isis' cult. "Sais seemed a poor village, not one where the royal house is."

"Tucked away inland it is, hidden among palms and vineyards, behind high walls."

Thoth's description proved accurate. Away from the Nile we proceeded, subdued, not ceremonial, on a road through lush foliage of date palms and cultivated grasses. With his false face, the ibis mask, God Thoth led on foot with his priests. I alone rode in an open carriage, one of Thoth's land transports, ornately inscribed with his cult's insignias. Dignified with my priestess garb, I upheld the staff of the Cult of Isis. Ahead, a thick wall covered with carvings of lotus flowers blended into the forest. Along the wall, sleek hounds roved a worn path, sniffing at the air when they caught our scent. With the speed of stallions, they bounded towards us.

"Don't move, Larthia!" Thoth's curt instruction left me motionless. "They're royal dogs—gazelle hounds—the pharaoh's breed. If we were enemies, they would have known instinctively and attacked."

The creatures with cold, vicious eyes encircled us, snouts quivering. I didn't breathe. Someone shouted.

Alerted, the hound's ears pricked up. Another command and the hounds slowly slouched back to the wall, as if anticipating a beating.

Eased by their retreat, we moved forward, unhurriedly so as not to incite them. Not from Thoth but from Isis, I had heard of these gangling hounds, hunters that belonged to mortals as guardians and were interred in royal tombs. I didn't want their hatred or wrath. They could tear me apart.

The gate was ahead. *Another trial lies before me! This pharaoh holds my destiny.*

Turbaned in gold shot cloth, wearing leather loin pieces over their genitals, sharp daggers hanging from ropes at their sides, a bevy of Nubian guards swung open the gate. They looked so ferocious that no one would defy them. When the leader spoke, he greeted our group with surprising serenity. "Pharaoh Amasis awaits you, God Thoth, and all that is yours. Descend from your cart, Priestess, and walk with the God."

The next gate opened into an enclosed field, a stone path dividing uniform rows of trees, more than twenty across and thirty deep.

"Pharaoh cultivates them for oils." Thoth pointed to some and named them as we walked. "Myrtle. Castorberry. Pomegranate. Tamarisk. Fig. Date."

Thoth tries to lighten my anxiety with distraction.

At the end of the path, the tallest man I had ever seen, dark-skinned and muscular, forcefully thrust open a huge metal door, inviting us to another court.

"Pharaoh Amasis experiments with coriander, mustard, samsuchum, and flowers here for fragrance."

Or does Thoth hint of how clever the pharaoh is?

Behind a second high, thick wall, a huge house gleamed with embedded glass stones, not the house of a rich noble, nor a poor laborer, but a palatial dwelling, a wondrous sight. We walked through hallways, courtyards and rooms, a labyrinth of confusing spaces, until we entered the palace gates proper.

A sparkling grand hallway led to the throne room. Floors were polished silver. Inlaid lapis covered the walls.

And there he was! A slim, bare-chested man, younger than Thoth, sat on a dais, his stiff gold skirt crushed by his pose. He didn't look my way, so that I had some breaths to fully take in the magnificence of Amasis III, grandson of the ruling Saite dynasty's pharaoh. Resting on his head, a close-fitted high crown carved with lotus and palm leaves, and symbols unknown to me. A necklace of precious jewels looped around his throat. Down from his armlets, his hand stroked one of those royal dogs, which indolently lowered his head.

"Great Pharaoh of Pharaohs, I've brought the Priestess Scribe of Isis."

Acknowledging that he heard Thoth, he petted the dog, unleashed it from its tether, stepped down and silently circled me, much as his guard dogs had. "There were once female scribes in Sumer, I am told." The pharaoh sniffed into a cloth. "In the land to the east. Northerly. But that was a thousand years ago. Sumer is no more. Yet you scribe in your land of Etruria. How is that?"

Beware! My rescuer, Thoth had told me. *Expect the opulence of the pharaoh. Be unfazed! Kiss the foot of the pharaoh!* I concentrated on what I had practiced on the river journey here. I already knew what I could tell him. Without divulging Etruscan secrets I would speak of my heritage, my origins, the land and people.

"Oh Royal Master! The gods have gifted me with this need, this talent. My family takes pride in our skills. I am a noblewoman descended from the clan of Laris, my father Master Road Builder Parth Vella, my mother Noblewoman Risa, Painter of tomb scenes. My grandfather, the great

Soil Sampler, Vel Porenna and his wife, Anneia the Healer of the sick."

"Impressive lineage. What of your husband?

"Master Hunter for Prince-priest Zilath of Tarchna."

"Does your prince-priest rule all of Etruria?"

"No. There are twelve prince-priests, one for each great city."

Amasis straightened his back and said smugly, "I rule all of Aegypt, Lower and Upper Aegypt—a vast empire."

"Etruria's region has different landscapes—mountains, valleys, lakes, pasturelands, meadows. Twelve prince-priests must manage commerce unique to their land."

"Hmm. Quick answers you give."

Amasis spoke to Thoth. "Her beauty is different from ours, her skin a lighter hue. You say she is knowledgeable of many parts of the world. Why is that?"

"The gods have willed it," Thoth soothed.

Yes. I know much. So much that words like 'world,' 'cosmos,' universe,' mean the same. How much I've learned throughout this bizarre life I've led.

The pharaoh sniffed his cloth again as he eyed me. "You know of Italic barbarians, the Hellenics, Phoenicians and us, I am told. Have you heard of the Pillars of Hercules?"

"Only that it's west of the watery cosmos."

"The cosmos, as you call it, is bigger than we think. We don't know of the Nile's source, but it is long and treacherous. There must be a great mass of land there. Rumor is that the blackest natives live in its midst. I'm sending a fleet of ships to find its end and bring back treasures."

Why is he telling me this?

Like Thoth had done, Amasis studied my face as if I could reveal all on the spot. "That's why I need to know your history."

Is he sincere? "I will tell what I can if you will let me go."

"You're right, God Thoth. She is bold." The pharaoh continued staring at me, his eyes becoming bright and dilated, his need for information almost tangible. "Priestess, you shall go when I am pleased with your explanations."

I strolled through the pharaoh's trellised garden of ripening grapes, through walkways of sycamore trees shading spice and herb beds, earthenware pots of blue lotus bordering fishponds and areas preserved for game. Thoughts of my encounter with Amasis whirled in my head as I inhaled the aroma of blue lotus, smelling some sweet unknown fruit. A gentle gaiety overcame me and I smiled within.

This day I challenged the elite Amasis! What more can I say without giving away laws that made Etruscans successful, laws from the Book of Tages?

"Are you different from us?"

"Pharaoh Amasis, you sneaked up on me!" Cockiness, perhaps from the blue lotus made me speak unlike I would have spoken to a superior noble. I felt I could do or say whatever I pleased! "Honored Pharaoh, Etruria has no desert nor pyramid nor sphinxes, but we live with enthusiasm, with fortitude inspired by our land's abundance of crops—deer, boar, pheasants and delicacies. We greet each day with eagerness, anxious to participate in ways of the cosmos. My people smile. They laugh. They make merry with banquet. They enjoy life with all it has to offer."

He snuffled at the cloth always in his hand, without noticeable reaction to what I relayed. Exuberantly I went on, unable to contain the expansiveness I felt. Truly the Hellenics would call it 'euphoria.' "Our gods have gifted us with the *Book of Tages*, our Discipline. They instruct our sacred priests to tell us how to forge for new ways to make our lives superior to Barbarians. All men and women are treated equally, discounting our spoils of war, the slaves of Carthage."

A look of disgust crossed the pharaoh's countenance. "Equally? What does that mean? Men think. Women have no thoughts of their own to be believed."

"I am a woman."

"Impertinent you are! You are a priestess, a ward of Isis. A guest in my palace."

He doesn't know how to treat me. He thinks I lie.

To his servant he ordered, "Give this priestess some tranquil chambers so that she might reflect on her thoughts."

Snapping his long bony fingers, he dismissed me. I hadn't satisfied him—and I had forgotten to kiss his jeweled toes.

I omitted telling Pharaoh Amasis the largest difference. The quality of our Etruscan joyous life surpasses Aegyptian seriousness.

He summoned me again, not inviting God Thoth to join me for this interrogation.

"Well?" His glazed eyes darted from my face to my clothes. "Have you more words?

"Etruria is centered in the middle of the cosmos. That's why our land has rich soil for its crops and . . ."

"And what?"

Was it the enchantment of that sweet blue lotus? Or is it a thunderbolt that reveals his interests! "Copper, lead and iron mines."

His eyebrows arched thin, like scratch marks of my scribing quill. "What else?"

"Tin. We make bronze from copper and tin. It is desired all over the Great Sea—the Mediterranean."

"Gold?"

"No, Pharaoh. Some silver but not much. Gold comes from the east. We trade for it." From out of my memory came the image of opening Princess-priestess Larthia's tomb, and how it had set my path. "Our gold crafters style beautiful necklaces, rings, crowns and exquisite bowls for tombs and banquets."

"Ah. What precious stones do you have?"

"None like yours. No lapis lazuli. No carnelian. Only garnets. Amber is traded from across northern mountains."

"Trade? Trade?" he asked emphatically. "Do your seafarers not pirate, too?"

"Our ships are the swiftest in the waters."

"Ha! So that is why Phoenician ship traders make us poor. They claim to get meager barter, and what they bring is worth more than it should. I suspect they lose our goods to Etruria's fleet."

My head spun, inspired by what I would say next. "In return for my passage I will take your wares for trade and send back copper and tin."

Where did I get this strength? Was it from my incarceration on Philae? Had Isis, in her seasons of instructions, given me power to blurt out those last words?

"We need iron. Is not the island of Ilva its source? The Phoenicians bring us iron from there, but their price is high."

"You mean that island off Etruria's coast?" Some force grew within me, becoming stronger. Then my internal power exploded! "I can do better than they. If you send me home with ivory, papyrus and perfumes, I will petition an exchange for iron with Ilva."

"You! A woman! A mock priestess of the Cult of Isis! Now an intermediary! You claim too much." He stroked his scrawny beard. "How would you arrange that?"

"Because I am a noble scribe to the prince-priest of Tarchna. I know how trade works."

"And what of the Cult of Isis?"

"I have promised to spread the word of the Goddess. Cannot both be done simultaneously?"

Almost unaware of what he was doing, the pharaoh paced around the spacious throne room, giggling, humming, puffing and snorting.

Could he be contemplating my idea?

With skirt crackling as he whipped around, the pharaoh pounced at me, smiling conspiratorially. "Perhaps we should deal with your people, not just with Phoenicians and Hellenics."

"We would be honored."

"You shall go, first by my ship and then with a Phoenician one, more seaworthy for distance than ours, and they will release you to your homeland. They shall bring iron from Etruria to my fleet waiting at Carthage, for now I know their shame of being pirated and will hold it against them should they not succeed. I'm sending the Nubian with you."

I bowed low to the pharoah, but did not kiss his foot.

Thoth waited in the garden for this discussion to end. "Your face shows triumph with Pharaoh Amasis. So he wants you to bring the message of the Cult of Isis. Smart he is. Isis is most beloved, for all sympathize with dilemmas of her myth. Then we will introduce me and after our other gods to your people."

Joy bubbled up within me like a fountain in Amasis' garden. "He wants more than that. I am to start trade between Aegypt and Etruria for him."

Thoth bellowed, a laugh that came from his depths. "I've helped you, but you go further! Have care. A woman trader now!"

"And I shall look as I do, like a priestess of Isis. How I have complicated matters, in my haste for any plan to go home."

We sat on a garden bench, each contemplating the benefits and drawbacks of this plan. Thoth hugged my shoulder endearingly, like a father to his daughter. His eyes lit up. "Your face hides nothing, but gives me answer to this problem. Stay here awhile."

I waited. The sun passed over the sky and dropped in the western horizon before Thoth returned from his palace quarters holding a bundle wrapped in cloth. He put it on the bench. "Your patience pleases me. Open it."

I unfolded the cloth. Inside was a wet papyrus mold.

With a dull knife, Thoth pried the shell off its mud base. "You will need to appear as many people, a priestess, an emissary and trader, a noblewoman, scribe, and—a goddess! The situation is like mine. I am the god of various aspects, but I am a man. What better way than we gods and goddesses do but mask our faces? No one knows who we are underneath and we are able to go about undetected."

"Your words overwhelm. Will I be able to rise to this task?"

"Remember who you are inside. Try this on." Deftly he pressed the shell to my face, around my nose, lips and cheeks. He removed it, measured and cut slits for eyes and nostrils then shaped it on my face again until it dried. From his tool pouch he took out a paintbrush and applied liquid shimmering gold leaf.

"You humble me with your cleverness, dear God Thoth."

"Wear it only when necessary. It will cause distance between you and those you encounter on your journey. Even seafarers will be fearful of your powers and won't harm you."

"I have not much to give you in return for your trust in me. But there is something I've scribed for you, a poem for you and Isis."

"For me and Isis?"

"You love her, don't you?"

"How did you know?"

"When you are together, your eyes meet in love"

He unrolled the papyrus and read to himself:

> *Gaze at me with shining eyes.*
> *Let me embrace you.*
> *I protect you with my flame*
> *Under the desert stars.*
> *Triumphantly we melt together.*

"You wrote this about us?" he asked.

"Days and nights are long in the desert. There are many occasions for thought." So as not to embarrass him further, I carefully held the mask, putting it on, taking it off, becoming used to my new face. "It's a radiant sun."

I must have touched Thoth's soul for I could feel a rise in our alliance. A rush of excitement came through my being. *He will truly help me return home.* Those words made me giddy, words denied so long, now uttered within me, bringing joy to my lips, the Etruscan smile that marked my people. *I'm going home to my husband, to my kin, to my life. I'm going home.*

17

Ari, The Dreamer

I thought I saw my precious sister yesterday but I couldn't have. It was a dream, of course, for Larthia is declared dead these past seasons, cooling, cold, warming and heat seasons, five times over. She is dead, having died at the hands of that barbarian Roman king whose clan defected from Tarchna several saeculae past. Etruscan traitor!

My night vision remained as I worked my men on the road that would give Tarchna access to the valley lands across the mountain chain. Pleased that I convinced Zilath that a winding road was feasible, there would be more trade with Clevsin and Perusia, distant Etruscan cities.

Like my deceased noble father, Parth, I sliced through brush, hacking stones to smithereens, pounding and packing dirt into usable paths.

"You're too introspective, Ari," Parth once said as I wielded scythe and hammer.

"Life works deep within me. My dreams deepen the clarity of my thoughts," I replied. "I serve Zilath as Road Builder, like you, Father, to keep our nobility."

Soon after Larthia vanished, Arun and I met at the prince-priest's court. Evasive he was, unable to keep a steady eye at me. Yet he searched for her to the north, south and eastern boundaries of Etruria, and said, "There's no reason to probe near the Great Sea. It's unlikely she's gone anywhere by ship, for a noblewoman certainly wouldn't travel that way." He gave up with excuse. "Zilath scorns my attempts to bring her home and the hunt is upon us."

There was a lie within Arun. I stopped believing him, he who was once my friend as well as brother-in-law. Arun knew more than he revealed. Was it my bitterness at his lack of interest to find Larthia that spurred me on? I saw the last hope in the disease-ridden swamplands, villages and ports near the Great Sea to the west where the sun dips every eve.

"Seek Larthia while we're unencumbered," Ranu, my wife and Larthia's dear childhood friend, urged not long after Arun quit his quest. "We won't need to prepare for harvest until next moon."

That gave me a handful of days. I sneaked away from Tarchna on the eighth day, when Tarchna rested from work and citizens filled the marketplace. On foot I traipsed to Gravisca, the hub of Tarchna's trade, from which nobles stayed away, sending servants or slaves. Uncle Venu had been an exception. He was a nobleman-turned renegade merchant-seafarer years past who made Gravisca his home port.

Prized sculptures and vases from Hellas were unloaded there. Etruscan pirates who had conquered enemy vessels and taken slaves from Carthage arrived. Seafarers lingered on the docks, awaiting work, telling fables of adventure with sea gods. The port teemed with gossip from around the cosmos. Larthia wasn't there.

Next season I trekked back to the port to see if, by chance, she had gone there. The latest hearsay was a most curious tale that everyone favored, about a woman aboard a ship heading to Sicilia Island to be roasted in the tyrant's metal bull for being a defiant, and badly behaved harlot. The tale was tainted from being retold many times. In some versions she was a shrew, a sorceress or a hag, in others she was sold to Athenai as a harlot. In every version, she was bold and courageous, invoking fear in crews.

She certainly wasn't my sister Larthia! Yet the weird story plagued and increasingly distressed me. Roman tradesmen who worked River Tiberis inspired its origins. Even Hellenic seafarers told a lewd version of how the woman was set upon. Perhaps it was true.

My night visions started. I dreamed Larthia was alive, the woman in the seafarers' story. She was somewhere in the vast cosmos. Like Tinia's creatures that change forms, from cocoon to butterfly, from fish to frog, Larthia transformed from noble to youth scribe to . . . could she be a harlot?

What thoughts I had when I awoke! *Could Larthia have been driven away from Tarchna by some evil gods who disapproved of her? Could she have become a sorceress?*

"How miserable it is that the gods made Larthia famous for leading a dual life," I told Ranu. "I will pay homage to her in Cisra's City of the Dead every heat solstice when Aplu's sun stays longest in the sky, for there the gods set her course. I can do nothing more."

"I'll prepare offerings for you to take to the gods," Ranu wept and packed me with votives to Vesta and bits of Larthia's scribing tools and slates.

And so it went on to the fifth heat solstice since Larthia opened Ancestor Larthia's tomb. The routine established, I journeyed to Cisra to praise the gods. The most convenient route to trek back to Tarchna was the port road, not deeply rutted, through Gravisca. It was also a way to hear gossip of fellow travelers. A second purpose was of commerce, to help me in my dealings with Zilath on where new roads should be built.

To placate absence from my family, I always traded for the finest goods to gift our tomb from the best markets at Gravisca's dock. As I strolled along the dock, commodities from Hellas, Carthage and Etruria's own fleets were being loaded and unloaded. Bales of wool were being hauled off an Etruscan merchant ship, a ship like *The Plentiful,* Uncle Venu's vessel that sank from old age not long past. Tarchna slaves, slinging sacks of withering grape vine saplings on their backs, waited their turn to board.

It was the man who directed laborers, not an overseer but the ship's helmsman himself, who interested me. From the care he showed for the handling of cargo, he was more obviously a merchant than a seafarer.

"An interesting barter!" I shouted to him.

"Do you need wool?"

"Thanks but no. We have enough." I couldn't help but gape at him. By Tinia's stars! He was the vintner I sought, the one who was at Zilath's court the last day Larthia was seen, one who left Tarchna soon after her!

He came across the rope gangplank, obviously trusting his men to work. "We take on saplings and Gravisca wine, not the best with this drought, but better than none this season. Our vineyards died without Tinia's rains. Our trade is sheep wool from my city, Curtun. Inner warmth for outer warmth." With concern, he asked, "Have you cause to glare at me, seafarer?"

"You! You!" I sputtered weakly, my mind not able to take this sudden encounter.

"Is there something amiss?"

"I'm not a . . ." The word "seafarer" never left my lips. Our conversation ceased as the dock master's shout announced a Phoenician vessel's arrival. Every seafarer stopped activity to watch it glide into the harbor.

"What a ship! Tightly fitted cedars, strong enough to battle salty waves and unfriendly winds, safe enough to keep seafarers from drowning," he admired, with reverence of a worshiper.

I found myself agreeing. "How fantastic this vessel! The size of Tinia's temple."

"The Phoenicians know how to craft a big galley for long voyages. Great distances they travel. This one came from Carthage, to be sure. Dry cabin boards. It's weathered much heat. There must be fifty . . ." the vintner counted, "or more oarsmen on board."

At the prow, a lone woman stood proudly, clad in bizarre costume, black straight hair bluntly cut below her shoulders, face painted bronze, her eyes rimmed with black outline.

We observed the woman together. My jaw tightened with a violence I didn't know I had. The vintner sucked in his breath. We stood there, a little stupidly.

He tapped my shoulder. "Are you stricken by her beauty? I can't take my eyes off her. She reminds me of someone I once saw."

"There's something familiar about her features."

At that moment, the wind gusted, turning the ship's prow towards the sea. With its movement, the woman disappeared from view as the crew hurried to right it.

"I remember now. It was at the prince-priest's court. So odd that it seared my brain. A man who looked like a woman assisted him, knowing all facts pertaining to commerce and barter."

The vintner reacted as I had. I shifted my balance uncomfortably. "Zilath's scribe."

"Yes! The scribe!"

"He appealed to all, male and female."

"The scribe was named 'Larth.'"

"The scribe was my sister, Larthia."

"Your sister? 'Larthia'?"

The vintner staggered backwards as if he had lost his land legs, sat down, rocking on his buttocks, chuckled, then laughed outright. "What a fascinating jest. To my shame, I wondered at the attraction I had for him." He stopped his amusement long enough to say, "Forgive my impertinence."

"Sometimes, too, I see its humor. She is no longer Zilath's scribe. Everyone in Tarchna says she is dead."

"Dead," he echoed. "Dead? Was she ill?"

"No. My sister left the court one night and hasn't been seen since."

I sat down next to him on the dock. In silence, we observed the ship's graceful turnaround in the harbor. Its crew had run to anchor the ship and it once again faced us. The woman was gone.

Then I began talking. He, a stranger, listened.

"If I could only shed what happened since Larthia disappeared! But I can't. It is always with me. For all I have to do is look at my shattered family and remember that Larthia caused so much misery. Not that I believe she meant to damage us.

"Arun, Larthia's husband, gave up his search for her, and I began mine in my own way. My plan was simple: start where Larthia was last seen, at Zilath's court, playing Scribe Larth. All of her associations were of the court, so caught up in her novel role of importance. I sought out magistrates, landowners and merchants who visited Zilath.

"No one kept track of visitors from far-off Etruscan city-states who came for wine harvests. It took the better part of that first heat season to track their whereabouts. By then most returned to their villages and cities. This task was only possible when my workday ended, so I wouldn't be missed. That's how I heard of you, Vintner Merchant from Curtun, Marc Vilemnas Partenu." I waited for his reaction.

"You've been looking for me since?" he asked quietly.

"I learned you questioned Scribe Larth's accounts, wanting everything recorded precisely, wanting receipts for your prince-priest at Curtun. The scribe accommodated you, designing a wax seal to affix to each wine amphora giving proof and naming quality, a procedure that has since become policy in Etruscan wine trade."

"Scribe Larth had common sense to figure out how to make commerce expedient. I was delighted, offering an extra fee to Zilath with some wine to Scribe Larth, recognizing worth for his able transaction," the vintner explained.

"You left the court, and Tarchna. Larthia went missing the next night. Zilath claimed there was no connection. Arun believed him enough to leave that idea cold. I wasn't so sure."

"I didn't abduct Larthia. I never went back to Tarchna."

The vintner didn't flinch.

"Why not?" I asked.

"My city needed me."

"The same happened to me. With the onset of the first cold season after Larthia's disappearance, Zilath required me to work further from Tarchna, insisting that was a crucial time for my men to tunnel through hillocks. Zilath's bidding was my first obligation. I was gone until the next warming season rains forced us to quit.

"Larthia hadn't returned. We, the family, feared the worst, but we had to go on with our lives. Zilath loaded us with constant work, assigned more labor since Larthia disappeared. We would lose our nobility if we defied him."

"Were you not suspicious of Zilath?"

"Yes I was. Zilath can be cunning. How I learned of my sister's fate was by cruel, harsh trickery of his words. Zilath always appears at his greatest when he speaks of glories of the afterlife. His eyes shine. He waves his arms at the sky gods to win their favor. That day he stood in front of the court—which is next to the marketplace where nobles and magistrates gather—and proclaimed, 'This heat solstice we host the Celebration of the Ancestors here in Tarchna! We'll show the other prince-priests of Etruria and their magistrates who soon arrive, the tomb walls of the most recently painted chambers that Noblewoman Laris has painted with Crafter Asba.'

"Just then an unknown voice from the crowd called out, 'Who opens a tomb this season, since your scribe opened the one in Cisra and stole the Ancestor's jewels?' Zilath replied, 'My Scribe Larth didn't steal jewels, but a vase worth more than jewels!' Then he had everyone's attention, and said, 'I have news, just arrived, of that thief! Scribe Larth paid dearly for his misdeeds. He is dead, killed by the Roman king. He spied for Roma against us and gave away our ancestral treasures.' How insincere Zilath sounded but his words made the crowd cheer! That voice in the audience could have been one of his very own servants, planted to bring up this announcement."

Visibly shaken, the vintner exhaled a low whistle. "Why do you think he did it then?"

"Zilath controls us. His message to the people is always, '*Don't go against me or your fate means death.*' I went on. "At the same time, Culni and I heard our mother, Risa, cry out. From opposite corners of the marketplace, we raced to find her. She had fallen in a faint and we dragged her to safety of a wall. Zilath hadn't finished his threat. Dramatically he told us, 'The vase is safe, back in Ancestor Larthia of Cisra's tomb!'"

"So it wasn't a tomb of Tarchna?"

"How confusing it must be to you, Vintner. The Celebration of the Ancestors is a yearly event in both Tarchna and Cisra. There's more. Do you want to hear it?"

The vintner smiled encouragingly.

"I had to revive Risa and begged her, 'Don't believe it, Mother! Zilath is malicious.' But Culni said almost merrily, 'Believe it, Mother. She is dead.'"

"Why was Culni so sure of Larthia's death?" the vintner asked.

"He can be hateful. He told everyone that his dead brat sister had the eye of the wolf like those he snared. Maybe it is callousness that it takes to be Master of the Hunt. Culni is loyal to Zilath as we must be. With announcement of Scribe Larth's death, and my mother collapsing at the news, the citizens rightly concluded that the scribe and the absent Noblewoman Larthia were truly one."

"Ahh," the vintner sighed sympathetically.

"After that, Tarchna buzzed with the scandal and our family took the brunt of it, ostracized from banquets, shunned by neighbors. The whole city was intrigued and chattered about Larthia's duplicity. They speculated about Arun, and how he felt about his deceased wife. Rarely had he been seen since the scribe supposedly stole Zilath's possessions. I don't see him often anymore, just a fleeting glimpse as he darts out on his stallion for the hunt, or walks with Zilath's men, as if he's guarded. His family home is closed to prying eyes, his relatives confined within its walls, with only servants going to market for provisions."

"How sad for you," the vintner said. "I'm sorry for your misery."

He hadn't shown deceit. Not a possible culprit! He couldn't have wronged Larthia.

"That's the whole story." Purged of it, I felt relief.

"We just saw a woman, didn't we?" the vintner took a scarf from his belt, mopped his sweating forehead and handed it to me.

"It must have been this muggy heat or perhaps we've seen an apparition. Women don't board ships." As soon as I said that, I remembered the woman in the seafarers' story of seasons ago. *Could she be the harlot of gossip?*

Without speaking we continued sitting on our haunches, contemplating our joint hallucination. Suddenly, a westerly sea breeze gusted towards the harbor, covering Aplu's sun with threatening clouds but no rain.

Tinia's lightning flashed against the foreign ship transmitting brightness across its prow. When it was gone, the same figure as before stood there but with face molded in a glittering gold mask. The mask was sculpted with symmetrical almond eyes, a straight, short nose with slightly flared nostrils and a full, closed mouth. Behind her, a tall black man whose features were as exaggerated as her mask was perfection, held an umbrella shading her from sun and wind. The vessel edged its way closer to the dock and let down a plank, not far from where the vintner and I sat.

Spellbound, we watched the cargo unload: baskets with bird feathers sticking through the weave, barrels piled with animal horns, trees with sword-like fronds, jugs, reed chests, shimmering cloth poking though slatted crates, numerous bundles, and carpets woven with gold. Smells of unknown fragrances, sharp and comforting, wafted in the air.

"Extraordinary goods." The vintner got up.

I stood also. We stretched our limbs and drifted closer to the ship's landing. "There can't be two women on that ship."

"Just one, I surmise."

After the baffling cargo was stocked into a nearby shed, the Phoenician commander came down the plank followed by the golden masked lady. He spoke to her in an unknown tongue, but her reply was too distant for me to hear. Her companion was a step behind, guarding her as closely as he could, as if she was the most precious being in the cosmos.

To discover how much the vintner knew of my sister, I divulged some of her qualities. "Larthia was clever, smart and as lovely as the first woman we saw. Feisty. She always needed adventure. Arun said her whim to dress as a man and scribe was 'a worthwhile activity.'"

"Dressed like a man and named one too. A scribe . . ." the vintner pondered, watching the masked woman move along the dock.

The mysterious lady covered her head with a mantle while the Phoenician commander sent for a Gravisca cart driver. Some exchange took place for the driver bowed his head respectfully, upturned his palm and the lady put small square objects in it. He seemed surprised, then pleased, beckoning her to his cart. The huge black man trailed, holding parcel and balancing umbrella, leaving the bulk of their effects with a seafarer enlisted to guard with his sword.

The vintner was fascinated with the woman. So was I. *Could Larthia have also dressed like a goddess?* "It could be Larthia," I broke in tersely. "I'm going to follow them. I think they go to Tarchna."

"My ship doesn't leave until dawn and our lading is on board now. I have this day for rest and might wander up to Tarchna."

"Unusual for a vintner to 'wander.' The golden-masked woman intrigues you enough to walk that uphill road?"

"A new adventure." The vintner grinned, his eyes sparked with challenge. "Aplu's sun shines on the Tarchna road."

"God Tinia smiles at our meeting. Call me Ari. I'm of the Laris clan, son of Parth Vella."

In newly made friendship, we hurried after the horse-drawn cart that bore the golden masked lady and her attendant.

"Your hopes may be false. The cosmos is wide and much comes from other lands that is new," the vintner advised solemnly

I nodded. "You reason well. Yet the Fates have introduced you and me on this solstice, you who I looked for many seasons past. And a foreign ship appears in the harbor bearing an exotic beauty. Coincidence? Perhaps it is only my longing to return honor to my family that I quest for Larthia. Whether it is false hope, my sweet wife, Ranu, awaits me. Share a meal with us, if you will."

"I bend to your hospitality. Are you convinced Larth—Larthia—is really dead?"

"Her corpse has never been recovered," I answered as we both headed through Gravisca's thoroughfare. "We cannot put her into the family tomb chamber."

18

Close To The Gods

What a story that burst, like an overfilled sack! The pharaoh's viziers squeezed the truth from Phoenician traders that indeed they overcharged Aegyptians for wares, particularly iron secured from Etruria's Ilva Island. That convinced Pharaoh Amasis that my role as emissary could prove worthwhile. He wanted to send grain and linen, but I insisted that Etruria had enough of its own. He had heard rumor of a devastating drought, but I dismissed it. Impossible! Our bounty was legendary, its climate temperate and constant throughout every saecula.

Generously gifted to me as part of our agreement, Hammad, the bald-headed Nubian slave, once the favorite of Pharaoh Amasis, was to come along. My dependence on him began when God Thoth divulged that the Nubian was a eunuch, castrated after boasting of his prowess in the pharaoh's palace. I felt safe that he was a eunuch.

Like a child tied to his mother's skirts, Hammad stayed near, fanning me with ostrich plumes as if I were royalty. He slept on a mat within my call, and asked permission to leave only for personal ablutions. The only other instances he left me were to haul our trade goods to the pharaoh's ship bound west for Cyrene, an Aegyptian outpost, or to deal with the Phoenician seafarers.

We left the palace of Sais and floated on one of the pharaoh's royal barges through the Nile's delta to the Mediterranean. From the flimsy Aegyptian vessel, we boarded a more durable Phoenician one that would sail us to Carthage, stopping along the Mediterranean coast at small sand-encrusted villages, Oes and Leptis. Under the fierce African heat, Hammad guarded me with a sun umbrella. Phoenician seafarers respected his size, and avoided me, thinking that I was a true priestess of Isis who incomprehensibly traveled to their homeport.

When Pharaoh Amasis ordered my passage through Carthage, I despaired. Would it be safe there? Etruria had an ambiguous relationship with the Phoenicians for generations, sometimes hospitable, sometimes dangerous. Would my Tarchna be allies or enemies? There was no one to ask, for I had postured as an authority to the Pharaoh. Odd how my self-belief had grown, first with blue lotus oil perfumed into my clothes at the palace, and then I simply grew into the task and showed knowledge of Etruscan commerce. I would be taken as a fraud if I didn't know what relations were between Etruria and Carthage.

No matter what it takes, I'll get that iron, traded for my freedom. I want no mishap, I often told myself.

Carthage, a settlement established by Phoenicians two saecula ago, had become a powerful city, proved by its architecture. Its circular harbor with an island of plants and trees in the middle was a stunning composition of thick stone columns supporting its quay. Luxurious houses and temples on low desert hills overlooked the sea and town. An anchored Etruscan ship showed answer to my questions. Cisra seafarers heading for eastern trade mingled peacefully with docksmen. We were currently on friendly terms.

To petition my cause, Hammad and I made our way on foot from the dock, through throngs of locals to the pristine white stone palace. Maskless, but bronzed with creams, I was presented as Priestess of the Cult of Isis.

"We receive you with pleasure." The Phoenician prince and princess smiled as warmly as the sun shone above us. He handed me a goblet of wine. She offered flat bread covered with chickpea paste. "Dine with us."

So keen were they for foreign company that they told the intimate history of Carthage's founding. Without boasting of their heritage, they informed me they were royal descendants of Dido, great-grandniece of notorious Jezabel, who escaped from tyranny of her brother, King Pygmalion.

What intriguing history they had yet they were interested in knowing about the Aegyptian past. As I told them of dynasties and pyramids, I gifted them with Pharaoh Amasis' alabaster image, rolls of papyrus and scarab gems. I drank their wine and ate of their bounty, choosing words carefully to relate my mission, to spread Isis' doctrine to the Etruscans.

"Can Isis save them from famine?" they asked. "Etruria suffers through her second year of drought and the people are losing faith in their magistrates."

I was shocked that they heard the same rumor as Amasis had. If only I had agreed to take grain, it might have proved more valuable than gems and grave goods.

"Goddess Isis' power might heal the land," I said. "I must hasten there."

Although the Phoenician rulers were annoyed that Amasis knew of their trade-bartering lies, they were agreeable and willing to help me.

"We give you transport across the Mediterranean to the Italic coast into Etruscan territory, if you take these," the sovereign prince said, as conversationally as if offering delicacies from a serving plate. But it wasn't food. He pressed a flat, gold sheet of foil in my hands and picked up another piece, then a third, all as thin as papyrus paper.

"If Prince-priest Maru accepts these dedications to our Goddess Astarte, who the Etruscans worship as Uni, and he hangs them in their temple at Pyrgi, we will also hang the same in our shrine. Our pact with Cisra will be assured."

"Pyrgi? Cisra?" I asked.

"Pleased you are!"

His delight was obvious. He mistook my perplexity for pleasure. They presumed I would go to Cisra! Pyrgi was Cisra's seaport. So Cisra and Carthage had ties of commerce! Tarchna did not.

"Your servant disclosed that you are scribe as well as priestess. One of these sheets is blank for you to translate into Etruscan after you master the tongue."

They had no interest in my purpose or destination as long as I did their bidding. The Phoenician sovereigns were no different from other scheming rulers I'd met. They wanted me to risk my life to present a treaty that would or would not be acceptable to Maru of Cisra! I would be indebted to them for passage.

On my lengthy journey, I had learned this crafty game. I too had hardened. With charm I said, "Gravisca is my destination, a small distance from Pyrgi. Can you get me there as well?"

"Pyrgi, Gravisca, no matter!"

They were too eager to help me. For all they knew there was no difference between Etruscan places. But there was. Every Etruscan city-state had its own laws and ways of thinking, competitive with each other.

What choice had I but to accept these golden sheets? Now I was chosen to represent the Phoenicians and Cisra's people. If I failed, what worth would my life be?

I lodged the golden sheets between layers of linen in the reed chest. On the voyage from Carthage, I engraved the letters with a stylus, poetically scribing homage that would bind Cisra and Carthage. Not Tarchna and Carthage but that could happen. *A scribe once more! Never would I have imagined that I would become an emissary, but the gods favor me with strength to do what I have promised.*

The sky and sea gods dealt fair weather as we crossed the smallest passage from the African continent to Sicilia Island, edging along the northern part, going up the Italic peninsula, passing the Hellenic colonies of Pithacusae and Cumae. *How many seasons ago did that evil mute drag me through these waters and his evil mother threatened to have me roasted in that metal bull?*

I hid behind my draped mantle as we anchored at the mouth of River Tiberis when the Phoenicians loaded salt sacks into their hold, trading gold and glass trinkets to the Romans. *How cruel the Romans were, abducting me, forcing me to reveal what I knew of Etruscan laws, branding me harlot. To exist, I must forget that shame, that humiliation and dishonor.*

What strangeness! When Cisra's port was spotted, the gods blew a cold north wind that churned the sea into fury. Had the Phoenician ship docked, it would have broken apart. With the golden sheets in my thoughts, my plan had to be rearranged. I had to take them to Tarchna. Later, I would present the Phoenicians' pact to Maru and propose Isis' doctrine to Cisra.

*   *   *

When this journey ends, I shall have fulfilled my fate, done these trials I was put in the cosmos to do. Will that be soon? Taking off the gilt gold mask that protected me from the Phoenician crew, I draped a scarf over my Aegyptian-tunic that clung to my body. Joyful tears slid down my cheeks when the Tarchna coast appeared, the city's walls above the coastal plain rising in mighty splendor. *Arun! Mother! Brothers! Family!* I stared at the shoreline, dismayed to see for myself the dried out land that had been so fertile when I left.

We moored in Gravisca, port entry to Tarchna. Tarchna—my rightful heritage! A misty cloud obscured the inland bluff where Tarchna perched. It would be a half-day's ride from this Phoenician vessel.

"You cannot go unmasked, Priestess! Please retain your covering."

"Hammad, you always shield me. Foolish of me in my joy to remove it."

Never far from me, the mask lay on the reed chest. Within the chest were my priestess garments and head-dress, covering the precious Phoenician gold sheets. Parcels of sculptures, a wall relief from the Temple of Philae and cloth-wrapped ostrich eggs that I knew would be craved by my people were clustered next to the chest. The rest of the deck was crowded with my Aegyptian trade, bundles of papyrus and ivory, baskets of amulets to ward off sickness, glass bead necklaces, perfumes, and potted date palm trees. How lovely it had been to select gifts for my family! A chain of gold for Arun, gold lumps from Punt for each relative to fashion into rings, lotus oil for Ranu, crushed colored rocks for Mother and Asba, silver and jeweled scarabs to bring good luck to all.

"You've become a friend to me as well as my protector, Hammad," I confided as we waited to go ashore.

"Priestess. I will be with you forever, for you are dear to me," Hammad vowed.

"What solace you give!" He might be difficult to explain to my family, but they would accept him. I scanned the dock to catch glimpse of anyone familiar; most were Hellenic immigrants who lived in the port town, those who linked Etruria's trade with the rest of the Mediterranean countries.

"Happy day! This sea journey is finally over! There's much to do." I listed the tasks ahead of us like a wife says to keep order in her house. "Hammad, I'm beginning to feel like a noblewoman again."

I almost danced down the gangplank with him. Laughing, we wobbled on land, adjusting slowly to solid ground after the rolling sea, relieved our voyage had been safe. Together, we spoke demotic Aegyptian, but daily on the confined ship, he had practiced Etruscan.

"We await our duties with you, fair Priestess," the ship commander called. "My most reliable seaman will guard your wares. He would not steal from you or pain of the lash be at him. We shall rest here until you send message granting permission to get iron from Ilva."

Like the Phoenician rulers, he knew no difference between Tarchna and Cisra, that each made its own treaties. It would not be me to inform him. I had to trust him for he brought me safely here.

On Gravisca's dock, I bartered Aegyptian ivory dice for a healthy stallion and fancy patron's cart which needed to be sent up to Tarchna anyway. That would impress the Tarchna. Shading me, as usual, with sun umbrella, Hammad sat behind, as we rolled through Gravisca and out to the crossroad. There it was, high above us,

Tarchna! But the sight of emaciated people begging by the roadside as we wound our way through the withered hills, dampened the thrill of being home. On top of the bluff, Tarchna stood as proudly as I remembered.

The gatemen at the city's fortified wooden doors let us pass, too surprised by Hammad's bigness and my fashion to question us. Within the walls, memories poured back and I felt even livelier. "Many times I used this road, going to and from market, seeing my family and friends. Many times I came to this corner, racing across this path, then that, going behind Mariscu or Ari and Ranu's home to escape watchful eyes of snooping neighbors to get to Zilath's court."

In Tarchna's streets, curious heads twisted as we rumbled by. I waved. None hailed greeting. What I must seem like to them, a masked creature, wearing a tunic of fancy style, adorned with armlets and beaded collar! *I've worn my priestess garb so much that they're more comfortable than those of Tarchna.*

"Don't turn around, Hammad. Two men pursue us. They've followed from the port, walking two hundred paces behind the cart. Whoever they are, friend or foe, they haven't come close. Concentrate on our rehearsed plans."

"Yes, Priestess."

Inanely I kept chatting, mostly to distract myself. "Arun's family home became mine in marriage. Most days of my life were there, preparing meals from harvest, spinning wool and flax, and banqueting. Very different from being a priestess."

"Banqueting?" Hammad asked.

"Eating, drinking, enjoying life to the fullest."

I omitted the drudgery, those common chores of household, cleansing floors and walls with family and servants, storing our harvest, labeling grains, oil, wine, curing stag meats and basting fowl, all which led me to boredom.

"Poor Hammad, you have to listen to all my stories."

"I don't mind. Your excitement is as it should be, gone so long." Hammad said no more, but his body set for fight.

In front of the prince-priest's court, citizens haggled over rations. Gaunt nobles minced over barter for measly fare, while scrawny servants drooped. The usual sounds I remembered were absent—no laughter, no rhythm of slaves beating sticks to mixing and grinding of grain, nor thumping of fruit and vegetables being tossed into bins.

With our presence all dealings stopped. In awe of the Nubian who strode before my cart, they flitted aside like skittish hares. It was the exact response I wanted, for I knew they had never seen such a huge, dark-skinned man, different from the emaciated captured slaves of our warriors. I didn't realize at first that they gawked in wonder at me, the exotic Aegyptian masked being he would introduce.

Hammad cried out in the Etruscan tongue as I instructed, "Make way for the Priestess of Goddess Isis, corn mother, earth mother who brings greetings from Pharaoh Amasis of Aegypt!"

I reined in the large, frisky stallion, glad that it was a manageable animal, and stepped down from the cart. With dignified noble manner, I ascended the platform that led to Zilath's receiving room. There he sat on his ivory stool as always, surrounded by nobles, patrons and magistrates. *My magistrate, the one who betrayed me, and forever altered the course of my life.* Silence fell in the court as my Nubian courteously ambled forward, bowed from his waist, and extended his hands outward gracefully, in supplication.

"You travel from the other side of the cosmos, servant.' Zilath greeted Hammad civilly but eyed me with uncertainty. "Your journey must have been long."

For a moment I was cowed by his penetrating eyes, remembering his authority, the power he had always wielded over my existence. Then I observed the magistrates who flanked him. They faltered and shrank back from my glance. I suddenly saw myself through their eyes, the masked, bejeweled emissary of the Pharaoh, and the embodiment of Goddess Isis.

What power I have! From deep within my being, a new voice rushed out. "O, great leader of Tarchna, of Etruria, we of Aegypt, have learned of the drought which has ruined your crops these past seasons and the famine which threatens your people."

"I am flattered that you take interest in our difficulties," he replied.

"It is Goddess Isis who sent me here, she who protects the earth, who blesses the soil and crops, and ensures bountiful harvest to her faithful followers. Goddess Isis can save you, if you can be saved at all."

Magistrates, nobles and patrons, astounded by what they heard, crowded within the columns. They were all there, the ones who daily attended Zilath, my brother Culni among them. My opening speech had whetted their parched appetites. I saw the Magistrate of Building, Velcha, one of the best magistrates, honest and sincere, contemplating my appearance.

Zilath leaned forward and struck a pose I recalled from seasons spent in his court. He meant to charm me. "Magnificent Lady—uh, Priestess! We should become acquainted with your goddess as we are surely in need of divine intervention."

One cannot have power over another without cruelty. Zilath is cruel. Rejecting his flattery, I knowingly went to the wall niche where his vases were displayed. "It will be necessary for you to undergo purification before I can intercede for you with the goddess." Out of the corner of my eye, I caught him exchanging a sneer with Spurinna, Magistrate of Commerce.

"My unholy being is at your disposal," Zilath concurred.

"Your being is of no concern to me." I picked up Larthia's vase, the precious vase I had last seen on that fateful day in Cisra when I entered her tomb at Zilath's command. "It is your tainted spirit I wish to restore."

A collective gasp came from magistrates and patrons. Zilath blanched, scowling at me, his eyes flickering back to the vase. "I shall bear in mind your foreign origins which have not bestowed upon you even the politeness of a boar in heat."

"I care not for your tawdry politeness. I have come to tell you your land can be healed, and Mother Earth will once again count Tarchna her favored child, only when there has been a full and honest accounting of the desecration and plunder of Ancestor Larthia's tomb."

A murmur rose up among the patrons and heads began to wag in alarm. As I walked towards Zilath with the sacred vase, he blustered, "There was a scribe in my court who removed some of the sacred objects. He gave them to the Roman king."

"And what of the objects which are in your possession?"

A wave of speculative muttering filled the air.

"There are none."

"Like Larthia's vase?"

"That?" He bent towards me condescendingly. "Pleasant though it is, it is a common flower vase."

"With every falsehood, Prince-priest Zilath, you condemn your city and your people to five more barren seasons."

His eyes tried to pierce my mask, seeking a clue as to my identity with which he could discredit me and end this meeting. Impassively I met his slyness, although beneath my costume, my being pounded which I was sure could be heard in all corners of the court.

The crowd of witnesses was growing in size. Word must have spread quickly, for citizens dashed from the city to hear what had become a volatile encounter. Whereas I had been the object of their inquisitiveness, Zilath now found himself the focus of their intense scrutiny. All he could do was deny my accusation.

As he opened his mouth to protest further, I said, "Have care. This vase has told me of its past and of the ring on your third finger plucked from the corpse of Ancestor Larthia's warrior."

Outrage at my revelation of Zilath's theft spread through the court, tinged with menace towards him. To them he protested, "Who would believe you, the word of a stranger, a masked one against the prince-priest of Tarchna, Zilath, son of Zilath and our Ancestors?"

Zilath regarded me with that special disdain reserved for lowly servants and slaves, but his hand trembled as he instinctively covered the ring. "I receive so many gifts. It's possible that another magistrate has unwittingly gifted me with this ring."

"Ten seasons drought," I announced.

Unable to contain themselves, a chorus of protest broke out in the court. Dread came to Zilath's eyes as he sank further into the muck of lies of his own theft.

"He had angered the gods and we are to pay for it with our very lives!" someone cried out.

"We are doomed!"

""By what right has he dishonored us, and traded our survival for the Ancestor's property?"

To quiet them, Zilath stood and raised his fasces, the iron double-bladed ax, the symbol of authority. "I bow to the needs of my people and the cosmic understanding of the goddess." He took off the ring and handed it to me.

"I will wait here while you bring me the rest," I said. "The golden brooch of ducks, the silver goblet, the unguent bowl, everything. Hold nothing back, Prince-priest Zilath. Believe me when I tell you that Tarchna's future depends on it."

Zilath jumped as if bitten by a viper. He glowered at me long and hard, and I questioned if I had pushed him beyond tolerance. Then he nodded to Magistrate Spurinna. The man set off for the inner chamber of the court and soon lugged a basket containing a variety of golden and bronze adornments for costume and body.

Zilath placed it at my feet. "May they bring the same gratification to your life, Priestess, as they have to mine."

"I have no desire to own them, only to set them to their rightful place."

"And how do you intend to do that? The tomb is sealed."

I ignored Zilath's furious glare and pointed. "He is trustworthy. Magistrate Velcha shall have the tomb unsealed."

Hammad hoisted the basket over his head and presented it to Velcha, who looked at me agog.

A hush fell over the audience. Some withdrew, ready to put space between us. Some dropped to their knees and invoked Tinia's name. Through my mask, I watched Zilath for one final moment before we departed. *Once he was a well-natured benevolent ruler, a friend, now unsound and wicked.* So that he wouldn't have me stabbed in retaliation, I backed away.

"Stop!" Zilath yelled, looking past me as I retreated.

Too late! My body hit something hard, its contours bruising my back. I swiveled around. The statue of God Tinia, usually mounted on the temple roof, had been taken down for repair to its broken stone fingers. Supreme God Tinia was known for his magical fingers that, according to legend, caused lightning when he flicked them. Tinia's tufa stone statue peered at me with amusement as if he had been listening. I regained my composure, given by his spirit. *Could it be that Tinia saves my life?* "Remember, Prince-priest, Zilath, I am close to the gods, both Etruscan and Aegyptian."

My heroic Nubian parted the crowd like a plow opening earth. I descended the platform through a field of bowed heads. As we walked away from Zilath's court, a thunderclap pealed across the sky. Nobles, magistrates and patrons streamed outside with eyes up at the gathering clouds. A wind blew in the direction of the uplands and raindrops began to fall.

"Surely Arun will delight in my homecoming."

With Hammad marveling at the novel phenomenon of rain, I mounted the cart and we drove through back streets to Arun's family home. Nervous and apprehensive as a new bride, I was excited to surprise Arun. Sweat dripped down my cheeks inside the mask. I shucked it aside. I wouldn't need it for my husband. The entrance was open and two children played, a boy of about eight seasons, a girl younger. "You've grown so." Their innocent faces reassured me that all was well with my family, although I couldn't remember to which brother or sister of Arun they belonged. The children rushed inside, and disappeared, leaving the door ajar.

"Everyone would be ending their tasks now, before the evening meal when Aplu's sun rests." Jittering with anticipation, I went in to wait for Arun.

There was enough delay to show Hammad some rooms. I had forgotten that an Etruscan dwelling differed from an Aegyptian one, not stark and gritty with sand on every surface. The courtyard was decorated with spontaneously drawn patterns on the walls. Cushioned couches lined the eating room with tapestries draped above. Bowls of fruit and flowers set on low tables. Family treasures lined wall niches, votives to the gods, bowls and jars for the upcoming family tomb.

Discomfort grows within me, a foreboding I don't understand.

A woman appeared, with the same two children who hid against her garb as if they had been naughty. "Who are you?"

"I'm Arun's wife," I stammered, irritated by who she was to ask.

"I'm Arun's wife," the woman crowed. "These are our children."

Accompanied by his parents, brothers and sisters, Arun hurried in from somewhere in the compound. He stopped short, not believing his eyes, as the woman hung onto his arm jealously. The family that I had known since the beginning of our union advanced upon me with hostility, like I was an enemy.

My Arun! I've come home! Why couldn't I manage to say these words I've thought many seasons? As if the cosmos had fallen away and the two of us were alone, we spoke.

"Larthia!" he sputtered. "You cannot be! You disappeared and are dead!"

"I was blinded, dragged, forced away from Tarchna, taking nothing but the scribe clothes I wore to be vilified in Roma, maligned in Hellas, then deified in Aegypt with the Cult of Isis. I am back from the nightmare of wrongful abduction and hideous lies upon my character."

"If you are who you say you are, you are the walking dead!"

"Scribe Larth is dead, but I, Larthia, the other half, lives."

"Alive! No!"

"The Aegyptians say 'to speak of the dead is to make them live again.' I waited for my words to sink in. "You're amazed at my homecoming?"

"It cannot be." How feeble he sounded, so dumbfounded by my presence. Dispassionately I gazed at the man I had waited to see. My husband. Stringy, thin hair over his forehead and eyes covered whatever feelings he held.

"I, your noble wife came back to reclaim my nobility and spread Isis' doctrine."

"No being is noble unless deemed by the gods," Arun's wife sneered.

"This woman demands our bed. What have you done, Arun? What has happened?"

"Zilath marked you thief."

"You know otherwise. Did you not defend me?"

"Zilath announced you were killed by Roma's king."

"See you a shadow before you? I'm alive, very much alive."

"You had no thought of me when you rushed about with fame of opening that tomb in Cisra, playing games of intrigue, knowing secrets from Zilath's court. What of the embarrassment that I endured with your deceit, your lies?"

What arrogance he shows, yet he wallows in his own pity. Vague feelings churned within me. He was not the brave hunter who commanded respect, the husband who grew up with me, who I once loved tenderly. Hoping not to appear as miserable as he, I asked, "Do you not care for me now or care about the love that once was?"

"I was told to marry. The Magistrate Matulnei's widow and her children are now my family."

His words, full of spite and venom, were as foreign as Roman or Hellenic. As if in a pall, I heard myself saying, with intent, "You have made up for your deprivation, for not having children with me."

Throughout this conversation, Arun's family listened to what would be a season's worth of remarkable gossip. I felt no shame for what had transpired, but darkness overcame me as if Aplu's sun had vanished from the cosmos.

Zilath plotted my downfall beginning at Cisra. Arun helped him, deliberately or otherwise, denying my existence, consenting to marry another. Zilath's treachery was clear. Arun's has come as a shock.

He looked at me helplessly, his eyes beseeching me to accept the inevitable. I stumbled away from the home I had called mine, and the life I dreamed I would have again.

In a stupor, numbed by my loss, I raced through Tarchna's streets, to the walls and out the second gate.

Hammad ran behind me bleakly, faithfully holding the gold mask. "Where go we now, Priestess?"

"There is a place where my mother, Risa, will be." Coastal fog had risen, blending with light rain. It shrouded us with enough protection to send us outside Tarchna's walls to the uplands. The drought had killed the long expanse of wind-blown grasses that held underground tombs for Ancestors and future Tarchna. I visited my family tomb first. It was sealed as it should be.

Without my mask, the frail Elder, guard of the Ancestors, looked at me queerly. "Who are you? You can't be Noblewoman Risa's daughter. She's dead."

"Take me to Risa," I ordered so strongly that the old man complied.

"She paints in that tomb yonder, with Crafter Asba." He indicated a grass mound where a stairwell led below.

I crept down the carved tufa rock steps leaving Hammad to stand watch, grateful for my consideration that he shouldn't join me underground.

The sepulcher was a perfectly squared room, carved from rock, its height just above that of the tallest Tarchna, pitched up in the center and upheld by stone beams. Empty beds for next patrons were niched in the walls. Above them, blank spaces were prepared with wet paint for friezes. The only light came from oil lamps focused toward one wall.

"Mother? Are you there?" As my eyes adjusted to the dim light, despair from my recent encounter embedded in my being, the most ghastly nightmare I'd ever known.

So shocked by my voice, Risa splattered her paint pot against one of the newly frescoed walls and swooned. Asba grabbed her before she fell, and laid her inert body down on one of the rock slabs that would serve an Ancestor as an eternal bed.

Warily, he held up a candle and glanced around the chamber, locating me at the foot of the stairs. "It is you, Larthia, isn't it?"

"Yes, Asba!" I hurried to my mother and cradled her limp form.

"Since your father's death and your disappearance, your mother suffers. Silently, but she is damaged."

As I kissed her pale cheeks, my own tears shed onto her closed eyelids. "Mother, please wake up. Hear me. I didn't mean to scare you."

Risa blinked, then her terrified eyes shot open, coming out of her faint. "Are you a vision, a specter?"

"No, it's your daughter, Larthia. I am alive."

Risa breathed more regularly, enough to let out a pleased sigh. "I thought naming you after our brave Ancestor Larthia would bring you good fortune. She was valiant, wise and comely. I was wrong."

"No you weren't. I've had many titles, most you don't know, but 'Larthia' suits best."

"With Turan's love . . ." She tightened her arms around me and laughed with rich, deep joy, "you've survived!"

The tomb walls were freshly painted where Risa's brush had been. A banquet scene of a reclining couple, eyes locked in loving devotion to each other was brightly colored, joyous in depiction. The woman held up the traditional egg that represented life, ready to eat it. Behind the couple, birds flew. A flutist played for a dancer on the next wall.

"You haven't missed me that much, Mother," I humored her. "I see you and Asba have been at work."

She sat up slowly, revived enough to say with satisfaction, "We paint well together. The seasons pass rapidly."

"This chamber is beautiful, like our family one."

"Our heritage is to be buried here on the uplands, yet you cannot be buried with us," Risa mourned. "You are dead to Arun and he is dead to you."

"Great distance I have traveled with calamity, Mother, from Tarchna to Tarchna. What I have done this day will ensure that more trouble is cast upon me." I looked at the tomb longingly. A stab of the worst sorrow entered my breast. I would never have a tomb this fine for my afterlife.

Risa held me to her bosom. "I curse the culprit who stole you away! I sacrificed my golden earrings to Menvra, throwing them into the waters of the Voltumna to beg your return."

Tears welled up in me. I wasn't the only one in pain. My loving, sweet mother had suffered from my fate. My throat was too dry to thank her, but she understood. Our bond had remained vital.

Voices from above floated down into the chamber, terse male voices who could only be my brothers, Culni and Ari. A third voice joined them, deep and masculine, without a Tarchna accent. Vigilantly, three men descended the stairs, stepping into the afterlife chamber.

"Wonder of wonders!" Ari wrapped me in his arms and hugged me with fierceness. I sobbed against his chest, relieved at his consoling welcome. Gently, he stroked my hair and said, "It was I who followed you from Gravisca."

"With what reason?"

"Curiosity, mostly. You were too exotic to let pass without knowing the mission of such a fascinating woman," he teased.

Through my tears, I gurgled a laugh. "My dear brother. Eyeing another woman? You so faithful to Ranu!"

"A bit of hope that it was you." Ari became somber. "Too dangerous for you to be here. Leave Tarchna now."

"I could have brought Zilath new trade with Aegypt and a peace invocation from Carthage, but in his presence I was overcome with anger for the wrongs I suffered at his hands. I saw an opportunity for revenge and took it. May the gods forgive me."

Ari emitted a low whistle. "Aegypt?" he asked incredulously. "Carthage? You've been to such places?"

"To Roma, Cumae, Athenai, the island of Rhodos, Aegypt's Nile, Carthage and back. I have circled the cosmos as if it were a round ball and incredibly I am in Tarchna."

"Only misery awaits you here," Culni, my eldest brother interjected, keeping apart from me as if I was diseased. "You gave secrets of our laws to Roma, our *Etruscan Discipline*! They paid you in gold and you went to live among them."

"How would you know where I was, unless? . . ." And then I knew Culni had recognized me.

"You've brought a blight to the family."

"Can you forgive me?"

Before Culni could answer, the man with my brothers came forward, his face blurred by the chamber's dimness. Softly he whispered, "Larthia, I'll take you with me. Be not afraid for I know a way to get you away from your devastation. We must be quick before your Zilath's wrath falls upon you."

The quality of his voice, calm and refreshing, soothes me. "The darkness of this tomb keeps me from seeing who you are."

"He is reliable, one who knew you as scribe at Zilath's court," Ari confirmed. "He'll take you to safety."

"But . . ." My words—*I don't know him*—were swallowed by the sight of Hammad flailing his arms as he almost fell down the stairs in panic.

"Men are coming towards this upland, Priestess. They walk with ugly stride."

"Zilath's henchmen," Ari said grimly. "He gives you little chance."

"No one believes you now. You're an evil creature from the netherworld," Culni spat malevolently. "Find your way from Tarchna or be killed."

"You're no son of mine," Risa moaned. "You defy the laws of family!"

Culni was one of Zilath's henchmen. He had told Zilath that the masked goddess was none other than his sister. Coldly I tore into this traitorous fiend who was of my blood. "Did you not see Tinia's rain? I am true. The wisdom of Isis protects me."

"Hurry!" the stranger encouraged.

"The gifts! Hammad must bring down the gifts for my family."

"How can you think of giving presents now?" Ari asked.

"Take care of my mother, now that my father is gone," I begged Asba urgently. The stranger yanked me up the steps.

"Run!" Ari ordered. "Run with Tinia's wind!"

19

Outcasts

We fled across the upland grasses as Zilath's henchmen pursued. The stranger grasped my hand and pulled me forward, moving with determination of a warrior going against his foe. Hammad bounced clumsily after us with bundles of ungiven gifts for Zilath, his load lightened by leaving some for my family. The gang of men, who must have numbered ten or more, armed with daggers, menaced by their advancing presence.

At the brink of the uplands, the path became a swath of scrub grass. Only an astute guide could see where a trail wound down the cliff. The stranger seemed to know which path would take us to Gravisca.

Smudged by dirt, stained and torn by brambles on the path, my once white tunic was ruined. No more did I look like a priestess or a respectable noblewoman. I was too weak to argue what course to take.

What companions I had! A ruggedly handsome man in plain brown tunic that blended into the earth, and a tall, huge dark-skinned slave. What a threesome we made with our dissimilar appearances! Wouldn't anyone be suspicious of why we banded together?

Branches and thorns blocked the path. Halfway along the wooded ravine, we looked back. Zilath's henchmen had stopped giving chase. The stranger paused to lean against a boulder. Hammad sank to the ground, his face a mass of twitches and puzzlement, laying the bundle on a fallen tree.

"They must have taken the sea road," I panted, trying to regain my breath and wipe sweat off my brow with grimy hands. "They could corner me there." I looked at the stranger. "I don't know your name."

"Marc Vilemnas Arnthal, Vintner from Curtun. I trek back and forth among Etruria's cities, bringing wines to my people in exchange for our wool."

"You're a foreigner. How did you come to be Ari's friend?"

"We met at the dock this morn."

"Today? And he put his trust in you?" A hand's worth taller than me, I looked closely at his face for the first time. High cheekbones, a strong jaw, beard roundly trimmed, and an even nose set off dark eyes, eyes that gently gazed back at me. "I've seen you before."

He gave me a wide silly smile. "More than once. Each time you seem to be different. I recall a noble scribe adept at keeping accounts and certifying quality of Tarchna's trade."

"It was *you* at Zilath's court years ago, when . . ."

"When you were 'Scribe Larth.' How fascinating it is that this day you are an Aegyptian priestess defying a prince-priest." While talking to me, the vintner gave Hammad a leather pouch. "Scoop water from the stream there with this."

"He knows only a little Etruscan," I said through chattering teeth, and translated to Hammad what the vintner wanted.

"Drink this." The vintner handed me a flask of hot honey water. "You shiver now in the heat season."

"There was no dignity in leaving Tarchna, fleeing those ruffians."

"They may still pursue from the sea road," he reminded me. "Is not escaping with one's life more important than one's dignity?"

"Of course."

The warm liquid spread through me, enough to restore control to my being. *His kindness softens this brutal coldness that has overtaken me.* "How will you trade at Zilath's court when they discover you helped me leave?"

"It was a mistake those men saw me. I can't return."

"Neither can I. We are both outcasts."

"Your Nubian makes three. Don't—" he shook his head, "don't dwell on it."

"How can I not think of what just happened? My whole cosmos went from triumph to total collapse. What tricks Etruscan gods play!"

As we reached the outskirts of Gravisca, I felt a twinge of something missing, forgotten in our flight. "The cart! The pharaoh's wares! The poor stallion! Surely, Zilath has them confiscated by now."

"You left them near the wall before you went to the tombs."

"How did you know?"

"I was at Zilath's court. While you had audience with him, you tethered the horse and baggage nearby. I wanted to learn what valuables a priestess would bring from Aegypt."

"You searched my things?"

"Not exactly. But I kept others from pilfering your load. I had to slice a thumb off a youth."

"What?"

"A slap on the hand wouldn't have stopped a group of nosy folks. Still, you came back too quickly. You didn't see us, but Ari and I followed, first to your husband's home, then to the uplands. Ari sent his road builders to drive stallion and cart to the dock."

"I saw you both, but only as two snooping men! After that, I was totally involved with Zilath to notice. Ari must have told you much about me."

"Some," he nodded modestly. "What other direction could you go?"

"Much consideration went into your plans, yours and Ari's."

"Spoiled by Zilath's men giving chase."

However enjoyable it was to talk with this man who saved my life, raucous noise from the wharf made it impossible for further discourse. The vintner guided us through a mixed crowd of seafarers and merchants, Etruscan, Hellenic and Phoenician, a blessing that none were interested in us. But the cart without stallion was at an Etruscan ship, not the Phoenician one.

Anxiously, I opened the reed chest. Intact. The gold foil sheets under my tunics lay undisturbed. Surprisingly, the bundled wares were undamaged from rough travel to and from Tarchna.

Hammad quickly brought out a fresh mantle, draped it over my torn clothes as I combed my hair. "I have a great amount of Aegyptian goods, not only these but others left in a shed near the Phoenician ship. I must go there. The commander thinks I am Aegyptian since . . ."

"No need to explain. I know."

"No, you don't. I made agreement with Pharaoh Amasis of Aegypt," I began, and told how it came to pass that I represented the holy ruler. "To assure my journey from Carthage I promised the Phoenician sovereigns I would consecrate Cisra's temple at Pyrgi with the golden inscriptions."

He was listening earnestly, without comment.

"A wind blew us away from Cisra's port. How uneasy I was! I still had the gold sheets. To gain passage to Gravisca, I promised the ship commander that I'd give him Tarchna copper and bronze utensils."

"You thought Zilath would welcome and supply you with this trade?"

"Yes," I said miserably. "The commander waits for those goods before sailing north to Pupluna."

"Pupluna? These seafarers must be iron traders."

"They are."

"Priestess, your choices are few. You're being pursued to the death, and you must appease the Phoenician. I offer solution."

"Many thanks. A muddle I'm in, but I'll fend for myself. There's more, Vintner. As a sign of integrity, in homage to Pharaoh Amasis, I needed to get weaponry from Tarchna to ward off Assyrian enemies."

The vintner gulped as if he couldn't get enough air.

"That shocks you? The Pharaoh, Thoth and Isis helped me in my peril in Aegypt. I must repay them." I headed for the Phoenician ship at the far end of the dock with Hammad wielding a spear taken from the cart, should Zilath's henchmen jump out from anywhere. Almost there, I turned to see the vintner rush towards me.

"Talk fast! Zilath's men just reached the port road." The vintner squeezed my hand.

An impulsive touch it was! I tugged away from him, warmth from his hand burning in mine. He disappeared into the throng of seafarers.

"Priestess, your expediency astounds me," the Phoenician ship commander approved as I arrived at his vessel.

"In good faith I came back. You brought me safely over the Great Sea from Carthage and I promised you copper and bronze, but I couldn't make agreement with the prince-priest. His barter was too high."

Anger boiled on the ship commander's face. Violence brewed in his balled-up hands, and I thought he would strike me. But he didn't.

Unexpectedly, the vintner reappeared like a dream that comes and goes during the night. He waved at the Phoenician in greeting, strode over to him and spoke in his language. "Ship Commander, my ship sails north like yours. Could you be persuaded to take wares of Pupluna instead of Tarchna's? I know crafters there who could fashion metals to your needs, household goods, bronze ware, candelabra, goblets, whatever you wish, although different styles."

"So you make up for the Priestess' loss."

"I can get you *best* quality, smelted iron from Ilva at *best* payment," the vintner bid.

The ship commander jerked his head upward upon hearing the vintner's persuasive words. "Your idea interests. What payment?"

"None."

"None, Vintner! The Priestess promised copper and bronze and couldn't get it. Now you say 'iron' without barter."

"None, I assure you. It would be agreeable to serve you for bringing Noble . . . uh, a priestess of the Cult of Isis to our realm."

"You believe in her still?"

"Of course. See those rain clouds over Tarchna? She has brought them to end the drought."

"Impressive." The ship commander looked at me with renewed respect, but continued speaking with the vintner, more a male-to-male encounter. "Vintner, could I not benefit you with goodwill?"

Inspired by the enthusiastic lying vintner, I barged in. "Please, hear me, Ship Commander. I can bring goodwill. I will give you a double load of iron for your help."

"How's that?"

"As service to Pharaoh Amasis of Aegypt, I must send iron spears and bronze shields. What I need is assurance that you deliver this weaponry to those Carthaginian seafarers who sail east to the Aegyptians at Cyrene. For that, I must oversee the barter and have passage to Ilva."

"To sweeten your work for the priestess, three bars of gold, each the size of a brick," the vintner added.

"What?" I exclaimed.

"The two of you now! A tricky proposition," the ship commander said suspiciously.

"I must speak to this Etruscan merchant alone." I apologized, and yanked the vintner's arm in my direction. "How would you get that gold?"

"Pupluna reaps gold from the east for much needed iron. They have gold bars. I'll trade wine I've just bartered from Gravisca to the Puplunians. Come to mind, wool skins are left in my chests unbartered, too."

"But your wine goes to Curtun."

"You could trade me those ivory tusks. Or the ostrich eggs. Or the papyrus. My people haven't opportunity to adorn their tombs like Tarchna and Cisra, being inland as we are, away from foreign trade."

"Your people expect you to bring wine!" I protested.

"They can drink honey water this season, a small price to pay for eastern luxuries that they will boast about."

"Why do you help me?"

"This is trade."

"Not only trade. You do a good deed."

"I don't search to do 'good deeds,' but if one comes my way, I can't refuse. And besides, I've never dealt with an Aegyptian priestess," he chuckled.

The Phoenician ship commander halted our hushed words, more excited at the proposal than annoyed at our private conversation. "My ship carries more than iron. If your bargain is sincere, I'll take your weaponry to Carthage and get them to the Aegyptians."

"One stipulation, Commander," the vintner said.

Acquiescently the commander sighed, "That is— goodwill."

"No. She must come with me."

"With you?" he asked.

"With you?" I echoed.

"Yes, Priestess of Isis. If we sail to Pupluna together, we can settle your Aegyptian trade. But to do it, I must be your Etruscan partner from Curtun."

"Partner?" I stupidly was repeating everything said. *So this is his solution. He seems determined to help me. A 'good deed.' Ha! It serves his purpose. Yet it might resolve my difficulty. Death nips at me. My reputation is slandered. His plan holds comfort for I would be dealing more with Etruscans than Phoenicians.* I would show him that I knew about trade. I came back to reality and smiled. "Done, Vintner."

He smiled back, a warm humorous smile, cheerfully contagious. "Marc," he whispered. "Honor by naming me."

"I depend solely on your word, Marc, " I replied, sealing the pact that could work or go askew. "But tell me first, where did you go?"

"To the sea road with my men. I spilled a load of amphorae so Zilath's men couldn't pass and had one of my men offer drinks all around to cause enough hindrance for awhile." His victorious smile was like Aplu's sun bursting out after a rain.

"How well you stopped them! What solution!" In spite of my most recent predicament, my load felt lighter.

"Fast we must fly, before the prince-priest discovers your cleverness at trade and wants you back. My crew will retrieve your goods from the shed." Marc grabbed my hand and we scuttled to his ship.

Miraculously, no one was after us.

Aboard the Etruscan ship of Marc's employ, a flurry of activity kept all occupied, as we made ready to sail. Hammad was recruited to package and fasten down our Aegyptian trade goods. Discreetly, I sneaked away to a hillock outside the port, close to the temple. With a piece of driftwood, I dug a pit in sheltered ground that would be dry and safe, folded the valued gold sheets in linen, and buried them. To retrieve them might be difficult, but my promise was to offer this sacred pact to Prince-priest Maru of Cisra from the sovereigns. It would be done.

Sea bound again. Escaping from Zilath's wrath, I stood covered in drab apparel of a common seafarer as we glided out of Gravisca dock. From further distance, the outline of Tarchna's walls became smaller, and disappeared from sight. *Within those walls I once had a husband, family and friends, a rich life filled with joy and abundance.*

All that could go wrong, had. Not only my home but also my past was no more, the final blow to years of yearning to get my life back. All left behind, ties severed, even the cart and stallion returned to its owner. Even the gold foil sheets destined someday for Cisra.

Was it my folly to want more by being a scribe? Under sail, I changed clothes. *I still dress and act as a priestess, now of a foreign cult.*

How dazed I was on those first mercilessly long, disembodied days! Four days both ships rode on the Great

Sea, four nights anchored in sheltered coves on land, heading to the most northerly reaches of Etruria. Not drifting out of land's view, the merchant vessel navigated the coastal waters. Never out of sight, the Phoenician ship rode in our wake.

Between his ship duties, Marc, the perfect sea companion, would come to the cabin where we had table and stools for repose. He would say words like, "It's easier to journey by sea than by road on this low coast. The land is filled with marshes, swamps and swarming insects. No one would live in that bleak territory."

He spoke easily of the cosmos, knowing more than I'd expect of a merchant. "Our Ancestors found the best places to live, up north coast. Pupluna on the mainland and Ilva Island are blessed with Aplu's sun and rich metal deposits. That's why we trade with them."

Dulled by my own plight, I hardly said a word, my being tangled with emotions. Most of the journey I spent on deck with little to do but absorb Aplu's sunrays, and tan my skin to golden brown, not something noblewomen did, but it brought me warmth, so cold my being was in the hot season. Marc's actions with his crew intrigued me. He treated them more like kin or friends rather than inferiors. Likewise, the seafarers were loyal to him, linked by seasons of working together.

How was it so? Plummeting from my mishaps landed me on another ship with foreigners! I am without a place to welcome me in its clans. No family life or traditions to uphold as my parents and grandparents had. No next generation to embrace. No afterlife tomb! My life is over.

His eyes read my stricken state. "You worry now from adversity. Yet from stories you told, the gods granted you a fuller life than most have."

"Which gods? Neither Etruscan, Hellenic, nor Aegyptian answered my worship."

He looked startled. "How could the gods fail you, Larthia? They kept you alive."

"They may hold up the sky, keep the seas nurtured and the land abundant, but they have forsaken me."

He called me by name. The word sounded like a caress to my ears.

New waters, new land! What had happened in Tarchna was over. I could never change my past—blunders or successes. I knew I would always remember that day, a day of the most delicious revenge and the most sorrowful heartbreak. As we sailed through Nefluns' sea sprays and Aplu's sunlight into new territory, my delight in that revenge grew so fully that it burst, destroying all bitterness and hatred. I was born into another being, one who could live again. Now I couldn't languish, occupied with my task to evaluate the worth of my goods against iron. I had no choice but to forge ahead with my obligation.

"Your beauty grows, Larthia, like the blossoming of wildflowers that fill the landscape where we soon moor," Marc said playfully as the ship rounded the headlands at Pupluna, a protruding mountain that sheltered a cove on the other side.

"What untrue words you speak!" There were wildflowers, but they were charred with residue from a sky that billowed with smoke-darkened clouds. The clouds drifted towards us, Pupluna's smoke, a layer of grime settling on deck and sail.

"The ironworks," he announced.

Row after row of smelting furnaces crowded the once sandy shore of the harbor. Half-nude savages stomped around cylindrical stone cones, each the size of a great oven, doing repetitive work that I couldn't understand.

Across the expanse of water, the island appeared far away, small and inactive. "When do we go to Ilva?" I asked.

*   *   *

As if the Etruscan gods got wind of my intentions, my deed was thwarted. Wearing my goddess gold mask, I sought audience with the magistrates of Pupluna. Even as they were enthralled with my presence, they frowned and one explained, "We don't sail there. Iron ore chunks are barged from Ilva and dumped here on the beach."

Another said, "Ilva is a dangerous distance from solid land."

There would be no passage to Ilva. We would be stuck at Pupluna until the iron arrived and crafters could forge weapons for the pharaoh. A half-moon to do commerce. It would inconvenience the ship commander and stain my reputation further.

Upset that our plan would be delayed, I questioned Marc. You knew of Ilva's situation, didn't you?"

"Yes."

"Why didn't you tell me?"

"You needed to get away from Tarchna's misery and your mission was strong."

"Relief comes from one less journey on this quest for iron. How dear you are to help."

Both Marc's ship and the Phoenician one joined a score of other iron merchants and laid anchor in the shallow harbor, the only convenient resting place since there was no dock. We disembarked and walked upon sand to the furnaces.

"Slaves heat the rock into 'blooms,' hammered to rid of slag. So much waste, but in the end precious iron ingots are wrought, the source of Pupluna's wealth," Marc instructed like a wise Elder.

"This is what we've come for. 'Pupluna's wealth' you call it. With our alliance, we'll increase wealth for our separate rulers. We'll prosper from these metals."

"You talk like a merchant already, Larthia."

No women were about, only grim-faced overseers, servants and slaves. The slaves sweated as they poured baskets of ore and charcoal into the furnaces, fanning them with leather bellows. If they missed the rhythm of fanning, the overseer lashed them with whip. With each punishing stroke, those sun-darkened bodies twisted into gnarled branches, like old trees.

"Are they not Etruscans? Where is the joy in these people?" I asked.

"Their labor is harsh with few rewards."

I almost wept at their tragic pain, and said, "Who am I to disapprove of them for no laughter? I have never seen such dismal toil."

"The townsfolk who live away from the fires, on that precipice there, do better. Their necropolis is on the other side." We strolled towards the village, through its small market place and past rows of houses crammed together, out to an idyllic cove not covered by the noxious smoke.

The sight was divine! The necropolis was filled with flowers, shrubbery and plane trees, sheltering the Ancestors in perfectly rounded stone drums, mounds of grass for roofs. "This garden setting here at the sea is exquisite, more life giving than Cisra's City of the Dead."

"How were you called upon to open that tomb?"

"How did you know?"

"You were the talk of all Etruria."

"Zilath wanted to claim Tarchna as first city to see the Ancestors' netherworld. He accoladed me with the honor and told the other prince-priests that my scribe name inspired the suggestion. They agreed, afraid to go in, afraid of angering the Ancestors."

"And you were not afraid?"

"At first yes. I was used as sacrifice. I was drawn into the chamber by the coolness of the tomb after the heat of day, a comforting, peaceful feeling. It was the chamber of my namesake, Princess-priestess Larthia. Unhappily, her corpse turned to dust with fresh air I brought in, but her life was revealed in that tomb. My fear dwindled when I saw her possessions. So potent! So lively in death! They seared me with her strength."

We came to the end of the necropolis wall and stopped. Struck by the words I had told Marc, the connection sunk in. *Larthia's tomb gave forth her power. What was her power but her spirit she touched me with? In her tomb, I received that spirit, her power passing to me, changing my life, shoving me from one journey to another. That's why the gods forsake me. My beliefs came not from them but from Larthia's power that now rooted within me.*

"Then you, Zilath's scribe, disappeared. What elapsed from then until now?"

His quiet voice and manner invited me to confide as we walked back to the ship. He wanted to know everything about me, and I, in grief, told him, ending with "Can you understand my calling?"

"Yes. I've heard the voices of the gods since I was a youth, calling me to serve my prince-priest, to make Curtun thrive. You are no longer a scribe but a priestess of one you call Isis. Your course strayed."

"Strayed? No! I scribed the stories of Isis. It gave me authority for I learned more than other priestesses."

"How is it you don't believe in the gods but you worship an Aegyptian goddess?"

"Worship Isis? No. Outwardly I must pray, but secretly I deny her. I am convinced of her glorious majesty, of the love and benevolence she showers on her followers. She is more sympathetic than Turan, wiser than Menvra. By anointing me with potions, Isis gave me stamina to survive her grueling demands. She was angry that I left, but knew I had to return to Etruria. With joy, I reciprocate her favors by bringing her word here."

Marc patted my shoulder gently, flooding my being with lightness. *It's nothing more than a sympathetic gesture. In brotherhood, he treats me like Ari did.* Yet his hand warmed me.

As we waited for our shipment of Ilva's iron, Marc and I scouted for crafters to hone the promised weaponry, haggling over barter as expected, striking bargains and arranging transport to the Phoenician ship. We wrote no agreement on stone, papyrus or metal. By verbal promise only, iron would be transferred to Cyrene and sail to the Nile delta on Pharaoh's Aegyptian reed boats.

Then Marc prepared for his journey to his home, Curtun, excluding me from his arrangements. He had done what he set out to do, rescue me from Zilath and leave me to make my way. We would part at Pupluna. His face lit up whenever he mentioned Curtun, a high mountain village of great distance inland from the sea, unpilfered by enemies. How fond he was of it. I never felt affection for Tarchna while I dwelled there. Only now that it was behind me did I appreciate its life and worth.

For the first time in my life I was alone with no one to make my decisions. In my godless life, whatever would come my way, I would choose to do or not. No one would choose for me but me! *What place will I go once my obligation to the Pharaoh is complete? The life of lies I've led now shames me. I loved being a noble scribe. To be a hetaera had its hidden pleasures, the songs and dance, the poetry. Yet what did that do for me but bring trouble, abduction, defilement, more lies, tossed from one city to the next, one country to another?*

I tried to imagine my future cosmos but drew blankness. *What journey awaits me? What road will I take?*

Awash in misery, I sat on a hillock near Pupluna's walls, expecting the Phoenician ship commander to declare his vessel's departure. *My journey ends with my promise kept to the pharaoh.* The image of Pharaoh Amasis in his gardens sprang to mind—intelligent, astute, sincere, an honest ruler. *He is more powerful than Zilath, ruling an entire nation, not only a city.* I envisioned the Nile, its force that gave life to the people with its annual flooding as the Cult of Isis regally floated on their barge, the banks lined with worshipers adoring them as they passed by. I remembered the reverence I was given when parading in hot sand villages as part of the wonderful Isis legends when the heat season's sun beamed down. *At least there I had position, a life cause. In Etruria, all my nobility has been damaged and stripped away. Perhaps my greatest enjoyment was neither scribe nor hetaera but priestess in the cult, under the protection of the mother goddess, made up to be beautiful, kohl lining my eyes, creams on cheekbones, lips reddened, hair brushed down, lavishly collared in gemstones. I became beautiful outwardly, and it thrilled me inwardly, my body's fluids replenished with vitality from potions of the mysteries.*

"Larthia, you must be in daydream. Could you not hear me call?" Marc had climbed the slope and knelt down besides me. "When you weren't at the ship, Hammad told me you'd be here."

"I can see the town's activities and am unseen," I gave excuse. "Hammad talks too much, now that your crew taught him more Etruscan in the last half moon."

Marc laughed. "He even tells them of Aegyptian cures to restore manhood."

"But he's a eunuch!"

"He hopes to recover."

"Recover?"

"He recounts an Aegyptian remedy. He says that if a man gets a dead fish, carries it to a running stream, blesses it with oil, throws it into the water and walks upstream, he will be strong again."

"It could be a Nubian remedy. Aegyptians have more wisdom than that. What else did Hammad tell?" I asked, joining Marc's mirth at the preposterous solution.

"He gives cures for love troubles. How to cause an intended wife to love her husband."

"Love troubles! He was castrated for entanglement with a vizier's wife at the pharaoh's palace!"

"He gave two methods. One is to take feathers from a rooster's tail and press it into a woman's hand. The other is put a dove into the mouth, talk to the beloved and she will love the man so dearly that she can't love another."

"Those remedies are more plausible." "Perhaps you will let him marry an Etruscan," Marc teased.

"He's mine. I hadn't thought of permitting him to marry. Amasis gifted me with Hammad as guard, in truth, Amasis probably wanted to dispose of him."

I know nothing of Marc, but that his eyes are as deep as the Great Sea. He places an enchantment on me with every glance in my direction, making me weak, making me want him. Such thinking is dangerous.

"My ship sails at dawn and so do the Phoenicians. What will you do?"

Casually he spoke, without more concern than for an acquaintance. *Why had I thought he might care?* His jests about Hammad must have been said to set me at ease before he could throw out the real intent of seeking me out.

"What will I do?" His question seemed to unravel the commotion in my mind. Suddenly it was crystal clear. *Aegypt! Return to Isis and the priestesses! They welcomed me once. Perhaps they will accept me again. There is no need to wish for anymore to do with Marc. His course is set and it is of another direction than mine.* "I will sail with the Phoenician ship, back to Carthage, to Cyrene, to Aegypt."

20

Marc, The Vintner-Merchant

What do I do now that Larthia leaves for Aegypt? Stumped by no answer, I had to get away from the stench of smelting iron, and walked through Pupluna to where the air was less pungent and cleaner. The road wasn't traveled by seafarers and merchants. Fields were planted with heat season barley, bringing to thought my own grapes that I must go home and tend. *Why do I feel as raw as mud turned up by the plow's blade?*

A man skittered towards me, a tall, lanky man of undetermined age, with a long, dirty robe that swept over the paving stones, whipping up dust with every step.

Firmly, he said, "You appear troubled. I'm named Haruspex of Pupluna. I can help. I live away from the city on the other side of the necropolis. Visit me."

He scurried away.

*   *   *

I risk nothing talking to this haruspex, unfamiliar as he is to me. At dusk, I found the dwelling, one that looked in need of repair, its clay walls stained with soot and age, the straw roof sagging from inclement weather, an unkempt garden full of weeds and night insects. The door was ajar and a shadow of light played against a most unsettling room. In various positions, small woodland animals lined shelves attached to walls: hare, squirrels and moles next to ducks, seabirds and bee-eaters, and a lone wolf. None moved nor made sound.

"Walk in, Master. Pay no attention. They're stuffed," a voice called from the back of the house. The haruspex appeared. Smearing bloodstained hands across the apron that covered a loose fitting tunic, he smiled serenely. In attempt to disguise the vile smell of rotting animals, he opened a bottle and doused vinegar over himself.

"You expected me when I didn't know I would come, Haruspex."

He cocked his head in answer. "After I read the entrails, I pick the best to preserve. For a wise man like you, a lynx will do."

"A lynx?"

"Tell of your Larthia."

"How do you know her name?"

"I just know." Clearing dust off a stool with the hem of his apron, the haruspex said kindly "Sit down, Master."

Halfheartedly, I began, "She portrayed a man, noble Scribe Larth, at Tarchna's prince-priest's court."

"Yes. Yes!" he encouraged.

More rapidly I added, "Standing close to him—her, the scribe—set my skin on fire and tortured my head. I didn't know what was happening to me, for I hadn't been attracted to a man before. So intolerable and shaken by the encounter, I left Tarchna the same day."

"Ah, your manhood . . ." the haruspex grinned.

"I lied to Ari."

"Ari?"

"Ari Laris, Larthia's brother. I told him I'd never been back to Tarchna after that, but I had. I went to Tarchna the next harvest season to trade wool for wine. Gossip was everywhere, word spread of Larth, the spy and thief! I afforded no time to it, shamed by my interest in the man, and I poured effort into trade to compensate. That was when our vineyards had suffered with frost and our wine was weak, tasteless. Tarchna had plenty. A cold season without wine would have Curtun riot now that there is fondness for the drink," I rushed on. "Our sheep are Etruria's finest and our wool is desired for its superior warmth."

"You ramble. Go on, Master."

"It's only because . . ."

"Because you've come here out of despair."

He understands me better than I understand myself. "While there, during one market day, Tarchna's Prince-priest, Zilath, announced that Larth was strangled by the Romans."

"You grieved for the scribe?"

I bowed my head, my voice sinking. "I felt sorrow. Fierce sorrow. A part of me died, too, but I shook it off, wondering of my sanity. After all, I didn't know him. Then relief, for I hadn't wanted a man, but a woman."

I balanced myself on the rickety stool that was offered, ready to rid myself of these remembrances. "Some seasons passed and I went again to Tarchna. The story had unfolded, talked freely about by the nobility. Scribe Larth turned out to be the married Noblewoman Larthia. A woman who posed as a man and succumbed for it! I couldn't . . . wouldn't believe she had been untrustworthy anymore than I believed her dead! Her husband was a master hunter. I was compelled to find out what this hunter, Arun, was like."

"You wanted to know what his disposition was, didn't you? If he was cruel, or wicked, making him at fault for Larthia's deception?"

"Yes," I confessed shamefully. "I found out where he lived and searched for him. I scaled the wall to his house and saw him. He acted like a man defeated, attended by a woman with young ones. My obsession was over, my lesson learned."

"What lesson was that?"

"Not to desire, to lust for anyone."

"The gods say it is human to want, even that which is unobtainable." The haruspex went to a corner of the room, opened a box lid and gathered up a dark-furred form.

"Other seasons passed. Our harvest flourished, our vineyards abundant with choice grapes, our wine of quality as excellent as Tarchna's," I continued, proudly thinking of the part I had taken to achieve those results. "I didn't journey from Curtun again until this past warming season when Tinia's drought destroyed the vineyards. Again I left my city to barter. My trade was successful everywhere I went, particularly with Zilath of Tarchna."

The haruspex carried a dead lynx back to the table beside me and repeated encouragement. "Go on, Master."

"This last heat solstice was the most notable day of my life. My ship was docked at Gravisca. A quirk of the Fates led me to meet Ari Laris, a landsman, a Tarchna noble. So in need to talk, he was free-tongued and told Larthia's story. In many ways, he and I are much alike, hopeful and adventurous. I took him for a friend."

"Friends with the brother," the haruspex ruminated.

"I pretended ignorance of his sister, and that's when I lied, feigning surprise as he explained her whole tale. I took my lie so far to show shock of Larthia's death."

"Lies gain more problems," the haruspex murmured, dragging the dead animal toward himself.

The haruspex was attentive. I recounted the story of what Ari and I did, sneaking up to Tarchna, going from place to place after Larthia. Then I named every enchanting detail that fascinated me about her.

"I was drawn to her, pierced with longing! I had not had a woman in so long that her shapely form captured me—slender, energetic—a form that would fit mine well. Am I cursed by Goddess Turan? Has she mixed up love's ways? Once a scribe, now I ache for the same woman who's a sacred priestess!"

"Smitten," the haruspex gurgled. "Confused."

Accidentally, I rested my arm on the table next to where the haruspex sat, brushing against the limp form of the lynx. "That wasn't all. Inwardly a fire rose up within me, spinning a madness of desire."

"What else of that day was remarkable?"

"It started to rain."

"An unusual circumstance. A break from the drought! On the heat solstice, you say?" The haruspex hadn't moved, listening intently as he cradled the lynx as if it were a baby.

"When she went to that underground tomb where her mother paints funeral scenes, I heard the priestess speak Etruscan. When she revealed herself, how joyful I became! I had never seen Larthia as a noblewoman!"

"More fire?" the haruspex asked, stroking the lynx.

"No! With relief she was truly the noblewoman! I respected that she returned to Tarchna to clear her name. Through wisdom that came from hardship, she comforted her mother in distress, while in danger herself. Her words of regret for the pain she caused, melted me."

I shifted my weight on the stool. "She would have been trapped by Zilath. He would have had his men hunt her like a deer and slay her with arrows. Anxiety grew within me. I wanted to save her life."

"And you did. Courageous, you are."

"Not courage, but desire. I jeopardized my own trade with Tarchna, and forfeited the trade opportunity I built so carefully. All for desire of one who didn't know me, one I didn't know but craved, not only her body but her entire being!"

"Ahh." The haruspex examined the lynx's corpse, opening its eyelids, turning it over, smoothing out the paws.

"I have taken her this far, here to Pupluna, a distance from her tricky situation. She is undefeatable and brave and will make her way well in the cosmos. Now that we have sailed these coastal waters together, I see she isn't false, but has a sincerity of purpose to keep her own respect."

"Your eyes glow as you describe your contact with Larthia." He bobbed his head up and down and then withdrew a sharp knife from his belt.

"She has a sweetness that makes me want to take her into embrace, but I cannot give up my ways to be with a woman."

The haruspex expertly sliced through the fur of the lynx. "Stubborn, you are."

I looked at the lynx, dull in death. Drained by my admission, I felt equally dull. "Larthia told me this day that she leaves with the Phoenician ship at dawn."

The haruspex didn't seem to hear me, concentrating on his work. Deftly, he put his fingers into the lynx's belly and pulled out a mass of bloody soft organs. Holding them up, he traced his fingers over the crevices and judged, "Your destinies merge. Go to her."

21

By Sea And Land

Goddess of Dawn Thesan had not yet awakened, but I felt her presence swerving around the small boat, curling waves in Pupluna's harbor. Hammad rowed us towards the anchored Phoenician merchant's ship that was ready to sail, weighed down by its cargo of iron weaponry and ingots. As if going against the water's push wasn't enough, the air had chilled more than usual. The end of this heat season was upon us. I pulled my shawl tighter around my priestess's garments to ward off any distractions that could change my decision.

Hammad's grim expression told me that he wasn't glad or grateful to return to Aegypt. Poor Hammad! He'd be treated as an Aegyptian servant, with less regard than he'd come to have among the seafarers.

"Every day, every season, I awake, unknowing what the day will bring. Through all its terror, there is a sliver of hope that something good may come," I said to comfort him. "So today we're bound for Aegypt!"

Hammad banked the oars and rested his muscles for the next strokes. Another small craft, similar to ours, headed towards us from another part of the harbor.

"Marc comes!" Hammad cried out, hailing him with sweeping arms.

"To say farewell," I replied miserably.

His boat gained speed and reached us. Both nudged each other, thrust by Neflun's waves towards the Phoenician merchant vessel's side. Immediately, hooks were lowered for Hammad to hoist up my bundles, fewer than before.

"They linger for me to board, impatient to be at sea."

"Don't go," Marc urged, straddling his legs across the boats. To my chagrin, Hammad helpfully emulated the merchant-vintner's movement so that the boats wouldn't drift apart.

I stood and poised my weight defiantly to resist his advances. "I will serve Goddess Isis, she who defended me from peril, who showed kindness. The Etruscan gods forsook me. Great Tinia cast me to the seas. Goddess Uni sent me into darkness. Menvra, who should have nurtured wisdom, withdrew mine. Even Goddess Turan took away Arun's love and gave it to another."

"The gods serve you now, willing me to give you sanctuary. They know our inner truths, what we really want," Marc retaliated, not moving from his uncomfortable position.

"How do you know what I want?"

Our adjoining rowboats floated in unison giving Marc a moment to take deep breath, then warned me calmly, "The way to Curtun is rough and hard, over water and land, but there you will be safe."

"Safe? What does that mean? I have no sense of safety or security anymore. The cosmos supplies constant threat and I feel its danger, even without war."

"Stay, Larthia" he pleaded, his eyes devouring me.

"I have no right to involve you further. Your life is elsewhere."

"Come with me," he coaxed provocatively. "I'll give you shelter."

"How can I, a woman of vanished background, enter a new village and be greeted?" I sagged onto the wooden bench, hugging my body, head bent so that he couldn't see my face, which must be contorted with the sorrow within. "I'm afraid, mixed in thoughts for an unknown future."

With lightning speed he bounded onto my boat. "Look at me." With his fingertips, he lifted my chin so that I couldn't avoid his eyes, rubbing away my frown with his touch. "Do I look fearful to you, Larthia?"

Oh, his eyes! His presence encases me. He says my name sweetly, with a care I haven't heard before. In answer, tears that I hadn't known before, escaped down my cheeks.

"You have but a passing fear. I am your future."

I'm unencumbered by family and home. It makes me wild. I crave a stranger more than I ever did my husband. I don't even know if Marc is married or has a family. Incapable of speech, I nodded.

Marc shouted to the ship commander, "The Priestess stays!"

With waves slapping against the vessel's side, the Phoenician may or may not have heard our conversation, but he grumbled and waved his fist as he lowered a pulley with my bundles attached.

The pulley, sent in irritation, almost splashed into the water instead of the craft. Marc caught the ropes and reeled the bundles towards him.

"So much for my integrity, " I exclaimed as we rowed back towards the harbor together, leaving Hammad happily repacking our possessions to haul to the Etruscan ship.

Have I made the right choice?

*   *   *

Aplu's sun shone high when the Etruscan merchant vessel sailed out of the harbor. Our sea journey continued north, manned by Marc's helmsman and seafarers.

"Your men aren't surprised by my presence now," I observed.

"No. They were more surprised to learn you'd board the Phoenician ship again."

I leaned against the rail so that he wouldn't see my blush. *He tempers my apprehensions with jovial words.*

"You have a wonderful smile, an Etruscan smile under an Aegyptian costume. My seafarers think you're a talisman of good luck, an exotic gift to bring to Curtun." Marc drew me towards him and held the palm of my hand in his.

A current of heat scorched my hand running through my being like a leaping flame breaking away from its hearth. His face registered shock. *He feels this fire too!* Dizzily I pulled away from him. *What have the gods done to me now?*

How improper it would have been to do anything but act as priestess aboard that ship. *Too many eyes watch us and I want no further scandal when we reach Curtun.* I avoided Marc's nearness by constant movement, conversing of trade with the helmsman, cleaning my scribing tools and honing pen tips, recording Isis' myths and Sappho's poems, listening to the crew's singing. Hammad joined in song and chores, ever ready to help, eager for acceptance with brethren aboard the ship.

Even with these ploys, Marc stayed close, protecting me by showing respect, offering nourishment constantly, more than I wanted. Once he gave me a honeyed fig cake, held out the wine flask and said, "Tell me more of you. Tell of Roma, Rhodos, and Aegypt."

I bit the sweetened delicacy and quenched my thirst. "You want to know of me but say little of your life."

Marc swigged down some wine. "You know me already."

He was kind, generous, and loyal. That's what I knew of him. Clever and witty, too. As he tramped to the other end of the deck, he checked sky and sea, tightened mast, sail and ropes, responsible for the welfare of ship and crew. But he baffled me with his moods. I didn't really know him at all.

When the helmsman signaled that the mouth of the Cecina River was in view, a change in the sea journey began. The brisk salt air of the Great Sea became a haze of dampness on a dismally brown river, its waters coursing from inland through a flat, bleak delta. Between thick cattail marshes, the ship slowly glided far up the tributary until it met solid ground. The seafarers busied themselves to disembark, and I was left alone.

Marc joined me as the ship bumped against a crude dilapidated dock. "We moor at this wayside refuge. An enterprising Etruscan and his laborers run it as industry."

Isolated away from the sea, it was a settlement of storage houses, oxcarts without oxen, and rows of small river craft. Silence hung over the site, except for buzzing mosquitoes, not pleasant or the most hospitable part of the cosmos, a part I would gladly not see again.

In contrast, jocular spirited teams of seafarers and laborers unloaded the ship's contents, which, to my awe, were almost the whole of it, except planks and mast. Amphorae, baskets squared and round, plants, sacks of grain, bedding, piled cloth, and the Aegyptian wares I had traded Marc—sculptures, rolled papyrus, and alabaster tomb ornaments I myself had bundled—were carefully transferred to oxcarts. The oxcarts were hoisted up by pulleys, swung over and lowered onto flat boats. The procedure repeated until all goods were removed and repositioned.

Work done, the seafarers rested and ate on the riverbank before filing back to the ship and going below deck.

"I thought you traded only wine and wool skins, but you have more than a town's worth of goods."

"Would it have been better to have nothing left? This journey isn't profitable unless many provisions can be bartered—barley, meats, berries, vines. It isn't worthwhile to be only a vintner or wool merchant. I journey in the warming and heat seasons to gather what Curtun needs. It's my livelihood."

The ship's crew reappeared, wearing landsmen tunics, dark heavy clothed, complete with sturdy leather sandals.

"Where is their seafarers' garb?" I asked, amazed.

"They're not slaves, Larthia, but servants to the high magistrate of Curtun, given to me to make this expedition possible. Walk with me now."

Together we strolled along the riverbank as Marc inspected the prepared caravan.

Just what authority does this man have? He has ability and equipment to do everything at once.

"We go inland by craft on navigable rivers until they end. Then we trek across roads, always heading east."

He stopped at one of the flat boats where an oxcart strapped onto the boat smelled of fresh paint. Prow and stern were carved with Isis' symbols of horns and sunball, sides painted colorfully like a Nile barge on parade.

"For you," Marc lifted me over the flat boat's rail before I could refuse.

The oxcart was decorated with cushions, blankets and tented tarp. In one corner, a basket was stowed, filled with Etruscan linen tunics and new sandals.

"How did you manage to do this?"

"It wasn't me. You charmed my men. It was a diversion from their labor to create a special place for you. In Pupluna, I was able to get some of the necessities, though," he said gruffly, and then became the vintner merchant again. "At night, we bed down in forest and mountain. You'll be away from my men and Hammad will guard you."

"The tunics—these cushions. How can I thank you?" I stammered, ambivalent to what his thoughtfulness meant. *He wants me to dress as an Etruscan, but how can I?*

"You're used to comfort and luxury."

"I once was. No more."

He gave me one of his most endearing smiles. "You're most worthy, Noblewoman Larthia, Priestess of the Cult of Isis, albeit of a foreign soil."

He questions who I am, yet I don't know either.

A land breeze met the sea wind as our procession of small riverboats, which I counted as sixteen, moved against the current into the saltless river. These craft were a motley lot, some crudely devised for cargo, pushed along the riverbed with long handled staffs, others with benches rowed by seafarers, now dressed as landsmen. Hammad and some of Marc's men rowed my oxcart boat, as I sat within.

The river changed, rippling as it narrowed, rapids cascading over the shallow rocky bottom until the delta led into a forest. Deep on the forest floor, the river became a trickle, end point of this river journey. There, a wooden planked ramp was the only dock. As each boat was hauled upon it, the landsmen attached wheels to the oxcart, and pushed it onward. At my turn, I swiveled my legs over the edge of my cart. "I'll walk along side."

"No, Priestess," one landsman protested. "It's tedious by foot."

We argued lightly, enough to delay the caravan's movement. From somewhere at the end of the group, Marc came forth.

"I might have known it was you, Larthia! It's not dignified for you to walk."

He too realizes what behavior is proper or not. "I'll ease the load for the uphill trek and seat myself before entering the city," I sputtered, embarrassed by his special treatment. "I've inconvenienced you too much."

"Feisty, you are!" Marc chortled and walked ahead, his stride and pace in rhythm with the land's crust, calling his men to follow. The oxcarts' squeaky cogs and unsteady wooden wheels creaked along over uneven earth. As a weak sun filtered through elm, oak and poplar trees, I hiked after them, listening to footsteps scuffling under dried leaves that carpeted the ground. The last berries shriveled on their stems with the end of warmth, the season fading, soon to be cold.

We ascended a slope of a mountain chain that grew from the forest floor into a pastoral landscape of grass fields dotted with shade trees. The mountains grew higher, steeper, more majestic, until the stone fortress walls of Velathri's city appeared above us. I took a breath to look down. We were high over the river we'd navigated from the sea.

The path we trod met an upward road that curved and twisted around the mountain's spine, climbing constantly to the city on the summit. Few people were on the road. Some local folks doddered with market carts on the incline. A horse rider, with small kill slumped over his back, coldly saluted our caravan, asking what we hauled.

"More spy than hunter. Say nothing," Marc hushed us. "Don't move until I give word."

Velathri's imposing portals looked like they could weather twenty saecula. Twelve rigid-faced, armed warriors, one for each of the number of Etruscan city-states, patrolled the walled city. Weaponless, Marc strode up to them and raised his hand in friendship. They relaxed.

"Welcome, Vintner of Curtun. What do you bring?" one friendly warrior asked. "Have you libations?"

Marc nodded and ordered one of his men to unpack an amphora. Interested in the drink, the warriors tossed down their long spears, and swigged the offered cups of wine. As they drank and refilled, we all waited, standing quietly in line with landsmen and carts. Only the warriors' chatter carried on the mountain air.

This was Marc's method of alliance. He had done this before, with the Tarchna henchmen who pursued us. *"It's not to drunken them, but to gladden them for they are murderers by fate and their lewd spirits are humorless,"* Marc had said.

"Who are they?" Another warrior ogled at Hammad and me mistrustfully, wiping off the wine stain on his lips. "Velathri is closed to foreigners."

"Have no worry. They're guests, not foreigners. The Priestess of the Cult of Isis brings wisdom of the East. The Nubian's a spoil of war," Marc lied smoothly in terms they could understand. "We'll need haven for my companions and me to bathe and rest. After we're refreshed, I'll gain audience with the prince-priest of Velathri."

The libations worked. Less reluctant, the warriors let us pass with Marc's men. I dared not look back in case daggers were pointed at us.

Placing our trade caravan inside the walls, we became household guests of noble Merchant Spantas, trader of alabaster vases and tomb ornaments.

Marc introduced me to the noble without hint as to our relation or trade. "Priestess Larthia is an emissary from Aegypt. She journeys to gift Etruria with Aegyptian knowledge."

Have the winds swirled the affection he had for me? Here he treats me with distance, not even as companion.

"Honored guest," the alabaster merchant bowed from his waist, "share our banquet delights, taste our specialties of boar and juniper sauces but know that our prince-priest and magistrates are cautious of the unknown. Why else should we have built our city away from other Etruscan ones, high on this mount?"

"Your words confirm the vintner-merchant's," I said politely to his bluntness. "I bring wisdom of Goddess Isis only to those who would accept."

Noble Spantas laughed. "The vintner-merchant does what he does well, going amongst the Velathri, bartering some of his load. Stay here, Priestess, and I will share our secrets of carving alabaster urns with you."

"She knows alabaster. It's found in her country," Marc scowled.

His frown showed disapproval, upset with either the noble or me. I had to charm Spantas to make sure we were favorable patrons. "Noble Spantas, your invitation pleases. I accept. Our alabaster is for carving pharaohs' statues and canopic jars for a deceased one's internal organs—heart, brains, liver, viscera."

"What words are those?" Marc asked. "They are not common to the Etruscan tongue."

"Aegyptians are an ancient people, knowing secrets of how the body works through dissection, cutting open the dead and taking out the entrails. We 'mummify' the dead, dipping the corpse in natron and wrapping it in linen. The ancients named body parts. As a priestess, my learning covered our science, history, scribing as well as rites of my cult."

"Science? What is that?" Noble Spantas asked.

"Calculations of the cosmos."

The alabaster merchant laughed again and turned to Marc. "She is clever. You are jealous that I take her and not you with me."

Marc's words to the warriors at the city gates had been very clear. Velathri's prince priest and magistrates heard of our caravan. I was not asked to be presented or attend. Velathri wouldn't welcome outside influences.

As Marc banqueted with the prince-priest and high officials of the city, I enjoyed the noble's hospitality of food and drink and his tour of the crafters' workshop. Alabaster dust covered a room of sarcophagi, each one the length of a corpse. Tapping hammers and scratching chisels sounded everywhere. I looked at one finished sarcophagus, its plainness apparent with only bands of horizontal and vertical patterns.

What was wrong with the alabaster sarcophagus was that it had smooth sides. I remembered the hieroglyphs at Saqqara. "It needs decoration."

"What decoration?" A crafter demanded, outraged by my criticism.

"Leaves. Flowers. Stories of the Ancestors."

He picked up a piece of charcoal from a cold hearth and handed it to me. "Scribe it then."

What have I done now, provoking these people? With swift strokes I drew a palm leaf, then a lotus blossom within the borders of the flat side of the sarcophagus.

From Ariela, the hetaera, I had learned the words of the Hellenic Homer, and drew the voyage of Ulysses entering of the afterlife of Hades. From what I had observed, perhaps these images would be appropriate for some local traits.

The group of crafters ceased their carving, laid down hammers and chisels and surrounded me. Noble Spantas broke the quiet. "Perhaps it can be done, pulling the drawings from the stone."

"You've been successful with the crafters," Marc seemed amused. "They are inspired to carve, and praise you, visiting Priestess of Goddess Isis."

"I won't stir them with comment again," I promised, feeling the restraint of this severe city. "It's just that the crafters were skilled and bored with monotony of routine work."

"These are the most stalwart of Etruscans, yet even they have taken to you. Spantas talks constantly of you. He wants you to stay and give expertise."

Does Marc taunt me? Does he want to leave me here? My head pounded, and I had to walk off my agitation. As unobtrusively as I could, I blended among the local populace, wearing cloak and covering my head with a scarf like the older women, studying Velathri for its uniqueness. I wanted to scream *how different from Tarchna or Cisra this city is! The noble is lively but most are somber, gloomy, and hostile until known. This isn't a place for me!*

Upon return to merchant Spantas's house, I pushed open the heavy wooden door. Marc waited in the hall, fidgeting like a youth.

He held out his fist. "Pry apart my fingers."

A carved alabaster amulet in the shape of an Aegyptian scarab was in his palm. "It was made by a Velathri crafter—for a lucky journey together."

I was relieved. Marc wouldn't leave me here. *Some days he treats me with care and fondness. Other days he is a stranger.*

22

The Pirate's Palace

We stayed less than a quarter-moon more in Velathri before trekking over the mountains on a ridge that afforded us views of deep luscious furrows, dense with trees and wildlife. The mountain chain dipped before descending into a broad valley that spread as far as my eye could see. The air smelled sweet, of earth and life. Breathing deeply, I walked next to my cart.

"Delight for the landscape enters you." Marc backtracked from the front of our caravan and walked at my side.

"The cosmos shows its wonders to Etruria. I never realized its vast loveliness."

Compatibly we hiked along, listening to the warble of mountain birds, ignoring the grinding carts' wheels crunching over the pebbled path.

"Does not this journey weary you?" I asked.

"No. That's what I do. It will take some days yet to cross these lands. We'll find shelter at settlements or villages along the way. Then the River Arbia will float us to our next respite."

"My bones aren't broken yet."

"You Tarchna are a hardy lot."

Don't remind me. Don't call me a Tarchna. I wanted to say but instead I smiled and complimented, "You Curtunians, too."

The season was fast changing, decaying leaves flying, ripped from branches. Evenings after a day's journey cooled more quickly with an early darkening sky. The seafarer-landsmen-turned hunters trapped pheasant, hare, a lynx, even a fox and wolf. Marc brought the wolf fur to me for a blanket, still stinking of life, but warming the chill. To his thoughtfulness, I gave a scarf of Aegyptian cotton to wrap around his neck.

We left the sluggish currents of River Arbia and circled hillocks, then climbed to a more rugged mountain range thickened with fir trees to a walled village. Like Velathi, it was patrolled, but by fur dressed men, spears in hand. Its outside walls were tiled with gilded decorations.

"This place is hidden to most. Murlo is an entity to itself," Marc sighed. "It's the only quick route east so we pass through it."

"What a bewildering setting. Who dwells within?"

Before he could answer, some unshaven guards encircled us. "Walk," they demanded and whisked us inside the walls.

Marc, the landsmen and I were enclosed in a grand courtyard, unroped and unchained.

"All stand a hand's distance apart," one guard ordered, "Silence!"

Tired from our day's expedition, we barely stood erect, wanting food and rest but receiving none, until the light of day dropped.

"What cruel play is this?" I whispered to Marc. "I wish I could bathe in a stream and sleep on soft pillows."

"They won't harm us if we show fortitude. This prince was a seafaring pirate. When chased, he escaped. By bringing his band of men to this spot, away from Etruria's eyes, he built this palace and created his own realm."

"A pirate! How odd he lives on this remote hilltop, outside Etruscan laws."

"Watch how you condemn him."

"Condemn him? I don't even know him. Having been condemned, I can understand why he left." I looked at Marc. "You've been here before, haven't you? He must trust you."

"Keep your head straight! That's better! He trusts no one. My men aren't always the same. I am observed every time for any change in character." Although speaking to me, Marc remained stationary, eyes forward. "He views us now with his augurs through slits in this courtyard wall."

The high stone walls led up to a slanted roof where the most unusual statues gawked down. Thirteen statues. I emulated Marc's posture and didn't move, counting these statues to keep me upright. Secured to curved ridge tiles, each solemn-faced god, with a square chin beard, wore the same expression, a vacant gaze. These statues were seated, hands resting forward on their kneecaps, like Aegyptian pharaoh statues. On each head was a cone-shaped, wide-brimmed hat, not a gold oak leaf crown of a prince-priest. They were the most different sculptures I had ever seen.

*   *   *

With twilight, we were hustled before the prince who sat on a throne-chair wrought of interlaced golden oak leaves. On his head was a cone-shaped, wide-brimmed hat. To balance himself, his hands rested forward on his kneecaps. His image matched the statues.

He makes silly images of himself! I contained a giggle at the pirate's conceit, the ludicrousness of his statues.

Inspecting us all, his eyes darted from one to the other. "Give your weapons to my guards."

Marc motioned to his men agreeably, and they withdrew knives from sheaths, piling them on the tiled floor. He bravely stood his ground. "Gracious Prince of Murlo, I bring wine, wool, and gifts for your consideration, with thanks for your obliging accommodation."

"Of course, Vintner of Curtun," the prince grinned as three old grandfathers shuffled in, "my augurs ascertained who you were at the courtyard."

The three augurs huddled together, a society unto themselves. They wore cloth of their order: the first adorned in feathers showing his rank of augur of flight birds: the second wore a plain linen tunic and held scrolls of *The Etruscan Discipline*; the third, lower ranking haruspex, a teller of fate, was covered by a muddied cloak, caked with blood from entrails of some freshly slaughtered animal.

The prince studied Marc. "They identified you but not the woman. Who is she, exquisitely costumed as she is, a jeweled traveler in the hinterlands?" Wantonly, he eyed me. "You are new to Etruria."

His vain suggestion was understood, that he could take advantage of an innocent newcomer. I almost laughed at his game. "I'm a priestess of the Cult of Isis, Aegyptian goddess of abundance."

"Charming. A priestess of Aegypt. You must like my statues, modeled as they are after your pharaohs. In my early days, it was so easy to outrun your fleet, your boats good just for the river, that I procured one statue, but it broke. Aegypt thinks it is center of the cosmos but it's not. Know you of Etruria? My augurs divine that Murlo is the center of our cosmos."

I doubted his last words. He demanded recognition that I knew I must give. "I am honored to be in your domain."

The prince turned to Marc. "And you, Vintner? Do you believe Murlo is the center of the cosmos?"

"It is center of your cosmos, but not mine."

The prince's brow puckered. "Etruria's lands extend from sea to mountain, from river to river and we're in the center."

What a difficult man, lonely, ready to argue, wanting opposition. I smiled pleasantly, hoping to smooth over a brewing rift between he and Marc. "For Aegyptians the pyramids are the center. For Athenai, the Acropolis. For Roma, the Forum. For Tarchna, the sacred well in the Great Court. Everyone thinks that their cosmos is chosen best under the stars, or they are lost."

"Best? A wise woman you are. You know the cosmos well."

Marc realized his mistake of not agreeing. "Prince, I just bring barter, not knowledge."

It was too late. The prince fussed, not happy with so much accord. "You are man and wife, aren't you?"

Embarrassed by the crude question, I flushed like a girl child.

"How clever you are," Marc replied briskly, "I've never brought a wife here before."

"Although old for marriage, you are recently wed?"

"I bring you goods, not my life story."

"There's a tension between you that shows." The prince beamed at his own intuition. "I guessed. A room will be given you at the north side of my palace. The sun enters late there. You will sleep peacefully."

"How could you lie to him?" Furiously, I yanked off my mantle and flung it on the bed. I unclasped my neck collar that reached from throat to shoulder and slammed it on the table. "The prince could slit our throats and none of Etruria might know our whereabouts!"

"I didn't lie, but worked words to advantage." Marc pressed his shoulder against the door to seal it, then scouted the room for a barricade, dragging a heavy bathing cauldron from the corner.

"Now we must bed together!" I paced, enraged by the curtness Marc showed our host. The palace guest room we had entered held a matrimonial bed with sumptuous linens on top of a feathered mattress. Adorned with carved trunks from Anatolia, vases from Hellas and silver candlesticks, it even had two drinking goblets from Tarchna and a flask of wine that a servant brought when he showed us our room.

"I want it to be so." He stopped my movement and whirled me around to face him, grasping my arms and drawing me into his embrace. Leaning forward, he brushed his bearded cheeks against mine.

Tenderly he released me. My head spun with pleasure from his nearness. *I lust for him to kiss my lips.* Not wanting to move, yet needing answer, I reluctantly pushed him away and asked, "What of your woman, your wife?"

"Wife?" he echoed.

"Have you children?"

A slight smile started at the crease of his lips. "Didn't your brother Ari tell you?"

Irritated, I threw back, "Tell me what?"

"He didn't, did he, when he took you aside in that tomb your mother paints."

"You tease but don't answer. You never speak of your life."

"My life is with you." He grabbed me again and kissed my mouth, tentatively, then with sweet strength. *His skin intoxicates me. I want to touch his cheeks, his arms. I want to feel his chest against mine.*

He pulled me down on the bed with him and said huskily, "Have you not realized that yet?"

The warmth of his arms melted me, forgetting my need to know the truth, sudden elation dissolving the strain of this rough journey. *I don't know where these feelings come from.* "What makes you hard to resist?"

"The same phenomena that makes you hard to resist. I fear that Goddess Turan has struck us with love for each other."

"You blame Turan!"

"Not blame. I honor the goddess with gratitude!"

"Turan!" I repeated, a smile emerging into radiance that must have emanated throughout the room. *A warmth not felt before grows within, a heat, a new fire kindled.*

"We're here together. All night." Marc kissed my throat and shoulders, caressing my breasts under my tunic. Delicately his hands swam over my back to my hips and buttocks, stroking and exploring my skin. Responding to his touch, my nipples hardened. Jolts of pleasure flickered down through me, awakening sensations that had been so long dead. Without hesitation, I brought my arms around his neck and fit my body against his. He pulled up my cloth to expose my sacred mound.

I moaned in agonized delight. *I need his warmth, his milk within me.*

Madly we tore at each other, not getting enough skin to touch, nor enough mouth and tongue to savor, our beings soaked with heat. He yanked up his own tunic, pressing his engorged shaft against me, finding entrance into my moisture, penetrating my core, taking but a moment to learn the rhythm, sliding in and out as if we had always been together in oneness, until our fire burst into flame, consuming us in its brightness.

"You rise late," the prince guffawed at Marc and me. "We've already eaten our barley cakes and drunk honey water."

In front of Marc's men, Hammad and the entire court, I felt as if I was a glowing candle, my being warm with memory of luster that had lasted the night, an intimacy that forever changed my wants.

"Your words brought new reflection, " Marc gave the prince a thin smile.

Uncomfortably, Marc averted my adoring eyes and downed the offensive meal. To me the barley cake tasted like stale bread, the honey water like vinegar. Marc hadn't openly admitted our union. He had been truthful. He worked speech to his advantage.

"I am wise, am I not?" the prince said pompously. "I took my augurs' advice and gave you a room to share since the gods brought you here together. I wasn't as rude as you thought me yesterday."

The cosmos is upside down. We've followed the words of a sea pirate turned lawless prince!

"Remain as my guests during the hunt. We shall celebrate your union with a regal banquet."

As he spoke, in the distant hills a flutist trilled his pipes. It was the same call I'd heard since childhood, the signal urging wild deer and boar to flee their forest homes. At that sound, the hunters gathered weapons, ropes and traps and left the court. How well I knew the routine from Arun. They would mount their steeds, prance with dignity, fan out in the hills, snare the unsuspecting animals and slay them. Surely we would banquet adequately.

"We take your hospitality briefly. By now, Curtun has had its hunts and the first frost. We are expected before the cold season is upon us," Marc said graciously but with purpose. "But first, Prince, let us bargain with satisfying trade."

"And I shall gift you with Aegyptian treats," I offered to show generosity, jumped up and brought forth ivory combs and an ostrich egg from the basket that Marc carried into the dining hall. I motioned to Hammad and he brought a bundle of gold threaded cloth to the prince. "You have given clarity to my life."

What insult this sleaze of a prince gave! He knew we weren't wed. He winked at me like I was a common harlot!

During the day Marc was aloof as he went about the palace, trading with the pirate-prince, tending to the needs of his men and the caravan, then each night heating our bed with desire, with love.

"What is our haste in leaving?" I asked as we continued our caravan over Murlo's hills. "We stayed only a few days."

"The prince would have kept you, enchanted you with his wily ways."

"His palace enchants with those statues and his lavish table."

"He enticed us, didn't he?"

He is no more wily than Marc. Sadness entered my being. The enchantment must have broken after we left the pirate's palace, seriousness replacing playful charm. *We must have been under the spell of the pirate and his augurs. They couldn't have been true augurs, but rogues, false diviners who put potions into our goblets, stirring us into frenzied sensuality.*

Marc ended the charm, staying with his men each eve
when the caravan bedded down near streams. Separately I
slept in my oxcart under Hammad's watch. *Now Marc
withdraws his love. It could not be otherwise for Marc must
have a wife and children. We haven't made a union after all.*

"There lies Curtun!" Marc proudly pointed.
"Where?"
"There."
It was a speck on the horizon, a spur of a mountain
chain across the wide expanse, with two valleys between.
"Each day we'll journey closer."
Our path sloped down, dropping to Etruria's
hinterland, the flat, wide Arbian River valley. Sheep and
oxen grazed on meadow grasses and munched brittle
stalks of grain they were fed, fattening their bodies to
ward off the impending cold.
Days blurred as the caravan slowly rambled across
that austere plain through dusty trails swept by harsh
winds, onto merchants' roads deep-rutted by oxcart
wheels. We rested at the occasional dwelling. Few others
traveled past harvest, staying indoors at Vesta's hearth.
Tinia's rain came and went, each storm cooling the earth
for the coming season.
Now, I walked with the caravan every day, all day,
stopping only for drink, against protests of the landsmen.
With heavy headdress balanced, and priestess garments
tattered at the hem, I walked. Through rain and mud, I
walked to rid myself of wanting Marc. Blisters chaffed
my feet. My legs cramped with strain. No matter what I
did, I could not stop wanting him.

Neither village nor town came into sight until we
reached the base of the greatest mountain range. Five

huge circular tombs, each as big as a hillock, announced the outskirts of Curtun, mounds covered with sheets of sod planted in wheat fields, open to the sky. Memories stirred at the sight, waking me from this dreary journey. How relieved I was to see an Etruscan necropolis. It proved I was still among our people.

"The Curtunians have common bond with other Etruscan cities, not with Velathri or Murlo, but more like places in the south. The funeral mounds are size and shape of ones in Cisra."

Hammad was gazing pensively at the necropolis too. "How different these tombs are from pyramids, not formidable or hard, but round and welcoming!"

"You have the enthusiasm of an Etruscan!"

"And different from Tarchna, Velathri and Pupluna."

"You've done well to learn their forms." Icy cold air hit my cheeks. "No matter what they appear, the tombs are a symbol of everlasting life. Shells of the Ancestors lie within them whose spirits float into the cosmos with wisdom."

"Priestess, how knowledgeable of the netherworld you are!"

"The augurs taught me our laws. What fate I have. There is no family tomb for me to be buried in. I don't have a place to die. Far I have strayed yet here I am, back in the lands of my Ancestors, not left to perish elsewhere."

What have I now become? A foreigner among my own people, journeying from place to place to seek refuge? Who pushes me on but the gods of each place I've been? Am I watched over by gods? A thunderbolt! *Etruscan gods destined this last journey for me! For almost a season, they sent me from Tarchna across Etruria, testing me with ordeals to show me ways of our cosmos, to find a place for my afterlife.*

"Why do you frown, then smile?" Hammad asked.

"I'm thinking what a freakish life I've led, and you with me."

"Priestess, I know your life story as intimately as my own. I see you are far away." Hammad peered closely at me and said in wonder, "You've just had enlightenment."

"Priestess, take to your cart," Marc ordered sharply as we approached the Curtun road from the foothills. "You are my guest. Ride!"

How I must embarrass him with my behavior! A noble who walks with the caravan! It is time to stop walking, to complete this journey with dignity.

"Of course."

"You will?"

Mortified by my obsession to walk with the landsmen, his anger had grown. Now it dissipated. One of his most infectious smiles played on his lips, reminding me of his sweet kisses.

To appear impassive, I looked upward. Buildings grew out of the cliffs high above. Like Velathri, the road wound around a vertical slope, curves switching back and forth to ease the climb.

I adjusted my golden mask and composed myself in the oxcart as an image of luxury, sitting tall on cushions, displaying Isis' symbols of abundance, sheathes of wheat on my lap. Four landsmen flanked my cart, ready to haul its weight. Hammad traipsed behind, getting used to his new leather skin shoes, wearing something on feet that had always been bare. The caravan began the ascent, from hillside to cliffs on the cobbled road edged by rows of leafless orchard trees and fields of vine roots matted with straw. The higher we went, the cooler the day, darkening with a coming storm. Marc weaved in and out of the caravan, among the oxcarts and men, encouraging them on a well-done journey as they worked their way up the last stretch of road before the city's walls. The closer we got, the more excited everyone appeared, chatting, energetic, and enthusiastic to return home.

"It' s too early for snow," Marc assured me as he halted my cart. Kindly now, he paused only to bundle an extra woolskin around my shoulders, "but frost might bite."

Is his gesture endearment or excitement? Or does he prepare to present me? I could no longer guess his meanings.

At Curtun's city gates, a number of townsfolk hailed the caravan and pushed the carts under the arch. No guards judged our passage through the gates. A steeper uphill road was beyond. At the top, solid houses and shops clustered on a long street. How high we were, almost above the clouds, with the valley floor far below.

The entire town was afoot to see the caravan. Women and children lined the curbs, all wearing fur cloaks, shouting out greetings of reunion. None were shabbily attired and most showed elegance in conduct. Laughing and singing, well-dressed youths walked alongside the carts, inquiring for stories of other Etruscan cities or excited to know what Marc and his men brought for the cold season.

It was my turn to parade. As my cart came upon each new group, they quieted, bewildered, I was sure, by my presence. When I passed, the crowd chattered again.

The citizens broke through the caravan's route to embrace husbands and sons with fondness, all rejoicing in homecoming. Marc mingled among them giving instructions, throwing bushels of grain to his men, relaying amphorae of wine in friendly pay.

The mood shifted as we moved along the street. One cart would slow and park on the side, another cart would disappear down an alley, some landsmen would break away from the caravan and go with women or children, others drifted off into the town. One by one all of the carts disappeared. I lost sight of Marc. He, too, disappeared with one of the carts.

Abruptly, this journey was truly over. Alone in my oxcart decorated with obscurely colored designs, encircled by Aegyptian bundles, gripping the bench, I sat not knowing what to do. *What kind of man is he who shows concern and walks away? My wanting him is over! How could I be so stupid! It's wife and children he goes to!*

Hammad shifted about nervously at the cart's side, holding a ready dagger in the fold of his skirt. No one else surrounded us, the street emptied of people. Marc and his men were gone.

Joyously they rush to their dwellings to reunite with kin. Their season is over. The long expedition arrived safely. What of me now, former noblewoman and scribe, priestess of the Cult of Isis? I am abandoned once more.

23

Far Journey

My oxcart sat beside a high-walled building of baked-clay, on a street as silent as a stone statue. The chill of nightfall drove me from the cart. Downcast, I alighted and stretched my legs, stiff from the cushions. Bored with waiting for danger that hadn't come, Hammad, used to flat desert land, slept sitting against the cart, drained by the hike up the steep mountainside.

A shadow came from within the dusk. Hammad shifted in his sleep.

"Shhh! Don't wake him!" Marc reached for my hand. "I've come to introduce you."

I pulled away.

"You didn't think I left you?"

"You callous brute!" I cursed under my breath.

"Canth demanded report of my journey."

"Canth?"

"The high magistrate of Curtun."

"You explain yourself now. Why did you not say that before?"

"Please come," he stuttered awkwardly. "This is my home."

"This one here?" I asked, flabbergasted that I had been sitting outside his dwelling like a stray. Grudgingly, without taking the hand he offered, I walked with him around the corner to the front entrance of the tall structure that nestled into the mountain incline. At the doorstep, a woman whose face was obscured by the cloth that blotted her streaming tears, then opened her arms to Marc.

I shrank back. *His wife!* He ran and lifted her, holding her in fond reunion. She squealed in delight and pinched his cheeks affectionately. "How late you are this season! I thought you'd never come, but the gods brought you safely to me."

Wretchedly I stood frozen to the ground, not from the cold that came with night. *What trickery he plays! He quibbles! He evades! Foolishly, I loved him!*

"Larthia! Meet Velina."

He said her name with such endearment that an attack of nausea hit my throat. Struck by his cajoling call, I grew hot, and then boiled at his impertinence, his slurring of my dignity. *I play not harlot to his wife.* I stormed back to the cart, pitched my gift of woolen skin to Hammad's awakened form, and ran past the village center where we had arrived, through the first street I saw, getting lost in a maze of zigzag alleys.

Uncontrollably I sobbed. Out of breath, circling Curtun's labyrinth of streets, I looked for exit from this walled puzzle. Quite a town! Built on a precipice, I couldn't fathom which direction to go, except up or down. From inside doorways laughter drifted out, probably of families starting evening meals. *How cruel the gods are. What honor do I have? I have no life, no loyal man, no family to eat with, no tomb!* I slid down against a rough stone wall, fraying my tunic and tearing my beaded neck collar. Frantically, I groped like a mad beggar to regain my scattered prized beads.

Racing footsteps come from above. Marc still pursued me. I hadn't outwitted him, too tired to go on, too sad to outrun him anymore.

Before I saw him, I felt his presence, the same intensity always felt when he was near. "Leave me be!"

He ignored my words and hugged me to him, kissing my hair and cheeks. "Forgive me," he murmured over and over. "I didn't think you'd come to mean all you do to me."

"You've a wife!"

"No wife! No children."

"Who's that woman?"

"Velina? How senseless I've been not to tell you. She's like an older sister, but no relation. After my parents died, she raised me." Before I could protest, Marc swooped me into his arms and carried me up the deserted path.

From my cradled position, I pounded against his chest. "Someone might see us. Put me down!"

"Not until you hear me out." He held me tighter and strode along. "My father was a sea warrior, lost in battle. My mother died in childbirth. Like you, she was a noblewoman, a kin of Curtun's high magistrate, disgraced by my father's unheroic death. In youth, when my friends married, I learned that no one would marry a nameless man. I went to Clevsin, in the lower valley we just crossed, and worked for a vintner who taught me his trade. Without a clan, I took to journey, bringing vine roots, then wine to Clevsin. Canth learned of my successful enterprise and claimed me for a native, fetching me here to my birth place, titling me with nobility." Out of breath, Marc reached his home, I still in his embrace.

"Put me down" I repeated more fiercely. "You embarrass me!" I twisted and wriggled from his grip, unbalanced him with my movement, until I stood properly to right my tunic. "And I am a nameless woman! You lied to me by saying nothing."

"You play priestess! You can't reveal your true Etruscan identity any more than I could reveal my heritage."

I ignored his last words and trod forward to meet Velina.

Graciously, Velina mentioned nothing about the spectacle of my arrival. Arms open, a sincere smile on her face, she welcomed me with warmth of friendship, not the animosity I expected from hosting an uninvited guest. "You'll be right in a wink. With thick bean soup to ward off the frost, barley cakes and wine, and a cauldron of hot water to soak and scrub off your journey, you'll sleep well."

By Etruscan code, we would sleep in separate rooms, behavior more fitting than at Murlo. Giving me the room I admired most, at the top of the unusual tower house, one with a view of that valley we had traveled, my wounded pride unbent a little.

After the night our journey ended, the shelter of Marc's dwelling comforted. Angry with him still I rebuked his advances and distanced myself, seething about his deception. *How can I trust a man who seems sincere one moment and holds his tongue the next?*

We moved separately within the house. He tried to make amends with considerate words and offers to do my bidding. Yet my stubbornness would not abate and I rejected him. Before he would enter the dining place, I'd slip away. Alone up high in my loft, I felt like a bird in its nest, eating food that Hammad brought.

Restless after constant motion of the past seasons, I wandered through the rooms, a terrible raw ache rising at what had befallen me. The dwelling was a myriad of cubicles, stairwells going from one to another up the mountain slope. Each cubicle had remembrances of Marc's journeys, an eclectic assortment of rich objects: metal votives, animal-shaped bucchero pottery, bronze containers, woven baskets, statues of the gods, colorful textiles, cushions and furniture brought home from his trade. These pieces were as appealing as the man. I had not been in a home as cozy, as loving as this, since childhood when mother had made our home special with ornaments.

From my perch, I glimpsed Marc as he left the house every day and guessed it was to trade goods, but I wasn't certain, nor did he tell me. *I've no friends to talk to, to share confidences. People would laugh if they heard my story, more preposterous than ever.*

Tinia's vengeance brought blowing snow that kept us indoors, all except Hammad. Wherever he was he hadn't come to serve my evening meal. My belly growled as I waited for him impatiently, annoyed that he had forgotten. *How easily I become angry. What has happened to me, so full of contradiction, irritation and even haughtiness if not fed?* In exasperation I descended the stairs to Velina's cooking hearth, composing myself, fidgety in the possibility of seeing Marc.

On the floor, Hammad lay on a pallet, shaking as if the Etruscan cosmos had over-frightened him.

"My servant just brought him in." Velina threw a blanket to me and took another for herself. Together we bundled my shivering Nubian, rubbing his hands and toes, dabbing compresses of hot pads on his chest.

"I'm dying!" Hammad cried desperately.

"Dying! How can that be?" Apologetically, I groaned, "What has happened to you, my strong, brave protector?"

"Priestess, these nights are frigid! Frost covers my skin, congealing my blood." He chattered deliriously. "Been sleeping in the cart."

"The cart? Why?"

"Priestess, you never thought to find bed for me." His freezing cheeks and forehead paled his dark skin and his huge frame shrunk beneath his clothes.

"I thought you bedded among Marc's landsmen." Tears welled up and I lamented, "Why didn't you tell me? Why didn't I ask? Why didn't I realize this cold season would harm? In selfishness I neglected you. Don't die, my dear friend."

"He has no strength to feed himself. A chill has overtaken him," Velina scooped a cup from the cauldron on the fire. "The best remedy is boiled soup of the vine. He'll stay here by Vesta's fire."

As one would feed a babe, I ladled the bubbling soup between his raw lips that he gobbled down ravenously.

"I'm mystified by this sight, nobles tending servants instead of the other way around," Marc said quietly. He had entered the cooking place and sat on a stool, watching our ministrations. He stooped over, pried open and examined Hammad's eyes. "How lucky you are to live, friend."

Lightened by Hammad's response to our treatment, both Velina and I laughed in relief, then companionably, closing the gap towards friendship.

"I'll tend him. My cooking room is always warm. He'll live here by the hearth and sleep by the fire," Velina pronounced with matronly authority and bustled about the room rearranging the space to accommodate him. Simultaneously, she glanced at Marc and me with a glint of amusement in her eyes. "You two eat there at the cushions."

"I'll take mine to my room." I chose a bowl and filled it with a stew of venison and tuber vegetables.

"Larthia, you share a meal with Hammad. Can you not share one with me?" Marc glared. "Are you not a guest in my home?"

So absorbed in my self-imposed exile, I've neglected Hammad. And now I've insulted the man I—I—by Tinia!—by Amun-Re!—I care for.

"Yes," I said humbly, avoiding his frown. "I'll eat with you."

Velina proved to be who Marc said she was, a sisterly dedicated friend to a parentless man, and a wonderfully loyal housekeeper. She kept thoughts and opinions to herself, not prying into Marc's affairs nor asking me of mine.

"Come to market with me." Velina tried to persuade every eighth day when the high magistrate distributed provisions. "Our neighbors busy themselves to know of you. My chores would go faster if I didn't have a constant stream of meddling folks at my door pretending to borrow some grain or bringing meats to share, to find out about the mysterious Aegyptian priestess and her attendant."

"What do you tell them?"

"That they shouldn't stick their noses where they don't belong."

"How lively you are!" I laughed. "I'm sluggish from the journey still. I have no energy."

Velina gave a quizzical smile and patted my shoulder with concern, not chiding me for being a weakling, or encouraging me to be stronger.

*　　*　　*

My listless spirit turned sleepless with the cold season's crisp air. Early one dawning I arose, my slumber distressed by twisted vivid dreams.

In their diaphanous tunics, the Ancestors flew at me, fighting me as I pushed stone boulders out of my way from one tomb to another, Priestess-princess Larthia's sepulcher, Veia's carved niche tombs when I was abducted from Tarchna, the pharaoh's chamber at Saqqara, even my family's eternal home. "What do you search for?" the Ancestors asked. "Something lost, unremembered by time," I replied. "I want to take it with me, to keep, to cherish." A flame shone ahead, an oil lamp lighting hieroglyphs on the walls of the pharaoh's tomb, words of The Book of the Dead. I brushed dust off the wall and it was revealed:

I am yesterday. I know tomorrow.

Agitated by my night visions, I traipsed to the highest slopes above the city, wrapped in the same drab woolen cloak that obscured my identity in Velathri. Few were awake except those who worked the most innocent, simple tasks. Farmers tended their stock, pitching hay. Servants graded the paths, strewing rocks for their nobles' passage.

A light breeze told of more approaching cold and snow, whistling through tall cypresses and rousing thrushes nested in cliffs. The exhilarating air was scented with pines and cedars. How different from Aegypt where air stifled and choked. In Tarchna, hearth fires smoked and lingered. In Hellas, blown sea salt invaded the nostrils, but here the air cleansed and purified my thoughts. *It is peaceful, quiet before everyone stirs.*

Another night I dreamed the same exhausting dream, leaving me too heavy to walk about. Yet when folks bedded down at dusk, I awakened and tiptoed out among the shadowed walls to reach the mountaintop where the stars were close, gloriously brilliant in the peaceful night sky.

Bless the stars sweeping across the cosmos majestically! They righted my paltry thoughts with their grandeur.

By the next eighth day, with more confidence, I donned my shawl instead of headdress, and entered the boisterous market place without Hammad because his presence drew too much attention. The drought had ended. Stalls were piled with grains and hanging meats, berries and roots. Servants scooped honey water into jugs and flasks. Nobles hardily gossiped as they procured the high magistrate's bounty, moving with assurance that there was enough for all, not having to fight for rations. The civil magistrates, denoted by their more elaborate tunics, smiled at each other as they met and talked of daily routines. Everyone knew I was Marc's priestess, brought from afar, but they greeted me with courtesy and kept their inquisitiveness in check.

They are Etruscan after all, not foreign rivals. Curtun may be different from Tarchna, but the customs are the same. If I am not in the city of my birth, at least I am in Etruria, dressed as an Aegyptian, with thoughts both Etruscan and Aegyptian.

After my nocturnal wanderings my dreams lessened. Calmness grew within me.

The three of us, Hammad, Velina and I, sat at the table to scrub, peel and chop the harvest's bounty for the cold season's reserve. There in Velina's cooking room Hammad revived, adapting to Curtun's cool, high elevation. When better, he remained often with justification he shouldn't chill. More reason was Velina herself. Beholden to the kindly woman, he kept close to her, bubbling with admiration. Likewise, she had a new ear to confide in, that of a big strapping man who brought stories of distant places she would never see, of pharaohs and pyramids, of the treeless land, the

Aegyptian desert, its customs and rituals. Sometimes I joined their banter and watched their mutual regard. *I'm envious of the simplicity of their talk. Marc and I once had that friendship but no more.*

How comforting those days were! How safe it felt to do homely chores. My appetite increased for I nibbled at food we fixed for storage. My belly grew plump with the cold climate, eating foods with desire. Even as I cleaned and bound herbs, drying them for use in stews as my mother and grandmother had done, I secretly lusted for Marc. He would leave the house at dawn and return at daylight's end.

A day came when a gust of Tinia's wind abruptly blew at the shutter and I dashed to close it. Looking down at the mountainside, I burst out, "Velina, where does Marc go?"

Velina's eyes twinkled as she grabbed my hand and brought me to the door. With a little push she said, "Walk down that path to the vineyard."

Rambling down the steep curving path that led below Curtun's walls through countless rows of planted vines was a new experience for me. In Tarchna, noblewomen weren't permitted on growers' land for worry of staining their dainty shoes. These vines were covered with frost, their entwined branches strung up on stakes, deadened by their need to sleep out the cold. *While I drank wine of my heritage, I never walked in a field, nor saw its flowering or demise.*

At the end of the rows, the pungent smell of fermented grapes increased, and I came to a vacant brick platform, with remnants of grape liquid stained on its surface. Familiar happy voices came from the large mud and thatch hut next to it and I peeked in the door. The seafarer-landsmen I knew were hauling huge bowls of liquid, slopping as they poured one after another into clay amphorae.

Marc hunched over a table, dipping a ladle into bowls. As the men greeted me, Marc spun around and quipped cheerfully, "Come sip the drink of the gods, this harvest's wine. Judge taste with me."

Warmed by my first swallow, I asked innocently, knowing the answer. "Do you come here every day?"

"It's part of my labor. Would you see the rest of our venture?"

How natural he acts here, so comfortable in his own surroundings. Guiding me through the hut, he pointed out stages of wine fermentation, from watery liquid to full-bodied drafts, a complicated process. From there we walked through the vineyards to a cypress-bordered garden to sample a jug of the most recent wine batch.

"This garden's tranquility intoxicates me, not the wine. How holy this garden is, enough to pray or reveal my every thought." I meandered among the late blooming flowers that seemed to revitalize with my touch and impulsively added, "Just as you have made your life worthwhile, I enhanced mine as a priestess of the Cult of Isis."

"Even though I am odious to you now, please stay," he pleaded. "We must be seen together to prevent scandal."

"Is all you want me for to prevent scandal? Scandal lies only within us, not with this city."

He flustered. "The magistrate requests the priestess who comes from afar. He grants us audience so that we may explain the Aegyptian trade."

"It's your trade now, done fairly for my need."

"You could sweeten the meeting with your presence."

"My presence?" I swirled the brilliant purpled liquid in my goblet. "Is he upset that you brought papyrus, not wine?"

"The papyrus interests him for it is practical and useful for his accounts. If you gift him with ivory vases, he'll be content. And those ostrich eggs would be a special acquisition for his tomb."

"But since there was little wine brought back from your journey and only a room's worth . . ."

Marc poured another goblet full and handed it to me. "The wine crop produced abundance after all."

"Then you lied to me about that, too!"

"I was gone. I was with you! How could I know?"

"Tinia grants you a surprise gift of good harvest. Even this wonderful garden blooms when the cold season approaches."

"Yes, surprises! Our village will drink wine this whole cold season, flowing from many storage amphorae. And herbs and tubers will grace the tables. Perhaps you are the harbinger of abundance from Isis, my mysterious lady."

"Could be," I kept my tone somber, unwilling to divulge how delighted I was by his compliment.

Then he smiled that same smile that endeared him to me so many moons ago. "So you'll come?"

The astounding garden uplifted my spirits. "When my best priestess' tunic is washed and dried."

I fastened the repaired beaded collar around my throat and smoothed it over my priestess's tunic. Freshly washed in potato water to give it stiffness, and pressed with a hot iron stone to take out wrinkles, the tunic lay around the contour of my body tighter than it had been. My body swelled at hips and belly. *I am with child. Another grows within, a tiny being. After so many childless seasons!* The idea aroused my senses as I ran my hands over my body blissfully, contentment in my fingertips. *Oh Turan! You have gifted me!*

Thrill poured through my being, a happiness I never had. *I'll bring forth a child for the ages, be it boy or girl,*

*and will nurse and lavish care as my parents did for me.
I'll plan my child's life to have the best I can put forward.*

Velina broke through my musings. She held a gold-thread-embroidered cloth covering and waved it in front of me like a banner. "I've made you a cloak to wear when you meet High Magistrate Canth."

Wait! What thoughts were those so advanced? How carried away I was by my new discovery. Velina jolted me back to this moment. Shortly, I would be presented to the magistrate of Curtun, who, like Zilath, was most powerful. A crucial event! Survival was all I should concentrate on. If I displeased him, he could banish me, even feed me to forest wolves. *Me, a priestess unwed, a noblewoman without husband.* I must hide my joy and find a way to make this condition acceptable. *What lies will I have to tell to go about the cosmos?*

"It's in the Aegyptian style!" I wrapped the cloak around my shoulders. "Many thanks, dearest Velina. How grateful I am for your discretion."

She knows I'm with child.

"What do I call the high magistrate?"

"'High Magistrate Canth.' No other," Velina answered, preparing her own clothes to accompany Marc and me to Curtun's court.

"What is Marc's title?"

Velina seemed surprised. "You don't know? Why, he's 'Prince Magistrate of Curtun, heir to Canth.'"

How blinded I had become in my rage at Marc! These sumptuous surroundings, this dwelling, grander than others on the narrow lane, rooms with every necessity of enjoyment, were of a noble. "I should have known. He doesn't always appear to be what he is."

"Marc isn't a brazen man."

"I would have thought a union would be requirement of a magistrate. It's odd, isn't it, that he hasn't married?" I strapped up my sandals, hoping that my words sounded more casual than nosy.

"So dedicated to his work as vintner, when his crops failed, he had to attest his worth to the high magistrate. He went afar to Cisra, Gravisca, Tarchna, and even further, to get vine saplings and bring home wine. The gods must have cursed him with wanderlust. Those who wander make poor husbands."

"You disapprove?"

"It's not for me to approve or disapprove. No need for a wife. It satisfies him."

Marc and I stood in the center of the high magistrate's court, civil magistrates and patrons gathered around the perimeter. I couldn't stop glancing at him, thinking, *Marc's child, his seed planted in my womb at the pirate's palace.*

"We wait with curiosity to learn of the exotic emissary from Aegypt." The high magistrate joined us, standing next to Marc as naturally as he would meet with a son.

He was unlike Zilath, Priscus Tarquinius or Pharaoh Amasis. Not demanding. Gentle. Yet, he was still a ruler who could change my fate. *I am here to deceive him with pretense of who I am.*

Uncomfortable at having the court's attention, I studied the ornamented ceiling, carved with scenes of Etruscan warriors against their Umbrian enemies, of the land east of the highest mountain, backbone of the Italic Peninsula. Suspended above the court was a bronze lamp of more than twelve parts, circular like a bowl, embellished with vines in relief. Between the vines, heads of the horned bearded God Flufluns, god of wine, and draped sirens with spread wings, while naked satyrs played flutes. From the bottom of the lamp, a huge gorgon's head complete with open mouth, tusks and tongue hanging out, surrounded by a wreath of writhing snakes, stared down.

Despite my poised demeanor, the shock of the lamp's grotesqueness made my throat dry and my stomach queasy.

"Do you like our candelabra, Priestess?"

"I've seen nothing like it."

"Nothing like it will ever be made again," the high magistrate said amiably and expertly switched topics. "You see about you our sacred village, where heaven-born Daedanus dwelt, he who left here to form the Trojan race. Our augur-priests prophesized we will be a mighty city."

I bowed my head in honor under his scrutiny.

"You know the story! Has my noble vintner-merchant told you it?"

"No," I admitted. "The story was well known to the Tarchna, jealous that their history had not such a lengthy background. I learned it as a scribe when reading Hellenic." *I should have said 'yes' and stopped there. But I ran at the mouth and said too much. Now I must guard my past carefully.*

Marc coughed to cover my mistake and gave me an encouraging smile.

"It is a popular story among the people," I finished lamely.

My answer hadn't bothered the high magistrate. "You have mastered Etruscan quickly but with a distinct accent."

"Aegyptian speech has similarities," I lied, a small lie to my bigger ones. I laid gifts of ivory, ostrich plumes, a carnelian and turquois breastplate on the altar for the magistrate. *I must complete this deception, these years of trials.* "I spread the word of Aegyptian Goddess, Isis, corn goddess. It was her influence that brings you prosperity of harvest this season."

"So she has!" He examined the gifts, touching them with reverence for their quality. "The treasures you have brought us are wondrous."

"Pharaoh Amasis of Aegypt selected them personally."

"When will you return to Aegypt?"

"She won't go back." Marc moved closer to the high magistrate. "I won't let her."

The civil magistrates, patrons and I strained to hear. The court stilled and focused on Marc. I couldn't take my eyes off him, fascinated by his intensity.

He spoke in a low firm voice. "I would have to go after her, and I want not to journey elsewhere again now that I have her."

The gods play tricks on my ears! My jaw dropped. My eyes opened fully. Marc's defiance struck me as forcefully as any gale of Tinia's storms, any thunderbolt, any vision of Ancestors attacking me in my distorted nighttime fantasy. I fumbled and dropped the alabaster vase I was about to present to the high magistrate.

Before it could shatter the floor tiles, Marc caught the vase and offered it to his benefactor. "The Priestess is noble, of the highest sort, for she has met the most painful trials and has won. She is a warrior against the highest enemies."

"What enemy has she killed?" the high magistrate asked.

"None. She's not a common warrior but the grandest commander who defeats her foe, not with weapons but with her wits. She carries no weapons except her scribing tools."

"She is higher than you, Prince?"

Swiftly, with urgency, Marc took my hand and kissed my palm, speaking to the magistrate. "Against the Fates, yes. She survived the hatred of two Roman kings, debated with those of the new social order of Athenai, worshiped at the great pyramids of Aegypt and is emissary to the pharaoh, besides being a Priestess."

"You petition for the Priestess?"

"Yes."

A feeling of perfect tranquility swept through my head, my trepidation, sorrow and inner torment diminishing. Clearly, I saw my dream anew. *The words in my dream were wrong. These are right: I am yesterday. I am tomorrow.*

From the back of the court, Velina started clapping her hands slowly, then faster and faster with delight. Soon smiles replaced the seriousness of the occasion, and applause started, contagious applause that became a rapid, happy roar.

High Magistrate Canth contemplated Marc and then his eyes bore into me with renewed interest. "Our gods spread love in your direction. You, my favored magistrate, noble Prince, and you, beautiful and intelligent warrior Priestess, who has voyaged infinite waters and journeyed rough roads, make a harmonious match. You will become one of us, Priestess Larthia of the Cult of Isis, and I will bless your sanctified union. Welcome to Curtun."

24

Silent Memories

"I've deceived Canth," I ranted, flouncing back and forth across the cooking room, arms crossed over to hold back distress. "I've lived a life of trickery! I've even deceived you, Marc!"

"Not me." Marc leaned against the hearth wall, infuriatingly calm.

"Yes," I spit out, "Most of all, you! I am with child."

"I know. It was in Murlo that we conceived."

"You—you have the boldness to smile about it!"

"Delighted." He undid my folded arms and pulled me towards his sensual warmth, then added passionately, "Our love is strong and always has been. Tinia and Menvra threw us together. Turan affirmed our bond. Your Isis threw her powerful love on the winds and sailed you to me. Our unborn is proof enough."

*   *   *

Little by little, like a reptile, I shed my Aegyptian image for an Etruscan one. So gradual that Marc, Hammad and Velina, my new family, hardly noticed, or if they did, said nothing. Too conspicuous to wear to market, I removed the Aegyptian jewelry, the bulky carnelian and turquois neck collar, silver armlet and gold disk earrings. For substitute, I wore thin strands of garnets with gold beads.

My body rounded with child, and I replaced frayed Aegyptian garments with colorful Etruscan tunics. I stopped shaving my scalp. My wig of straight black tresses sufficed until stubbles grew to become the hair I once had, dark naturally buoyant waves. When my hair lengthened, I fashionably plaited it to gain favor with other noblewomen. A shallow tribute that brought less gossip.

How sufferings stay, punishment for years of deception. These silent memories linger at the back of my mind, but some escape when Uni's full moon is most penetrating.

Cleansing away my night's sleep, I splashed cool water down my cheeks and washed my hands in a bronze oval basin that one of Marc's crafters made. Unable to contain myself, I burst out to Marc, "In my dream last night I was in a courtyard of a huge dwelling in some unknown village. Closed, planked wooden doors were framed in its walls, so heavy that I had to push with both palms just to open one. Visions rushed out, transparent forms that swirled into the courtyard, jumping up and down with glee as they spiraled around. They were horribly familiar forms—those miscreants who seized, abused, and tortured me. As they flew by I named them: Zilath's scheming thieves; King Priscus' henchmen; the younger

Roman king; the Hellenic mute; the hypocrite Alexis, the merchant."

"They're in the past." Marc picked up a cloth, dried my moistened face, and kissed me tenderly.

"If only they wouldn't live in my mind."

Marc nibbled at my throat and shoulders, working his lips down to my breasts.

"You distract me! Let me finish!"

"Sit on my lap and tell the rest."

A request that I couldn't deny. To touch his skin always brought pleasure. "Trying to escape from my enemies, I raced to the second door and hammered against it with my fist until it opened. Inside there was a large plain room with my family, each at their daily chores. Mother was painting a tomb wall with Asba, laughing, holding a cup in one hand, a paintbrush in the other, while Father measured a corner with his groma to check for accuracy. Culni and Ari were youths, scrapping over a game of kottos. Uncle Venu watched his Hellenic crafter, Nikosthenos, at his pottery and cheered his production. Aunt Arith brushed her hair, bemoaning an exquisite sarcophagus she craved, one her husband wouldn't give her. I begged and cried to each kin to shelter me in their house."

"You were a child in that dream. Surely, it must mean you miss them sorely. Was Arun there?"

"He was dressed in leathers, honing arrows, preparing to leave for the stag hunt. He didn't see me, nor did the others for I was invisible."

Marc wrapped his arms around me. "You're here and very visible."

"There is more!"

"In the same dream?"

"At the end of that stark room, a third door opened by itself and an unknown force beckoned me into a dark space, chilly and damp. A voice called from somewhere in its hollow recesses, and I knew immediately it was the cave of that Hellenic Prophetess Sibyl. Not bestowing an oracle, she sang the same words the hetaerae taught, of Homer and Sappho. Irresistible poetry of valor and courage! Then her song dimmed. At the end of the cave, light of the day sky drew me onward. Dust and grit blew and settled on me, clinging as I sweated in the intense heat. Then the ground rumbled. Thrust up from the sands the Aegyptian Giza sphinx appeared, the great carving with the head of a man and body of a lion! He opened his mouth as if to yawn, but instead he asked if my journey satisfied. How jumbled it all was, not like what happened all those seasons."

"Did the sphinx's words scare you? What did you answer?"

"Words choked in my mouth. I rushed away. His monstrous image shrank back. Ahead, one of the wooden planked doors of the courtyard opened."

"And?"

"And I woke up."

"If I could undo the wrongs committed against you, I would." Marc poured us each a goblet of fresh harvest wine as we awaited Velina's grilled quail and bean stew that eve.

Balancing my drink, I snuggled into the cushions and shut my eyes. Images rapidly flashed—the same images that constantly haunted my dreams or disturbed my days. In one, I was locked in my room and starved in Roma's Forum. In another, a boulder catapulted from Aphrodite's acropolis in the Rhodos' moonlight. And the one dream that occurred most was of those awful crocodiles that slithered up the banks of the Nile, snapping, vicious jaws, chasing me to the Temple at Philae.

The wine warmed my strength. "They can't be undone. The Fates willed my destiny, and sometimes the challenge was too appealing not to do. There will always be sadness for experiences regretted or missed."

Marc sat next to me and traced the contours of my face with his fingertips. His caresses on my skin were ecstasy. "Your dreams are seeded within you, returning to perpetuate your wisdom. You're my goddess of wisdom."

"I'm not a goddess, just a mortal. How drained I am of my dreams."

Had the Fates at my birth bestowed the destiny of a discontent? They gave me the magic of scribing, yet had me conform to a noble's ordinary way of life. Then they doomed me to be childless and set me on an unwanted journey. With union to Marc and settling in Curtun, I was righted to become the noblewoman of my heritage.

Our new life began together as Marc promised. He stopped those journeys to Etruscan cities and ports, designating other Curtun merchants to the tasks. Through them, my messages passed to ship pilots who sailed the Great Sea to Aegypt. I reported to Isis of our triumph in spreading words of her cult. The ways of the cosmos are mysterious. Of those Curtun citizens interested in my exotic Aegyptian life, I told of Isis' myths and legends, and gifted them with grave goods. How paradoxical that they became cultists.

Outwardly, my life was occupied. When Marc inherited leadership as prince-priest magistrate of Curtun, I became "Princess-Wife." I was not only an Aegyptian priestess. I became a mother. Goddes Uni granted me, who had been barren, a beautiful healthy child! Born after our sacred union, Velia, my darling girl, was given an auspicious fate by Curtun's sacred priests.

Dear Hammad remained my faithful friend, posing as servant and adoring nurse to Velia. I was his protector in a cosmos that had no others like him and he was mine. He and Velina could never marry, but they lived together under our roof of "the tower house" as I called it, with plans to build a tomb for their afterlife.

Those narrow-minded citizens who thought being a scribe was an unacceptable female occupation, came to learn that skill was more important than gender. Marc understood my vocation, but hadn't fully realized how my talent was part of my essence, not just a fleeting enjoyment. Not secretly as in Tarchna, I scribed daily, and even kept Marc's accounts, amidst household duties and care for Velia. Other magistrates wanted my scribing services, but I declined. Never would I record for another, not even another prince-priest!

Most of the time I was of good humor, yet inwardly there was a void, left by my tumultuous past. For consolation, I scribed hieroglyphics, beautiful mystical inspirations for the *Papyrus of Ani*. In Hellenic, I rewrote Sappho's poetry on linen strips. Even as I exhausted my craft of copying everything I knew and supplies were low, my urge to scribe remained. Compulsively, or was it to keep my fingers nimble, I scribed on cloth scraps, flat pebbles or broken bucchero, and collected bird quills, picking up bits of charcoal to hewn into points. I siphoned wine dregs for ink.

Inspired by Sappho, I wrote poetic verses that came from the core of my being. For amusement, I wrote a funny story of one of Uncle Venu's adventures, then of my grandfather's discovery, his mix for bucchero. Soon I took comfort in scribing about each of my kin's history, and went on to chronicle my entire heritage. Although far away in Tarchna and lost to me, my cherished family lived on in my scribings. Stacks of linen scrolls accumulated which I stored in boxes.

How strong my need for tranquility was that I had vowed to myself not to talk about that odious journey, yet I couldn't avoid its memory. Those encounters with men who used me for sexual exploits were kept in my most intimate thoughts, of the mute who chased and ravished me in front of his crew, of dancing in transparent costume for the Athenian men whose semen spilled as they lusted, of Alexis who wanted me as his personal hetaera. With heaviness I wrote of my anguish and burned those scrolls in the hearth when no one was about. Somehow my scribings lifted me and I breathed more freely, as if the air was of fresh season.

Would Marc have loved me if he knew of those lurid episodes? I didn't want the answer. Had Arun learned of those men, he would have exposed me like Roman men did, or thrown me out in the woods to die. My feelings for Arun had died that fatal day in Tarchna when I unsuccessfully returned to reclaim my past.

From my long, dangerous odyssey I was not the being I once was, nor could be again. How strange! The gods of my people had clasped me to them, then cast me away and now reached out. Tinia's hand that touched my being in childhood with love, struck with wrath in my cresting and then rose insistently in Curtun. Who had I become but a composite of my experiences?

All of the gods, be they Etruscan, Roman, Hellenic or Aegyptian, must laugh at what they created. I too was sometimes tickled, sometimes enraged by their new creation of me. Had I not had death of one life, rebirth into another? Was not another fate given me, forming me into a revitalized being? It must have been Goddess Turan who brought Marc on that destined day in Tarchna, when my life was torn apart, never more to live among old family and friends.

"When dawn rises, when eve comes, I have you and you have me," Marc said as we left Velia in Hammad's charge and walked down the slope from Curtun. "Overjoyed I am with our issue but you are dearer."

I savored his loving words. Our first lust had given way to shared endearments and harmony of spirit. Openly, he showed me tenderness. Openly, I gave to him kindness, not the kiss of bees as when I first came to Curtun.

On this path birds sang in the air above, and the smell of lemons and grapes wafted. Marc led me past his vineyards to the cypress-bordered garden that I marveled at when I had newly arrived in Curtun.

The garden now bloomed with the heat seasons' flowers and shrubbery. How different it was! Instead of the table where we had sampled wine, a square platform, open to the sky, was laid with flat polished stone.

Marc ushered me up its seven steps. "An altar for you to worship Isis."

Tears watered my eyes. "Honor the goddess here!" The setting was pure, serene and holy, a place to truly establish my credibility as priestess to the people. Easily I imagined praying for abundance, sharing the beauty of Isis' myths. "How did you know this place was right?"

"You selected it with your instinct. Turn around," Marc said, his voice full of excitement. "For you, my Larthia."

At the far end of the garden, a domed slab structure sat under the shade of a great, ancient oak tree—a tumulus unlike Tarchna or Cisra's, uniquely of Curtun stone. From the altar to the tomb was a short distance, but in the moments I took to reach it, a change entered my being, a flutter of happiness.

"What sight is this so divine? I've journeyed through the cosmos and never saw such beauty." Filled with gratitude and inexplicable joy, I traced my fingers on the side of the precise half-sphere.

"Come. Our vault lies within."

Cut into the rock, a narrow hallway led to three small chambers, one completed, the other two unhewn.

"This one is ours. We could furnish it in a few seasons."

It was empty except for smooth plain walls, arched ceiling and a niche at the farther wall, ready for a painter's ornamentation.

Inspiration, brought on by the comfortable chamber design, coursed through me. "Our sarcophagus should go into that niche with painted vine leaves and thrushes overhad."

"Sarcophagus for both of us?"

"Yes. With us portrayed on the lid. If only Mother and Asba could paint friezes on the walls!"

"Hmm," Marc considered, and added helpfully, "What else?"

"You might place your razors and weapons here and your biga and horse bits there. My scribing tools and tablets might fit in this corner. Incense burners, banquet plates and goblets for the afterlife can surround our biers. The mourners can strew lavender petals over whatever other cherished possessions we have."

"Our family and generations to come will rest here."

Generations to come! Marc's words stuck like a dancing song. *Generations to come!* Since the journey that destroyed my past, uncertainty had clouded every moment. Missing from my new life had been the tie of heritage to future. Now with this wonderful tomb chamber there would be security and protection for the afterlife.

What I had been, and what I had become, solidified as strong as this tumulus, our eternal home.

The veil of chaos lifted with Marc's gift. Fresh sensations surged through my being, a brightness that illuminated from my countenance to toes. I was glad to be alive, to be loved and fulfilled. *My trials now end. I will dwell here on this precipice in peaceful harmony with my beloved and our child, far away from all I've ever known. There's no one else I want to be with and nowhere else I want to go.*

"No tomb is more perfect." Gently, I kissed Marc's lips, tasting the delicious honey of his soul, desiring him all the more. With a lightened heart, I stepped out of our chamber and faced Aplu's sparkling sun.

Author's notes:

What is now between Rome and Florence, Italy, was once the realm of the Etruscans. Their spirit must live in the soil and air, for this region has been home to creativity and prosperity for more than two millennia. The Roman arch was actually the Etruscan invention. Water channels and road construction that were used by the Romans (and are still in use today) are based on Etruscan design. Our English alphabet holds root in the Etruscan one. Dante, Boccaccio, Michelangelo, Leonardi da Vinci, Botticelli and other great Italian painters, sculptors, and craftsmen hailed from Tuscany. The ruling dynasties of the Medici, Ghibellines, Guelphs and popes planted their seed in Florence. Some of the most succulent food originated and was inspired from the land. Authors, actors, artists and cinematographers have been inspired to set marvelous work in the last century.

The Etruscans called themselves "Rasna" or "Rasenna" (perhaps referring to the Rhaeti people in the northern Alps). The Greeks called them "Tyrenhoi" (coming from the Greek word for "sacrifice"). The Romans called then "Tusci" or "Etrusci."

Historians of Western Civilization have overlooked the Etruscan civilization since the early Latin chroniclers (Seneca, Cicero, Livy). Their origins were suspect. Their language was not Indo-European and is not decipherable. The Etruscan personality was of a different spirit and attitude, not to Roman and Greek liking. Dionysius of Halicarnassus wrote that the Etruscans were "a people who don't resemble any other, either in their language or in their customs." It was a culture where men and women shared property rights and banqueted together. It is generally thought that women had equal rights.

The Etruscans were a religious people, whose beliefs and philosophical attitudes were steeped in mythological, somewhat superstitious, ritualized laws known as "The Etruscan Discipline." Each chief leader (perhaps called "king-priest" "lucumo" or "Magistrate") of the twelve major Etruscan cities also meted out religious law. Therefore in this book, I name him "prince-priest" or "maru." Augurs—diviners identified as "fulguriatores," specialized in the flight of birds, or "haruspices"(singular: haruspex), read animal entrails.

The Etruscans adopted and renamed Greek gods and goddesses (divinities), retelling myths and legends.

Mentioned in this book:

Etruscan	Greek	Roman
Tinia (greatest god)	Zeus	Jupiter
Uni	Hera	Juno

(goddess of the moon, wife of greatest god)
Turan   Aphrodite   Venus
(goddess of love)
Menvra   Athena   Minerva
(goddess of wisdom)
Aplu   Apollon   Apollo
(god of the sun)
Nethuns   Poseidon   Neptune
(god of the sea)
Flufluns   Dionysos   Bacchus
(god of the vine, of wine)

Seafarers in the Mediterranean region, the Etruscans held power over the seas in the sixth century B.C.E. Their decline began in sea battle with the Syracusans. Over the next few centuries, Rome warred against the twelve individual city-states, systematically destroying them. Simultaneously, their own slaves revolted. By 91 B.C.E the Etruscans were either assimilated or wiped out by the Romans.

Our knowledge of the Etruscans is through burial sites and archeological evidence of inscriptions on stone or metal. From tomb paintings, sculpture, craft (pottery, jewelry, weaponry, tools, sarcophagi, etc.) and cemeteries (necropolises), we are able to glimpse an unusual, but enlightened, society. Their colorful paintings depict playful scenes of lively banquets, sports and competitions. On sculptures, facial expression is usually stylized with a knowing smile, one of contentment and peace.

For all of the above-mentioned explanations, these people are referred to as "The Mysterious Etruscans."

Rosalind Burgundy's enchantment with the Etruscan's amazing culture began when she worked as Technical Illustrator and Curator for an archeologist in the Roman Forum. After some 30 years as educator, wife, mother and world traveler, Ms. Burgundy returns to her life-long interest to create *Odyssey of an Etruscan Noblewoman.* Two other novels on the Etruscans, *Song of the Flutist* and *Tuscan Intrigue* are part of this trio. She divides her time between the Central Sierra in California and Palm Beach Coast in Florida.

LaVergne, TN USA
30 October 2009
162490LV00001B/70/A